The Black and White Club Series of Novels

The Black and White Club: Genesis

The Black and White Club: Illuminology

The Black and White Club: Illuminology

Peter Bergeron

ISBN (Print Edition): 978-1-09836-690-2

ISBN (eBook Edition): 978-1-09836-691-9

Special Thanks to my beta readers

Debbie Bergeron

Tina Romero

Georgia Grillo

Mr. George Clark

Col. Dan Elmore, USAF (ret)

Mr. John McConnell

Thank you to my wife Debbie for always asking me,

"Did you finish your words for the day?"

THE BLACK AND WHITE CLUB

Illuminology

PETER BERGERON

CHAPTER 1

I don't want to die. She fought the panic that started to grip her body. Everything was black, and she couldn't breathe. *What's happening? This isn't right.* She tried to move her hands, but they were bound at her waist and attached to something. She wiggled her index finger across a smooth, hard surface. *How did I get from a frat party to standing here with a bag over my head?*

A slow scrape sounded on the floor behind her, followed by footsteps closing in. She tensed as strong hands gripped her biceps from behind, holding her in place. Another set of hands released her restraints and pulled the bag off her head. Her eyes winced involuntarily at the brilliance that suddenly replaced her darkness.

To recover balance, she placed one hand on—what was it? A huge white marble altar. It felt so cold. She held up the other hand to shield her eyes. *Where the hell is the light coming from? Dear God! It's bouncing off mirrors. The mirrors are hovering over people's heads. No. They're stuck on the front of hats. No. They're built into a line of chairs on the altar. Four, five, six, seven of them!*

She squinted to try and make out the faces of the seven motionless people in the chairs. They wore robes of gold. She couldn't see through the blinding light, so she tilted her head and wondered why she was wearing a white graduation gown. *What the hell is going on?* She shook her head to clear the fog. The last thing she remembered was drinking a glass of punch at the Delta Faros party, and now she was standing in front of some marble table in blinding light wearing a white robe.

"Has the selection been made?"

"Yes, we made the selection."

She turned her head left at the sound of the voice and noticed she was not alone. Six girls were lined up next to her in robes of white.

They were also shielding their eyes and holding on to the altar. One girl down the line looked familiar. She had long red hair. Tracy from Biology, or was her name Tammy? She turned her gaze away from the other girls when a wave of dizziness gripped her. She reached for the altar with both hands and sensed movement to her right.

Two men came out of the shadows in black robes and grabbed her arms. They started pulling her into the darkness—more like carrying.

Her feet barely touched the floor.

They walked down a dim hallway lit only by rows of night-lights at the base of the walls about a foot off the floor. They turned left down another corridor and stopped at a door. One of the escorts opened it, and the second grabbed her arm and waist, then pushed her into the room. The floor night lights illuminated the dark space. The escorts pushed her over to the wall. She bumped her head on a wooden X, which was attached to it. She felt the guards grabbing her arms and pulling them over her head. She was powerless to resist. She could barely stand. They pressed her face-forward against the wood, placing her arms on each limb of the X and buckling them into place with leather straps.

Oh fuck, this is not good. She pulled on the straps, which bit into her wrists, but her arms were tied in place. The door opened and closed, and a breeze touched her cheek, and the scent of lavender filled her nostrils as the escorts left the room. The air of silence was thick in the place.

"Hello? Is anyone in here?" She turned her head to see if anyone was behind her. Nothing but blackness and floor light, then she heard breathing over her right shoulder, and hot breath caressed her neck, sending chills down her spine. A firm hand pressed on the small of her back, pinning her to the X.

"Hmmm. A nice slice of lettuce!"

CHAPTER 2

FBI Special Agent Josh Martin leaned against a birch tree to catch his breath. He dropped his forty-five-pound rucksack on the ground with his left hand. At six feet tall and 205 pounds, six months of combat training had hardened his frame. His brown hair was cut razor short, and Maui Jim tactical shades hid his green eyes. He wore a woodland camo uniform with a full combat load. He smacked the butt of the thirty-round magazine on his Colt M4A1 Carbine to make sure the mag did not come loose during his trek across forty miles of North Carolina hills. It seemed like the western side of North Carolina was built on a mountain. Josh also visually inspected the seven thirty-round magazines stuffed into the pockets of his tactical vest and the four seventeen-round magazines for his Glock 17 Gen 4 9mm. Nothing came loose. Showtime.

Josh pulled a pair of M22 binoculars out of his rucksack and stepped deeper into the stand of birch trees on the edge of a hillside. He leaned the side of the binoculars on a tree to steady them and scanned the base of the slope. According to the digital display, the cinder blockhouse target was 320 yards in the distance as the crow flies, all downhill. A little longer on foot since the gravel road curved a bit rather than charting a direct course. A single door hung open about 30 degrees on the east side to the far left. He shifted his gaze to the roof. A single sentry stood there on the northeast corner, facing Josh directly and scanning the hillside with binoculars. The dash from road to door would have to happen when the guard stood on the opposite corner. The odds favored Josh during his descent through the shade if his opponent was using infrared because the afternoon sun would be heating the whole canopy above him. Josh timed his path. Roughly twelve minutes to complete a 360-scan of the terrain around the house. So, Josh had six minutes to get to the side of the house before someone spotted him.

Josh lifted the rucksack off the ground and slipped the straps over his shoulders. When the sentry moved to the northwest corner, Josh broke from the tree line and sprinted to the road. The pack cut into his back as it bounced up and down. He ignored the pain and kept his eye on the edge of the roof and the door. If anyone appeared, he would have to engage the target and still close the gap to the door.

No-man's-land was dead-man's-land.

Josh kept his legs churning as the distance to the wall closed. He crashed into the wall with his chest heaving, trying to catch his breath. He looked back at his starting point, and he saw the trail of dust, which followed his exact path to the wall. *Game over, if the sentry saw it.*

"Fuck me." Josh heaved off his pack, shouldered his rifle, and went through the door.

CHAPTER 3

Captain Aimon Moreno stood on the starboard bridge wing of the container ship *Garcia Asombrosa* and looked across the container yard of the Aztec Shipping Company. Forklifts were ferrying containers along the twelve streets of the yard like ants swarming a sugar pile. Three overhead dock cranes were busy loading 350 containers on his ship, which was docked starboard side to berth one at the Aztec facility in Vera Cruz, Mexico, just past Fort San Juan de Ulua. The Port of Veracruz is Mexico's third-largest port, just having completed a $160-million-dollar expansion in 2018, which included the construction of Latin America's longest breakwater at 4.3 kilometers long. He shifted his gaze from the port to the sealed yellow eight and a half by eleven-inch envelope in his right hand. "Captain Moreno, Eyes Only" was written on the front in black magic marker. A courier dropped it off at the gangway, and the ship's third mate brought it to him along with a cup of coffee that sat on the bridge wing railing with steam rising from the hot liquid. The envelope arrived every couple of months, so he knew what was inside, but it still gave him butterflies. He slipped his left index finger under the flap and pulled the envelope open.

Inside was the picture of a young girl on a swing with a smile on her face and pigtails flying in the wind dressed in a white T-shirt and pink shorts. There were other children in the background chasing a soccer ball. Behind the photograph was another piece of paper with two six-digit numbers:

061025 and 102127. Captain Moreno took another look at the picture and put it back in the envelope along with the piece of paper. He picked up the coffee mug, took another sip, squinted his eyes to hold back tears, and walked into the pilothouse.

Josh moved left and kneeled after slipping through the entrance. He scanned a hallway that extended about fifty feet into the building and ended in a T intersection. There was a single doorway on either side of the hall. A closed-door was on the right. The door on the left was open at 90 degrees. He strained his ears to listen. All quiet, he inched forward, keeping his rifle pointed at the end of the hallway and covering the entry on the left. When he was abreast of the opening, he took a quick peek. Nothing. Josh took three deep breaths and stepped into the room, ramming his shoulder into the open door, driving it hard against the wall. He felt resistance behind the wood and a surprised cry of "What the fuck?"

He leaned all his weight onto the wood, trapping the tango between the door and the wall. The door bucked back and forth. As he kept his pressure on it, he spotted a camouflaged figure in the corner straight across from him, fumbling to bring an AK-47 to bear as if he had just been napping on his feet.

Josh centered his red dot on the second tango's forehead and squeezed the trigger. There was a silenced *schwack*, then the man's head snapped back, and he slumped to the floor. Josh drew his sidearm and slipped it behind the door and squeezed off six shots to cries of "Ahhhh, son of a bitch." The door stopped bucking. Josh did a quick look behind the door. The tango sprawled on the floor with six body shots.

Josh trained his rifle on the door on the other side of the hallway. It didn't open. He did a quick peek down the corridor—nothing. Josh eased around the corner of the doorframe and sighted down the hallway. A head poked around the left corner, and Josh shot it right between the eyes. The tango dropped, and his weapon clattered onto the floor. A rifle muzzle snapped around the right corner, and a string of bullets whizzed down the hallway, striking around the doorframe, driving Josh back into the room. The door across the corridor opened, and another hail of bullets chased Josh farther into the room. Josh quick-stepped to the corner behind the door. Anyone trying to get in would have to enter the space to shoot instead of just sticking the barrel in and spraying the room. He propped the limp body of the door-dancer between the metal door and the wall to avoid getting trapped and provide space to maneuver. He ejected his magazine, which clanged to the floor, snatched another magazine from his vest, and rammed it home.

He sighted down his rifle at the crack between the door jam and the door. It was about three-quarters of an inch wide. A flash of movement filled the space, and Josh squeezed off three shots, which found their mark, impacting flesh—a body sprawled into the doorway, and an AK-47 clattered to the floor.

Another burst of gunfire lit off from the doorway, the impacts stitching the far wall, sending bits of concrete and dust flying. When the firing stopped, Josh pivoted sharply into the opening and leveled his weapon at the soldier, trying to reload in the room across the hall. Josh fired two shots center mass and one to the head, which snapped the tango's head back and dropped him to the floor.

Josh hustled through the door and started down the hallway. At the T intersection, he did a quick peek right—a dead end. Another quick peek left revealed an empty hall with a straight shot to an exterior door. Josh sprinted down the hallway and exited into the bright sunlight to cheers of "Granite, Granite, Granite" from an assembled group of Delta Force commandos.

CHAPTER

4

Director Vincent P. Santiago took a sip of Diet Coke and looked at his watch: 0950, ten minutes until his next appointment. Vince was Latino with black hair cut military short, dark brown eyes, and a scar over his right eye courtesy of deployment to Mogadishu. A former Delta operator and CIA paramilitary officer at forty-two years of age, he could still ace the Rangers' physical fitness test at five-foot-ten and 180 pounds. He wore his D.C. power suit, Calvin Klein charcoal-gray spring collection with a white shirt, red tie, red pocket square, American flag pin on the lapel, and gold cuff links with the Army A engraved on the front to remind him of his distant past.

The light flashed on Vince's secure phone, and the voice of Lisa, his executive assistant, came through the speaker.

"Senator Alonzo is here."

Vince pressed the speaker button. "Is her chief of staff with her?"

"No, sir."

"Roger—send her in." Without the chief of staff, they could discuss Black and White Club issues. Elaine Bishop was the senator's chief of staff and not read into the program.

Vince's office was small for someone who had twenty-four-seven personal access to the President of the United States. There was a sitting area to the left of the incoming Senator. A leather couch sat against the wall facing a glass coffee table and two leather chairs. A flat fifty-five-inch 4K T.V. hung over the sofa tuned to CNN. Every intelligence office in the DC, Virginia, and Maryland areas had a T.V. tuned to CNN. The goal was always to get information to the boss before he saw it himself. With the intelligence resources of the Black and White Club, Vince never lost to CNN when calling the President about vital incidents around the globe and within the United States. A cherry conference table with seating for eight was next, followed by two leather executive chairs facing his desk. His office had no windows because, like the rest of the third floor of the New Executive Office Building, it served as a Sensitive Compartmented Information Facility (SCIF).

Vince opened the door for Senator Donna Ruiz Alonzo. She rushed into the office—a woman on a mission, dressed in a gray pantsuit with a white shirt. Her brown hair was pulled back tight in a ponytail, and her brown eyes were red, seemingly from crying. She slammed the door behind her and stopped in front of Vince. Rage filled her face.

"They took my baby, Vince! Somebody took my baby!

CHAPTER 5

Josh smiled at the sound of his nickname, "Granite," from the assembled group of commandos. It meant he'd completed the six-month Operator's Training Course for the First Special Forces Operational Detachment-Delta (1st SFOD-D), often shortened to "Delta Force" or "The Unit." The final test was a forty-mile trek in full combat gear, carrying a forty-five-pound rucksack over rough terrain, culminating in an assault on a shoot house staffed with Delta operators waiting to rain vengeance on the recruit. Josh was far from a rookie since he was already a Navy SEAL. Director Santiago thought Josh needed some combat hardening before joining the ranks of the Black and White Club's Black Operative Directorate, and he needed some diversion and focus after losing his wife and unborn baby to a car bomb planted by a cartel operative.

The commandos parted, as a weather-beaten figure walked toward Josh.

"Not bad for a puddle pirate and a squid." Colonel Ted Gangsei extended his hand. He wore an Army combat uniform. His red hair was cut short, and he was clean-shaven, unlike his band of commandos, who looked like a motorcycle biker gang with long hair and beards. The sand of many deserts had blasted his face, leaving his complexion a mishmash of sunburn red, tan, and pale. Crow's feet framed his piercing blue eyes.

Josh shook his hand with a firm grip. "Thank you, Colonel. I hope I didn't shoot up your training team too bad."

"Well, why don't we find out?" Colonel Gangsei slapped Josh on the back. "All right, boys, come on out."

In Delta tradition, anyone shot during a combat drill paraded in front of his peers at the end of the exercise. The door of the shoot house banged open, and a line of commandos started to exit the building. Most of them were marked with two fluorescent-green splotches in the center of their chests and a single blemish in their face shields or helmets. Sergeant Jamison brought up the rear of the procession with a hitch in his giddy-up and six fluorescent-green marks over his entire body, including a nut shot, which brought derisive laughter and catcalls from the assembled group.

"Oooh," Colonel Gangsei said. "That's going to leave a mark."

The simulation rounds of soap with a fluorescent dye exited the weapon at regular velocity, so they hurt like a bitch to serve as a reminder to not get shot.

"All right, all right, simmer down," Colonel Gangsei told the howling commandos. The mayhem quickly silenced. "It gives me great pleasure to acknowledge another member into our brotherhood of warriors. Lieutenant Joshua Martin, call sign Granite, you are now officially a member of Delta Force. Congratulations! Tonight's celebration is on you!"

A loud cheer rose from the gathered commandos.

"Way to go, Granite! Bring your credit card."

Vince ushered Senator Alonzo to his couch, grabbed a box of tissues from the glass coffee table, and sat next to her. He handed her the tissues. She took a handful and dabbed her eyes. "So, Donna, what's going on?"

Donna took some deep breaths to slow down and gain her composure. As the only heir to the largest sugar conglomerate in Florida and the U.S. Senate Majority Leader, she was not used to getting emotional, especially in public. She steadied herself.

"Sorry about that, Vince, but sometimes a parent's love takes control. You have kids, so you know. I have two daughters, Bri and Deborah. Bri is a sophomore at the University of Central Florida. Like a good daughter, she's called me every Saturday morning for the last ten years. Last Saturday—no call. So, I tried to call her—straight to voice mail. I called her roommate. Bri went to a party Friday and didn't come back; she hasn't been seen since. I alerted the capitol police, called the FBI, and talked to the UCF Police Department. No one seems concerned about a missing college student. They think she shacked up with a boy after a wild weekend. Vince, I know my daughter. This is not right. Call it mother's intuition, but I know something is wrong. Something is seriously wrong." The tears welled up in her eyes again. "Can our people look into this for me?"

Vince sat back on the couch, contemplating what to do. *We usually don't get involved in missing persons or kidnapping, but we do have a new FBI Agent as a member of our Black Operations Group. I could call it a presidential favor and have Josh take a trip to Florida.* Donna looked like a worried mother, not a member of the Black and White Club executive committee who could end someone's life with a single vote.

Vince reached out, took her hand, and peered into her eyes.

"We'll do whatever it takes to find your daughter."

Calm returned to Donna's face because she knew what that statement meant. The Black and White Club would find her daughter using the best intelligence apparatus in the world. An elite cadre of trained and equipped agents would apply all necessary force to bring her back. She squeezed Vince's hand and stood up.

"I can't tell you how much this means to me, Vince. Thank you! Thank you! I trust you to call me right away the minute you learn anything. She walked over to his office door, stopped, and looked down. "I know you'll find her. And Vince, when you find those responsible, I want justice." She opened the door and walked out.

Vince leaned forward on the couch and put the tissues back on the table. *I wonder if Josh completed his training yet. He must be close.* Vince rose slowly, strode purposefully to his desk, and pushed his lips together while taking his seat. He picked up his cell phone, swiped his access pattern, scrolled through his lists of contacts, then pressed the green call button. The phone started to ring.

CHAPTER 6

She sat on the edge of a small bed dressed in white hospital scrubs, white sneakers, and white socks. She had found the clothes laid out on the bedspread when they finally led her to the room and locked her in. So far, no one had touched her except the creepy doctor who tore off her clothing and verified she was a virgin after they strapped her to the X. Haunted by the piercing screams, she had recoiled from minutes ago when the screams vibrated from the other side of her wall. She braced to lose her virginity to some ugly monster of a man who would revel in her pain and humiliation. The thought sent a shiver up her spine. A single dome light lit the windowless room. A bathroom with a toilet and tub/shower combination was attached. There was nothing else except a table with toilet paper, a toothbrush, toothpaste, dental floss, a single bar of soap, a stick of deodorant, and a towel arranged in a neat row.

She stood up from the bed and walked to the center of the room, sat in the middle of the floor in the lotus position, closed her eyes, and started to meditate. She focused on her breathing and calming her anxiety. She concentrated on the tenets of surviving a hostage situation she'd learned at the Center for Advanced Survival Training. Thank God her mother insisted on the training for both her and Deborah. She recited the creed in her head: *Remain calm. Be a person, not an object. Be valuable. Don't lie if there's any chance of getting caught. Help in your rescue. Eat and stay hydrated. Exercise.*

Feign compliance. Adopt a survivor mentality. Establish a bond with your captors. Plan your escape. Find the reason for your abduction. She took another deep breath, unready to open her eyes. *I don't think they abducted me for ransom, but I also don't think they know who I am.*

She opened her eyes at the idea. *Did anyone in that weird lineup know who I am?* She tried to remember, but it was mostly just a fog.

Tracy? Tammy? Biology? Red hair? Not good. Fuck me! She rolled over into a pushup position and cranked out twenty-five pushups, then followed up with twenty-five sit-ups.

Then the thought hit her: *This place probably has cameras.*

CHAPTER

7

Josh placed his hands on the edge of the bar and leaned down to stretch his back to get out the kinks. A forty-mile stroll with a forty-five-pound rucksack. *At least in the Navy and Coast Guard, we got to swim with no ruck.* He stood back up and took a sip of his Dos Equis Amber beer. The Lafayette room at the Iron Mike Conference Center in Fort Bragg, NC, was rocking. The Stone Age Juliets were belting out "Honky Tonk Women," and a bunch of drunk Delta troopers was gyrating on the dance floor with their significant others. Thirty round tables for eight surrounded the dance floor on the blue and gold carpet of the Lafayette Room under white tray light ceilings and gold walls. Colonel Gangsei and his wife, Jan, Major General Tim Day, his wife, Ellen, and Captain Nancy Nesbitt, the General's Aide de Camp, sat at the head table with all the services' battle flags lined up behind them. The ash and trash who usually accompany a general officer did not get invitations. That would prevent any misunderstanding regarding Delta warriors' opinions on military bearing, etiquette, and appearance.

Josh took another sip of beer and noticed Colonel Gangsei stand up from the head table with his cell phone pressed to his ear. The colonel nodded his head twice and looked straight at Josh. He put his phone back in his pocket and tilted his head left. Josh nodded in agreement and headed to the lobby.

Josh, attired in a dark-blue Zegna blazer with tan pants, a light blue shirt, and brown Johnston & Murphy shoes, looked great despite his limited wardrobe after six months of training. He'd gotten through Delta training the same way he did the SEALS: focused on the next second, the next minute, and the next hour to accomplish the task at hand. No looking ahead. All the indoc and physical hazing were mental games. It had taken him a month to get rid of his civilian sloth. Six months in, he was rock-hard and laser-focused. He gained twenty pounds of muscle from all the rucksack marches and hitting the weights daily. As his brother JJ would say, he had functional fitness. Millions of dollars in DOD research determined the number-one attribute for excelling on the battlefield was physical strength. You could either carry your two-hundred-pound wounded comrade two miles, or you couldn't. Josh set the record for the obstacle course and could outshoot anyone in his training cadre. No one wanted to meet him in the battle ring—MMA for grunts. Every new Delta graduate got a call sign. They called Josh "Granite" because he hailed from Lancaster, New Hampshire—the Granite State.

Josh weaved around the tables to the exit and pushed through the door into the foyer. Colonel Gangsei was waiting for him. He felt two zaps on his wrist from his Rolex watch, but he already knew the colonel was a black operative for the Black and White Club. Most Delta Force members were part of the club.

"Nice party, Josh. Usually, we just get a couple of kegs and some takeout pizza. Sit-down dinner for three hundred plus an open bar and a live band must have set you back a little bit."

Josh shook hands with Colonel Gangsei and smiled. "It's all good, Colonel. I put it on the corporate card."

Colonel Gangsei laughed. "Vince is going to enjoy that. Speaking of Vince, that was him on the phone. He called earlier this afternoon to check on your status. He needs your talents on an urgent matter in Florida. I have a car outside ready to take you to Simmons Airfield. A Black Hawk is waiting on the tarmac for a hop down to NAS Jax. You'll get a mission brief there.

That's all I got. Sorry for the last-minute tasking; I know you were planning on a couple of weeks off."

"No worries, Colonel. What about my gear?"

"I'll have your stuff packed up. Send me an address where you want it to go. You'll have to get outfitted at Jax."

"Roger, sir! Thank you for all your guidance over the last six months." Josh stuck out his hand.

Colonel Gangsei shook his hand, pulled him in for a bear hug, and whispered in his ear. "You can call me Ted, and if you ever need anything, and I mean anything, I've got three hundred Delta troopers ready to cover your back."

Josh stepped back. "Thanks, Ted, and if you need any help with parking tickets or arrests for solicitation, you can give me a call." They both laughed. Josh headed for the exit.

"Hey Josh," Ted said. "I almost forgot—a special guest is going to meet you in Jacksonville."

Josh waved his hand over his head and pushed through the exit into the great unknown.

CHAPTER 8

Captain Aimon Moreno stared at the bank of four computer monitors strapped to the desk in his cabin. They were for administration, weather, navigation, and the status of ship systems. He looked at the navigation screen. The track legs for the trip to Tampa displayed on the screen with 917 nautical miles. At fifteen knots, the *Garcia Asombrosa* could make the trip in sixty-one hours, depending on the weather.

The weather screen showed a front passing through the Gulf of Mexico in the next forty-eight hours, so a delay seemed likely. He took a note on a scratch pad to call the Tampa agent with an updated ETA. The *Garcia Asombrosa* made regular runs between Tampa and Veracruz carrying finished car engines for G.M., Fiat, Chrysler, and Ford into the United States and returning to Mexico with parts and assemblies to build the engines. Captain Moreno looked up at the sound of a knock on his door.

"Enter." Captain Moreno pushed his chair back from his desk and looked at his cabin door.

Lope Calma pushed through the door. "We're all loaded, Captain." Lope was the first mate. He had long black hair pulled back in a ponytail with a tattoo of a wolf on his right forearm. He was about six feet and 190 pounds with dark brown skin and the look of a man who made his living at sea.

"Did our friends arrive?" Captain Moreno asked.

"Yes, Captain. Two men signed on. Their papers are in order."

"Two? There's usually only one for special cargo."

"Must be a large shipment." Lope scratched his head at the thought. "They asked me to speak with you."

"Okay. Call for the pilot and tugs. Tell our friends I'll see them when we clear the sea buoy."

"Aye, Captain." Lope backed out of the cabin and pulled the door closed behind him.

Captain Moreno looked at the manila envelope on his desk. *How do I get out of this madness?* Money is only useful if you live long enough to spend it.

Josh walked down the steps of the Iron Mike Conference Center, slid into the passenger seat of the waiting vehicle, and turned to speak to the driver. "Oh, shit, how are the family jewels?"

Sergeant Mike Jamison winced as he turned his head. "They're turning all kinds of black and blue. Docs say no permanent damage, but light duty for a couple of days. Teach me to hide behind a door."

"Sorry for the nut shot, but it's all reflex when the bullets start flying." Josh clicked his seat belt.

"Yeah, no worries." Sergeant Jamison wound through Fort Bragg to an entrance gate at Simmons Airfield. A sentry flagged him down at the gate. Sergeant Jamison lowered the driver's side window and flashed his I.D. "I got one for a ride to NAS Jax."

The guard checked the I.D. and shined his flashlight at Josh. Josh passed over his FBI credential for the guard to review. "Your bird is the second on the left. They just finished pre-checks, and they're ready to go." The guard stepped back and waved them through.

Sergeant Jamison pulled up to the edge of the safety circle around the Black Hawk on the tarmac and put the car in park. Josh hopped out and walked around the vehicle to the driver's side window.

"Thanks for the lift." He handed Sergeant Jamison a twenty.

"What's this?"

"Tip for the taxi ride," Josh said with a laugh. "Buy yourself some frozen peas for the family jewels." He tapped the car roof twice and started walking over to the helo.

"Good luck, Josh. You're all right for a fed," Sergeant Jamison shouted out the window.

Josh turned, tapped his chest twice, and pointed at the car as he walked up to the waiting flight crew.

CHAPTER

9

Bishop Stephanie "Steph" Avery leaned back in her white marble chair with gold-trimmed purple seat cushions to survey her domain. In front of her was a white marble altar with a gold cross in the center. Flanked on either side were three golden chairs occupied by the lightkeepers, named after the archangels: Michael, Raphael, and Gabriel were on her left. Uriel, Raguel, and Remiel were on her right. Saraqael was seated on the far right of the Sanctuary near the access to the stage. The lightkeepers wore robes of gold. A large video screen hung over the main altar so all of God's creations could see the wonders of the Church of Illuminology from the cheap seats. Beyond the screen were velvet floor seats for the true lights of God, who donated more than a million a year to the church. Behind the true lights of God was the control section, who beamed the church's weekly services on the Gospel Broadcasting Network and Night Vision Television Network as well as local channels in most major U.S. markets. On either side of the floor, the seats expanded upward like a basketball arena with a lower and upper bowl, finally topped by a ring of skyboxes for the truly enlightened. The total church capacity was sixteen thousand per service, with two ninety-minute services each weekend on Saturday and Sunday. It was always standing room only. Not bad for a preacher's daughter from Melbourne, Florida.

Bishop Avery stood, and her white robe flowed around her. At five-foot-three and a toned 120 pounds, she wore three-inch heels to appear taller.

Her red hair was cut short and fell just below her ears. A plain gold cross hung from her neck and draped across her chest. She wore stage makeup so she would look fantastic on T.V. and the video screen. Her blue eyes sparkled in the light of God. The congregation rose in unison as she stood.

With outstretched hands, she said, "May the light of God shine on you and keep you safe until we meet again in this holy place. Please, go with the grace of God. Peace be with you."

"And also with you," the audience responded.

Bishop Avery walked off the stage to the right with her white robe trailing behind her. She stopped in front of Saraqael just off stage, who unzipped her gown from the back. She stepped out of the gown, grabbed the hood, and handed it to a waiting guardian dressed in a black suit, white shirt, and black tie. The guardian hurried off with his charge to have it cleaned for the next service.

Bishop Avery turned to Saraqael. "Can you please find Annie and have her come to my office to get this crap off my face? Then stop by and let me know how we did Friday night and how many we have en route."

CHAPTER

10

The flight from Fort Bragg to Naval Air Station Jax took a little over two and a half hours. Josh slept most of the way. He woke up when the flight mechanic told him they were twenty minutes out. The lights of Jacksonville flew by the window until he saw the distinct markers of a runway. The helo transitioned from forward flight to a hover, and NAS Jax, the third largest naval installation in the world, appeared out his window. The chopper settled on the landing pad just off runway ten, and the pilots cut the engines. Two General Electric T700-GE-01C engines started to wind down, and the blades came to a stop. The flight mechanic popped the door, and Josh stepped out on the tarmac. A dark-blue Tahoe parked next to the pad flashed its lights, and Josh walked over to climb into the passenger seat and extend his hand to the driver.

"Josh Martin."

"Petty Officer O'Zaki," came the reply as they shook hands.

"What's your first name?" Josh asked.

"Art. Captain Andy White sends his regards. He's the base Commanding Officer." Art started the engine and headed off the tarmac.

"Thanks for coming to get me, Art. Any idea where I'm staying?"

"You're booked into one of the Heritage Cottages. They're really nice. My instructions are to drop you off and let you know someone will meet you in the morning." Art drove through the airfield gate and turned left toward the cottage recreation area.

"Any idea who?"

"No, sir. Above my pay grade."

"Roger that." Josh sat back in the seat and watched NAS Jax pass by the window. *Back to the land of the big P.X.*

It was a quick trip to the cottage. Petty Officer O'Zaki pulled in front of a tan building with a green roof, white shutters, and a red door. A screened porch with a white door enclosed the entrance.

He put the Tahoe in park and handed Josh a white plastic key card across the console. "This is your key to the palace."

Josh took the key and opened the car door. "Thanks for the lift, Art. Have a great night." He stepped out into the fresh night air, shut the door, and gave Art a wave. The Tahoe backed out of the driveway and headed off into the night.

Josh turned to look at his accommodations. A single light to the left of the front door lit the porch. He opened the screen porch door and walked up to the red front door. He flashed the card at the lock, the light blinked green, and he pushed through the door.

The cottage looked and smelled like a thousand DOD rooms across the country with light green walls, GSA furniture, and G.I. disinfectant. The cabin was basically one big room with an attached bedroom and bathroom. Two fabric living room chairs in a green floral print were on the left as Josh entered the cottage. An end table with a lamp sat between them. A small green sofa was angled at 90 degrees from the chairs and faced a small flat-screen T.V. on a wooden folding table. A little brown wood coffee table sat in front of the sofa with a black binder, which probably contained the cottage rules and regulations. The room continued into the kitchen, separated by a small oval dinette table with four chairs. The kitchen formed an L shape with a dishwasher, sink, stove, and refrigerator. A microwave and toaster sat on the counter with a coffee maker in the corner. Attached to the side of the coffee maker was a basket with sugar packets and creamer pods.

Josh walked to the refrigerator and opened the door.

The refrigerator contained bread, eggs, bacon, O.J., deli ham, mustard, lettuce, tomatoes, and milk. A six-pack of Dos Equis Amber beer was chilling on the bottom shelf. Josh reached in and pulled out a beer. He found a bottle opener in one of the drawers, popped the top, and took a sip of beer. Cold and refreshing. He owed somebody a considerable favor. He walked into the bedroom, which contained a queen-size bed flanked by two nightstands with lamps and a clock radio on the left stand. The bed faced a dresser with another T.V. on top and a remote next to it. Laid out on the bed were two sets of clean towels, toiletries, underwear, and three sets of Navy PT gear, including shorts, T-shirts, socks, sweats, and Nike Air Max running shoes. He checked the sizes. They would all fit. A small, folded card sat on top of the towels. Josh flipped it open.

See you in the morning.

Becka

PS—I'm bringing a friend.

CHAPTER 11

Captain Moreno lounged in his recliner and sipped a can of Diet Pepsi. A soccer game between Mexico and Colombia played on a fifty-five-inch T.V. mounted to the ceiling in front of him. Mexico led two to nothing. On his left, beyond an identical recliner, a brown leather couch reached from the entrance to the bulkhead. It sported dark blue pillows with gold anchors stitched in the corners. A desk sat across from the entrance under a porthole. Beyond it, he could see an identical porthole through the open door of his sleeping quarters. An eight-person conference and dining table occupied the space behind him. He took another sip of his Pepsi and looked at his watch. They cleared the sea buoy about thirty minutes before. No guests yet.

As if on cue, he heard a knock on his cabin door. He retracted his recliner footrest, climbed out of the chair, walked over to his cabin door, and opened it. Lope and two unknown faces were waiting for him.

"Come on in, gentlemen." Captain Moreno waved his guests into his cabin.

"Thank you, Captain." Lope walked in. "This is Amado Arias and Berto Sala." They were Colombians, both about thirty years old, with dark-brown skin, black hair, and black mustaches. They wore *Garcia Asombrosa* dark-blue coveralls and looked like crew members, except both carried silver attaché cases.

"Welcome, my friends," Captain Moreno said. "Let's move over to my table and sit down. Can I get you anything? A soda? Coffee?"

"No, gracias," Amado said. "Thank you for taking the time to see us."

They walked over to the table and took seats. Captain Moreno sat at the head with Lope on his right. The other two sat across from them and placed the cases on the table. It was the same game each month. Sometimes twice a month. Usually, it was only one package. This time it's two. The boxes were containers added to the ship's manifest. The game also called for additional crew members to ensure the packages' arrival into the United States and the return cargo back to Mexico.

The escort couriers were always different. They placed the cases on the table, popped the latches, opened the lids, and turned them to face the Captain. Each case contained twenty-five stacks of twenty-dollar-bills banded in $2,000 increments, a total of $50,000. Each of the twenty-one-member crew received a $2,000 payment in cash for each shipment. The first mate and chief engineer received $50,000 for each load, and Captain Moreno received $100,000 per shipment. Their funds were deposited in offshore accounts in the Cayman Islands via wire transfer. Captain Moreno kept any excess cash in his safe if they had to pay off an unexpected Customs official or dock worker.

"Looks good, gentlemen. Thank you," Captain Moreno said. "I'll update you on our arrival time when I know our transit speed based on the weather. There's a storm building ahead of us." Captain Moreno stood up, followed by the escorts and Lope.

"Thank you, Captain," Amado said. "I'll tell our compadres." They all shook hands, and the couriers exited the cabin.

Lope walked over to the cases, took out four stacks from each case, and put them on the table. He closed the cases and picked them up. "I'll distribute this to the crew," he said as he headed to the door.

"Thanks, Lope." Captain Moreno sat down and looked at the money. *I wonder how much cocaine or heroin we're carrying. It has to be drugs for this much money.* He knew the value of a kilo of cocaine depended on the form. It was cheap during production at the point of origin in Colombia, Peru, or Bolivia. It went up to between $5,000 and $10,000 a kilo, depending on the "staging area" of Central America, the Caribbean countries, other islands, or Mexico. Once the kilo arrived "safely" in the U.S. (on the West Coast), the price doubled and increased with farther distance eastward. A kilo of 85 percent pure cocaine on the East Coast cost approximately $32,000. Prices also depended on relationships between buyers and sellers, geography, and other factors.

How many kilos do we have? Captain Moreno stood up, picked up the stacks of cash, and walked over to his safe on the left side of his desk. He punched in the code and put the stacks next to the money pile already in the safe. He picked up the manila envelope on his desk and slipped out the picture of the little girl, and smiled at the image of his daughter, Isabel. She was getting big. They always sent a recent picture before every shipment—a reminder there was no way out.

CHAPTER 12

Josh took a sip of coffee and put the cup down on the cottage porch's patio table. The previous night's sleep was amazing. He wasn't sure when his guests would arrive, so he got up at six, took a shower, and got dressed in Navy PT gear. He made bacon and eggs with toast for breakfast, and there was nothing left on his plate except some yellow smear. A cool breeze blew through the porch screen and rustled through some long green grass planted next to the cottage. A faint rumble broke his first quiet moment in six months. He tilted his head toward the distant noise and couldn't quite place the familiar sound. It came closer. When he moved to the porch, his chest vibrated in resonance with it. A ruby red Ford F150 Platinum crew cab roared around a stand of palm trees next to the neighboring cottage and headed in his direction.

"No fucking way." Josh stared in disbelief as the Shelby F-150 pulled into the cottage parking lot and cut the engine. A barking dog was jumping around in the front seat. Tears filled Josh's eyes. "No fucking way." *She's supposed to be at Mom's in New Hampshire.* "Oh man, no fucking way." The driver's side door opened, and a babe with short blonde hair hopped out, followed by a shrieking hair missile who sped past the blonde and sprinted straight for Josh. He bent down and caught her full in the chest—seventy pounds of excited Belgian Malinois, happy beyond belief.

"Syrin. I missed you so much." Josh pulled her in close for a hug and felt pure joy in his arms. He let her go and stood up. "Who's my good girl?" Syrin danced around Josh, doing her booty shake and barking. He grabbed her snout and gave it a shake, getting happy growls in return. Syrin ran to the stand of palm trees and went on kennel point. "You have to clean that up." Syrin scratched in the grass, ran back over to Josh, and rubbed on his legs to mark her property.

"Some girl is happy to see her man." LCDR Becka Kendall extended her hand. She wore a dark-blue polo shirt with tan pants and white sneakers. "Glad to finally meet you in person. I'm Becka."

Josh shook her hand and felt two zaps on his wrist from his watch. She didn't look like other black operatives. This one you'd bring home to your mom. "Becka? As in Becka, who stocked the cottage?"

"That would be me."

"You are a true angel. I slept like a baby last night and ate my best breakfast in six months. How much do I owe you for the food and clothes?"

"Not a thing. I put it on the company card." She scratched behind Syrin's ears, who clearly liked the attention.

"I hear there's a lot of that going around," Josh said with a laugh. "Nice truck. It sounds like a Shelby. How'd you get it?" Josh walked over to the truck and opened the door to look inside. The interior was black leather and smelled brand new.

Becka trailed behind him. "Not my truck. It's yours. Title and registration are in the center console. I'm supposed to give you this." She handed Josh a white envelope with the presidential seal.

Josh opened the envelope and pulled out a notecard, also with a presidential seal. He flipped it open. *It was the least we could do. Brian.* Josh stared at the truck in disbelief. "How did they get a Shelby? They only made five hundred." Josh climbed into the front seat and rubbed his hands on the steering wheel. Syrin stuck her nose in the truck.

"The President is good friends with the CEO of Ford." Becka stepped up on the running board. "They made this truck as an exact copy of a Ford Shelby with some modifications from the Defense Advanced Research Projects Agency. The body of the truck is ceramic armor supported by a ductile backing of nanite composite materials. The glass is a nanite shield. Unlike your old truck, which had all the additional weight from ballistic protection, this truck is the same weight as an original aluminum F-150. Still, it's bulletproof from conventional small arms. The glass won't fail after five AK-47 rounds."

"This is amazing," Josh said like a kid at Christmas.

Becka stepped off the running board and opened the rear cab door. She reached in and hit a silver disk on the floor of the truck, and the back seat flipped up to reveal a gun safe. "They also installed your old armory, complete with Benelli shotgun, go-bag, gas mask, flashbangs, and M67 grenades."

Josh turned in his seat. "You're shitting me."

"Nope. You have all the gear and seven hundred horsepower under the hood." Becka reached into the truck and pulled out a black canvas duffle bag with a lock on the side. "As much as I'd love talking trucks with you, we have a time-sensitive mission to discuss. What do you say we chat inside?"

"Roger that." Josh climbed out of the truck and shut the door.

CHAPTER

13

Bishop Avery took a sip of morning coffee from a fine white china cup with a gold inlay rim and a picture of the Cape Canaveral Lighthouse, the founding symbol of the Church of Illuminology. Attired in a knee-length white skirt and white blouse separated by a wide black belt along with matching two-tone black and white shoes, she leaned back in her chair to enjoy the morning. The gold cross still hung around her neck. She set the cup on a white saucer and pressed the control button on her keypad. The homepage flashed on. She moved her cursor to a video camera icon and left-clicked the mouse control. A bank of seven camera views filled her screen.

Each view showed a picture of their holding rooms and the occupants. She saw six girls curled up in fetal positions on their beds in various stages of crying. The seventh girl was exercising. *Hmmm. Six sheep and one lioness.* She hit replay on the video stream and watched six sheep cry and wail for over eight hours and cringe every time food was delivered. Their plates were untouched, and they said nothing. The lioness exercised, greeted everyone who brought food, and ate and drank everything. She would also meditate in various positions on the bed and floor. Bishop Avery checked her notes from Saraqael's brief. *Marvelous! This one's a virgin. Some raghead is going to pay dearly for this prize—twenty-three more en route. Holy Ship is underway. Double shipment.* She picked up her encrypted cell phone from the edge of her desk and punched in a number. The call was answered on the second ring.

"Yes?"

"We are going to have an outstanding quarter." Bishop Avery turned to look at the lush green lawn out her office window. It reminded her of the fairways at Augusta during the Masters.

"Excellent," came the reply. "I plan to make a sizeable donation to the President's reelection campaign."

Josh held the cottage door open for Becka. Syrin ran in ahead. "Looks like someone forgot her manners."

Becka followed her in. "I think she's claiming her position as top dog," she said with a laugh. Syrin sniffed around every nook and cranny in the cottage.

Becka walked over to the dinette set. "I love what you've done with the place." She set the bag on the table and took a seat.

Josh followed her and walked into the kitchen. "After where I've been for the last six months, this place is like the Ritz. Do you want some coffee?"

"I'd love some." Becka pulled out her phone, found the app, and pressed a button. The lock on the canvas bag popped open.

"Do you want anything in it?" Josh got two mugs out of the cupboard and filled them.

"Nope, I take mine black." Becka unzipped the canvas bag and pulled out some manila folders.

"I guess no pink lady jokes and lipstick on the mug, but in your case, that might be an exception." Josh walked over to the table, sat down opposite Becka, and pushed a coffee to her.

Syrin finished the security recon of the cottage. No mice, food scraps, or tennis balls, so all clear. She walked over and lay down on Josh's feet under the table.

"Really? A bed, a couch, and two living room chairs, but you have to lie on my feet?" Syrin let out a sigh and shifted to get comfortable.

Josh took a sip of coffee. "So, what is so important I miss thirty days of recovery leave?"

"This." Becka opened a manila folder and slid it across the table to Josh.

Josh stopped the folder with his left hand, picked it up, and flipped it open. "I haven't looked at paper documents in a while." On the left side of the folder was an eight-and-a-half-by-eleven picture of a smiling redheaded teenager. *Looks like a senior yearbook photo.* The name "*Bri Castillo*" appeared in black Sharpie at the bottom of the image. The other sections of the folder contained names and addresses of known associates, car registrations, phone numbers, and background information for the last ten years. Josh flipped through the pages. "Okay. Why do I care about Bri Castillo?"

"Bri went to a party last Friday night, and no one has seen her since. No activity on her phone, no credit card usage, and GNOSIS shows no facial recognition on any camera system or mention on social media except that she's missing." Becka took a sip of coffee. "This is pretty good for a coastie."

"Do you know why there's no ice on the sideline of a Navy football game?" Josh asked.

"No, why?" Becka replied.

"The cadet with the recipe graduated." Josh closed the folder.

"Ha. Not bad. What do you know about GNOSIS?"

"From what Vince told me, it's a reprogrammable quantum computer at the University of Maryland, and we reconfigured it to run our system called the Buxton D-Wave Quantum Computer in honor of our first director. The

Buxton D-Wave runs our GNOSIS system, which is Google, on a global scale for intelligence, which provides keyword searches on anything."

"Wow. I'm impressed." She took the folder back.

"Now it's my turn. How do you fit into all this? I felt the double zap when we shook hands, but you don't look like any black operative I've met." Josh moved his feet from under Syrin to keep them from falling asleep. Syrin repositioned to lay back on his feet.

"I'm in charge of our East Coast intelligence center. Our facility's in an underground bunker about a mile from here at the Navy Munitions Command. I'll be your Black and White Club case officer for this mission." Becka slid another folder across the table. "This is why you care about Bri Castillo."

Josh opened the folder. The left side had an official portrait of Senator Donna Ruiz Alonzo. "Oh, shit! So, what's the plan?"

CHAPTER 14

The lioness looked at the clock on the wall—almost noon. *Lunch should be here soon.* She sat down on the bed and waited. A toothbrush with the end sharpened to a point was under her left leg. She'd fashioned her makeshift shiv in the middle of the night by rubbing it on the edge of the metal bed frame. If they had infrared cameras, her bid for freedom would be short-lived. So far, no room searches. There was a knock on the door.

"I'm on the bed." She was required to sit on the bed any time someone came into the room.

The door opened, and a girl and boy about her age entered the room. They were both dressed in white shirts and black pants. The boy always blocked the doorway while the girl carried a tray with food and a carton of milk, like lunch at the high school cafeteria. The girl would set the tray on the table and turn to leave. She would walk out of the room, and the boy would pull the door closed.

She contemplated her options. *There's no way I'm going to get both of them. All the boy has to do is pull the door closed, and I'm screwed. I'm sure they're not concerned about the welfare of a single cult girl.* She lay back on the bed to think through the problem and slipped the toothbrush shiv under the fold of the bed covers. *No one is concerned that I can see their faces, which means I'm not going to be around for the trial.*

Becka took another sip of coffee and pulled the folder back from Josh. "Bri Castillo's real name is Bri Castillo Alonzo. Castillo is her grandmother's name. Somewhere along the family tree, someone married an Irishman or woman, which is how Bri wound up with red hair. Otherwise, Senator Alonzo was getting some on the side, but we found no indication of that. She uses Castillo for security purposes."

"Not a bad idea, given the current political climate in the country," Josh said. He slid his chair back and extricated his feet from under Syrin, who raised her head off the floor. "Feels like you put on a couple of pounds from Grandma's cooking." Josh looked back at Becka. "Sorry, someone was putting my feet to sleep."

"So, Bri went to a Delta Faros Fraternity party on Friday night. She didn't make her weekly call to her mom, and her roommates said she didn't come back to the apartment. Her apartment is at The Oasis, an off-campus housing complex for the University. Senator Alonzo alerted the FBI, Orange County Sheriff's Office, the UCF Police Department, and the Capitol Police. No one was distressed about a missing college student who didn't return from a party. They figured she shacked up with a significant other."

"Makes sense to me. I've never heard of Delta Faros. Who are they?" Syrin moved over and got back on Josh's feet. "Really?" Josh bent down and scratched her head.

Becka scanned through some notes in the folder. "They're affiliated with the Church of Illuminology. They have fraternity and sorority chapters at two thousand colleges and universities across the country."

"And what about the Church of Illuminology? Sounds like bullshit to me, or a tax dodge."

"The church's annual budget last year was ninety million, so that's a whole lotta bullshit." Becka reached into the duffel and pulled out a Glock 22, Gen 4, four-inch, forty-caliber Smith & Wesson, two full magazines, and a Sig Sauer P938 9mm. "These are your firearms. We weren't sure if you switched weapons after your Delta training, but I figured this was a start. You also have the Benelli in the truck armory, and we installed an M4 carbine under the back seat.

Josh picked up the Glock, ejected the magazine, and jacked the slide to the rear.

He checked the barrel. It was spotless. The action was smooth. "Someone worked on the gun."

"Our armorer checked out everything." Becka pulled out a black canvas carry bag. "I wasn't sure how you were going to carry in Florida, so I got you this." She tossed a black canvas fanny bag over to Josh and pulled a cell phone out of the duffel. "This is your encrypted cell phone. I transferred all of your previous contacts and installed contact info for me, Director Santiago, Dave Tuley, and Colonel Gangsei." She slid the phone over by the bag.

Josh pulled his feet from under Syrin and stood up. Syrin climbed out from under the table and provided escort service to the sink, where Josh put his coffee cup. "What are we going to do about her highness?" Josh bent down and grabbed Syrin behind her ears and hugged her.

"She's going with you." Becka pulled another folder out of her bag. "You aren't the only one who went for training. We sent Syrin for four months of training at the military working dog school at Joint Base San Antonio. She graduated at the top of her class. Her only shortcoming was bonding with her trainer." Becka tossed the folder on top of the gun bag. "These are her official papers. We even got a special waiver from the director of the FBI, since all FBI dogs are Labrador retrievers."

"What was her training language?" Josh stood up, and Syrin jumped up and put her paws on his chest.

"German." Becka pushed her chair back and got up. "Your orders are to proceed to Orlando and find out what happened to Bri Alonzo. Call Director Santiago when you're on the road."

"Roger. Can I give you a lift somewhere?" Josh got free of Syrin and walked over to the table.

"No thanks, I'm good. I have a car on standby, and I need to erase your presence from this cottage." She zipped up her duffel and closed the lock.

"Okay. Syrin, are you ready for a road trip?" Josh asked. Syrin barked and walked to the door. "I take that as a yes."

CHAPTER

15

Captain Moreno looked at the raging sea from the bridge of the *Garcia Asombrosa*. Fifteen- to-twenty-foot rolling white caps were slamming the bow, and sea spray blew across the deck. A driving rain with fifty-knot winds was howling around the superstructure. The clear view screens on the bridge windows worked overtime to keep up with the rain and sea spray—nothing like a tropical storm to keep things interesting.

"What is our speed of advance?" Captain Moreno gripped the front bridge handrail to steady himself as the ship rolled to starboard.

"We're turning for ten knots, Captain, and making about four," came the third mate's reply.

"Have the deck crew check the tie-downs on our special cargo. We can lose an entire lot of boxes, but we cannot lose those two. I'll be down in my cabin." Captain Moreno turned to leave the bridge.

"Aye, Captain."

Saraqael, the angel of death and protection for the Church of Illuminology, knocked on the door and walked in. She wore a black suit and open-collared white shirt with black tactical Low Pro shoes. Her brown hair was pulled back into a tight ponytail. At five foot ten and 140 pounds, she was a professional soldier. "Bishop Avery?"

"Sari, I'm at my desk," came a reply from another room.

Bishop Avery's office was two rooms separated by an expansive wooden archway. Sari walked into an all-white conference and reception room. A white marble conference table with polished silver corner accents sat at the far end. Four high-back white fabric chairs adorned each side, and two captain chairs occupied each end. A crystal chandelier hung over the table. A bank of white-framed windows with a view of the sweeping church lawn dominated the far wall. The rest of the area was open space for church functions with various pictures of church events adorning the walls. The church photographer would change them out every month.

Sari walked across the gleaming white marble floor to the archway. On the left side of the arch was a built-in wine refrigerator with eight stacked wooden trays holding ten bottles of wine, each at precisely 50 degrees. The fridge featured Château Lafite Rothschild 2016, Bodegas Vega Sicilia Unico Tinto 2006, Château Mouton Rothschild 2015, and Louis Latour Château Corton Grancey 2015 for the guests. On the right side of the arch was a framed picture of Bishop Avery and her dad in front of the Cape Canaveral Light on Easter Sunday. Sari touched the portrait as she walked by.

"The ship's going to be late." Sari walked into the office. The thick, padded white carpet squished under her feet. The office contained a glass desk on the right, which faced another expanse of white-framed windows. Two beige leather recliners in front of the windows faced left toward a wall-mounted 8K T.V. A door to the exterior terrace was behind the chairs. Sari sat on one of two art deco white mocha metal swivel chairs, which faced the desk. A computer monitor sat next to a keyboard, a mouse pad with a picture of a flying dove, and a desk blotter with a pad of paper. To the left, a bud vase held a single white rose, which the gardener replaced every day.

Bishop Avery turned to face Sari. She took off her glasses, tossed them onto the desk, and rubbed her eyes. "What's the problem?"

"Tropical Storm Cory. I just got a text from the ship. They slowed to ten knots due to the weather, but they're only making about four through the water. No ETA yet." Sari shifted in her chair. "These chairs really suck."

"Yeah, I know, but they help keep meetings brief. When are the rest of the girls arriving?"

"Two days. We can't keep twenty-three girls here." Sari stood up and walked over to the windows. A landscaper was bent over in a flower bed across the lawn, pulling weeds.

Bishop Avery leaned back in her chair. "What do you suggest?"

Sari turned back from the window. "I think we should use the conference center—the next scheduled event's in two weeks. We should be able to move the girls out well ahead of it. The building's easy to secure."

"Okay, sounds good. You also need to let our distribution folks know the shipment is running behind schedule. Come look at this." Bishop Avery moved her mouse pointer to the camera icon and brought up the holding room cameras on her computer. She clicked on lioness's video feed.

"What's that?" Sari walked over and stood behind Bishop Avery.

"One of your charges made a shank." She froze the video of the charge, sliding her shiv under the fold of the bed.

"Holy shit. Which one?" Sari peered at the screen. "Looks like a toothbrush."

"It's the red-headed virgin. She's not your typical sheep." Bishop Avery played the video with the girl meditating, working out, eating, interacting, and observing.

"She's been trained. We need to check her background. She's not your typical princess. Someone's going to come looking for her." Sari walked back to the front of the desk.

"See what you can find out. Also, introduce yourself, so she doesn't get any ideas about sticking one of our members." Bishop Avery put her glasses back on.

"Roger, boss." Sari turned to leave.

"One more thing. Make sure you're right. I don't want to disappear a million-dollar asset unless I have to."

CHAPTER

16

Josh set the cruise on the truck to eighty and followed the traffic flow on I-95 South. Syrin slept in the shotgun seat. He pressed the Bluetooth button on the steering wheel. "Call Vince Santiago."

Vince picked up on the third ring. "I would have picked up right away, but I was checking to make sure my car warranty wasn't going to expire. Where are you?"

"About forty miles south of Jacksonville, heading south on I-95. I should be in Orlando in about ninety minutes."

"How's your partner doing?"

Josh looked over at Syrin. "Snoring like a sailor after a port call in Bangkok. I can't thank you enough for sending her down. Also, please thank the President for the truck. I can't believe I'm actually driving another Shelby."

"It's the least we could do for you. Thanks for taking this assignment. You can catch your recovery leave after the mission. Colonel Gangsei had nothing but great things to say about you. He wanted to know if he could keep you."

"I hope you told him no. Hiking up and down hillsides is not my forte. Also, rucksacks suck."

“That they do. I told him Black Ops had first dibs. Speaking of which, your present assignment is not a sanctioned Black and White Club operation. You’re operating as an FBI agent. FBI rules of engagement apply. If anything changes, let me know, and I’ll brief the executive committee.”

“Roger.” Josh signaled left and passed a blue Mercedes. “Anything else?”

“One more thing. I’m sending you help. She’ll meet you at the UCF Police Department. I’ll text you her number. Good luck. Call Becka if you need anything.”

“Roger. Talk to you later.” Josh ended the call and looked over at Syrin. “Hey, Snore Queen, you could keep me company.” Syrin didn’t move.

The lioness sat in the middle of the floor in the lotus position with thoughts of walking the beach in Saint Marten. The sun heated her back, and the water-cooled her feet while she walked through the shallow surf. A knock on the door snapped her back to reality. *Not lunchtime. So, not good.* She got to her feet and moved to the bed. “I’m on the bed.”

The door opened, and a woman in a black suit with a white shirt walked in. Her brown hair was pulled back in a ponytail, and she moved like an athlete. She walked into the center of the room and looked at Bri. “I think you have something for me.”

“I don’t know what you mean,” Bri said, trying to keep her voice from cracking. Her brain didn’t register the quick hand that slapped her face, snapped her head back, and knocked her into the wall. A firm grip twisted her left arm behind her back and pressed her face into the bed with the weight of the woman on her back. The point of something sharp pressed against her neck. *Oh shit. Oh shit. Oh shit.*

“No, please!”

CHAPTER 17

Josh took a right on State Road 50 West and exited on Alafaya Trail.

He took another right and continued to University Boulevard, passing a sign which said *Welcome to the University of Central Florida*. He continued through the campus, turned into the parking lot for the UCF Police Department, and pulled the truck into a visitor's slot next to three flag poles flying Old Glory, the Florida state flag, and the flag of the university.

"Yo, your highness, we're here." Syrin raised her head and sat up to look around. "I'll leave the truck running with the A.C. on. You protect the valuables."

Josh slid out of the truck and looked up at the front of the three-story building. It had a brick front with the bronze symbol of the UCF Pegasus emblazoned on the side and large bronze POLICE letters over the emblem. "Must be the place." On his way to the door, Josh read a plaque next to the statue of a fallen police officer; *UCF Police Corporal Mario Jenkins was shot and killed in the line of duty on Saturday, September 24, 2005.*

Josh tapped the plaque twice. "Rest in peace, brother. We got the watch." Josh walked up to the door and pulled it open.

Sari pushed the sharpened toothbrush into the side of the lioness's neck about a quarter-inch and drew blood, which trickled down her throat. The girl didn't make a sound. Sari released her arm and climbed off the bed, looking at the pink toothbrush, tipped with blood. "Not bad. It would have done the job. So, now you know we have twenty-four-hour surveillance, including lowlight. No more creativity or I will come in and break both your arms."

The prisoner nodded her head in agreement but kept her head down. Sari walked over to the door, pulled it open, and stopped halfway through.

"Save your strength for your final destination. You're going to need it."

Josh walked into a waiting room where fifteen brown lobby chairs in a U pattern surrounded a table covered with magazines. Doors stood on both sides of a plexiglass-enclosed reception desk with inset speakers on either side of a slot. He approached. A black female uniformed officer with a "Torres" name tag gave him the once over and scowled at his Navy sweatsuit. Josh pulled his FBI credentials from a pocket and pushed them through the slot. "Special Agent Josh Martin with the FBI. I need to see someone about a missing UCF student."

The police officer flipped open the case and compared the picture on the credentials with Josh's face. Her scowl turned to a smile. "Laundry day? It's not often we get federal agents in workout gear." She pushed the creds back through the slot.

"Long story." Josh retrieved his creds.

"Detective Friday is expecting you. He called down to say you were coming by. I'll let him know you're here, and he'll come down and get you. He also has a U.S. Marshal with him." Officer Torres picked up the phone, and Josh walked over to an empty chair that faced the door with a wall at his back. It wasn't a long wait. The entrance to the right of the reception desk buzzed, and two people walked out.

Josh stood up and watched the same perplexed look on both faces. A black female in a gray pantsuit with a white shirt stood next to a white male with a burgundy sport coat and light gray pants. The female was about thirty with short black hair, a perfect white smile, and a small diamond scar on her forehead. The male, probably a little older than his escort, had brown hair cut military short with a scruffy Irish face.

"Josh Martin?" The guy in the sports coat extended his hand. "Joe. Friday."

Josh started laughing. "Detective Joe Friday? You're shitting me." They shook hands.

"Nah, that's me. My mom liked the show. What's with the outfit? Someone didn't tell me it's casual Friday?" Joe started laughing.

"Touché," Josh said. "I got pulled out of a military training exercise, so no time to get civilian clothes. My orders were urgent."

Josh turned to the woman and extended his hand. "You must be the U.S. Marshal."

"Elena Diaz." She shook Josh's hand. They both felt a double zap on their wrists. "Before you ask, I don't know Tommy Lee Jones, and I didn't memorize the outhouse speech."

"Isn't that required training at Marshal's school?" Josh asked.

"Nope, but you'd be amazed how often we get the question. What do you say we find our missing college student? Detective Friday…"

"Joe," Detective Friday said.

Elena said, "Joe showed me video footage of our girl escorted out of the frat party into a white van. She could barely walk. It looked like she was drugged, not drunk. I sent video stills of her escorts to Becka to get an I.D.

We're headed over to the frat house to talk to the future of America and see what they know about our missing girl."

"Sounds good to me," Josh said. "Elena, why don't you ride with me so we can compare notes. We'll follow you, Joe. I'm driving the ruby red Ford F-150 with a princess in the back."

"Princess?" Joe said.

"You'll know what I mean when you meet her. Let's go find our Richard Kimball." Josh walked over to the exit.

CHAPTER

18

Bishop Avery walked back and forth on the church stage, practicing for the weekend service. She still needed to get with the church music director to review the song selection. She caught movement out of the corner of her eye and turned to see Sari crossing the stage, carrying a plastic bag. "What's in the bag?"

"The shank I took off your lioness." Sari held up the bag. "She made it out of a toothbrush. Clever girl."

"What's the red stuff on the tip?" The bishop leaned in for a closer look.

"Blood. I needed to make a point to our guest, pun intended, and I wanted to get a DNA sample. Nothing better than blood. I'll send it off to the lab. We should know in a couple of days. She didn't make a sound as I was sticking her with the shank, so she's not a normal college student."

"How long will the results take?" Bishop Avery resumed walking around the stage. "I also just got a message from the ship. No updated ETA. When are you taking a ride out to our distribution group to tell them the shipment will be a little late?"

"I'll put a rush on the order. We should know in forty-eight hours. Let me go find the girls for the road trip." Sari turned and walked off, leaving Bishop Avery to her performance.

Josh hit the truck fob, the lights blinked twice, and the doors unlocked. He walked over to the driver's side and pulled the door open. Syrin greeted him with a kiss. He grabbed her head and kissed her between the eyes. "Who's a good girl?" Syrin's tail thumped the leather. "Back seat." Syrin hopped into the back, and Josh slid into the seat and shut the door.

Elena pulled her door open and climbed in. She turned to greet Syrin. "You must be the princess." Syrin put her front feet on the console and gave Elena a lick. "Oh, thank you for that. You are a good girl. What's your name?"

Syrin barked.

"Her name is Syrin." Josh started the truck. "Any idea what Joe's driving?" Josh scanned the lot for an approaching police vehicle.

"No, he was in his office when I got here." Elena stroked Syrin on the head. "Syrin is such a pretty name for a princess."

A white Ford Explorer exited a chain-link fence enclosure across the parking lot and headed toward them.

"I think I see Joe. White Ford Explorer." Josh backed the truck out of the parking spot, waved to Joe in the Explorer, and followed him out of the parking lot. The two-car caravan turned left on Libra and then right on North Gemini Boulevard. Traffic was light, so they made it across campus in about fifteen minutes. Joe made a left turn onto Greek Court and pulled to the curb in front of a large Southern plantation building with white columns.

Josh parked behind the Explorer and cut the engine. Both Elena and Josh slid out of the truck. Elena carried her large black purse. Josh opened the rear door and let Syrin out.

"Syrin, sit." Josh reached in and pulled out her green FBI working dog vest from the truck. He cinched it around her chest. "Syrin, heel."

Josh walked over to Joe and Elena, who were waiting for him at the back of the Explorer. Syrin followed him close on his right hip.

"So, this must be the princess." Joe reached down and scratched her head.

"Syrin, shake." Josh looked at Syrin. She extended her right paw to Joe.

Joe shook her paw. "Nice to meet you, Syrin. What do you say we go in and meet some rich assholes?" Joe started walking toward the frat house, followed by Josh, Elena, and Syrin. "They call this place the mansion. It's the largest and wealthiest fraternity on campus. They have a hundred and sixty brothers in the chapter; twenty-five brothers live in the house. They're funded and sponsored by the Church of Illuminology."

"Brothers?" Elena said. "This looks like the Massa's house."

"Yeah, not that kind of brother. Fraternity brother. Another name for rich, white, privileged asshole. Every kid here is the son of some wealthy businessperson, lawyer, or politician. They have a fleet of chapter cars parked on the side of the house, including Benzes, Beamers, Audis, and a Ford truck. They'll probably make an offer on your truck, Josh, when they see it."

They walked past a flagpole with the U.S. flag and the UCF flag flapping in a light breeze. On the right side of the flagpole was a replica of the Canaveral Light House with black and white stripes. On the left was a six-by-six-foot brown marble slab on a black steel pedestal. *Fraternity Delta Faros* was etched into the stone. After the display, a manicured path of painted red bricks led to the mansion porch. The mansion was a gray brick two-story with white trim and black shutters around each window. Seven white columns fronted a granite veranda porch that stretched across the front of the building. Two sets of white double doors led into the mansion. The lawn was meticulously maintained, and oak tree clusters grew on either side of the main house. Four large, evenly spaced, trimmed bushes screened the front of the porch. Syrin went over and "watered" the shrub on the right.

"You probably should have saved that for the house," Joe said. He walked up the three stone steps to the porch and over to the double doors on the right. He pressed the doorbell on the right, pulled his credentials out of his pocket, and held them up to a camera mounted over the door. When it buzzed, he pulled it open and walked into the foyer. Josh, Elena, and Syrin followed him. The sound system started playing the theme song to *Cops* when they entered the house.

The foyer was large with a single round card table against a wall encircled by four folding chairs. The floor was dark brown mahogany with wide planks. The fraternity logo, complete with the Cape Canaveral Lighthouse, adorned the floor in the center of the room, surrounded by five stanchions connected with purple museum ropes so no one could walk on it. The walls were painted a dark royal blue, and white double doors graced each end of the room. The doors on the right swung open, and the music stopped.

"Sergeant. Friday? To what do we owe this honor?"

"Hi, Chad. Nice music choice," Joe said. "This is FBI Special Agent Josh Martin and U.S. Marshal Elena Diaz. Guys, this is Chad Brown. He's the president of the fraternity." Josh and Elena shook hands with Chad. Chad looked like an athlete, about 180 pounds, with shoulder-length blond hair, a tan, and a surfer vibe. He sported a short-sleeved, dark royal blue polo shirt with the fraternity logo over the left breast, black gym shorts, and flip flops.

"So, what can we do for UCF's finest today?" Chad looked at Joe.

"We need to ask you some questions about Friday night. Is there someplace we can chat, or would you prefer to come to my fraternity house?" Joe asked.

"Why don't we talk in here?" Chad walked over to the set of doors he walked through and held the door open.

Joe, Josh, Elena, and Syrin followed Chad into the next room.

"Please, have a seat." Chad gestured to a large maple conference table with five black leather office chairs on each side and a single chair on each end. "This is our study room."

The room was painted in the same dark royal blue as the foyer with a bank of floor-to-ceiling windows trimmed in white along an entire side of the room, providing a view of a parking lot full of expensive European luxury cars. Chad took a seat at the head of the table. Josh sat to his right with Joe and Elena across from him. Syrin sniffed around the room and lay down next to a white air vent in the wall across from the bank of windows. She barked.

"Someone probably smells Delilah. She's our fraternity golden retriever." Chad looked over at Syrin. "She's a beautiful dog. Is she a German Shepherd?"

"No, she's a Belgian Malinois," Josh said. "Her name is Syrin."

"Oh, yeah, they say that breed does not have an off switch." Chad laughed.

"That about sums her up," Josh said. "So, back to business. We're looking for Bri Castillo. She's a UCF student, last seen at your party on Friday night. Elena, do you have a picture?"

Elena pulled an eight-by-ten photograph out of her purse and slid it across to Chad. Josh could tell by the picture it was her high school yearbook photo. Josh felt a buzz in his pocket. He pulled out his phone and looked at the text. It was an attachment from Becka. He tapped it twice, and two photos appeared on his screen: Kyle Furman and Dillion Kling.

Chad looked at the picture. "There were a lot of girls at the party. She could have been here or not. I don't know, and I didn't see her." He pushed the photo back to Elena.

She retrieved the photo and put it into her purse. "You know, Chad, unlike our local police, lying to federal agents is a felony offense. I can think of a bunch of guys in federal lockup who would like to make you their girlfriend. What do you think, Agent Martin?"

"I definitely think he would be the president of the local sorority chapter." Josh leaned over to Chad and put his phone in front of him.

"Tell me about Kyle Furman and Dillion Kling." He tapped his screen, and the photos appeared on the screen. The blood drained from Chad's face, and his pupils dilated.

"Elena, do you have the video?"

"I do." She pulled her tablet from her purse and touched the screen. The frozen video appeared on the screen. She hit play.

The video started to run. Kyle Furman and Dillion Kling were supporting Bri Castillo under each arm and carrying her down the front steps of the mansion into a waiting white van.

"So, Chad, where are Kyle and Dillion now? We need to talk to them." Josh sat back in his chair.

Chad stood up. "I think it's time for you to leave. I'll call my dad, and next time you can talk to our family lawyer. You can show yourself out." Chad walked out of the study room.

Josh, Elena, and Joe stood up and headed toward the door.

"Syrin, come," Josh said. Syrin followed them out of the house. They walked down the steps and out to the vehicles.

"Well, that was a whole lotta nothing," Joe said with a look of disgust on his face. "What were you thinking?"

"We're thinking he's going to call somebody," Josh said. "We can always come back and round up the brothers, but you only get one shot at an emotional response. These Einsteins did not plan this. Something else is going on."

"How are you going to trace the call? We don't have a warrant," Joe asked.

"We have special technical means and authority through the National Fugitive Act," Elena said.

"Speaking of warrants, how about you go back to the office and draft a search warrant for the mansion and the white van parked in the corner of their parking lot," Josh said.

"On what grounds?" Joe pulled his phone out of his pocket to take notes.

"Suspicion of felony kidnapping based on the videotape, and the sale, distribution, and manufacture of narcotics," Josh said.

"Where do you get the narcotics angle?" Joe typed notes into his phone.

"When Syrin laid down by the air vent and barked, that was a narcotics alert. You'll find a stash of narcotics in the air vent space. When you finish the warrant, I'll get a federal judge to sign off on it." Josh pulled his phone out of his back pocket.

"Damn," Joe said. "Remind me not to piss you off. I can't wait to see the expression on their privileged faces when we serve the warrant. Do you want in on it?"

"No. We're going to track down whoever is on the end of the phone call. Just call me after you guys do the takedown. Thanks for your help, Joe." Josh patted Joe on the shoulder.

"You got it." Joe walked over to his Explorer.

Josh punched a number into his phone. "Are you ready?"

"Yes, sir. The bird is overhead."

CHAPTER 19

The lioness sat cross-legged in the middle of the floor with her eyes closed, focused on her breathing. She played her interaction with the crazy bitch over in her mind. The weight on her back pushing down, feeling the strength on top of her like a jungle cat playing with her prey. A shiver went down her spine. She didn't make a sound when the toothbrush pierced her neck. Half-expecting her life to be over. No amount of self-defense training would overcome the bitch. She did have an accent, almost Jewish. Probably Israeli.

The room had cameras with low-light capability. She couldn't beat the bitch in a fair fight. *Don't try anything here. They're eventually going to move me.* She needed to leave a trail for searchers to find proof of life. Her mom would send an army to locate her. *Stay alive until they come. So, what to leave behind?* The thought finally came to her. She stood up and walked into the bathroom.

Elena scratched Syrin behind the ears as she stood on the center console. "So, where to now?"

"Three things." Josh turned left onto North Gemini Boulevard. "I need to find an ice cream shop to pay off the princess for finding the dope. We need to get something of Bri's at her apartment to use as a scent imprint for Syrin. And I need to find a clothing store so I can change out of the Joe Leisure Navy PT uniform." Josh punched up "ice cream" on the truck's navigation system. Two and a half miles later, they pulled into the parking lot of Knight's Ice Cream Parlor.

"Do you want anything?"

"Sure. A twist cone with chocolate sprinkles. What about you, Syrin? What kind of ice cream do you want?" Syrin's tail whacked the seat at the words "ice cream."

"Syrin's flavor of choice is vanilla. She'll help me finish mine when I clean off all the jimmies." Josh pushed open his door.

"What are jimmies?" Elena hugged Syrin.

"New Hampshire speak for chocolate sprinkles." Josh rolled out of the truck.

Syrin bounced her front feet on the console and made spin moves in the back seat when she spied Josh returning with three ice cream cones. Josh walked up to Elena's window and passed her cone through the opening.

"One twist cone with chocolate jimmies for the marshal."

Josh walked around to the driver's side and climbed in. He held Syrin's cone over the center console. She licked the ice cream, which dripped on Josh's hand. "You make a mess; you're cleaning it up."

Josh finished his jimmies just as Syrin crunched the last bit of her cone. He ate his ice cream down to the cone with Syrin watching every lick. He gave her the cone, which she chomped down in two bites. He grabbed her head. "Who's a good girl?"

Syrin shook her head and growled.

"All right, back seat." Syrin hopped up on the back seat.

"That is some good ice cream." Elena wiped her face with a napkin.

"It's okay. You haven't had real ice cream until you've tasted fresh Martin Ice Cream with maple syrup from the North Country of New Hampshire." Josh started the truck.

"You own an ice cream store?" Elena pulled out her phone, punched in her contacts button, and scrolled through to Bri Castillo's address.

"A couple. What's her address?" Josh pressed the truck's nav button.

"Three-oh-one Dalhausser Lane, Oviedo, Florida. The complex is called The Oasis." Elena put the phone back into her purse.

Josh typed in the address, backed out of the parking spot, and pulled into campus traffic.

CHAPTER

20

Zeus leaned his six-foot-two and 305-pound frame back in his chair and stretched his arms over his head. He still felt the burn from his morning shoulder lift. Everything seemed to hurt when you got past thirty. Pushing thirty-two, he didn't know how many years he had left. Life expectancy for a motorcycle club president wasn't great. His cell phone buzzed on his desk. He snapped the chair back, grabbed the phone, and punched the green accept button.

"Yeah, this better be good; you're interrupting my morning stretch."

"We got a problem." Chad Brown could barely get the words out. "The feds came by looking for the redhead chick from Friday night."

"Feds? Why would the feds care about a missing college slut?" Zeus sat upright at the mention of feds. "What kind of feds?"

"An FBI agent, a U.S. Marshal, and Detective Friday from the UCF Police Department. They also got a video of Kyle and Dillion dragging her to the van. They know their names, and they're looking for them. What are we going to do?" Chad sounded on the verge of tears.

"Calm down. Did they get anything on the van? Plate? Description? Did they see the driver?" Zeus was turning over options in his head.

"No. Nothing on the van. Only a white Ford panel van. My dad's going to kill me."

"From what you told me, you're in the clear. All you did was have a party. You had no idea what Kyle and Dillion were doing. We'll take care of it."

"What does that mean?"

Zeus heard fear in Chad's voice. "Just make sure you have an alibi for the next couple of days." Zeus disconnected the call and punched in another number.

The caller picked up. "What can I do for my favorite biker?"

"We've got a problem. How soon can you get here?"

"Funny, you should ask. I'm about ten minutes out."

"That's it up on the right." Elena pointed to a flagstone wall with *The Oasis* in gold letters framed by brown wooden beams.

Josh turned right and pulled into the complex, which was a cluster of apartment buildings and cottages on either side of the road. He followed the main office signs and pulled into a slot in front of a white building with the same flagstone facia and wooden beam trim as the entrance sign.

They all hopped out of the truck. Syrin was still wearing her FBI vest. They walked up to the covered entrance and pushed through a set of double doors into a large reception area with gray tile floors. Two diner-style booths flanked the entry, set against windows with overhead lights. Two semi-circles, blue-striped pattern couches faced each other in the center of the room with a large flat-panel TV screen mounted on the wall to the right. UCF basketball was playing on the screen. An extended counter ran along the entire left wall with dark barstools in front of individual hookups for internet and charging ports.

"Wow. Nice place," Josh said. "Sure beats Chase Hall."

A voice came from under the TV. "Can I help you, please? Oh, dogs aren't allowed in the complex."

Josh looked at the source of the voice. A dark-haired Asian kid stood behind a reception desk.

"She's working." Josh pulled his badge out of the Navy sweatsuit and walked up to the counter. "FBI." He placed his credentials on the desk. "My name is Special Agent Martin, and this is Marshal Diaz."

Elena waved. Josh looked at the nameplate on the counter: Glenn Tan.

"Oh, sorry, sir. I thought you were a parent in the Navy."

Elena snickered at the comment.

"No, Glenn, I'm not a parent, but you can help me. Looking for cottage one-oh-three."

"Yes, sir. Walk out the opposite end of the building from where you came in. Go around the pool to the left, and you'll see cottage one-oh-three on the left at the end of the pool. You can't miss it. Go Navy!"

"Yeah. Go Navy. Beat Army. Thanks for the help, Glenn." Josh tapped the counter twice.

"Come on, Dad. Let's find your daughter," Elena said with a smile. She started walking with Syrin to the exit. Josh caught up and held the door for the girls.

Through the exit door was a vast free-form resort full of college students laughing in lounge chairs and kids splashing in a pool. A beach volleyball court was on the right, with a game in full swing.

Josh, Elena, and Syrin made their way through the crowd of students. "I definitely went to the wrong school," Josh said. "Although I don't think I would have got any studying done here. What about you? Where did you go to school?"

"Eight years of Army training, sir, and then two years at the University of Miami. I lived in an apartment, so none of this stuff." Elena looked around at the party. "I wonder if this goes on every day."

"I would say yes. There's cottage one-oh-three. It's the red one on the left with green trim." Josh pointed to a two-story red building and headed in that direction.

A covered stone porch ran along the entire front. A second-floor terrace above the porch looked out over the pool. There were two windows to the right of the balcony, probably a bedroom. They walked up the three steps to the porch. Josh raised his fist to knock on the door and stopped.

A loud crash of breaking glass came from the other side of the door, followed by a slap on bare skin. "I don't know what you want. Please don't hurt me."

CHAPTER 21

A blue strobe light over the bar started flashing, and the sound system played "Bad to the Bone." Zeus glanced at the security monitor. Four black Harley-Davidson Low Rider Ses were waiting at the back gate. The riders wore black leather with black helmets. One of them held up a middle finger. Zeus laughed and pressed the gate remote. It slid open, and the sound of four Hog engines resonated in the parking lot. Zeus got up from the table and walked out the back door of the club.

The four Harleys pulled into slots and cut their revs to zero. The riders slid off their bikes, removed their helmets, and revealed the beauty underneath. The God Squad had arrived.

"So, what kind of problem are we talking about?" Sari asked.

"Why don't we go inside to get out of the sun, and I'll fill you in." Zeus held the door for the ladies. Sari led the way, followed by Rafi, Michael, and Gabi, all angels of the Church of Illuminology. They wore black leather pants, black T-Shirts, and black leather jackets.

The three angels headed to the bar, and Sari followed Zeus to a corner table. Sari noted the high-class feel of the Lightning Strikes Motorcycle Club. Not a typical biker bar for sure. She walked past a full bar on the left and eight tables for four on the right with bright green banker lights hanging over each table. Two regulation pool tables occupied the center of the room.

Beyond them lay a gleaming white tile dance floor. A hallway in the rear led to a full kitchen, three bedrooms, and a gym. A five-bay garage spread across the parking lot in the back. All the bays were empty except for one, which contained a white Ford panel van.

Zeus pulled up a chair in front of Sari. "Can I get you something?"

"Iced tea would be lovely. Sweet, no lemon." Sari wiped the sweat from her forehead and slipped out of the leather jacket. "These leathers are hot as fuck but better than road rash."

Zeus signaled to a prospect behind the bar. "Iced tea. Sweet. No lemon." The prospect nodded his head.

"So, what's the problem?" Sari cocked her head while she stared at Zeus.

"I just got a call from Chad Brown." Zeus ran his hands across the table. "He said a couple of feds and a campus cop just stopped by the fraternity looking for the redhead we picked up Friday."

"You're shitting me." Sari leaned forward in her chair. "What kind of feds?"

"A U.S. marshal and an FBI agent." Zeus leaned to the right, and the prospect set the iced tea in front of Sari.

"Thank you, sweetie." Sari took a sip of the tea. "This is not good. Feds don't go looking for someone unless you are someone. We have thirty girls in the pipeline—seven at the church and twenty-three at the conference center." Sari lowered her forehead to the table and bounced it twice on the wood.

"It gets worse." Zeus watched Sari to gauge her reaction.

Sari raised her head off the table and looked at Zeus. Her eyes narrowed, and a cloud came over her face. "What does that mean?"

"Don't kill the messenger," Zeus stammered out a response. "The feds have video of two of the fraternity boys dragging the redhead to our van."

"Oh, Christ, how is that possible?" Sari stood up and slammed her hand on the table. Zeus slid his chair back. She looked him in the eye. "Is the white van in question the one in the garage in the back?"

"Yes. Do you want me to get rid of it?" Zeus took a deep breath since he had more bad news.

Sari pursed her lips to think. "Is the van registered to the club?"

"Yes," Zeus said.

"Okay. Get some of your boys to clean it inside and out. Use bleach. Then take it out to the middle of nowhere and drive it into a swamp. Make sure it sinks." Sari took a sip of tea.

"Do you want us to report it stolen?" Zeus looked around the club and motioned for the prospect.

"Yes. If the feds start checking for white vans, they will eventually get to you." Sari pushed in her chair. "On another bad news note, the shipment is going to be late."

"How late? We're getting low on supply." Zeus stood up.

"A couple of days. The ship ran into Tropical Storm Cory. You'd think they could find a better name than Cory. Must be a boy's name because it's hanging around like an ex-boyfriend." Sari looked over at her angels. "Are you ladies ready to roll?"

Rafi gave a thumbs-up, and the girls spun off the stools and headed toward the door. Sari took her jacket off the chair.

Zeus stopped Sari. "One more thing. The feds have pictures and names of the two frat boys who dragged the chick to the van."

Sari looked at Zeus. "Text me their names and pictures, and save a couple of seats in the van. You may have some passengers."

CHAPTER 22

Josh put his hand on the doorknob and twisted it. It moved in his hand, *unlocked*. He looked back at Elena. Her feet braced for entry, and her Glock 22, Gen 4 in .40 caliber held steady in her hand. Josh pointed to Syrin and gave a thumbs-up. Elena nodded. Crying and unintelligible screaming came from the other side of the door.

"Syrin, bite." Josh pushed open the door, and seventy pounds of ice-cream-fueled rage flew through the door. Josh followed close on her heels. A hallway with wooden floors opened into a living room. A set of stairs on the left led to a second floor. Syrin's nails scratched on the wood, gaining traction as she made a beeline to a white male, who was holding a struggling Asian female. Josh caught a glimpse of "holy shit" on the subject's face before Syrin hit him square in the chest and latched onto his right arm. The force of the blow sent dog and target flying over an end table onto a couch with a table lamp and a vase full of wilted daffodils crashing to the floor. The female screamed and headed toward Josh.

Josh stepped around the fleeing female and reached the end of the hallway to hear, "Ahhhh, motherfucker," as 195 pounds of bite pressure bore down on the male's arm. He writhed on the couch with an angry ball of fur pinning him down.

Josh turned the corner into a kitchen just in time to see a second white male throwing a right-hand punch at his head. Josh stepped right, blocked the blow with his left forearm, grabbed the subject's wrist, hooked his right arm under the armpit, twisted his right hip into the body, and flipped the target over his back, slamming him to the floor with an *oompf* as the air escaped his lungs. Josh drilled him a straight right punch in the jaw. Lights out. He stood up to calm his adrenaline.

Elena made it to the corner in time to see Josh knock the guy out. She holstered her gun and pulled out her handcuffs. She flipped him over, checked his pulse and breathing, and snapped the cuffs on him.

Josh walked over to the mix of dog and screaming kid. "Syrin, *lass es*."

Syrin released and stepped off the couch, snarling and barking.

"That fucking dog bit me."

"You shouldn't attack girls, Dillion," Josh said.

"How do you know my name?"

Josh grabbed a towel off the counter and tossed it to Dillion. "Because we've been looking for you. Wrap the towel around your arm."

Josh looked over at the second girl, a caucasian cowering by the sink. A red imprint of a hand marked the right side of her face. "It's going to be okay. Who hit you?"

She pointed down at the figure cuffed on the kitchen floor. "Kyle. He and Dillion tried to force us to tell them about our friend Bri."

"How about you come over and take this dirtball's place on the couch after I move him? What's your name? No answer. My name's Josh, and this is Elena. We're federal agents, and these scumbags won't hurt you anymore. Dillion, get your sorry ass off the couch and go stand by Kyle."

Dillion got off the couch, clutching the towel to his arm, and moved over next to Kyle. He leaned on the refrigerator.

"Syrin, guard." Syrin snarled and positioned to cover Dillion. "You move, and she's going to munch on your other arm. Capisce?"

"Yes, sir." Dillion cringed and watched Syrin.

The girl moved around Kyle and took a seat on the couch. "My name is Gisele Fay. I'm an exchange student from Paris. My other roommate is Ji-Min Choi. She is from Korea."

"Hi, thank you for your help," came a tiny voice from behind Elena in the hallway.

"Why don't you take a seat next to Gisele." Josh motioned to Ji-Min.

"Elena, why don't you talk to these young ladies while I arrange transport for our fraternity brothers?"

He turned toward the kitchen. "How's that arm, Dillion?"

Josh walked down the hallway, opened the door, and stepped out on the front porch to find a crowd of college students and four UCF police officers pointing guns at him.

"That's him. There's also a black woman and a dog."

"Freeze. Let me see your hands."

Images of Corporal Mario Jenkins's statue flashed through Josh's mind.

CHAPTER 23

Sari hit the throttle on the Harley Low Rider S and leaned forward inside the windshield as the bike rocketed to 110 miles per hour down West Irlo Bronson Memorial Highway. The empty fields on either side of the road blew by in a kaleidoscope of green. Old Irlo Bronson used to own land on both sides of the highway all the way from I-95 to Kissimmee. Selling property to Walt Disney to build Disney World was his claim to fame. Bronson became a trivia question in history. The locals called the highway "Route 192" or "the road to good intentions."

Sari eased off the throttle about two miles before the church turnoff and leaned into a left-hand turn on to Church of Light Boulevard, formerly Holopaw Road, before the church bought the land. Two seventy-five-foot replicas of the Cape Canaveral Lighthouse dominated either side of the entrance, complete with working lights. "Church of Illuminology" adorned the side of each lighthouse in bright white letters. The letters lit up at sunset to mark the path for the enlightened.

Sari looked back to make sure the angels were behind her. They were all coasting in her wake, zigzagging down the road. She smiled and turned right down the Road to Heaven, which would lead to the promised land or the Church of Illuminology complex. The church occupied the remains of Eight-mile ranch, forty thousand acres, complete with citrus groves. Two miles through a winding patch of orange groves, the road opened into the complex.

A vast sea of parking spaces and trolley stops for sixteen thousand of the enlightened extended to the right. On the left was a sloping green lawn, which reached to the church building. A full-size replica of the Cape Canaveral Lighthouse, at 151 feet, dominated the exterior. A church gift shop in the base sold sermon collections and six bestselling books by Bishop Avery. It also offered T-shirts, mugs, pens, and anything else that could hold a logo and a pithy saying.

The Angels cruised past the light and pulled into the underground garage for church employees. They pulled their bikes into slots in front of the elevator marked with *Reserved for Angel Parking* signs. Sari shut off the engine, kicked the stand down, and stepped off the bike. The other angels followed suit. She took off her helmet, smiled at the signs, and walked toward the elevators. *I wonder if God has a sense of humor.* She pushed the elevator's up button. *If she did, the sign would read,* Fallen Angels. *Time to fire up the wrath of God.*

"On the ground, dirtbag. Extend your arms out from your body and cross your legs. Do it now." A big black cop in front was doing the talking. The other three fanned out on either side.

"Easy, fellas, I'm an FBI Agent. My ID is in my back pocket." Josh got down on his stomach, crossed his legs, and extended his arms out from his side at ninety degrees.

"If you're an FBI agent, I'm the Sheriff of Orange County. I've never seen a fed in a tracksuit. Cuff him, Jimmy." The black campus cop made a waving motion with his gun.

Jimmy came from the left and snapped a handcuff on Josh's left wrist and bent his arm to the center of his back. He tapped the center of Josh's back. "Right hand." Josh moved his right arm to the center of his back, and Jimmy hooked him up.

“Call Detective Joe Friday. We’re working on the case together. My partner, U.S. Marshal Elena Diaz, is inside.” Josh lifted his head to look at the cop. “Check my credentials.”

At the mention of Joe Friday’s name, the black cop got an “oh shit” look on his face. “Check the man’s back pocket.”

Jimmy patted Josh’s back pocket and found his credentials. He pulled them out and flipped them open. “FBI Special Agent Joshua C. Martin.” Jimmy looked at his boss.

Detective Joe Friday pushed through the crowd of students. “What in Christ’s sake are you morons doing? Get him up and get those cuffs off him, and for the love of God, put away those guns.”

The cops quickly holstered their guns, and Jimmy fumbled with his cuff key, trying to unlock the cuffs. He succeeded on the third try and popped the cuffs off. Josh stood up, and Jimmy handed him his creds.

“Sorry, Agent Martin. We didn’t know you were FBI. Are you undercover?”

Detective Friday walked up to the black cop. “Billy, why don’t you back these students up?”

“Yes, Sergeant.” Billy gathered his crew. “All right, everyone back up. Nothing to see here. Move back.” He turned to Friday. “The man’s wearing a tracksuit.”

Friday smiled and turned to Josh. “Sorry. Might be time to retire that outfit.”

“That was our next stop after picking up a sample of Bri’s clothing here as a reference scent for Syrin. We heard screaming girls, yelling guys, and hands slapping skin. The door was unlocked, so Syrin went in for a look-see. She got to know Dillion. He’s going to need some stitches. Kyle took a swing at me. He's going to need a concussion protocol. I was about to call you when the posse showed up." Josh gestured at the cops dispersing the crowd.

"You got Kyle and Dillion?" Friday asked.

"Yup. They're inside in the kitchen. Elena is talking to the girls. You can charge them both with assault on a federal agent. Let's go inside." Josh turned to open the door.

"Billy? We got two for transport," Detective Friday shouted.

Billy turned and gave a thumbs-up. "Okay, let's go."

Josh and Joe walked into the cottage.

CHAPTER 24

Sari rode the elevator to the fifth-floor executive office suite. She dumped her helmet and leather jacket into her office and went down the hall to Bishop Avery's office. Eleanor Davis looked up when Sari walked into the outer office, which consisted of a lounge area with a round white marble table, six chairs, and a Keurig coffee set up on a small credenza alongside fresh chocolate chip cookies. Sari grabbed a cookie and walked up to Eleanor's desk. The woman was in her late sixties with short gray hair just off her collar. She wore a white blouse with a lace collar and black pants—standard uniform for church employees. Eleanor had worked for the church for the last thirty-five years and knew the burial place for all of the skeletons. She sat behind an enormous mahogany desk, which had belonged to the Reverend William Hancock Avery, Bishop Avery's great, great grandfather. He started the family's smuggling business during prohibition.

"Is she in?" Sari took a bite of a cookie. The chocolate melted in her mouth.

"Yes. She's expecting you. Jean-Paul did a nice job on the cookies," Eleanor said with a smile.

Sari finished the cookie. "Excellent job. I don't know how you can sit here and not eat the entire plate." Sari walked past Eleanor's desk and into the reception area of Bishop Avery's office.

"I'm watching *Downton Abby*," came a voice from the office.

Sari walked across the white tile floor, through the archway, and into Avery's office. The bishop was kicked back in the recliner with a glass of red wine watching TV. An open wine bottle was on the small wooden table between the chairs.

"Come join me. There's another glass on my desk." Bishop Avery motioned to her desk with her wine glass.

Sari retrieved the wine glass and picked up the bottle. "What are we drinking?" She poured the dark red wine into her glass, swirled it around, and put her nose in the glass, and inhaled. "Mmmm, black fruits, rich tannins, great concentration." She looked at the wine. "Dense, dark core." She took a sip and swirled the wine in her mouth, and swallowed. Full, rich flavor, smooth, no aftertaste. I'd say it's a twenty-fifteen Rothschild."

"And you would be correct." Bishop Avery offered her glass for a toast.

Sari clinked her glass, took another sip, and sat down in the opposite recliner. "What are we celebrating?"

"The ship just called. They're back underway. ETA to the pier at Tampa is forty-eight hours. How did you make out with Zeus?" Bishop Avery took another sip of wine, picked up the remote, and turned the TV off.

"We have a complication." Sari ran her finger around the lip of the glass.

"What kind of complication?" Bishop Avery set her glass down. The celebration drained from her face. "Don't tell me. Our fucking virgin."

"And you would be correct." Sari took another sip of wine. "Zeus said he got a call from the fraternity. Two feds showed up looking for our girl—an FBI agent and a U.S. marshal."

"Damn." Bishop Avery snapped the recliner footrest back and stood up. "We grabbed the wrong girl. What do you think we should do?"

Sari took another sip of wine. "It gets worse. They have a video of the two clowns who dragged the girl to the club van, and I just got a call from our friend at the campus PD. Our two feds picked up the clowns at the girl's apartment."

"What were they doing there?" Bishop Avery went over to her desk and sat down.

Sari finished her wine, set the glass on the side table, and stood up. "Our source doesn't know. They're getting booked for assault on federal agents. One of them has a concussion, and the other one has a dog bite."

"A dog bite?" Bishop Avery scrolled her mouse to bring up her computer screen.

"Yup. Apparently, one of the feds has a dog."

Bishop Avery leaned back in her chair. "I think it's time you girls earned your pay."

Sari looked at Bishop Avery. "Do you want us to contract or keep it in house?"

"Keep it in house. We have too much exposure with thirty girls and a double drug shipment." Bishop Avery picked up a pen on her desk and tapped it twice on her blotter.

"Roger." Sari turned to leave. "What about the girl?"

Bishop Avery twirled the pen in her fingers. "If we can't move her in forty-eight hours, call the Dibble brothers. Also, take another ride out to Zeus's and tell him he has a pick-up in two days."

CHAPTER 25

Captain Moreno stood on the starboard bridge wing of the container ship *Garcia Asombrosa* and looked at the gentle swell of the sea off the bow. Tropical Storm Cory finally blew through, and calm weather always follows a storm. They were full ahead for twenty knots, trying to make up for the lost time. He took a sip of coffee and went back inside the pilothouse. He grabbed the satellite phone off the rack on the starboard bulkhead and dialed a number. The caller picked up.

"Yes?"

"We're finally back underway with an ETA of 0600 to the pier on Thursday into Tampa. Make the call."

"Roger." The phone went dead.

Captain Moreno put the phone back in the rack. *Nothing to do now but wait and pray.*

Josh walked into the cottage and down the hallway to the kitchen, with Joe bringing up the rear. Elena walked over to meet them.

"Both girls identify Kyle as the slapper and Dillion as the restrainer. They gave me one of Bri's T-shirts out of her laundry bag." Elena held up a

Ziplock gallon bag with a black and gold UCF T-shirt inside. "What was all the commotion outside?"

"UCF's finest did not appreciate my tracksuit. Do you guys have any holding cells?" Josh motioned at Kyle and Dillion.

"We've got three cells in the basement. Mainly for holding the drunk and disorderly from football games. Let me get Billy in here." Joe walked to the door.

"Syrin, *lass es*." Syrin gave Dillion a final growl and walked over to Josh, wagging her tail. "Who's a good girl? You may need an update on your shot record. No telling what you could catch from the nasty frat boy." Josh scratched her head.

"Really, dude? Is that necessary?" Dillion glared at Josh.

Josh's face hardened, and his focus narrowed. "How about I come over there and slap you around a few times like the girls?"

Dillion slunk farther into the corner of the kitchen. "No, dude. We cool. I'll just shut the hell up."

"Good choice." Josh turned to see Joe and the UCF cop walking up the hallway.

Joe motioned at the two fraternity brothers. "Take these two Einsteins to holding. Put them in separate cells at either end."

"Roger." The UCF cop put handcuffs on Dillion and lifted Kyle off the floor with the help of Josh. The side of Kyle's face was swollen, and his left eye was almost shut.

"Damn. I bet that hurts. Teach you not to hit girls. Let's go, boys." Joe escorted the boys out of the cottage.

Elena turned to the girls. "Are you ladies going to be okay?" They both nodded their heads yes. "Thank you for this." She held up the T-shirt. "You have my card. If you need anything, call me." Josh and Elena walked out of the cottage.

On the porch, Josh caught Elena's arm. "We got a hit on Chad's phone."

CHAPTER 26

Chris Del Toro leaned back in his chair and stretched his arms over his head. He sat up again and sipped coffee from a Customs and Border Protection monogrammed coffee mug. He looked out the third-floor window at the sprawling Port of Tampa Bay. Tampa was Florida's largest port (by size and tonnage), handling over thirty-seven million tons of cargo per year and encompassing over five thousand acres. The port served as a distribution center gateway to Florida with easy access to trucks and rail.

Chris ran his hand through his silver hair. In six months, he would celebrate his fifty-first birthday and his thirtieth year as an intelligence analyst for Customs and Border Protection. His retirement orders were already approved. In half a year, he would leave all the traffic and congestion of the Tampa/St. Pete region for a relaxing forty-acre spread with a cabin on Smokey Mountain Lake in Tennessee. He had made cash payments on the property for the last five years. Two more payments and he would own it outright.

Chris's phone buzzed on his desk. He checked the text message.

Garcia Asombrosa – Hooker's Point – Berth 211 – 48 hours

Empress Express – Hooker's Point – Berth 212 – Container number 759933

He picked up the phone and called the duty watch desk.

"Watch desk, Cody."

"Cody, it's Chris. I have some info on a shipment. *Empress Express*. Her ETA is in forty-eight hours. She's going to Hooker's Point, Berth two twelve. The container number is seven, five, nine, nine, three, three."

"Seven, five, nine, nine, three, three, I got it. I don't know how you do it, Chris, but you're the best. We're going to miss you."

"Thanks, Cody. Let me know what you guys find. I'll send you a post-card from Tennessee. Have a good one." Chris clicked off.

Josh backed the truck out of the slot in front of The Oasis clubhouse and headed to the exit.

"So, who did Chad call?" Elena turned in her seat to face Josh.

"The number was a burner phone, but we did get a location. Someplace called Strikers in Palm Bay. Look it up on your phone."

Josh turned left at the complex entrance and headed back to the Knight's Ice Cream Parlor. "You're going to get fat eating all this ice cream." Josh looked in the rearview mirror at Syrin in the back seat. She was doing her regal queen pose because she knew a good job when she saw one. "Woof," the queen spoke.

"That's right, you tell 'em, girl. He should look so good." Elena reached back and scratched Syrin behind the ears. "Strikers is a bowling alley and family fun center in Palm Bay, Florida. They have franchises in all fifty states, the District of Colombia, and Puerto Rico."

"Why would Chad call a bowling alley?" Josh pulled the truck into a slot at Knight's Ice Cream Parlor. "Do you want any ice cream?"

"No, I'm good, and no idea. Maybe he likes to bowl." Elena put her phone in the center console cup holder.

"Why don't you call Becka and get her to do a background on Strikers, and I'll get the queen an ice cream." Josh opened the truck door and stepped out.

"Will do. Syrin, you got a promotion from princess to queen. What a good girl." Syrin danced in the back seat at the sound of her name and "queen."

Josh shook his head and shut the door.

CHAPTER 27

Sari felt her phone vibrate in her back pocket. She pulled it out and looked at the text message. *Kyle Furman is in holding cell #1. Dillion Kling is in holding cell #3.*

She punched a number into her phone. The caller picked up.

"Yes, my love. How can I help you?"

Sari smiled. "Subject one is in cell one. Subject two is in cell three. Are you good to go, and what about the second op?"

"We're all set for both operations tonight. I'll call with an update when we're complete. Have an illuminating day." The caller clicked off.

Sari put the phone back in her pocket and walked down the hall for another chocolate chip cookie.

Josh slid into the truck and handed Elena the vanilla cone with no sprinkles. "Why don't you feed her highness. She always gets slobber on my hand when I feed her. What do you say we head over to Palm Bay, find a place to eat, a place to stay, and a place for me to retire the tracksuit?"

"I think that sounds like a fine plan. Don't you, Syrin?" Syrin was too busy dripping ice cream all over Elena's hand to answer.

Josh fought his way through resort traffic to Route 192 and cruised at eighty-five miles per hour to I-95. He slowed a bit as they passed the twin lighthouses of the Church of Illuminology entrance. He followed the truck's GPS to the Melbourne Square Mall and parked. It took them about ninety minutes.

Elena kicked the door open. "I hope they have a good place to eat. I'm starving." She hopped out of the truck.

"They have a Brazilian steak house, Estampa Gaucha; how does that sound?" Josh opened his door, and Syrin jumped through the center console and followed Josh outside. "Hey, who said you could come?"

Josh grabbed her head in his hands and kissed her.

"Sounds like heaven to me. We should probably update your wardrobe before they stick you in the kitchen with the help." Elena shut her door and headed over to Syrin and Josh.

"They have a Macy's. I'll have to slum it and get some stuff off the rack." Josh headed to the entrance.

They found Macy's. Josh bought two blue blazers, a pair of tan and gray dress pants, a light blue dress shirt, and both black and brown shoes with matching belts, socks, and underwear. He changed into one of the blazers with a light blue shirt and tan pants and walked out of the dressing room.

"Nice. You clean up pretty good. Spin for Syrin." Elena laughed. "What happened to the tracksuit?"

"It didn't make it past the dressing room trash can. What do you say we drop off this stuff at the truck, and I buy you dinner?"

"Now, *that* sounds like a great idea. Come on, Syrin. Never turn down a free meal from a handsome man in a blue blazer."

Sari pushed the up arrow on the elevator, and the door opened. She walked in and put her right index finger on a biometric scan pad.

The pad turned green. She pushed the P button for the penthouse. The door opened, and two large men greeted her.

"Evening, Boss. She's in the dining room."

"Thank you, Julius." Sari walked across a marble foyer into a waiting room with three chairs on either side of a white double-door entryway. The door buzzed, and she walked in.

Bishop Avery lived in the four-thousand-square-foot penthouse apartment on top of the ten-story office complex attached to the church stadium. From that headquarters, 380 employees oversaw the church's legitimate enterprises and ninety-million-dollar annual operating budget.

The apartment's open floor plan had baseboard-to-ceiling windows on three sides with a sweeping view of the church grounds. A wrap-around deck surrounded the apartment with a lap pool on the west side so the bishop could swim laps and watch the sunset. An open-air kitchen and bar accompanied a stone fireplace for evening drinks by the fire. The bishop was seated at the end of a glass-top dining table with gray fabric chairs. Sari walked over and sat down.

"Would you like something to eat? Chef Jean-Paul just made an exquisite filet with a red wine reduction sauce." Bishop Avery took a sip of wine.

"No, thank you. The girls and I are headed out, but I will have a glass of wine." Sari poured some wine into her glass from the crystal decanter, swirled the wine to get the aromas flowing, and inhaled deeply, enjoying the fragrant aroma of a classic wine. She took a sip, swished the wine in her mouth, and swallowed. "I think this is the best perk working for you. Your wine is always exceptional."

"Life's too short to drink bad wine." Bishop Avery raised her glass in a toast. "To the vices of men—may they always keep us in good wine." They clinked glasses. "So, tell me, what is the wine?"

Sari took another sip. "The aroma and flavor are off the chart with a heavenly array of blackcurrants, cedar pencil, graphite, tobacco, and incense. This one's easy. It's the Château Lafite Rothschild 2016."

Bishop Avery shook her head. "You always amaze me. You could be a sommelier in another life. So, are we ready?"

"Yes. We have everything in place for tonight, and we will move the girls to the staging location tomorrow. In three days, we'll have two tons of dope in the pipeline, thirty girls en route to a new life, and the virgin bitch will be gone." Sari drained her glass of wine.

CHAPTER

28

Elena finally flipped her card from green to red to signal the waitstaff at Estampa Gaucha she'd finished eating, and they didn't need to bring any more food. Josh had indicated defeat twenty minutes earlier.

Josh took a sip of wine. "Finally, I don't know where you put all that food."

Elena put her napkin on her plate. "Hey, a girl's gotta eat, and the food was fabulous. How's Syrin doing?"

Josh looked under the table. "She's sleeping on my feet. I'm surprised she's not snoring." Josh leaned in. "So, we really have not had time to talk about our partnership. How did you get involved in our organization?"

"By organization, you mean Vince?" Elena did a quick look around the restaurant. They were at a back table, and the nearest customers were four tables away.

"Yes, tell me about your backstory and how you got into all this." Josh tapped his watch.

"Well, when I graduated from high school, I didn't know what I wanted to do, but I wanted to get out of the neighborhood, so I joined the Army. I always thought about a law enforcement job, so I became a military police officer out of basic. After three years as an Army cop, I applied for the Criminal Investigations Division. I checked all the diversity boxes—female, black, Latino—and I speak fluent Spanish. They welcomed me with open arms. I completed the fifteen-week CID Special Agent course at Fort Leonard Wood. My first posting after graduation was the Third Military Police Group in Stuttgart, Germany. I quickly found my niche tracking down wayward soldiers and wanted felons. I did two years in Germany and another two in Seoul."

"Did you learn any German or Korean?" Josh asked.

"Enough to get by. After eight years in the Army, I wanted to be a U.S. marshal to track down scum bags full time. I earned my associate's in criminal justice in the Army. I got out of the Army and went back to school at the University of Miami to complete my bachelor's degree on the GI Bill. While I was at the U, my…." Elena's voice trailed off, and her eyes started to water.

Josh reached out and touched her arm. She grabbed his hand and squeezed it.

"Sorry, I always find it tough to go back. Elena dabbed her napkin at the corner of her eyes. While I was at school, my baby sister Jennifer was also a student. She was walking back to our apartment from the library, and she either stumbled across a mugging or drug deal. The police weren't sure. Some mutt called 'Demon' shot her in the head and left her to die on the sidewalk. The police finally caught up with Demon, but he walked on a technicality. The arresting officer who read Demon his rights didn't speak Spanish, and Demon allegedly didn't speak English, so the case got tossed."

Josh leaned back in his chair. "And then Vince came for a visit."

Elena looked up in acknowledgment. "Yes. I was having lunch at a corner coffee shop. Vince pulled up a chair and showed me his White House credential. He invited me to Washington and made the sales pitch. Join our group, and he would make Demon disappear. I said yes, and here I am four years later. They found Demon floating face down in the Miami River.

The cops came looking for me, but I was in Washington when old Demon went into the river. He was conveniently wearing a watch, which gave the date and time he went for a swim."

Josh laughed and signaled for the waiter. "What's your specialty? We all have a certain skill."

"I find people." Elena smoothed the napkin with her hand on the table. "What's your story?"

The waiter walked up with the bill. "That's a story for a different time." Josh handed him his credit card. "It's getting late. How about we find a hotel and swing by Bass Pro Shops? I need to get a couple of holsters and two ammo pouches. I think there was a hotel right at the exit off I95."

The Lioness climbed into bed and curled up with her pillow. She ran over her preparations in her head. If someone came looking for her, they would find enough breadcrumbs to know this was her room. Unfortunately, she was running out of time. Her attendants could not look her in the eyes. They knew she would be leaving soon. Whether that meant this place or this life, she didn't know.

She felt tears welling in her eyes. The thought of not seeing her family got to her at night. No one could see her cry. She closed her eyes tight and pushed those thoughts out of her head. One way or another, she was getting out of this room.

Hopefully, the bitch woman would not be present during the transfer.

CHAPTER 29

Josh pulled the truck into the valet lane at the Tropical Suites Hotel, put it in park, and hit the unlock button for the doors.

He exited the truck and tossed the fob to the approaching attendant.

"Are you checking in, sir?" The attendant wore tan shorts, white sneakers, and a purple floral print Hawaiian shirt. His name tag said, "Jason."

Josh said, "Yes, we are, Jason." He handed him a twenty-dollar bill. "This baby is my pride and joy, so park it somewhere safe." Josh pulled the flap back on his blazer to show his gold badge and his gun in his newly purchased holster. "If nothing happens to my truck, there'll be another twenty in the morning. If something is wrong with the truck, you get to explain it to my partner." Josh opened the rear door, and Syrin hopped out and stared at Jason.

The attendant took a step back. "Yes, sir. She'll be absolutely fine. Do you need any help with your luggage?"

"Yup. Get all the bags out of the back, including the dog food and dish."

"You got it." Jason handed the valet slip to Josh. "Front desk is through the entrance doors and to the left. You have a good night."

"Thanks, Jason. Come on, Syrin, let's go find us a nice bed."

Josh walked around the front of the truck with Syrin in heel position sporting her FBI vest. They followed Elena into the hotel.

The Tropical Suites Hotel had twenty-five floors of suites in a circle around a central courtyard with koi ponds, cascading waterfalls, and tropical green foliage.

Four glass-enclosed elevators on each side of the courtyard moved guests up and down as they watched the world below. Smartly dressed attendants at a concierge desk could make any Disney dream come true. Beyond them, the front desk lay hidden from the main traffic flow behind a row of giant ferns. A serious-looking Asian man was helping two tourists. Beside him, a bubbly blonde waved for Josh and Elena to come over.

"Good evening. Are you checking in?" She wore the same print shirt as the valet, but with "Hannah" on her name tag.

"Yes, we were hoping you had a room available." Elena stepped up to the desk and slid her credit card and driver's license across the counter.

"How long are you staying?" Hannah punched something into her computer.

Elena looked back at Josh, who shrugged his shoulders in the reserve salute. "Let's say a week."

Some more typing. "We only have one suite available for that time. It'll be two fifty-nine a night plus tax, and fifty dollars a night for the beautiful dog."

"We'll take it. Can you also send up some extra bedding and pillows? Someone will need it for the couch." Elena looked back at Josh.

Josh scratched Syrin's head. "Now, isn't Marshal Diaz nice? She's getting some extra bedding for you on the couch."

CHAPTER

30

Corporal Billy Witherspoon stepped into the reception area at 0530 in the fucking morning. He had the 0600 to 1400 desk shift for the next week because he cuffed and stuffed a fed. *How was I supposed to know the motherfucker was an FBI Agent? He was wearing a fucking tracksuit. Twenty years as a New York State Trooper, and now I gotta listen to the dog shit parade for a week.*

Billy waved at Officer Weeks behind the counter. She smiled at seeing her relief and buzzed the door. Two food trays were on the counter when he walked through the door. He asked, "Do you want me to take these trays down to our overnight guests?"

"That would be great. I'll finish the shift logs before you get back," Officer Weeks replied.

Billy picked up the trays and stacked them on top of each other. He walked down a long hallway to a locked door. His ID card was attached to a retractable lanyard. He stretched the cord and placed the card on the reader to the right of the door. The door buzzed. He pulled it open and stepped through to a landing at the top of a set of stairs.

The overhead lights blinked on as a motion detector sensed his presence, and an overhead camera activated to record his entry through the door. He walked down the stairs and turned left to another locked door. He went through the same entrance procedure; the door buzzed, the lights flicked on, and another overhead camera started recording.

Beyond the door, bars of three holding cells alternated with haze gray concrete walls on the left. Each cell would accept a food tray through a slot onto a shelf. Each also contained a simple set of stainless-steel bunks, a toilet, a sink, and a bench. Billy thought of this place mostly as a drunk tank for rowdy fans on football nights.

"All right, ladies, time to rise and shine. I have the finest in powdered eggs from the cafeteria." Billy walked up to the first cell, which contained Dillion Kling, and put the trays on the shelf. He looked into the cell. Dillion was on the bottom bunk, and he wasn't moving.

"Come on, asshole. Don't make me come in there and drag your ass out of bed." He bent down to get a better look. There was something wrong with Dillion's face. He looked closer. There was a dark spot where Dillion's right eye should be and a dark stain on the pillow and sheets.

"Oh, Jesus, Mary, Mother of God, no fucking way." Billy hustled down the hall to check on Kyle. Kyle was in the same position on the bottom bunk—a dark hole where his right eye should be and a dark stain on the sheets.

"Oh, fuck me." Billy ran back down the hall. *I wonder if the New York State Police are hiring.*

Carolyn Apicelli strolled up the front walk of manicured red bricks and climbed the steps to the mansion's front porch. She had made the same walk every morning for the last thirty-five years. There would not be many more walks. She had just turned sixty-five, so she was planning on hanging up her apron. She made breakfast for "her boys" every morning, rain or shine.

Her kitchen was open from 0700 to 1100. Most of the boys showed up at 1059. Momma A tried the front double doors on the right.

They were locked. She looked up at the camera and waved. No response. She tried the doorbell. No answer. *Hmm. That's weird.* She dug her keys out of her purse, put the key in the lock, and turned. The door unlocked with a thunk. She pushed the door open and detected a faint smell of almonds. *Some of the boys must be making flavored coffee in the study room.*

Momma A walked into the foyer and put her purse on the card table. She walked across the dark mahogany floor and pushed the door open to the study room. Three of her boys were slumped on the table next to their laptops with their eyes open, looking at the great beyond. Their skin had a cherry tinge, and their lips bore a faint shade of blue.

"Oh, sweet Jesus, please protect me." She made the sign of the cross and bolted out of the room. She grabbed her purse off the table and ran for the door, knocking over one of the museum rope stanchions protecting the fraternity crest etched on the floor. She fumbled with the doorknob, pushed the door open, and ran down the steps to her car.

CHAPTER 31

Josh's phone started playing the theme song to Dragnet. He opened his eyes to see a hairy paw on his face and part of a dog on his head. It took him a while to process the situation. Hotel, fold-out couch, Syrin, phone ringing. He pushed Syrin off and grabbed his phone.

"Yeah."

"They're all dead," Sergeant Friday shouted into the phone, his words running together.

"Slow down, Joe. What do you mean they're all dead?" Josh stood up, wide awake.

"The morning shift at our HQ found both Dillion and Kyle dead in their cells this morning. They were both shot in the head. Then, our deputies responded to a nine-one-one call of dead bodies at the Delta Faros Fraternity. They found three dead bodies in the study room, and a quick sweep of the house found dead bodies everywhere. Somebody is cleaning house in a big way. Literally, cleaning the fucking house."

"Where are you?" Josh looked for his pants.

"I'm at the fraternity. You guys need to get here quick. I got every agency in the alphabet here, and everyone is asking about you and the marshal."

"Roger. We're rolling now." Josh walked over and pounded on the bedroom door. "Elena, get up. We've got a situation!" Syrin looked at Josh and put her head back on the pillow.

Sari scanned the Golden Pineapple menu. The other angels were spread out around the table, sipping coffee. At their go-to breakfast place, everything tasted homemade. They always stopped there on their way back from Orlando. The waitress showed up to take their order. Everyone chose pancakes and bacon. Sari took a sip of almond-biscotti-flavored coffee and suppressed a laugh.

"Okay, anyone have a problem?" Everyone shook their head no.

"Great. We'll finish breakfast, and if we hurry, we can get back for the morning Bible session."

Elena and Josh showered and dressed. They were in no hurry to get to the circus. The dead weren't going anywhere, and the first folks on the scene usually had no clue what was going on or what to do. Then the brass would show up, and they would have even less of an idea what to do other than point fingers and say it was someone else's problem. Best to show up after the real investigators made an appearance and the brass headed to the press conferences.

Josh and Elena walked out of the hotel, followed by Syrin. "This is going to fuck up breakfast," Elena said.

"Yeah, we can drive through Dunkin' and get coffee and some sandwiches." Josh handed the valet a twenty when he rolled up with the truck in perfect condition.

"Thank you, Mr. Martin. We parked her in our best spot. Not a scratch, and no bird shit."

"Thanks, Jason." Josh opened the rear door for Syrin, watched her hop in, and climbed into the front, followed by Elena. He eased out of the valet lane and turned out of the hotel toward I-95. They did a quick drive through Dunkin' Donuts and took the on-ramp to I-95 North. In a couple of miles, he took Route 192, set the cruise to seventy-five, and hit the call button on the steering wheel.

"Call El Jefe."

The phone rang twice, and Vince Santiago picked up. "Good Morning, Josh. Is that you in Orlando? Becka just called and filled me in."

"Yes, sir. I'm here with Elena; we're headed over there now. The two who got whacked in the cells were Dillion Kling and Kyle Furman. We picked them up yesterday. They were the two subjects in a video of Bri getting escorted—dragged—to a white van."

"Oh, shit," Vince sighed into the phone.

"It gets worse. Both Dillion and Kyle were members of the Delta Faros Fraternity. The same fraternity that got hit last night also hosted the party where Bri went missing. I think it may be time to change our rules of engagement."

"Roger. I'll set up a meeting with the executive committee. Let me know if you need anything."

"Will do. One thing, though. You may want to check on the senator. This doesn't sound like your typical operation. Someone has some pros."

"I was thinking the same thing. Stay safe." Vince clicked off the call.

"You don't think it was the mom, do you?" Elena looked at Josh and took a sip of coffee.

"If it were my daughter, I would have killed every one of those rich assholes and burned the place to the ground."

"Fair enough. You may want to leave that part out of the official report." Elena took another sip of French Vanilla. "Not bad, but not like back in New England."

CHAPTER

32

Vince Santiago picked up the small oil lamp that sat on the front of his desk. The light of freedom. *Let it forever shine on the cause of democracy*, or something like that, according to legend. FDR was the original owner, and it sat on his oval office desk during WWII. He gave it to Colonel Ned Buxton, Jr., the first director of the Black and White Club, when he signed the founding document on January 17, 1945. It rested on the desk of every director since the colonel. It didn't travel very far. Colonel Buxton had it in Providence, Rhode Island until he died in 1949. It then spent twenty years in the Old Executive Office Building, called the Eisenhower Executive Office Building, after Clinton signed legislation renaming it in 1999. It moved to the third floor of the New Executive Office Building in 1969 when the building opened. *Now, it sits on my desk; I'm director number six of the Black and White Club.*

He put the lamp back on the desk and picked up a secure phone. No need to dial; it was a direct line. President Brian C. Byrne picked up.

"I thought you would call, Vince. Is it Orlando?"

"Yes, Mr. President. We have two assets on the ground. I'd like to schedule a meeting of the executive committee as soon as possible."

"On the ground already, how is that possible? I know you're good, but that's almost impossible."

"I can explain at the meeting." Vince swiveled in his chair and picked a pen out of an Army coffee mug. There was a pause on the phone.

"Okay, eleven hundred today. I'll make the calls."

"Roger," Vince scrawled the time on a note pad. "Thank you, Mr. President. One thing—I'd like to make the call to Senator Alonzo."

"Any particular reason?"

Vince could hear the question in his voice. "Everything will be clear at the meeting."

"All right, Vince, see you at eleven hundred." The line went dead.

Vince picked up his office phone and buzzed his executive assistant.

"Yes, Director?"

"Lisa, can you please set up a phone call with Senator Alonzo. Tell her it's urgent."

"Yes, sir."

"Thank you." Vince clicked off. "What am I going to tell the mother?" He slumped back in his chair.

Josh turned into the Dunkin' Donuts at Collegiate Way on the edge of the University and parked the truck. They made the trip in about ninety minutes. "Do you want anything?"

"No, I'm good. I'll keep Syrin company."

"Okay, I'll be right back." Josh hopped out of the truck and walked into the shop. The smell of fresh doughnuts rushed out of the store when he pulled the door open. The place was empty except for one college kid waiting for his order. Josh walked over to the *Order Here* sign.

A smiling girl with braces and a "Mindy" name tag greeted him. "Can I help you, sir?"

Josh cringed at the sir. Elena would be laughing. "Hi, Mindy. I have a pretty big order. I'd like eight dozen assorted doughnuts, eight large Boxes of Joe, and all of the cups etcetera to go with it."

Mindy rang up the order, and the staff of four started running around stuffing doughnuts into boxes and pouring coffee. "That will be two-twenty thirty-one."

Josh slid his card across the counter and noticed Mindy was expecting. He turned his head and blinked a few times to will the tears back into his eyes. He never knew what would trigger the thought of his beautiful wife, Kat, and his unborn child, lost to that motherfucking Rob McDonald and Nick Lacava. *I hope Rob's enjoying his time in hell, and Nick's enjoying his new boyfriend at Camp X-ray in Gitmo.*

Mindy ran his card and handed it back to him, wrapped in the receipt. "Thank you, sir! You can pick up your order at the end of the counter."

Josh put the card back in his wallet and pulled out four hundred-dollar bills. He put one of the hundreds in the tip cup. He rolled the other three into a tight roll. "Mindy?"

"Yes, sir?" She walked back to Josh and did a double-take at the hundred-dollar bill sticking out of the tip cup.

Josh handed her the tight roll of bills. "This is for the baby."

Mindy took the roll of money, and tears welled in her eyes. "Thank you." She went back to packing the order, trying not to cry.

It took Josh four trips to get everything loaded into the back of the truck. He stacked the last four boxes of doughnuts on the floor. "These aren't for you, Syrin." Syrin thumped her tail against the back seat and barked. Josh climbed into the front seat. "Never arrive at a local crime scene, especially in the morning or late at night, without bringing a little something."

Josh turned out of Dunkin' Donuts and hit the first roadblock within a mile. Two orange and white barricades blocked the street with two Orange County Sheriff, white-and-green cruisers stationed at either end of the barrier with lights flashing. A Deputy approached the truck.

Josh rolled down his window and handed the deputy his credential. He also passed him Elena's.

The deputy scanned both credentials. "Agent Martin, Marshal Diaz, good morning. Could you please wait here a second?" He walked back to the second deputy with a clipboard and checked their names against a list. The first deputy waved them up.

"You're good. They're expecting you at UCF Police Department." The deputy handed their credentials back through the window.

"Hey, you guys want some coffee and a doughnut?" Josh gestured to the back of the truck.

The deputy looked in the back window. "You're kidding me."

"Nope." Josh opened the door and climbed out. "Josh Martin." Josh extended his hand.

"Chris Cardinal, and that's my partner, John Brady." They shook hands. "Hey, John, they got coffee and doughnuts." Chris waved his partner over.

Josh opened the back and got cups and lids, and handed them to the deputies. "How do you guys like your coffee?"

"Black is fine," Chris said. "John also takes it black."

Josh poured two cups of coffee and offered them a selection of doughnuts from a box. They each grabbed a chocolate glazed. Josh closed everything up and shut the door. "Call ahead and tell your guys we got coffee and doughnuts. I'll park the truck and put everything on the tailgate."

"You guys just made my day. You need anything in Orange County, just give me a call." Chris handed Josh a business card.

"You got it, Chris. Stay safe." Josh climbed into the truck and headed to the police department.

Another mile down the road, they could see a UCF police officer waving them to the left into a parking lot jammed with marked cruisers, unmarked government cars, and a medical examiner vehicle. Josh turned into the lot, and another cop pointed him to an empty slot. "Gotta love the valet service."

Josh put the truck in park and left it running with the AC on. "Syrin, stay. I left the AC on, so no whining. Also, don't eat any doughnuts." Josh and Elena climbed out of the truck. He hit the tailgate release on the fob, and the gate dropped down. They stacked four boxes of doughnuts and four boxes of joe on the tailgate. A line had already started to form.

"All right, boys and girls, have at it, courtesy of the FBI and the marshal service," Josh said.

Josh and Elena weaved their way through the first responders and parked vehicles over to the statue of Corporal Mario Jenkins. Josh held the door for Elena and followed her through.

CHAPTER

33

The phone buzzed on Vince Santiago's desk. He pressed the blinking light. "Yes?"

"Senator Alonzo is on line one."

"Thanks, Lisa." Vince pressed the transfer button. "Senator Alonzo, good morning."

"Good morning, Vince. What's urgent? Is it about my daughter? Oh, God, don't let it be Orlando."

"It's not Orlando, but it's related to your daughter." Vince tapped a pen on his pad of paper. "We have a video of two fraternity members dragging a girl who looks like your daughter from a party to a white van. Our assets arrested those individuals yesterday. They were the victims in the UCF Police Department double homicide."

"You're kidding me. No sign of my daughter?"

"Not yet. We're still looking. I want to convene an executive meeting today at eleven hundred to discuss the case. Can you make it?" Vince underlined 1100 on his pad.

"Absolutely. Thank you for pursuing this, Vince. I knew my daughter was not shacked up and sleeping it off. See you at eleven hundred." The senator clicked off.

Vince looked at the phone for a couple of seconds, remembering what Josh said about professionals, and put it back in the cradle. He picked up his secure cell phone and punched in a number. Becka picked up immediately.

"Good morning, Director. What can I do for you?"

"Good morning, Becka. Please do a complete communication sweep of all our executive committee members, including a deep financial dive."

"Roger, sir. What time frame?"

"Go back a month and keep a continuous sweep until I tell you to stop."

"Will do."

"Becka, one more thing. My eyes only."

The police officer at the reception desk saw Josh and Elena enter and waved them over through the crowd. Reporters crammed into every inch of space in the reception area, typing away on laptops. They barely looked up when the two walked across to the desk. The door buzzed, and Josh pulled it open. Joe Friday was standing at the entrance.

"I wish we were meeting under better circumstances," Joe said. They all shook hands. "This is a first-class goat rope."

"So, bring us up to speed," Elena said.

"Kyle and Dillion were executed in their cells last night while they slept," Joe said.

"Executed? What makes you say that?" Josh moved in and leaned on the counter near the reception desk.

"Only way to describe it. Someone shot both subjects in the right eye multiple times from outside the cell with a small-caliber weapon. No exit wounds and minimal trauma going in. All rounds went precisely through the eye." Joe rubbed his hand on the side of his head.

"Can we get a look?" Elena asked.

"Sure, follow me." Joe headed down the hallway. "This is the only way to the holding cells." He stopped at the door. "This door is locked and requires key card access."

"The desk officer didn't see anything?" Josh looked back down the hall at the reception desk. A half-wall coming out from the entrance door obscured the view of the waist-high counter.

Joe buzzed through the door. "No, claims she didn't see a thing. Once you get through the door, a motion sensor will turn on the lights, send an alarm to the desk for door open, and start video surveillance." Joe pointed to the overhead camera trained at the door. They continued down the stairs and turned left to another door. Joe pressed his card on the keypad, the door buzzed, and he pushed it open. "The same thing happens here." They all walked through the door.

Two ambulance gurneys lined the walls of the gray cement walkway next to the open cell doors. Camera flashes came from both cells. Two guys in dark-blue suits approached them.

Joe Friday did the introductions. "This is Special Agent Felix Najera and Special Agent Dan Sullivan from the Florida Department of Law Enforcement. They're the lead investigators for this case. This is FBI Special Agent Josh Martin and U.S. Marshal Elena Diaz."

Agent Najera was a little shorter than Josh, with a slight build, slicked-back black hair, and a five o'clock shadow. Dan Sullivan was as Irish as they come, with a pale complexion, short brown hair parted to the left, and glasses.

Najera jumped right in. "So, if you don't mind me asking, how do two federal agents get involved with the arrest of two fraternity kids?"

"They were involved in a missing person case we were investigating as a kidnapping. We found them at the missing girl's apartment yesterday.

They were beating on the roommates. My dog didn't like how they treated girls, being a girl herself, so she put the bite on Dillion. Kyle took a swing at me, and he found out what it's like to assault a federal agent."

Both FDLE agents suppressed a laugh. "We," Josh motioned at Elena, "turned them over to the UCF Police Department for holding, and here we are. Can we get a look at the bodies?"

"Unfortunately, that's going to be a problem. My resident agent in charge said no federal, county, or university involvement is allowed. This is strictly a state investigation."

"You're kidding me. This is our investigation." Josh put his hands on his hips, and his focus narrowed.

Elena saw the coming storm. "Josh, why don't we call D.C. and straighten this out?" She put her hand on his arm, pulled out her cell phone, and walked back through the stairway door to make the call.

The two FDLE agents walked back down the cement walkway to observe the crime scene technicians.

"Sorry, Josh. I told you it was a goat rope. FDLE bigfooted everyone. Orange County Sheriff is also not happy." Joe glanced at the two FDLE agents.

"What does the state get out of strong-arming this investigation? It doesn't make any sense. Who takes on twenty-five homicides? It's twenty-five, isn't it?" Josh looked at Joe.

"Only twenty-two. Three of the fraternity brothers were sleeping with girlfriends." Joe checked his notes. "David Cinalli, Howard Shaw, and William Martinez. They picked an excellent time to get laid." Joe closed his notebook.

"Are you rounding them up? Not a good time to be a Delta Faros member." Josh leaned back on the door.

"As we speak. We're also notifying the other one hundred thirty-three UCF fraternity members who don't live in the mansion to be aware of their surroundings and report any suspicious activity. I have your requested search warrant. We were going to execute it this morning." Joe turned at the sound of a knock on the door.

Josh moved off the door and pulled it open. "Any luck?"

Elena walked in and looked down the walkway to the FDLE agents. "Wait for it."

As if on command, Agent Najera started patting his suit pockets to find his phone. He found it inside his coat pocket, put it to his ear, and almost came to attention. His head started doing a lot of affirmative bobbing like a bobblehead on a car dash, and they could hear a lot of "Yes, sirs" bouncing off the cement walls. It was a short call. He slipped the phone back into his suit jacket pocket, lowered his head in resignation, and started the walk of shame, followed by Agent Sullivan. They stopped about three feet short of Josh.

"Agent Martin, Marshal Diaz, I'm sorry for the confusion. I honestly don't know what the fuck is going on. The lieutenant governor called my RAC personally this morning and told him this would be an exclusive FDLE investigation. No outside assistance. That phone call was from Governor Fred Call. I have been with FDLE for thirteen years, and I have never met the governor, let alone personally talked to him. Now I've got him chewing my ass for following the orders from the lieutenant governor. So, let's start again. Agent Martin, Marshal Diaz, we would appreciate any help you can give us with this investigation, and FDLE will support you any way we can."

"Thanks, Felix. Can you show us the crime scene?" Josh suppressed a *Yes, motherfucker, now that's what I'm talking about. Marshal Diaz is kicking some ass.*

They all walked down the cement corridor and stopped at the first cell. Dillion Kling was lying on his left side with a black hole that used to be his right eye, staring at them. A technician in full personal protective equipment was snapping photos with a Nikon camera.

"Can we get a copy of all photos?" Elena handed Felix her business card.

"Yeah, no problem." Felix put the card in his pocket and handed his card to Elena.

Josh simulated sighting down a gun and pointed his right index finger at the black hole. "How far do you think it is from here to Dillion's head?"

"Fifteen feet, six inches," came the reply from the crime scene technician. "Same thing for the kid in the other cell. Almost an identical scene."

"How many shots?" Elena looked over Josh's shoulder.

"More than one. We won't know the exact number until autopsy." The technician stopped taking photos and walked over. "There are no exit wounds, so it was a small caliber round. I'm thinking .22 hollow point. Based on body temperature, rigor mortis, and lividity, I would put the time of death around zero two-thirty. Identical for the kid in the other cell. We found no shell casings, so the shooter, or shooters, policed their brass. We got nothing from the crime scene."

"Thank you." Josh walked away from the cell.

"Do you guys want to see the other scene?" Felix motioned at the other cell with his hand.

"No, thanks, I've seen enough dead kids, and we still have to visit the frat. Thanks for your help, fellas. Sorry for the fuck up with the governor. We're all just trying to do our jobs and get home safe. Can you call ahead to your guys at the mansion and let them know we're coming?" Josh extended his hand.

Felix shook his hand. "You got it, Josh. We'll be in touch."

"Roger. Marshal Diaz, are you ready?" Josh motioned to the door.

"Yeah, I'm coming. There's one thing I don't understand."

"Only one?" Josh pulled the door open.

CHAPTER 34

Bishop Avery sipped a fresh cup of French press coffee and took another bite of Jean-Paul's waffles as she looked out the windows of her apartment. The complex was rousing to life with cars entering the parking lot and lawnmowers crisscrossing the vast green lawn. They reminded her of golf course greenskeepers. A small dish of maple syrup flown in from Vermont sat next to her plate, along with a bowl of fresh berries. She liked to dip bits of waffle into the syrup instead of dumping it across the whole stack. Mozart's Serenade Number Thirteen played softly in the background. Avery wore white shorts and a yellow flower-print shirt with matching earrings and her signature small gold cross around her neck.

The phone buzzed on her dining room table. She turned it on its edge to check the number, picked it up, and hit the green accept button. "Yes?"

"Both crime scenes are clean. No leads in the case. Unfortunately, no success in turning off the feds. No idea why."

"Okay, thank you. Let me know if anything changes." She ended the call and took another bite of waffle. *Hmm. The lieutenant governor can't protect an investigation in her home state. Somebody's got some juice.*

She turned at the sound of heavy footsteps on the white marble floor and smiled. Julius, the mowing Samoan from Florida State University, was not subtle no matter how hard he tried. He started at left tackle for four years with dreams of an NFL career until a devastating knee injury ended those dreams in his final bowl game. He always reminded her of The Rock.

"Yes, Julius?"

"Sorry to disturb your breakfast, but Miss Sari is here to see you."

"Oh, great, send her in." She took another bite of waffle dipped in maple syrup. The butter and maple flavors were exquisite.

"Did I make it back in time for Bible study?" Sari walked across the floor. Unlike Julius, she made almost no sound, like a Jaguar in the jungle. She pulled out a chair and sat next to the Bishop so she could see out the window and keep an eye on the front door.

Bishop Avery laughed. "No, you missed Bible study. Can I get you breakfast, or did you stop at the Golden Pineapple?"

"Yeah, we stopped for breakfast. I'll take some of that coffee."

"Of course. Jean-Paul, some coffee for Sari."

"Yes, Bishop, coming right up," came a voice from the ceiling.

An older black gentleman slightly stooped, walked in from the kitchen dressed in a white chef's uniform. He set a white china mug monogrammed with a gold cross in front of Sari, and steam rose from the hot liquid.

"Thank you, Jean-Paul. It smells great." Sari picked up the mug and blew across the top to bring down the heat. She drank out of a coffee mug because it reminded her of field training.

"Can I get you some waffles? They're delicious," Jean-Paul offered.

"No, thank you, Jean-Paul. I already ate breakfast."

"Very well, Miss Sari. I'll be in the kitchen if you need anything. Can I get you a refill, Bishop?"

"No, I'm good. Breakfast was wonderful."

"I'm glad you liked it." Jean-Paul shuffled back to the kitchen.

"So, how did things go?" Bishop Avery watched for Sari's response.

"Everything went as planned, except we missed three, who were not sleeping at the mansion. They're probably going to be under protective custody, so they'll be tough to reach. Not impossible, but tough." Sari rubbed the side of her mug, trying to gauge the drinkability of its contents.

Bishop Avery sat back and pursed her lips. "No, I was most worried about Chad and the two in the holding cells. I don't think the other three are worth the risk. Are we ready to move the girls?"

"Yes. The bus will be here tomorrow to load the seven and then get the remaining twenty-three at the conference center. We'll stage them at the warehouse before loading them into containers for embarkation on the ship." Sari took a sip of the coffee, which was outstanding. *Like her wine, never pass up a cup of the bishop's French press coffee.*

"What are you doing today?" Bishop Avery plopped a fresh strawberry into her mouth.

"I'm heading over to Zeus's to work out the distribution plan for the coke. We have to ship product to all state chapters. That's a lot of moving parts."

"Okay. Take someone with you. I couldn't turn off the feds. They're still snooping around." Bishop Avery pushed her plate into the center of the table.

"Will do." Sari stood and took a final swig. "Have a blessed day." She pushed in her chair and padded across the tile floor.

Bishop Avery picked up another piece of waffle with her fork, dipped it into the maple syrup, and placed it in her mouth. She tapped the fork on the syrup dish. *Maybe one more loose end.*

CHAPTER 35

Josh, Joe, and Elena walked out of the UCF Police Department building and stopped by the Jenkins statue.

Josh turned to Joe. "Let's take two vehicles over to the mansion. My back seat is full of doughnuts, dog, and coffee. I'm hoping the doughnuts are not in the dog."

"Roger. I'll get the Explorer and meet you over there. FDLE called ahead, so you should have no problems getting in." Joe headed to the UCF lot.

Josh and Elena headed to the truck. Josh hit the key fob, the lights blinked, and the doors unlocked. He opened the door and climbed in, followed by Elena. Syrin jumped off the back seat, placed her paws on the center console, and licked Josh's face.

"Oh yes, dog kisses. You don't look any fatter." Josh patted her rib cage, and Syrin barked. Josh put the truck in reverse and backed out of the slot. "What was the one thing you didn't understand?"

Elena looked at Josh. "What?"

"When we were walking out of jail, you said there was one thing you didn't understand." Josh turned on Libra and then North Gemini Boulevard.

"Oh yeah, how did our shooter know the boys were in UCF holding? We could have put them in Orange County, Orlando, a federal detention center, or some other lock up."

"I was wondering the same thing. Plus, how does someone bypass all of that security on less than twenty-four hours' notice? I think there was only one shooter." Josh moved left to get around a snowbird lost in traffic.

"What makes you say that?" Elena scratched behind Syrin's ears and looked at Josh.

"Someone put two or more rounds in a target with a diameter less than a quarter at fifteen feet, six inches, and they did it under stressful conditions. I couldn't do that at the range on a beautiful sunny day, and I'm a pretty good shot. I'd be surprised if more than five people could make that shot. Someone may get lucky and do it once, but twice, no way. That was one shooter. With two shooters, someone's missing."

Josh turned left onto Greek Court and pulled behind a slew of cop cars parked at the curb. He put the truck in park, then he and Elena hopped out. Syrin did a don't-leave-me dance in the back seat. The two of them moved all the coffee and doughnuts to the tailgate, and the cops on the scene started lining up. Joe Friday pulled in behind them.

"You know how to win friends and influence people." Joe walked up.

"You've got a mole in your department." Josh opened the rear door to let Syrin out. She jumped down.

"Chief thinks the same thing. He ordered polygraphs for the entire department. No exceptions." Joe grabbed a plain doughnut out of the box.

"Well, that's a start. I'd also flag everyone's bank account. Someone's likely to disappear. I'm sure they didn't sign up to hold the bag for twenty-two dead college kids." Josh snapped a leash on Syrin. "What do you say we go find some dope?"

CHAPTER 36

Director Santiago appreciated his view of one of the most secure conference rooms in the world. One could reach this nondescript concrete box, two-hundred feet beneath the New Executive Office Building, only by elevator. The elevator came straight from his office, with the only two other possible stops being the ground floor and a Leadership Subway station. Instead of using buttons, it required a biometric hand scan and voice recognition.

The Eisenhower administration built the Leadership Subway. It connected the White House, the Pentagon, Congress, the State Department, and the Supreme Court. It allowed the country's leadership to meet at various locations without prying eyes, including the press. It also provided security to move leaders around the city in times of war or unrest. Access to the Leadership Subway was granted only to the president, vice president, Speaker of the House, Senate Majority Leader, chief justice of the Supreme Court, the secretary of state, the secretary of defense, and the chairman of the Joint Chiefs.

The Black and White Club conference room was even more exclusive than the subway system, with only six members. Director Santiago placed name placards around a circular table since every member in this chamber was equal: president, vice president, Speaker of the House, leader of the Senate, and the chief justice of the Supreme Court. Santiago was a member but didn't get a vote. He placed the placards at random from one meeting to the next, so no one got the impression of a personal seat. Large video screens surrounded the table on each of the four walls so that one could get an unobstructed view no matter the location of their chair. A refrigerator in the corner contained each member's favorite non-alcoholic drink. Next to it, a modular bar in the shape of a wine barrel opened to access each member's favorite alcoholic beverage. Ike donated the bar when he built the conference room. A coffee cart with two Keurigs recessed into the wall held a carousel of flavors.

The elevator door chimed, and a green light shone over the doors, which opened in due course. The Speaker of the House walked in behind Bri's mother, the leader of the Senate.

"Good afternoon, Vince." Katherine F. Rich was the Speaker of the House from California's Twelfth District in San Francisco. Dressed in a lavender jacket with a matching skirt and a light cream blouse, she exuded elegance. She parted her short brown hair to the right and paired the outfit with pearl earrings and a matching pearl necklace.

"Good afternoon, Madam Speaker. Can I get you anything?"

"No, thanks, Vince. I'm just going to get some coffee." She walked over to the coffee cart.

Donna Ruiz Alonzo, the senior senator from Florida, heir to a sugar fortune and top Republican in the Senate, located her placard and sat down. Her long brown hair fell loose below her shoulders. She wore a dark-blue dress with matching pumps. Her lips were pursed in grim determination, and a mole on her right cheek distracted just a little from her penetrating brown eyes.

"Vince, is everyone going to make it?" Senator Alonzo looked at the director.

"Yes, Senator, we should have a quorum."

"Any more news on Orlando?"

"No, Senator, just what we talked about this morning."

The elevator chimed again, and the doors opened. President Brian C. Byrne and his vice president, Amelia Evelina, walked through the doors. The president carried a large black leather briefcase. Inside was an aluminum case that contained the nuclear launch codes for all U.S. nuclear forces. The military aide on duty usually carried the "football." This was the one place off-limits to the military aides and Secret Service personnel. The Air Force presidential military aide and the vice president's Army military aide waited topside on the subway platform along with Secret Service details.

"Ladies, how are you doing?" President Byrne smiled.

"We're fine, Mr. President." Speaker Rich poured a cup of coffee and added some cream and sugar. "Good to see you again."

"Same here, Katherine." The president walked over to Vince, and the vice president walked over to get coffee.

President Byrne was an athletic, forty-five-year-old former Republican governor of Iowa, dressed in a tailored dark-blue power suit, solid maroon tie, crisp white shirt, and shined classic black shoes. He had piercing blue eyes with a short military haircut cut close on the side of his head to hide his gray hair. He exuded power and money.

"Anything new on Orlando?" Byrne shook hands with Vince.

"No, Mr. President. Not since I talked to you this morning."

"Okay, Vince, thanks." He set the case on the floor and looked at his watch. "Anyone seen Carlo?"

"He was wrapping up some oral arguments when I talked to him this morning," Vice President Evelina said. She walked over to the table, carrying her coffee. Amelia Evelina, the former Republican Senator from Georgia, was the first African American female elected vice president of the United States. She and Byrne looked right together. With long black hair piled in a tight bun, she wore a dark pantsuit and white blouse. Her matching dark blue shoes sported flat heels to keep her from towering over the commander-in-chief. Her smile, figure, and confidence would make her a contender in a beauty pageant. Amelia took her seat at the table, stirring her coffee and watching Vince.

The elevator chimed again. "That's probably Carlo." President Byrne turned toward the elevator doors.

The doors opened, and in walked Carlo Virgilio, chief justice of the Supreme Court. He looked like a college professor, and he fit the job description. Nominated to the Supreme Court while he was a law professor at Harvard, Carlo was pushing seventy. He had a receding gray hairline, beard, and mustache, and he walked with a slight limp from a mountain biking accident in Colorado. He took off his wrinkled gray sports coat and draped it over his seat.

"Sorry I'm a little late, folks. The lawyers wouldn't shut up." Carlo pulled out his chair and sat down.

"Lawyers are long-winded? Say it isn't so." Katherine walked over from the coffee cart and sat down.

Vince nodded at the leader of the free world. "Mr. President, I believe we have a quorum. Would you please call the meeting to order?"

"All right, Vince." Byrne opened a black binder in front of him and started reading: "Under the purview of Executive Order nine-five-one-three, addendum A, this meeting of the Black and White Club is called to order. All actions taken by this committee must be by unanimous decision and based on the best judgment of each member without consideration to position, political affiliation, or current United States law. The only guiding principle is the preservation of the democratic institution, which is the United States of America, and the defense of our constitution against all enemies, foreign and domestic. All proceedings and decisions made during this meeting shall never be divulged beyond these members."

He looked up. "Does everyone agree?"

Brian scanned the table. They ignored official titles and positions once the meeting started. It was one person, one vote. Everyone nodded in agreement.

He nodded back. "Okay, Vince, the floor is yours."

"Thank you, Brian." Vince pressed a button on a remote. A map of the United States appeared on the screens with a star over Orlando.

"Sometime last evening, a suspect, or multiple suspects, entered the University of Central Florida Police Department and executed two college students who were in holding cells one and three.

"This is Dillion Kling." Vince showed a side by side of Dillion Kling's senior year picture and a shot of him lying on the cell bunk with a black hole in place of his right eye.

"Oh, dear God," Carlo said.

"This is Kyle Furman." Pictures of him filled the screen.

"How is it possible to kill two kids in a jail cell in a police department?" Katherine looked at Vince.

"We're investigating." Vince took a sip of coffee.

"Earlier this morning, you said we already had assets on scene. How is that possible?" Brian leaned forward in his chair.

"I can answer that." All eyes looked at Donna. "Last Friday, my daughter Bri went missing from a fraternity party. She always calls me on Saturday mornings. Last Saturday, she didn't call, and her roommates said they hadn't seen or spoken to her since the party. I contacted the Capitol Police, the Orange County Sheriff's Department, and the University of Central Florida's

Police Department. They all guessed she must have shacked up with some boyfriend. Number one, she doesn't have a boyfriend, and number two, she would have called. I asked Vince for help."

Katherine reached out and grabbed her hand. "I'm so sorry."

Brian looked at Vince. "I don't mean to be insensitive, but why were agents dispatched without this committee's authority?"

"Really, Brian? What if it was one of your kids?" Katherine glared at Brian.

"Let me explain." Vince rubbed his hand across the smooth wood table. "The agents I dispatched are Josh Martin and Elena Diaz. They were operating under the rules of engagement for their agencies. Since this is a missing person case and the possible kidnapping of a senior government official family member, it's under the FBI's purview. Josh is an FBI agent. I sent Elena because she's our best at finding people."

Brian sat back. "Sorry, that makes sense. I thought Josh was still in Delta training."

Vince pulled up a video. "He'd just finished the final exercise when I called Colonel Gangsei. Ted wanted to keep him for Delta Force."

"I hope you told him no." Amelia took a sip of coffee. "That man's a patriot and a hell of an agent."

"Amen," Carlo said.

Vince hit the clicker again. The video of two young men dragging a stumbling girl to a white van played on the screen. "The abductee is Bri. The abductors are Dillion Kling and Kyle Furman. Josh and Elena arrested them yesterday."

"What were the charges," Carlo asked?

Vince looked at him. "Assault on a federal agent. Both gentlemen were slapping around Bri's roommates, trying to discover her real identity. One of them took a swing at Josh, which was not the best career decision."

Carlo leaned back. "Real identity?"

"For security reasons, her name is Bri Castillo, which was her grandmother's last name," Donna said.

"Ah, that makes sense." Carlo stood up and walked to the refrigerator to get a soda. "Anyone want a drink?"

"I'll take a Perrier," Katherine said.

Carlo got a can of Diet Coke and a bottle of water from the fridge and walked back to his seat. He handed the water to Katherine.

"Thank you." Katherine twisted hers open.

"You're welcome." Carlo pulled the top on the Coke and sat down. "Sorry, Vince, but I know what's coming, and I'm not in a hurry to see it."

"Yeah, the next slides aren't pretty." Vince pressed the remote. "This is a shot of the Delta Faros Fraternity. It's the largest fraternity on campus with one hundred sixty members. Twenty-five of them live in the frat house."

He clicked through the slides: three dead boys, facedown on a table, vacant eyes staring at nothing. Chad lying contorted on a bed with his right arm hanging limply off the side, touching the lifeless body of a golden retriever. Another young man sprawled on a pool table.

"I think we've seen enough, Vince," Brian said.

All the members were looking at the floor. Vince clicked off the computer, and silence filled the room.

"How many dead?" Brian looked up at Vince.

"Twenty-two." Vince put the remote on the table.

"Lord, have mercy." Carlo took a sip of Diet Coke to settle his stomach. "How did they die?"

"Some type of gas attack—we won't know for sure until we get the forensics. We also don't know the delivery method. Everything was locked up tight. No obvious signs. All gas lines were intact." Vince opened a folder in front of him, then passed out a single sheet of paper to each member. "This is a direct-action request against any organization, company, or persons involved in the killing of twenty-two members of the Delta Faros Fraternity at the University of Central Florida."

Everyone around the table reviewed the document. They knew direct action meant to remove, kill, or prosecute anyone connected to the Delta Faros killings without the benefit of a trial. Sometimes the best solution was the thirty-eight-cent solution—a bullet to the back of the head.

"We have a motion before the committee for direct action," Brian said. "All those in favor?" Everyone raised their hands. "The motion carries. Please sign the document."

Everyone signed the documents and handed them back to Vince, who slipped them back into the folder.

"Any other business?" Brian looked around the table. No response. "Meeting adjourned."

Everyone stood and headed to the elevator.

"Mr. President, could I please have a minute of your time?" Vince put the folder under his arm.

"Sure, Vince. What's up?" The President picked up the football and put it on the table near Vince. The elevator chimed, the doors opened, and the other members of the executive committee departed.

"When our agents arrived on scene at the University of Central Florida, the lieutenant governor tried to freeze everyone out except FDLE. I had to call Governor Call to get everything straightened out. He had no clue about her order, and he wasn't happy. I know the lieutenant governor is one of your biggest supporters and financial backers. I figured you should know."

President Byrne pursed his lips. "That doesn't make any sense. I'll give her a call. Thanks for the heads-up."

CHAPTER 37

Joe, Josh, and Elena signed in to the crime scene and started up the red brick walkway.

"Who found them?" Elena walked up the three steps.

Joe checked his notes. "Carolyn Apicelli—she's the fraternity's dorm mom, for lack of a better term. She cooks them breakfast and makes sure the cleaning staff does a good job. She found the three in the study room, ran out, and called nine-one-one."

They all put on shoe covers, gloves, and N95 masks at the door. Josh walked into the foyer first with Syrin on a lead. They turned right and entered the study room. The three bodies were already gone, but the tape outlines of where they had fallen remained.

"Syrin, seek." Josh unclipped her lead. Syrin made a quick dash to the air vent, barked, and lay down. "Good girl. Syrin, come." Syrin walked back over. Josh clipped the restraint back onto her. "I'm going to put her in the truck. Since this is probably a gas attack, I don't want her getting any residual." Josh walked out of the mansion.

Elena and Joe walked over to the air vent. Elena slipped a knife out of her pocket and snapped the blade open. She moved an edge behind the air vent cover, pried it open, and set it on the table. "We should get the register dusted for prints."

Friday took a flashlight from his belt and flicked it on. He shined the light into the duct. "Bingo." He pulled out individual-size bags of pills, coke, and heroin and piled them onto the table. He also pulled out four-kilo-size bricks of something wrapped in plastic. The symbol of the Golden Knight marked every individual bag. Someone wrote *ILL* on every kilo package in black marker. "Holy shit, I think we just found the Holy Grail."

"What are you talking about?" Elena looked at the pile of dope.

"The Golden Knight is the primary drug supplier on campus. We've been looking for them for years." Joe held up a baggie with a white powder. "Nine times out of ten, you would find one of these bags at a campus overdose for the last decade. I gotta call the chief." Joe pulled out his phone and headed to the door just as Josh was walking back in.

"Where's he going?" Josh jerked his thumb in Joe's direction.

"To call his chief; look at this dope." Elena held up a bag of pills.

Josh looked at the pile of drugs on the table and whistled. "Wow, that's not personal use."

"Nope. Joe thinks it's the main campus supplier." Elena shook the bag of pills and tossed them back onto the pile. "So, what do you think?"

"I think we got girls and drugs. The only thing missing for the trifecta is guns. Do you like to bowl?" Josh gestured at the door.

"I thought you'd never ask. What about the dope?" Elena headed to the door.

"Joe can have it. We still need to find a girl and some scumbags. I'll call Vince and see if our rules of engagement have changed. I'm betting, yes." Josh pulled out his phone and hit send.

CHAPTER

38

Sari and Michael walked out of the elevator. They headed past the row of black Harley-Davidson Low Rider Ses to the Barcelona Blue BMW M8 competition convertible parked three slots over. Both angels wore matching tan tactical pants, white sneakers, and green polo shirts. Michael was the same size and build as Sari, but she had blonde hair cut short just off the collar. They both wore tinted Wiley X Romer sunglasses, and each carried a Leslie Crossbody bag, which contained Heckler and Koch VP9SK 9mm pistols with two extra ten-round magazines.

Sari pressed her fob, the car doors unlocked, and both women slid into their seats. The fifteen-position alpine-white leather seat automatically reset to her preferences. The 523 HP 4.4-liter twin-turbo V8 rumbled to life at the touch of a button. Sari backed out of the slot, eased out of the parking garage, and took a right toward the Highway to Heaven. Just past the Cape Canaveral Lighthouse, she stopped. "What are you in the mood for?"

Michael shifted in the seat to get comfortable. She knew what was coming. "Play something country."

Sari pressed the sound button. "Play song 'Homecoming Queen.'" She also hit the button to release the top, letting in bright sunshine and a cool breeze. The 1,375-watt Bowers & Wilkens Diamond Surround Sound System started to crank Kelsea Ballerini. She pressed the power button for the Escort Redline EX radar detector, and the system blinked to life. The top closed into the back, and she stomped on the gas. The M8 accelerated like a rocket, pushing them both back into their seats. The digital speedometer passed sixty miles per hour at two-point-eight seconds and one hundred miles per hour at seven-point-four seconds before she eased off the gas to make the turn onto Church of Light Boulevard.

"The Bishop would kill you if she knew you drove like that on her road." Michael checked the side mirror to see if they had run over any pedestrians.

"Nah, she loves me. Why have a sports car if you're not going to drive it fast?" Sari turned right onto Route 192 and stomped on the gas again, but she kept it under eighty—no need to get pulled over for a ticket with so much going on." They exited on I-95 South and eventually turned into the parking lot near a neon sign with a bowling ball hitting three pins. A strike of lightning appeared over the word *Strikers*. It looked better at night.

She headed to the right of the main building and stopped at a chain-link fence shrouded with black canvas to mask what lay behind it. Two cameras on either side of the gate covered both the driver and any passengers. Sari looked up at the lens. The barrier slid open. She drove in when the gate cleared the front of the car. The portal closed when she went by a sensor on the side of the building.

"Now *that's* a nice car." Josh watched the Barcelona Blue BMW M8 turn into the Strikers parking lot, pass through the back gate, and disappear around the building. From their vantage point parked in a CVS parking lot across the street, they had a clear view of Strikers Family Fun Center.

"Were you watching the car or the two babes driving it?" Elena put her binoculars on her lap and reached for her phone. She punched up the number for Becka.

"I can neither confirm nor deny. Did you get the license number?" Josh did another scan of the parking lot and building, then looked at Elena.

"I'm sure, just skipped right over them. I'm calling it in now." Becka picked up. "Becka, this is Elena. I need you to run a license plate: Alpha, November, Golf, Echo, Lima, number one. Correct. Also, put a rush on the record check for Strikers Family Fun Center. We want to know who owns it. Thank you. I'll tell him." Elena put the phone back in her purse. "Becka says hi."

"Did you just say 'angel one?'" Josh looked at Elena.

"I did." Recognition crossed her face. "You think they're connected to the church?" Elena picked up her binoculars and looked at the fence. "We need to see what's in the back. I've never seen a family fun center with a security perimeter. Got any ideas?"

Josh stared out the window at the parking lot. "Vince said we're operating on Black and White rules of engagement, so anything goes. We could come back at night and do a sneak and peek, but I have a feeling we're running out of time on Bri. Do you still have Agent Najera's business card?"

"Yeah, I got it right here." Elena pulled the card out of her pocket. "What for?"

"I got an idea. We need to gear up." Josh reached in the back and hit the button on his armory.

CHAPTER 39

Sari pressed the button to close the roof. The back shell popped open, and the top rose, then locked into place in less than fifteen seconds. Sari and Michael popped open their doors and slid out of the car to see a smiling Zeus on his way out of the club.

"Nothing better than seeing two fine women getting out of a gorgeous automobile." Zeus wore a black T-shirt with a stick figure fucking the Y in *Your Feelings*, tan surfer shorts, and flip flops. His softball-size biceps filled out his shirt.

"Nice shirt. We get 'fine,' and the car gets 'gorgeous.' What's up with that, and why is the stalker van still on solid ground?" Sari pointed to the white cargo van still sitting in stall five.

"I thought you said there might be a passenger for the van." Zeus cricked his massive neck to the left.

"Nah, the passengers caught a different flight. Get rid of it. Let's go inside. It's hot as balls out here." Sari walked past Zeus, patted him on the abs, and pulled the door to go into the club.

The cold air hit her in the face. She held the door for Michael, dropped it on Zeus, and followed Michael to a table. The place was empty except for the new guy. He stood behind the bar wearing a black T-shirt, which said *Prospect* in white letters. She came close enough to see the rest of him over the counter. He wore khaki shorts and shit kickers with white socks sticking out over the tops. Zeus's muscles dwarfed those of the prospect, whose full beard and long black greasy hair made him look like a biker. Zeus looked like a surfer from Venice Beach.

"Are you girls hungry? The prospect makes an awesome cheeseburger." Zeus pulled up a chair opposite the girls.

"I'm starving," Michael said.

"Sounds good to me." Sari hooked her gun bag on the back of the seat.

"Prospect? Three cheeseburgers, french fries, and sweet iced tea." Zeus pointed around the table. The prospect nodded his head.

"So, what brings you, ladies, out today? Are you looking for a little Zeus time? We got a couple of beds in the back." Zeus flexed his right bicep.

"As tempting as that offer may be, I don't think you could keep up with the angel experience since you slipped past the magic age of thirty," Sari said. Both Sari and Michael laughed.

"Now, now, ladies, in the immortal words of the great philosopher Toby Keith, 'I ain't as good as I once was, but I'm as good once as I ever was.'" Zeus leaned back in his chair and put his hands behind his head.

The prospect walked up with a tray and placed silverware wrapped in napkins in front of everyone along with glasses full of iced tea, a bottle of ketchup, mustard, and relish.

"We'll have to pass on the offer. The holy ship arrives tomorrow." Sari smiled at the prospect. "Thank you, sweetie. Can I get a straw?"

The prospect pulled three straws out of his apron pocket and put them on the table. "Anything else?"

"No, we're good. Make sure you don't burn the burgers." Zeus gave him a look, meaning *get the fuck outta here*. The prospect hustled back to the bar. "The ship arrives tomorrow. That's fantastic and great timing. We're doing our annual beach bash rodeo at Clearwater. Everyone can pick up their shit on the way out of town."

"Excellent. That was the purpose of our trip out here—to make sure you had enough time to make arrangements to move the load. It's a double shipment." Sari took a sip of tea.

"Oooh, we can't move that much in a single rodeo. We'll have to warehouse some. I'll make arrangements with the stash houses. We should be able to move most of it. Most colleges will have graduation parties, and finals are always a prime sell season." Zeus looked up at the prospect, who was walking with a food tray. He always had a sixth sense about the arrival of food. "Smells good, prospect."

The prospect set the tray on a nearby table and transferred plates of cheeseburgers and hot fries in front of everyone. "Fries are really hot. Bon appétit." He retrieved the tray and walked back to the bar.

Zeus took a big bite of the cheeseburger, and grease oozed out of the corner of his mouth. He dabbed it with a napkin. "What did I tell ya? The kid makes the best cheeseburgers. I may just tell him to fuck the club; let's open up a hamburger joint at the beach." Zeus took another bite of cheeseburger.

The door between the club and the family fun center burst open, and the front desk clerk rushed in. "Cops! We got a bunch of cops in the front parking lot, headed our way."

Zeus looked up at the security cameras just in time to see a red F-150 slam through the gate.

CHAPTER 40

Josh hit the gas, and the Shelby pancaked the gate like JJ Watt heading to a quarterback. He raced along the side of the building and jerked the wheel hard left, which fishtailed the back of the truck into a left turn. He accelerated and hit the brakes, sliding to the stop behind the blue BMW. Josh piled out of the F-150, pulling an M4 Carbine with him. Elena exited the passenger side with a Benelli shotgun. Josh pulled the rear door, and Syrin, with her green FBI vest, rocketed out of the truck to Josh's left side.

Josh did a quick visual sweep of the back parking lot. A five-stall garage across the lot from the family fun center had a white van parked in the end stall and other motorcycles in other bays in various states of repair. The blue BMW sat in front of the rear entrance below a giant neon sign, Lightning Strikes Motorcycle Club. Two Harleys were parked nose-in about fifteen feet from the door.

Josh sprinted to the door, paused, and Syrin ran in front of him, nose to the door. Elena closed to his six. Josh pushed on the door. "Syrin, guard." Syrin rushed through the door and jumped up on a table, snarling and barking at the room. The two Beemer beauties were sitting at a table with a big dude while another male in a black T-shirt stood behind the bar. The back door of the club hung open.

"Hands. Let me see your hands." Josh pushed into the club to the left. Elena went right, while the snarling queen of dairy took the middle. The Beemer chicks calmly placed their hands on the table in front of them and surveyed their options. The big dude was moving his hands over his head like he was doing the wave. The guy behind the bar made a run at Josh.

"Fucking feds." He sprinted from around the bar and threw a right roundhouse punch at Josh's head. Josh leaned back and watched the punch pass in front of his face. When the punch cleared, he jammed the butt of his M4 into the guy's stomach. The man dropped like a sack of potatoes retching on the floor, followed by seventy pounds of pissed off Malinois snapping at his head. Josh dropped to his knee and cuffed the subject.

"What the fuck? Do I have a sign on my back that says hit me?" Josh kicked the prospect to emphasize his point. He looked at the big dude. "Anyone else here?"

"No, man, just us, the fun center staff in the front, and customers. What's going on? Do you have a warrant?" The big dude looked from Josh to Elena.

"Local police got a call of an active shooter." Josh looked around. *Pretty swanky for a motorcycle club.* The door to the fun center opened, and Sergeant Gary Hartlage from the Palm Bay Police Department walked in. They met him in front and offered to help when all the units started rolling in.

"Agent Martin, Marshal Diaz, thanks for your help. It looks like a prank. You folks can put down your hands." Sergeant Hartlage looked at the prospect cuffed on the ground. "What did he do?"

"Took a swing at me." Josh looked at the prone figure.

"I'm gonna sue. Both you, your bitch, and this fucking dog." The prospect tried to raise his head.

Josh bent down. "What did you say to me?

"Take these cuffs off me, and I'll show you how to satisfy your black bitch partner," he said and then whispered, "Code blue."

Josh grabbed the prospect's arm and hauled him to his feet. "We'll take him into federal custody and let the US Attorney sort this out. Syrin, come." Josh walked over to the exit, banged the prospect into the door to open it, and pushed him through.

"Hey, you can't do this." Zeus stood up. "Gary, this ain't right." Gary raised his hands in defeat and walked back into the club.

"Who's going to pay for my gate?" Zeus complained.

Elena pulled a business card out of her pocket. "Call this guy, and he'll take care of the damages." She tossed Agent Najera's card on the table and walked out.

Sari stood up. "Fuck me." She snatched her bag off the back of the chair and kicked it across the room. It slammed into the bar and fell over.

Zeus stood up. "Hey, what the fuck? Take it easy."

"Take it easy? Are you really that stupid? Two federal agents and a dog? Remember? They just SWATTED us. They got pictures of you, us, our car, and that white fucking van parked in your garage. Damn it!" She slammed her fist on the table.

"Oh, shit." Recognition crossed Zeus's face. "Oh, man."

Michael looked up from her seat. She never got excited, no matter the situation. It always ruined the shot. "So, what do you want to do?"

Sari took three deep breaths and pushed the emotion out of her system. She paused for a couple of seconds, looked down at Michael, and said, "They gotta go. And Zeus, get rid of the fucking van."

CHAPTER

41

Josh turned left out of the Strikers parking lot and hung a right on Palm Bay Road toward I-95. He looked at the prospect in the backseat in his rearview mirror. "We're clear. Who are you?"

"Special Agent Jeremy Guzman, DEA. Thanks for getting me out of there."

Elena turned to Josh. "You're kidding me. How did you know?"

"He gave me a code blue when he was offering to take you on a date. Who's your case officer?" Josh watched for Jeremy's reaction.

"Special Agent Fred Gonzales; he's out of the Orlando office. Can we get these cuffs off? Your dog's giving me the eye." Jeremy moved farther to the door.

"Her name's Syrin. She thinks you're buying her ice cream." Josh hit a button on his phone. "Call Becka." She answered on the third ring.

"Hi, Josh. What can I do for you?" came out of the truck's sound system.

"I'm here with Elena and a guest. I need you to check on an undercover operation. The undercover agent's name is Jeremy Guzman. The case officer is Fred Gonzales."

"Wait, one." There was a pause on the line. "Checks out. A registered case for drug trafficking involving the Lightning Strikes Motorcycle Club."

"Roger. Thank you. Also, can you run facial recognition on our body cams? We just paid a visit to the Strikers Fun Center. I want to know about the big surfer dude and two chicks sitting at a table. There's a white van in a garage across the parking lot. Run the plates. Did you get anything yet on ownership of the fun center?"

"Not yet. There are about a dozen shell companies in the loop, including three offshore. Something's not right. I don't know what."

"Okay, thanks." Josh clicked off the call. "Syrin, *lass es*." Syrin lay down on the back seat. "You still owe her ice cream." Josh pulled over onto the right shoulder. He got out of the truck, opened the back door, and unlocked Jeremy's cuffs.

"Thanks." Jeremy rubbed his wrists.

"Sorry for the butt stroke and bouncing you off the door." Josh climbed back in the truck and pulled into traffic.

"No worries. I'm just glad you didn't have the dog bite me. Can I use a cell phone?" Jeremy reached over the console.

Elena pulled her phone out of her pocket and handed it to Jeremy, who punched in a number.

"Fred, it's me, Jeremy. I borrowed the phone. We've got to meet. I think we finally got them."

Bri heard the knock on the door. She got off the floor and sat on the mattress. "I'm on the bed."

A male attendant cracked the door and peered in. He stepped back, and one of the female stewards walked in, carrying fresh linens, towels, and a dark-blue garment. *I guess the white hospital scrubs are getting replaced.* The male attendant stood at the door and watched her as the female left the room.

"Be dressed and ready to go at zero six hundred. Do you understand?" The male attendant opened the door wider.

"Yes, I understand. Do you know where I'm going?" The door shut. "I guess not."

She got off the bed, went over to the pile of towels and linens, and picked up the dark-blue garment. It was a pair of coveralls. There was a patch on the left breast pocket with *Garcia Asombrosa* in white stitching. *Amazing Grace, what is this?*

Lieutenant Governor Rachel Avery Collier from the great state of Florida picked up the phone and dialed a number from memory. The president of the United States picked up on the first ring.

"You're on my list of people to call today. Your ears must have been burning."

"The checks in the mail. How are you doing, Brian?" Rachel pulled the front of her navy-blue pinstripe suit to smooth a wrinkle.

"I'm doing fine, Rachel. I hear you're making waves around the UCF investigation."

"Not too much; I'm trying to keep everything in-house so we can control the message. Apparently, two of your agents did an end run. I got an incredibly angry call from Governor Call. That wasn't you, was it, Brian?"

"No, Rachel, that wasn't me, but you need to steer clear of those agents. They're not your average pencil pushers, and they're very dangerous."

"Is that a threat, Brian? I can send those sixteen thousand individual donors to someone else." Rachel could feel her temper starting to rise. *Elected politicians have a way of forgetting who got them elected.*

"Not a threat, Rachel. Just a fact."

"So, there is nothing you can do about them?"

"I'm afraid not; in fact, I shouldn't be talking about them. I have to go, Rachel. Give my best to your sister. I'll tell my guys to look for your donation." The line went dead.

She looked at the receiver. He hung up on me. *What on earth would spook the president of the United States? So, if he didn't call Governor Call, who did?*

She put the receiver back in the cradle, picked up a bottle of Tom Ford Lavender Extreme, put a couple of drops on her right index finger, and dabbed behind both ears and her wrists. The sweet smell of lavender always calmed her.

CHAPTER

42

They arranged to meet at the local FBI office in Melbourne, Florida. Josh pulled the truck into the lot and parked in front so Agent Gonzales would know they arrived. The FBI office was in a nondescript office building off Wickham Road. They walked into a lobby with gold and black marble tile and various tropical plants scattered in large planters.

Syrin walked over and sniffed a plant near the elevator. "Syrin, no. You can't water these plants." Josh walked over and grabbed her snout. He pressed the up button for the lift.

In the elevator, Jeremy pressed five. The elevator lifted with a jerk, and the door opened on the fifth floor.

"It's over here on the left." Jeremy pointed to a dark maroon door with a doorbell and speaker to the left and a black-tinted camera dome overhead. There were no markings on the door. Jeremy pressed the button.

"Can I help you, please?"

Jeremy looked at the speaker. "Agents Jeremy Guzman, Josh Martin, and Marshal Elena Diaz. My SAC, Fred Gonzales, should have called ahead." The door buzzed. Jeremy pulled it open, and they walked to a small vestibule with a reception window protected by thick bulletproof glass and a two-inch slot between the counter and the glass edge. There was a reinforced government green door to the right of the window.

A thick middle-aged woman in a black dress with a silver pendant of a crab around her neck looked out from the glass. "Credentials, please?"

Josh and Elena slid their credentials through the slot in the window.

"I don't have an ID with me," Jeremy said. "I work for the DEA."

"We can vouch for him," Josh said. "He still owes my dog an ice cream."

The green door buzzed, and Josh pulled it open. He followed everyone into the office, where they retrieved their credentials.

"Welcome. My name's Bonnie. You're going to be in here." Bonnie pointed to a conference room. "What's the beautiful dog's name?"

"Her name's Syrin." Josh patted her head.

"Can I pat her? I have two dogs of my own." Bonnie reached out to touch Syrin's head.

Syrin stepped back to stay out of reach and walked behind Josh.

"Sorry about that; sometimes she's not in the mood for social interaction. Where is everyone?" Josh gestured around the office.

"There's an active shooter exercise at the port. I'm holding down the fort. Let me know if you need anything." Bonnie strolled back to her desk in the bullpen.

"Thanks, Bonnie." Josh walked into the conference room, which was typical of such rooms in hundreds of FBI offices across the country. A large cherry-finish table had six high-back black leather chairs on each side and a leather captain's chair at each end. A large monitor dominated the far wall, and a ring of chairs lined walls for backbench personnel. They each took a seat, and Syrin found a spot in the corner.

Bonnie returned to her desk and looked back through the door to the room with her visitors. No one was visible. She took out her phone, punched in a number, and waited.

"Yes?"

"They're here," Bonnie whispered into the phone.

"How many?"

"Three, plus the dog, like you said. They're waiting for a third agent."

"Thank you."

"One more thing. Your third guy with the beard and the long black hair is not under arrest. He's an agent with the DEA."

"Fuck me." Sari clicked off the call.

CHAPTER 43

Sari looked at Michael in disbelief. They were standing outside the elevator in the church complex.

"What is it?" Michael pushed the up button.

"Zeus's prospect is an undercover DEA agent." Sari walked into the elevator and leaned on the wall.

"Shit, are you sure?" Michael pressed the five.

"Yeah, one hundred percent. That was our contact at the FBI."

Sari's phone buzzed for a text message. She looked at the text. *Your DNA results are available.* She clicked open. *Subject – Bri Castillo 99.9% confidence. Sister – Deborah Castillo 99.9% confidence. Mother – Donna Alonzo 99.9% confidence. Father – Hector Alonzo 99.9% confidence.*

"Well, we know the name of our lioness." She showed her phone screen to Michael.

"Who's Bri Castillo?" Michael walked out when the door opened.

"No idea. Maybe the boss knows." Sari headed to Bishop Avery's office with Michael trailing in her wake. Eleanor was not at her desk, but there was a plate of chocolate chip cookies on the corner. They each grabbed one and walked into Bishop Avery's outer reception area.

Bishop Avery was seated at the end of the reception area table with papers spread out in front of her. She looked up when the girls walked in.

"Ladies, welcome. Are you the bearers of good news? Can I get you a glass of wine?" Bishop Avery held up a glass of red wine.

"We'll take some coffee." Sari held up her cookie.

"Jean-Paul. Two coffees, please," Bishop Avery said.

"Yes, Bishop." The voice came from the ceiling.

Sari and Michael took seats on either side of Bishop Avery. Jean-Paul walked in with two steaming mugs of coffee, a plate of chocolate chip cookies, and some napkins. He put coasters with prints of Cape Canaveral Lighthouse in front of Sari and Michael and set the mugs on them. He put the plate of cookies in the center of the table along with the napkins.

"Anything else, Bishop?" Jean-Paul peered over his glasses in his freshly pressed chef's uniform.

"No, Jean-Paul, thank you." Bishop Avery picked up a cookie from the plate. "Should go well with wine." Jean-Paul shuffled back to the kitchen. "So, what's the news?"

"We just got back from Strikers. They can take delivery. They may have to warehouse some since it's a large load," Sari said.

"That's good news." Bishop Avery took a bite of a cookie.

"Yes, but we got played. While we were having lunch, half the local police department raided the place along with the two feds and the dog." Sari felt the edge of the mug. Still too hot.

"You're kidding me." Bishop Avery stared in disbelief.

"Nope. They said someone called in an active shooter. So, the two feds got pictures of us, and the morons still had the white van in the garage, so they got the license plate." Sari took a sip of coffee. It burned the roof of her mouth. "The feds also picked up one of Zeus's prospects. It turns out the new guy is an undercover DEA agent."

Bishop Avery slumped back in her chair and rubbed her hand over her face. "How did you find that out?"

"Our contact at the FBI field office called it in. We asked her to let us know when two agents and a dog showed up with a suspect. She just called and said the suspect was not in handcuffs, and he identified himself as a DEA agent." Sari took a bite of chocolate chip cookie and burned her mouth again on the coffee.

"They've got to go." Bishop Avery pushed her piles of paper together.

"Already one step ahead of you. I called Zeus. He'll take care of it. We got the DNA analysis back on the lioness." Sari pushed her phone over to Bishop Avery. "Does the name Bri Castillo mean anything?"

"No. Never heard of her." Bishop Avery picked up the phone. She scrolled through the names. *Deborah Castillo, Donna Alonzo, Hector Alonzo*. "Holy Mother of Christ, we snatched the daughter of a U.S. senator. This day keeps getting better and better. We need to clean things up, and right now. Those feds are not going to stop, and we need to remove any trace of the daughter."

"Roger. I'll call the Dibble brothers. We'll take her over in the morning." Sari took another bite of cookie and nodded at Michael. "Do you want us to remove our other connection?"

"Yes, clean everything up. We need to lay low for a couple of months." Bishop Avery stood up. "I need to go practice my sermon."

CHAPTER

44

Josh swiveled in his chair. "So, tell me about the Lightning Strikes Motorcycle Club."

"We started the investigation about two months ago." Jeremy looked from Josh to Elena. DEA intelligence reported that Lightning Strikes was a distributor for a major cocaine importer. We placed agents in clubs around the country both in the fun centers and the clubhouses."

"Wait a minute." Elena leaned forward. "You mean there are other fun centers with motorcycle clubs in the back?"

Jeremy answered, "Yes, every single one. Like you, we can't find any information on the ultimate owner or owners. A different entity owns every center. There are one hundred eighty-three centers and clubs across the country, covering all fifty states."

"Damn, that's one impressive distribution network with a great cover. Mom, Dad, and the kids go bowling in the front, and cocaine goes rolling out the back," Josh said.

Josh turned to find Syrin. She was in the corner directly across from the doorway, sleeping. She picked her head up at the sound of the front door buzzer.

A Hispanic male filled the doorway. He looked forty-ish with dark black hair pulled in a ponytail, a full black mustache, jeans, a Miami Dolphins

T-shirt, and Doc Martin boots. Syrin growled, got to her feet, and walked between the door and Josh.

"Don't bite me. I'm a good guy—Fred Gonzales." Agent Gonzales walked into the room.

"Syrin, release." Josh stood up. Syrin walked over and sniffed the new guy, and wagged her tail.

"You're a beautiful dog." Agent Gonzales scratched her behind the ears.

"She has her moments." Josh walked over and shook his hand. "Josh Martin and this is my partner, Elena Diaz. I'm with the FBI, and Elena's with the Marshal Service."

Elena stood up and shook his hand. "Nice to meet you."

Agent Gonzales took a seat next to Jeremy. "What did I miss?"

"I was just filling them in on the M-C and the fun centers," Jeremy said.

"Pretty good distribution network. How did the FBI and Marshal Service get involved?" Agent Gonzales looked at Josh.

"We didn't know anything about the drug connection. We're looking into an apparent kidnapping. One of the subjects in our investigation called the fun center when we applied a little pressure. Now he's dead, along with twenty-one of his classmates. Someone mistakenly called in an active shooter at the center. We were in the area, so we joined the party."

Agent Gonzales laughed. "Just happened to be in the area."

"In another life, I was in the Coast Guard—*Semper Paratus*, always ready." Josh turned toward Jeremy. "What can you tell me about the white van parked in the garage, the big surfer-looking dude, and the two females at his table? They looked a little high-end for a biker spot unless they were slumming."

"The big surfer dude is Adrian Stanhope. His club name is Zeus. He's the club president. He came from a middle-class family in North Carolina, went to Eastern Florida State College, no priors, clean record. He got a degree in business. In fact, most of the guys in the club are not stereotypical bikers. They're all educated with no prior involvement with law enforcement except a couple of parking tickets; they just look the part. Long hair, biker clothes, tattoos."

"So, straight out of central casting," Elena said.

"Exactly. They haven't been arrested for any felonies yet. They camouflage themselves to look like criminals and their clubhouses to look like family establishments.

"What about the white van?" Josh took his cell phone out of his pocket and set it on the table while furrowing his brow at Jeremy.

"Nothing special. It's the club van. They use it for part runs, and it follows the pack with luggage and supplies for group rides."

Elena looked at Jeremy. "What about the two females?"

"Sari and Michael—they're half of the 'God Squad.' I don't know their last names, but the other two are Gabi and Rafi. All four came to the club yesterday. Three of them sat at the bar, and Sari talked to Zeus alone."

"Why do you call them the God Squad?" Josh tapped on his phone, nervously.

"They're members of the Church of Illuminology."

Josh stopped tapping. "You're shitting me."

"No. They're regulars. Sometimes they ride Harleys over, and sometimes they take the BMW."

Josh said, "The fraternity where the members were all killed, Delta Faros, was affiliated with the Church of Illuminology. I don't know about you, but I don't believe in coincidence."

Josh's phone buzzed on the table. He looked at the caller ID. *Text from Becka.* He tapped the notification. A picture of a woman appeared on the screen over the name *Aria Rafael.* He swiped to the next image. It was the brunette at the club, *Maya Sarno.* In the following picture, he didn't recognize *Mila Gabel.* The next photo was the blonde, *Romi Michelson.* He passed the phone to Jeremy. "Do you recognize anyone?"

Jeremy took the phone and swiped through the pictures. "These are photos of the God Squad. What's their story?"

Jeremy handed the phone back to Josh, who opened the attachment.

CHAPTER

45

Captain Moreno lounged in his bridge chair on the starboard side of the pilothouse. A fresh breeze with the smell of salt air drifted through the open bridge wing door. The sound of the propeller churning through water and the rock of the ship eased his tension on the pending delivery. *This never gets old.* First Mate Lope Calma dismounted from the main deck ladder and broke his reverie.

"Permission to enter the bridge?"

"Granted." Captain Moreno turned to his first mate.

"Good afternoon, Captain. We're all set for tomorrow. Pilot pick-up is at zero five hundred, and we should be at Berth two-eleven by zero nine hundred. We should start container offload around eleven hundred, depending on Customs."

"Thank you, Lope. Sounds good. Is everything set for our special off-load and onload?" Captain Moreno stood from his chair and walked to the starboard bridge wing, followed by Lope.

"Yes, Captain. I just got the confirmation before I came up here. Everything is ready to transport the two containers tomorrow. We'll offload them around containers two hundred to two-ten. The other cargo will load the next day along with our load of outbound containers. Lope leaned on the bridge wing railing and gazed at the trailing wake from the ship.

"All we can do now is pray." Captain Moreno walked back to his chair.

Josh read the attachment. "I knew they looked different. You can never hide military."

"Well, ours or somebody else's?" Elena looked at Josh.

"Israeli. They operated as a Mossad direct action team until about five years ago when they disappeared on an operation in Syria. They were listed as killed in action. It also explains the .22 caliber used to eliminate Dillion and Kling."

"What do you mean by that?" Elena asked.

When the Mossad took out the Black September terrorists who'd massacred the '72 Israeli Olympic team, their weapon of choice was the Beretta Model 70 or 71 in .22LR. However, their execution method was to empty the magazine at close range and not put three rounds through the eye. Spielberg made a movie out of it in 2005—*Munich*." Josh laid his phone down. "So, we have a professional hit team working for a church. How does that make sense?"

Elena crossed her arms. "Jeremy, what made you call a code blue?"

"I've been undercover for about three months. We knew a shipment was coming in, but we didn't know when. The chicks from the church said the ship was arriving tomorrow. They called it the Holy Ship. I had no way for immediate communication, so you guys provided the best opportunity." Jeremy looked at Fred.

"The Holy Ship? What the hell is that?" Fred looked around the room.

Jeremy replied, "No idea, but it's going to offload a bunch of dope in Port Tampa Bay tomorrow. The club is doing a beach bash rodeo tomorrow at Clearwater Beach. Chapters from all over the country are riding in. That can't be a coincidence."

“No, that sounds like a distribution party, and you guys have your work cut out for you. I wish we could help, but time is running out on finding our girl, and I think it involves the church somehow. If we hear anything about drugs, we’ll let you know, and if you hear anything about a girl, please let us know.” Josh tossed his business card across the table.

“You got it, Josh.” Fred passed his card over. “Don’t put any SWAT calls on me.”

“I don’t know what you’re talking about.” Josh stood up to leave. “Syrin, are you ready to go to church?” Syrin answered with a bark.

CHAPTER 46

Zeus turned the white van into the parking lot for the Taste of India restaurant and pulled into a space with an unobstructed view of the commercial building entrance next door. "Guys, there's the red truck parked in front of the building, so they're still there. When you're done, a van from A1 Electric Company will pick you up at the rear exit. Are you clear on the target package?"

"Yes, we're clear. Do you also want us to eliminate the dog?"

"Yes, the mutt's part of the package. I'll wire one hundred thousand to your account after successful job completion."

"Cool." Four members of the Aryan Brotherhood of Florida exited the van wearing sport coats and open-collared shirts and carrying black backpacks. The group walked over to the building and entered the lobby.

The shooter watched the Ford Explorer exit the UCF Police parking lot and turn from Libra to North Gemini Boulevard. The shooter drove a white Ford Flex rental, one of about thirty thousand white rental cars in the Orlando area. The Flex pulled behind the Explorer about five cars back. The driver felt no need to maintain a close tail. The destination wasn't a mystery.

Jeremy walked out of the conference room. "Excuse me. Is there a men's room close by?"

"Down that hallway past the elevators; you'll see the sign." Bonnie pointed.

"Thank you." Jeremy headed out of the room, followed by Fred, Josh, and Elena.

"I think I'm also going to use the ladies' room." Elena looked at Bonnie.

"Right next to the men's room. You all have a great day." Bonnie gave them a wave as they filed out of the office.

Fred, Josh, and Syrin walked over to the elevator lobby to wait on Jeremy and Elena, who headed past it to the restrooms.

"Pretty dog." Fred kneeled to scratch Syrin's head. "What is she?"

"She's a Belgian Malinois. We used them in the teams. I decided to get one for myself."

Fred stood up. "You were a SEAL?"

"Seems like many years ago. I went to the Coast Guard Academy and then applied for SEAL training when Admiral Allen made coasties eligible."

"How'd you get into the FBI?"

"That's a long story for a different day." Josh watched Jeremy walk up. "Did you find the right door? Elena would kick your ass if you went in the wrong door."

"I heard that." Elena walked up behind Jeremy. "And, yes, I would kick your ass."

Josh walked over and punched the elevator's down button. The doors chimed and opened. The boys let Elena and Syrin get on first. Josh filed in next and stood next to Syrin in the back. Fred and Jeremy stepped in directly in front of the doors. The doors closed, and the elevator started to descend.

The white Explorer turned into the parking garage for The Yard at Gibraltar Apartment complex.

The shooter pressed the comms button on an eight-hundred-megahertz encrypted radio. "Are the cameras down?"

"Roger. The cameras are down," came the response from Rafi in the earpiece.

"Thank you." The shooter turned into the complex and headed to the fifth floor of the parking garage, then turned up the incline to the fifth deck and watched the Explorer pull into a spot marked 524. The Flex stopped just at the top of the slope, and the shooter did a quick scan of the parking area. All quiet. The driver's door on the Explorer opened and paused. The shooter pulled the Flex up to the opening between the Explorer and a red Nissan with the passenger door facing the target.

The shooter pulled the latch on the door, kicked it open, turned in the seat, and stood up, keeping the Beretta 70 with a six-inch silencer obscured behind the car. "Excuse me. I'm lost." The shooter walked around the front of the Flex.

An older woman with black hair pushed the Explorer door closed and turned at the opening door's sounds and the voice. "What are you looking for?"

The shooter closed the gap to about three feet, raised the Beretta, and squeezed the trigger three times in rapid succession. The Beretta cycled three times with practically no sound, just the pistol jacking rounds and the shells bouncing on the cement floor. Three CCI Stinger copper-plated, hollow-point 32-grain bullets exited the muzzle at 1640 feet per second and exploded through the target's left eye, then fragmented after striking the back of her skull. The target's head jerked back three times with the impact of each bullet, and she slumped to the garage floor with her head banging on the cement. She didn't feel a thing. She died when the first bullet bounced off the back of her head.

The shooter bent down and picked up the three casings before checking the target. She was not breathing, her right eye was locked open, and a trickle of blood was draining from her head, filling in a crack in the cement. *Considerably easier than popping those two clowns through cell doors.* The shooter did a quick 360-degree scan of the garage—no sound or sight of anything—then slipped back into the Flex and pulled the door closed. The Flex headed for the exit.

CHAPTER

47

The elevator jerked to a stop on the bottom floor, and the doors opened. Fred and Jeremy stepped off and turned right, followed by Elena. Syrin followed Elena off the elevator, stopped, looked left, and took off with a snarl.

"Syrin." Josh lunged after her and missed. He turned to see two white males pulling HK MP5s with thirty-round magazines and assault grips from black backpacks. Syrin hit the target on the right square in the chest and bit down on his right arm before he could get the MP5 clear of the bag.

"Gun." Josh drew his Glock 22, Gen 4, pointed it at the white shirt button of the other male and squeezed off two shots. The gun smacked his hand twice. Two 180-grain Hydra-Shok bullets sped to their target at a thousand feet per second. He looked at the bridge of the target's nose and squeezed off another round. The first two rounds each clipped a piece of button before slamming into the target's chest, obliterating his heart. The third round hammered through the bridge of his nose and jellied his brain before it could register that the heart ceased to exist. The subject dropped to the ground, and the MP5 skidded across the tile floor.

Josh moved the gun right. The second gunman was jerking around with seventy pounds of angry Malinois gripped on his arm, shaking for all she was worth. He couldn't risk a chest shot with Syrin swinging in and out of the target area. The male's head turned to scream at Syrin. Josh looked at the target's left temple and squeezed the trigger. After another smack from the gun, the Hydra-Shok found its mark, blowing through the flopping male's head from his left temple and exiting out the right in a spray of blood and bone. The grisly mix covered lobby plants and floor tiles. Syrin gave the corpse a final shake before it dropped to the floor.

The entire sequence took about five seconds. Two MP5s opened up to his right with a deafening roar that echoed through the confined lobby, jarring his focus. Josh dove behind a large planter in front of the elevator doors. He looked across at Elena, who had tucked herself behind another planter by the opposite set of doors. There were no planters for Jeremy and Fred. They each took a full auto burst from an MP5, which drove them jerking back past Josh and Elena. Dozens of bullets impacted the planters, the walls, and the glass doors at the far entrance, which shattered in every direction.

Unlike in the movies, real-life automatic weapons run out of ammo quickly on full auto. An MP5's rate of fire is eight hundred rounds per minute or thirteen bullets per second. Both shooters went Winchester in five seconds.

When the bolts clicked to the rear, Josh stood up and sighted at the target on the right, who was trying to eject his magazine and pull another one out of his backpack. Josh looked at the bridge of the nose and squeezed the trigger. No need for two to the chest since the MP5, bag, and magazine obscured the target. The target's head snapped back, and he dropped to the floor, scattering his gun, clip, and pack. Josh moved left to target two, who was already jerking from the impact of six rounds of center mass from Elena. He dropped next to his partner.

Josh looked at Elena. "Are you okay?"

"Yes, I'm going to check the front for a driver." She sprinted to the lobby entrance and pushed through the doors.

Josh checked both Fred and Jeremy. They were gone. He pulled his phone from his pocket and headed through the shattered doors of the other entrance with Syrin on his six. He stepped through the doors and did a quick check of the parking lot. An electrical contractor van pulled away from a curb and headed to the exit. Nothing else was visible. Josh holstered his Glock and called 911.

"Nine-one-one operator. What is your location?"

"FBI field office, Melbourne. This is Special Agent Josh Martin, FBI. Shots fired at this location. Officers down. Send all available units, including an ambulance. Plainclothes agents on the scene."

"Roger. Rolling now."

Josh clicked off the call and pressed the contact number for Becka. "Good afternoon, Josh; what can I do for you?"

"Elena and I just got ambushed at the FBI field office building in Melbourne, Florida. We have two agents down and four suspects. We need a cleanup crew and some interference. The investigation is moving fast, and we can't get sidelined in paperwork and shooting investigations. The two agents down are DEA. Send their investigation team. Also, move our air asset from the fraternity to the Church of Illuminology complex."

"Roger. Copy all. Call Director Santiago when you get a chance." She ended the call.

Josh put his phone back in his pocket and looked down at Syrin, who was staring up at him. He squatted down to her level and gave her a big hug. She licked his face. "Great job, baby girl. We wouldn't be here without you. I think Elena owes you some ice cream. What do you say we go ask her when she's paying up?" Syrin barked yes.

CHAPTER 48

Detective Sergeant Friday stopped his Explorer at the parking garage entrance and powered down his window as an Orange County deputy approached. He showed the man his credentials and said, "I got a call to come to a homicide at this address."

The deputy checked his list. "Yup, you're good. Park on the fourth level and walk up to the fifth." He stepped back and waved him through.

Joe turned up the ramp, wound his way through the garage to the fourth level, and pulled into a slot marked for Westphal Associates. *I don't think they'll need their space for a while.* He put the Explorer in park, killed the engine, and swung the door open, careful not to ding the silver Mercedes next to him. He walked to the up ramp and started climbing. At the top, he ducked under a yellow crime scene tape and walked over to a gaggle of first responders clustered around a white Explorer and a red Nissan.

One of the men, who wore a gray suit, white shirt, and maroon tie, stepped away from the group and walked over to Joe. "Hey, Joe. Thanks for coming." Detective Jerry Shealy had served as a Marine and kept his brown hair short—not quite a jarhead cut, but close.

They shook hands. "No problem, Jerry. What've ya got?"

"Unfortunately, Joe, we've got one of yours." Jerry handed Joe a UCF Police identification badge with the smiling face of Margaret Thorne, Assistant Director of Information and Technology.

Joe looked at the picture. "What happened?"

"That's why we called you over. We've got a mystery." Jerry walked over to the space between the Explorer and the red Nissan. Crime scene techs were snapping pictures.

Joe peered between the cars. Margaret's corpse lay sprawled on the pavement with a trail of dried blood from her head to a low spot under the vehicle. "Let me guess. Shot through the eye multiple times with no brass or forensic evidence."

One of the techs looked up. "How did you know that?"

"We had two with an identical MO in our jail cell the other night." Joe turned away from the scene.

"So, what do you think?" Jerry followed Joe.

They walked about ten yards and stopped. "This stays between us."

Jerry nodded his head.

Joe pointed toward the corpse. "We have a mole in our police department, and I think she's the one lying on the pavement. Somebody's cleaning house to distance themselves from our murders and the twenty-two at the frat house. These are professional hits. Do you guys have anything?"

Jerry shook his head no. "It's like you said. No brass or physical evidence." One of the tenants walking to the elevator found the body and called nine-one-one. Unis are canvassing the area, but so far, nothing."

"Any video?" Joe ran his hand through his hair.

"No. The system went down about noon." Jerry looked back at the swarm of cops.

“There’s a lot of that going around.” Joe pulled a card from his pocket and handed it to Jerry. “Text me your number, and I’ll keep you informed. Please let me know what you find out about Margaret. I need to know how she got turned.”

They shook hands, and Joe started the trek back to his car. He pulled out his phone to call the chief. Jerry’s contact information flashed on his screen.

CHAPTER

49

Josh walked back to the crime scene with Syrin on his hip. He tried to avoid the broken glass—n*o need for the hero to cut her paws.* The siren of every emergency vehicle in the county wailed in the distance, getting closer. Josh walked through the door. Elena was draping the bodies of Jeremy and Fred with green floral curtains she'd pulled from entrance windows.

Josh nodded at her. "Anything?"

"No." Elena walked over and hugged Syrin. "Good girl. You know, if it weren't for both of your quick responses, we'd be lying next to Fred and Jeremy. You dropped three guys in less than ten seconds with headshots, and you could cover your two to the chest with a quarter. Now I know why Vince paired us; I find people, and you put them away."

"Something like that. We still got one more." Josh watched a fleet of approaching Brevard County Sheriff vehicles through the lobby doors and curtainless windows. Four deputies sprinted to the entrance with guns drawn. Josh pulled his badge from his pocket and held it over his head. "FBI. Shooters are down."

"Keep your hands where we can see them." One of the deputies, Sergeant Compagnoni, approached Josh and took his credential. "It's him. We're clear."

The deputies holstered their guns and looked around. “Holy shit. What the hell happened?” Sergeant Compagnoni had the heft of a weightlifter with a bald head and piercing blue eyes.

“Long story. We still need to take one more. Can I get a couple of deputies to come with us?” Josh motioned at Elena.

“Sure. Where are we going?” Sergeant Compagnoni gestured for another deputy. “Jim.”

Josh pressed the button for the elevator. “Fifth floor.”

Sari pushed the last rep of three sets of ten squats with 225 pounds. She stepped forward to set the bar in the squat rack clips and eased the weight down. She grabbed a towel from the rack and wiped the sweat off her forehead, and looked at her watch. Michael should have been back. Her phone started playing “Something Bad” by Miranda Lambert and Carrie Underwood while Zeus’s number flashed on the screen. She swiped to answer.

“Tell me some good news.” Sari leaned on the squat rack. Her legs were burning.

“Not sure who we hit, but all four of our shooters are down. I know we missed the two feds with the dog. One ran out the front and one out the back after the shooting, looking for getaway vehicles.”

“Shit. What about the DEA agents?” Sari grabbed her towel and started heading to the locker room.

“I think they’re down. A nine-one-one call reported officers down. Shots fired. Our on-scene contact reports six bodies in the lobby. Someone draped two bodies with a green covering. I’m assuming those two are DEA.”

“Okay. On the plus side, the shipment is still in play with the two narcs down. Enjoy your time at the beach. Call me when you have the product.”

"Will do." Zeus clicked off.

Sari scrolled through her contacts and stopped at Bonnie. She hit the call button. *I wonder how much she knows. Probably should call Michael.*

Bonnie picked up on the second ring. "Yes?"

"They're coming for you." Sari ended the call.

The blood drained from Bonnie's face, and she dropped her phone onto the floor.

Sari then called Michael, who picked up on the first ring.

"Yes, madam, what can I do for you?"

"The Nazis missed. Time for plan B." Sari pushed through the locker room door.

"Roger. Rafi has everything set up. I'll head over there now."

Josh, Elena, Sergeant Compagnoni, and Deputy Jim Reynolds walked into the elevator. Josh hit the button for the fifth floor. The elevator jerked and started to rise. "We're looking for the FBI's receptionist. We think she tipped off the shooters in the lobby. She's the only one in the office. The rest of the staff is at an active shooter drill at Port Canaveral."

"How do you want to do this?" Sergeant Compagnoni looked at Josh.

Josh hit the stop button on the elevator, and it bounced to a halt. "There are two doors into the office: an outer door from the hallway into a small reception area and another door from the reception area into the office. The hallway, reception area, and office are under video surveillance, which is why we need you guys. She knows us, so she's not going to open the door. But she may for you. She doesn't know we survived. Tell her you're checking on one of the agents killed in the lobby shootout. Show her my credentials." Josh passed his credentials to Sergeant Compagnoni.

"Okay, then what?" Sergeant Compagnoni put Josh's credentials inside his gun belt.

"When you get through the first door, hold it open while you wait to get in the second. When you get access to the second door, keep it open, and we'll come in to negotiate with her. Got it?"

Josh hit the start button, and the elevator started to rise.

Sergeant Compagnoni looked at Deputy Reynolds, who nodded his head yes. "Okay, we're good."

The elevator dinged for the fifth floor, and the doors opened. Josh hit the elevator stop button again. Sergeant Compagnoni and Deputy Reynolds stepped off the elevator.

"Turn left, straight ahead. Press the doorbell," Josh said. Both Josh and Elena drew their sidearms. "Syrin, guard."

Sergeant Compagnoni walked up to the door and pressed the doorbell. "Brevard County Sheriff's Office. We need to talk to someone about a Special Agent Josh Martin." He pulled Josh's credential from his belt and held the picture up to the camera.

The door buzzed. "Come on in."

Sergeant Compagnoni pulled the door open and stepped into the reception area. Deputy Reynolds held the door open. The second door buzzed.

"I'm in the back. There's no one else in the office. Come on in."

Sergeant Compagnoni pulled the door open and stepped into the office. Two 9mm rounds slammed into his chest, and the sound of gunfire roared in the confined space.

CHAPTER 50

Bri looked in the bathroom mirror and adjusted her hair. She picked up a bobby pin, put it in her mouth, and pulled it out, biting down at the same time. The small rubber tip came off the end. She spit it into the sink and ran some water to make sure it went down the drain. She slipped the bobby pin in her hair over her right ear and checked herself in the mirror. It was not apparent at a glance. She shook her head, and the pin remained in place.

She walked out of the bathroom, sat cross-legged in the middle of the floor, and slowed her breathing. She filled her thoughts with the sound of waves crashing on the beach and running up the sand to cover her feet. She knew it was her last night in this place. One way or another, the next day would be her last in captivity. *I hope the bitch is not part of the transfer.*

At the sound of the gunfire, Josh, Elena, and Syrin sprinted for the door. They caught it just as Deputy Reynolds let it go to help his partner. Josh hurried through with his gun in his hand. Sergeant Compagnoni had his butt on the floor, his back to the wall, and one foot holding the door slightly open, which provided cover from the gunfire. Five more rounds boomed off in the confined office space and smacked the reinforced bulletproof door in rapid succession like a sledgehammer pounding on a metal roof.

"Get me the fuck outta here." Sergeant Compagnoni tried to inch into the reception office.

"Hold the door." Josh reached to grab Sergeant Compagnoni, and Elena pushed on the door. Josh caught the Sergeant around the ankles and heaved him into the reception area. His bulletproof vest had stopped both rounds, which lay flattened in the outer fabric.

"Deputy? Go get medical help; we'll take care of this." Deputy Reynolds sprinted out of the office. Josh looked at Sergeant Compagnoni. "Are you okay?"

"Hurts to breathe, but I'll live. Next time, you go through the door."

"Roger that. Syrin, ready? Bite."

Syrin flew through the door, followed closely by Josh. Bonnie pointed a Beretta 92FS 9mm at the door. She moved her gun down to shoot the rushing dog. Josh raised his Glock, looked at the buttons on her blouse, and squeezed off two shots. He looked at her nose and fired another round. The first two rounds impacted her chest at almost the same time, and the third round hit right between the eyes. The impact drove her back, and she flailed to the carpet. Syrin skidded to a halt.

Elena came around the corner and saw Bonnie sprawled like a broken doll. She stopped near Josh. "Black and White Club rules?"

Josh nodded, yes. "Black and White Club rules."

CHAPTER

51

Michael walked through the front entrance of the Tropical Suites Hotel, stopped at the concierge desk, and looked at the on-duty concierge's name tag: Manny. "Good afternoon, Manny. I'm looking for the employment office. I need to pick up some uniforms. I'm supposed to start work tomorrow." Michael flashed her *you-might-get-laid* smile.

Manny's eyes got wide. "Awesome. Welcome aboard. Let me take you over there." Manny headed to a door to the left of the reception desk and walked through, followed by Michael. He stopped just inside.

"It's the second door down on the left. Ask for Lisa. If you need anything else, just let me know."

"Thanks, Manny. I'll see you around." Michael started walking down the hallway.

Manny watched her walk away. *I need to put that beautiful piece of ass on the hit list.* He shut the door and walked back to his desk.

Michael smiled as she strolled away. She knew what Manny was thinking and what all men were thinking. If he wasn't careful, he'd be on the hit list. She found the second door on the left: *Human Relations*. She knocked and stepped in. "I'm looking for Lisa. I'm supposed to pick up some uniforms."

An older woman looked up from her desk. She was forty-something with brown hair going gray that was pulled back in a ponytail and glasses perched on the tip of her nose. "What's your name?"

"Samantha Stewart. I'm supposed to pick up some uniforms."

Lisa punched Samantha Stewart into her computer. "Housekeeping. You start tomorrow. Is that correct?"

"Yes." Michael scanned for exits and weapons. Some habits were hard to break.

Lisa stood up from her desk and walked into a back room. She came back with five purple floral print Hawaiian shirts and two name tags, one with *Samantha* etched into the gold plastic. "Here you go." She handed the bundle to Michael. "You need to wear tan shorts—nothing too revealing—and white sneakers. Report to the head housekeeper tomorrow at fifteen hundred. You have the night shift tomorrow from three to eleven. You can pick up your key card at the front desk."

"Okay, thank you." Michael backed out of the office and headed to her car with the shirts slung over her back and the name tags stuffed into her pocket. She cruised past the reception desk and the vacant concierge stand. *Manny must be out bothering some other woman. I might do the women of the world a service if I see Manny on the job.* She walked outside and put her shirts in the trunk of a red Toyota Corolla. She couldn't remember the last time she drove an economy car. She climbed in, started the engine, and headed to the exit. She hit the phone button on the steering wheel. "Call Sari."

"Calling Sari" came over the car's sound system.

The phone rang three times. "How was your job interview?"

"Peachy. I got five ugly shirts, and I start tomorrow at fifteen hundred."

CHAPTER 52

Josh, Elena, and Syrin walked out of the office just as two EMTs and a bunch of Brevard County deputies rushed in. The two EMTs headed over to Sergeant Compagnoni, who was still bitching about his chest. The deputies headed over to Josh and Elena.

Josh pointed at the interior office. "The shooter is down inside the office. We'll give statements to the shooting team."

"Are you Agent Martin?" Deputy Clark looked between Josh and Elena.

"Yes, and this is Marshal Diaz." Josh nodded his head at Elena.

"There's a bunch of suits in the lobby looking for you. You guys had a busy day. You may want to go out the back." Deputy Clark chuckled.

"Yeah, thanks for that. You guys got this?" Josh patted Syrin's head.

"Yeah, we're good. We'll tape off the scene until the suits make their way up here. You guys have a good day. Five fewer scumbags in the world. By the way, who's the combat shooter?"

Elena pointed at Josh. "Dropped three guys in ten seconds."

"If I see you in the town, I'll buy you a beer." Deputy Clark shook their hands and went into the office. "Holy shit. Another double-tap."

Josh, Elena, and Syrin rode the elevator down to the first floor. The doors opened onto a beehive of activity. They moved along the outer edge of the cluster fuck among DEA, FBI, and the Brevard County Sheriff's Office and walked out of the entrance.

One of the suits broke away from a gaggle near a black SUV and headed their way. "Agent Martin, Marshal Diaz—my name's Trevor Knight. I'm with the FBI director's Special Projects Branch. Director Santiago sent me." Both Josh and Elena felt two zaps on their wrists. They all shook hands. "Anything I need to know about this?"

"We had a meeting with Agent Gonzales and Agent Guzman in the FBI field office. The only other person present was the office admin assistant—Bonnie…something. After the meeting, when we stepped out of the elevator, four Adam Henrys pulled out MP5s and let loose on us with a full clip of spraying and praying. The two DEA agents were leading the pack and took the initial bursts. Luckily, Syrin spotted the two in the rear before they could clear their MP5s from their backpacks. She latched on to the prick on the right. I dropped the one on the left. Then I took care of the one who was dancing with my four-footed partner." Josh patted Syrin on the head. "We both hit the deck behind some planters." Josh gestured at Elena, then the fragments of pottery and dirt. "The two in the front buzzed through their ammo in about ten seconds. We popped up and dropped them. Case closed."

Trevor looked at Elena. "Anything to add, Marshal Diaz?"

Elena shook her head. "No, that about sums it up, except my partner is a little modest. He dropped those three in ten seconds with bullseye headshots, and if Syrin didn't grab onto the fourth one, we'd be lying next to those DEA agents."

"I saw the shots. Special Forces?" Trevor looked at Josh.

"In another lifetime," Josh said.

"One more thing. What about the shooting in the FBI office?"

"We knew the admin assistant called in our meeting to someone who sent the Hitler youth," Elena said. "We went up to make an arrest, Bonnie put two in the chest of a sergeant with the Brevard County Sheriff's Office, and Josh put her down."

"Okay. Sounds good to me. I'll get all the paperwork together for your review and signature. I'll also handle all of this." Agent Knight made a sweeping hand gesture at the organized chaos. "Should be an interesting food fight. Why don't you guys take off before the FBI ASAC gets back and finds his admin assistant graveyard dead in his office?"

CHAPTER 53

Josh turned left on Wickham Boulevard out of the FBI parking lot. "I don't know about you, but I'm starving, and Syrin is starting to show a little rib cage." Syrin stuck her nose over the console at the sound of her name, and Josh hugged her. Her tail thumped on the back seat.

"What are you thinking?" Elena pulled out her phone to look up restaurants.

"How about barbecue?" Josh pointed to a place on the left with two dancing pigs in chef outfits in pink neon lights: *Henrietta's Pig-Out Palace.* "It's got a cop car parked out front, so it must be good."

"Sounds good to me. I love me some barbecue. What do you think, Syrin?" Syrin gave Elena a lick. "I take that as a yes."

Josh turned into the parking lot and pulled into a slot next to a Brevard County Sheriff's Office green and white cruiser. When they stepped out of the truck, Josh grabbed a bag of Syrin's food and a dish. *Hopefully, they have outside seating in the back.* They walked through the front door, where the hostess grabbed two menus and took them toward the back. Two deputies looked up to gauge a threat when they came past. They spotted Syrin's FBI vest and gave Josh a head nod. He returned the gesture.

Picnic tables with red and white checkered tablecloths spread across a wooden floor stained by years of dropped sauce. The smell of fresh barbecue filled the air, and smoke drifted off a couple of smokers in the back. Syrin turned and gave Josh a *fuck the kibble* look.

"I know. I'll sprinkle some barbecue juice on your delicious nuggets." Josh stroked Syrin on the head.

The outdoor seating area looked like the main restaurant, but the floor was cement, and it was surrounded by an eight-foot vinyl fence and covered with a canvas top. Four fans ran in the corner to circulate air, and an AC duct dumped cold air on top of the fan nearest the building. The area was empty aside from four large male customers dressed in Henrietta T-shirts and jeans chowing down on all-you-can-eat pulled pork. They looked like it wasn't their first visit.

"Cops out front, regulars in the back; this place must be good. You really know how to treat a lady." Elena flipped open the menu. "I wonder what's good?"

"I hope it's not the pulled pork because I don't think they have any left." Josh gestured at the good old boys, and Elena laughed.

A blonde teenager with a perky bounce to her step emerged from the kitchen and headed to their table. "Good evening. My name is Alyssa, and I'll be your server tonight. Can I get you something to drink?"

"What do you have on draft?" Josh looked up from his menu.

"We have Bud, Bud Light, Coors, and Heineken." Alyssa tapped her pen on her order pad.

"Do you have any Dos Equis?" Josh closed his menu and put it on the table.

"We have amber and lager."

"I'll have amber with a full rack of baby back ribs, coleslaw, beans, and a corn muffin." Josh looked at Elena.

"Sounds good to me. I'll have the same thing." She handed her menu to Alyssa.

"So, I got two full racks, two Dos Equis amber, coleslaw, beans, and corn muffins. Anything else?"

"Yes. And one more thing. Please add the bill for the two officers in front to our check, and can you bring a dish of barbecue drippings in a bowl?" Josh handed Alyssa his menu.

Alyssa gave Josh a weird look. Josh tilted his head at Syrin.

"Of course." Alyssa laughed. "That's so nice. Your beers will be right out." Alyssa turned and walked back into the restaurant.

Elena looked at Josh. "What do we do now that the DEA just got taken out of the picture, and we're still no closer to finding the girl?"

CHAPTER 54

Bri sat on the edge of the bed. It was feeding time at the zoo. Someone rapped on the door. "I'm on the bed." The door opened, and a large black man walked into the room carrying her food tray. He looked like a bouncer at a local club. Another large man blocked the doorway.

The large black male put the tray on the table and turned to look at Bri. "Oh-six hundred. Ready to go. Don't be late."

"Yes, sir." Bri kept her eyes down.

The men walked out and pulled the door closed.

Shit. No more college kids. These guys looked like professionals. Probably a hired transportation crew. Getting away just got more complicated.

Bri stood up, went to the table, and picked up the lid from her food tray. *Mystery meat, a scoop of mashed potatoes, peas, coagulating gravy, a carton of milk, and a container of fruit cocktail. I hope this isn't my last meal.*

Nine flights up, Bishop Avery looked at her dinner: a one-and-a-half-pound fresh Maine lobster flown in that day surrounded by a ring of steamers and red potatoes with an ear of corn on a side plate. She picked up a glass of her favorite German Riesling and took a sip.

"The meal looks fabulous, Jean-Paul. Thank you." Bishop Avery looked up at the ceiling. She took another sip of wine, savoring the melon taste, and set the glass down.

"You're welcome, Bishop Avery," came the response.

She picked up a steamer, took out the clam with a small fork, dipped it into a side saucer of butter, and popped it into her mouth. "Mmmm, that is so good. New England does seafood right." She pierced a piece of lobster meat still in the crusher claw. Jean-Paul served his lobster ready to eat. He slit and cracked all the claws with a knife. The tail was free of the shell, placed on top, and cut into bite-size pieces. She was about to take a bite of lobster when she spied Julius's large figure lumbering across the tile floor with her glowing phone in his hand.

"It's your sister." Julius set the phone on the table and trudged back to his station at the front of the bishop's residence.

Bishop Avery wiped her hand and mouth with a napkin and picked up her phone.

"Rachel, how's the life of a corrupt politician?"

"Not too bad; the governor got his panties in a wad over the fraternity investigation, but he's back to playing golf. I still can't figure out why the president shut us down. Something's got him spooked."

"I know why. One of the girls we grabbed is Donna Alonzo's oldest daughter, Bri. You were at her induction."

"Oh shit, the virgin?"

"Yup, that's the one. They sent a special team to get her back. Sari just called. They dropped all four members of some friends we sent to remove them from the playing field. Took them like ten seconds."

"This is not good, Steph, especially with the shipment coming in and the girls going out."

"Don't worry, big sister. I'll handle it. The girls go out tomorrow, the shipment arrives in port, and Senator Alonzo's daughter goes on a swamp boat tour of the Saint Johns River Marsh."

"Okay, that sounds good. I think we need to start divesting ourselves of certain businesses if I'm campaigning to become president of the United States."

"I thought the same thing. This will be our last run. I'm getting too old for this shit, and we make a ton of tax-free money on the church. The risk would outweigh the reward. When Rachel Avery Collier gets elected president, we'll make a fortune."

"I like the sound of that. You take care. Love ya." Rachel clicked off the call.

Bishop Avery set the phone on the table. *I wonder how big the offices are in the West Wing.*

CHAPTER 55

Josh pushed the plate away and drained his Dos Equis Amber. He looked down at Syrin, passed out on the floor after her meal of kibble soaked in barbecue juice. She would be snoring any minute. Elena still nursed her beer.

Alyssa sashayed to their table. The four all-you-can-eat buffets had sauntered out of the restaurant when Josh and Elena's food arrived. One of them wanted to comment about Syrin but thought better of it when he saw her vest and the look on Josh's face.

"Do you guys want any dessert?" Alyssa took the plate from in front of Josh.

"I'm good." Elena waved her off.

"I'd like some coffee," Josh said.

"Okay, one coffee, and I'll be right back with your check. She walked off, carrying both plates.

Elena looked at Josh. "You know my story. What about you? I've seen a lot of things in the Army and the Marshals Service, but nothing like today. That was a whole different level of kickass. You are not your typical FBI lawyer or accountant. I know you told Trevor 'Special Forces.' Since we're partners, what's your story?"

Josh looked at her and drew his finger around the top of his beer bottle. He had not told his story to anyone since Kat died, let alone a hot woman with a gun.

"I grew up in a small town called Lancaster in northern New Hampshire, about fifty miles south of the Canadian border. My family owns and runs a dairy farm and a maple sugar business. We also have a string of ice cream retail stores in New Hampshire, Vermont, and Maine. I worked the farm every day of my life until I was eighteen. My dad died of a heart attack when I was a freshman in high school—one of the saddest days of my life. I remember walking up the driveway and seeing my sister crying on the front steps. I can still hear her words: 'Daddy is dead.'" Josh took a sip of beer.

"Do you have any other siblings?" Elena started peeling the label off her bottle.

"One brother, JJ. Let me show you the dumb ass's picture." Josh picked up his phone. He pressed "gallery" and scrolled to a picture of JJ and himself sitting on the end of a dock, fishing on Martin Meadow Pond, and then another picture of JJ in his Marine dress blues.

"Now *that* is one fine looking brother. When this is over, you need to give me his phone number." Elena stopped peeling her beer bottle.

"Don't say that too loud; his head's big enough already. We don't want it to get all swollen up." They both laughed.

"So, the obvious question. Not many black folks in New Hampshire?" Elena pushed her bottle to the edge of the table.

"JJ's dad, Big Jim Johnson, came to run our farming operation when I was about five. JJ came along as a package deal. We've been brothers ever since. In fact, Pops—that's what we call Big Jim—is engaged to marry my mom."

"When's the wedding?" Elena looked left at the sound of the door opening and Alyssa bringing a steaming mug of coffee.

Alyssa swapped the check tray for Elena's empty beer bottle, and she slid the coffee in front of Josh. "Anything else?"

"I think we're good, Alyssa." Josh put his credit card on the tray.

"Okay, I'll be right back." Alyssa picked up the card and the tray and headed for the door.

"I don't know yet. I've been in Army training for the last couple of months." Josh blew on the mug of hot coffee.

"Well, continue with your story."

"So, I graduated from White Mountain Regional High School in two thousand one and went to the US Coast Guard Academy. I graduated from there in oh-five, and my first assignment was a two-hundred-seventy-foot cutter out of Boston, USCGC SPENCER. The Coast Guard signed an agreement with the Navy to allow coasties to become Navy SEALS. I got accepted into the program and completed BUDS and follow-on training to earn my trident."

"So, that explains the Special Forces training. How did you become an FBI Agent?"

Josh saw Alyssa walking through the door with the receipts. "That story will have to wait for another day." He stood up from the table. "We need to get back to the hotel and check in with Vince and Becka. We're going to need some help." Josh signed the restaurant copy. Left zero for a tip on the receipt and slipped a hundred-dollar bill under the clip. He handed the tray back to a stunned Alyssa. "Don't spend it all in one place."

Josh, Elena, and Syrin walked toward the door.

"And when you finish your story, tell me how you have so much money to throw around. It sure isn't on an agent salary."

"I told ya. I got the corporate card." Josh held the door for the two girls.

CHAPTER 56

"All stop." Captain Moreno checked the radar for any traffic with a CPA of less than two miles. It was all clear. The seven targets in the vicinity were loitering in place like the *Garcia Asombrosa,* waiting their turns for the transit into Port Tampa Bay.

"All stop. Aye, Captain." The mate pushed the engine indicator to all stop. "The engines answer all stop."

"Very well. Distance to the pilot station?" Captain Moreno turned to look at his navigator.

"Fifteen miles, Captain. What time do you want to make the run in?"

"Underway at zero three hundred. Turn for eight knots and adjust speed as necessary. Put me in for a wake-up call at zero two hundred. I'll be in my cabin. Have a good watch." Captain Moreno walked off the bridge.

It was a quick ten-minute trip back to the hotel. Josh pulled the truck into the valet lane, put it in park, and hit the unlock button on the doors.

He exited the truck and tossed the fob to Jason.

"Are you in for the night?" Jason was sporting the usual tan shorts, white sneakers, and purple floral print Hawaiian shirt.

"Yeah, we are, Jason." He handed him a twenty-dollar bill. "You know the drill. Also, keep it somewhere close. We may have to leave in a hurry." Josh opened the rear door, and Syrin hopped out, stared at Jason, and wagged her tail. "You're moving up in the world, Jason. She likes you."

"Thanks, Boss. We'll keep a close eye on the truck. It's a beautiful ride. Do you need any help with baggage?"

Elena opened her door and hopped out.

"No, I think the marshal can get to the room by herself." Josh winked at Jason, who laughed.

Josh walked around the front of the truck with Syrin in heel position wearing her FBI vest, and Elena trailed them into the hotel. The cold air of the hotel lobby hit them in the face, and cascading waterfalls added to the ambiance. They rode the elevator up to their twenty-fifth-floor suite, exited the elevator, and proceeded to the corner room. Josh took the room card out of his pocket, held it on the touchpad, watched the light turn green, and pushed through the door. He pulled his holster and gun out of his waistband and set it on the side table near the hotel phone.

"I'm going to call room service for some ice cream cones. Do you want anything?" Josh picked up the receiver.

"No, thanks, I'm going to take a shower. I need to wash off. Are you going to call Vince?"

"Yes, I'll call him after I order the ice cream. Do you want some company in the shower?"

Elena gave him a surprised look.

"Syrin could use a rinse job."

Elena laughed. "Nah, I think that experience is all yours." She walked into the bedroom and pulled the door closed.

"Two scoops or one?" Syrin barked three times. "You're not getting three. How are you going to run down criminals with an ice cream gut?" Josh picked up the phone and pushed the button for room service.

"Good evening, Mr. Martin. How can we be of service to you?"

"Do you have any ice cream cones?"

"We do. Chocolate, strawberry, and vanilla."

"Do you have any chocolate jimmies?"

"I'm sorry, sir. I'm not familiar with jimmies. Please wait a second. Oh, chocolate sprinkles. Yes, we have them."

"Great. Two double scoop vanilla ice cream cones, one with chocolate jimmies."

"Yes, sir. It will be about twenty minutes. Have a good evening."

"Thank you." Josh hung up the phone and sat on the couch. Syrin piled in next to him. "You know, there's another half a couch over there." Syrin put her head on his lap. Josh buried his face in her fur. "Who's my good girl?" Syrin's tail thumped on a cushion.

Josh pulled his cell phone out of his shirt pocket, scrolled through his contacts, and called El Jefe.

Director Santiago picked up immediately. "I was wondering when you were going to call. You've had a busy day. Are you guys, okay?"

"Yeah, we're fine. A little tired after the adrenaline wore off. Elena's in the shower now. Syrin and I are sitting on the couch in our room, waiting on ice cream cones. Any word on the four shooters?"

"They were hired help from a white supremacist group, the Aryan Brotherhood of Florida, so other than extensive rap sheets for assault, attempted murder, extortion, and various weapon and drug charges, no help on this case."

"What about the admin assistant? Bonnie something?" Josh stroked Syrin's head.

"Bonnie Tyler. She was with the FBI for eighteen years and probably dirty for ten. We found a bank account in the Cayman Islands with a little over one-point-six million. Monthly deposits of twenty thousand started about ten years ago. We can't trace the source of the payments, but we did add the one-point-six million to your corporate credit card account."

Josh laughed. "Who ratted me out?"

"Colonel Gangsei. He thanked me for your graduation party."

"I bet he did. Troopers can really chow down on free food and an open bar."

"That they can. Any movement on finding our girl?"

"The only thing that connects everything is the Church of Illuminology. They sponsor the fraternity. Their Israeli God Squad are regulars at the Lightning Strikes Motorcycle Club with suspected ties to drug smuggling and transshipment. So far, the girl is a ghost. Can you get Becka to move our air asset from the fraternity to the church complex? I also need to find out any information on something called the Holy Ship, who's who in the zoo at the church, and any information on suspected drug shipments into Port Tampa Bay."

"Roger. Copy all. Anything else?"

"We need some help. We got unknown assholes shooting at us, and we have a lot of ground to cover. I could use a couple of tac teams."

"Okay. I'll see what I can do."

Josh looked up at the sound of three knocks on the door and a voice saying, "Room service."

"Thanks, Director. Gotta go. Syrin's ice cream is melting."

CHAPTER 57

Sari leaned back in her office chair and stretched her arms over her head. "Man, these late nights are starting to get to me. We need to plan a ladies' cruise after all this shit is over."

"I'll drink to that." Gabi took a drink of Gatorade. Her black battle dress uniform clung to her body, matched with black Under Armor Valsetz RTS 1.5 Tactical Boots. Her blonde hair was cut razor short, and she wore no makeup. She had the same build as Sari, but leaner. She just completed her fifty-state marathon quest the month before with the Orcas Island Trail Run in Olga, Washington. It was wet but beautiful. Her resting pulse rate was fifty-two, which was perfect for shooting.

"Are you clear on the target?" Sari stood up.

"Yes, I reviewed the target package. No problems. Do you think Eleanor has any chocolate chip cookies left?"

"I don't know. Let's go find out. If she doesn't have any, I know where Jean-Paul keeps his stash." Sari walked out of her office with Gabi on her six.

Bri set the alarm clock on the table for a 0430 wake up, climbed on top of the bed, and lay down. She didn't bother to get undressed in case 0600 was a cover, and they would come for her earlier. She checked the pin over her right ear for the tenth time. It was still there. She glanced at the clock: 0959. *This is going to be like Christmas Eve, except with dread in the morning and not joy.* She closed her eyes and slowed her breathing to try and get some sleep and work the problem.

There are two issues: I need to get away from my captors and reach a haven. There will be some type of transportation tomorrow from wherever this place is to my new destination. The new facility will be either another holding location for more transit or a final destination. I don't think it's a final destination—too many girls. Probably headed out of the country, which will make the second half of the problem—refuge—extremely difficult. So, I need to make the break tomorrow before I leave the country.

She drifted off to sleep at the thought. A bang outside her door startled her awake. *I wonder how long I've been asleep. Probably a couple of hours.* She rolled over to look at the clock: 10:12. *Fuck, Christmas Eve with no Santa Claus.*

Josh swiped the next page of *Blue Moon* by Lee Child on his Kindle. Elena was sleeping in the bedroom, and Syrin was snoring next to him, curled up on the pull-out couch. His phone buzzed on the end table next to the sofa. He looked at the caller ID: El Jefe.

"Hey, Boss, working late?"

"Yeah, D.C. is the city that never sleeps, not New York. Did I wake you up?"

"No, I'm lying here reading a book and listening to Syrin snore. What's up?"

"Just calling with an update. I got you two tac teams: Dave Tuley's group and some Delta troopers. Where do you want them?"

Josh thought for a moment. "Send Tuley's group to Tampa near the port and send the troopers to my location. We're staying at the Tropical Suites Hotel in Melbourne, Florida."

"Roger. Tropical Suites Hotel. Also, the air asset is currently on top of the Church of Illuminology complex. The church is jamming communications, so we have no intercept capability. It's military-grade equipment. From the profile and parameters, it looks Israeli."

"That makes sense. The church has an ex-Mossad team on the payroll." Josh closed his Kindle.

"That's right, Becka gave me a rundown on the team. I also got her working on the church, the Holy Ship, and drug shipments into Port Tampa Bay. She goes on watch at midnight. That's all I got, sailor."

"Thanks, Vince. I'll call you tomorrow to give you an update. I think we're running out of time."

"Yeah, I was thinking the same thing. I have no idea what I'm going to say to the mother."

"Hopefully, it doesn't come to that. Good night." Josh clicked off the call and put his phone back on the table along with his Kindle. He reached over, killed the light, and tried to get some sleep to the dulcet tones of Syrin snoring. *Tomorrow, she sleeps with the marshal.*

CHAPTER 58

Becka Kendall turned right on Birmingham Avenue from Route 17 and eased to a stop five cars back from the Birmingham Gate entrance to Naval Air Station Jacksonville. Only the far-right lane was open. The Navy petty officer on duty checked IDs with a handheld scanner and waved people through when they passed the screening. He wore a blue camouflage uniform. He waved her up with his right hand. She hit the button on the door, and the glass rolled down.

"Evening, ma'am," Third Class Petty Officer Curtis Johnson said.

"Evening, Curtis. I see you're still riding the midnight train." She gave him her ID card.

"Yes, ma'am, but I like the quiet." He checked her military ID and handed the card back to her. He snapped to attention and rendered a sharp salute.

Becka took her ID and returned the salute. "You have a quiet night, Curtis."

"Thank you, ma'am."

Becka drove through the checkpoint, leaving the window down. The night breeze sent a chill down her spine, and the fresh air felt invigorating. It would be another twelve hours until she breathed fresh air again. She turned right on Allegheny Road, left on Akron Drive, and pulled into the gravel parking lot of the Navy Munitions Command. She parked next to a gray 1979 F-150 pickup. *I guess Max has the shift tonight.*

The Navy Munitions Command was a series of prefabricated buildings which now contained office spaces. As she stepped out of her new Toyota Camry, her boots crunched on the small stones underfoot. She stared at the sky awash in stars like a million pinpricks in the fabric of the universe with the light of heaven shining through. She located the Big Dipper, followed the two stars that formed the front edge of the cup, found the North Star, made a wish, and headed to work.

She bypassed the Navy munition buildings and made a straight line for the haunted house, about fifty yards from the parking lot through the grass. It was a medieval-looking stone building, about forty by sixty feet, with brown shutters and no windows. The only illumination was a single dome light over the door with a number four covered in green patina. The stone mausoleum wasn't alone. There were twenty-four identical buildings lined up behind it, but number four was the only one with a light. It was also the only one with a two-person security team in the woods, which bordered the building. She scouted the tree line. No movement, but they were there. They checked in every hour with the intel team for an "ops normal."

She took her common access card out of her pocket, inserted the chip into the reader next to the door, and punched in 8823. The door buzzed. She pulled it open and walked into a dark room. The door shut behind her with a metallic clank as the locking bolts slid back into the wall, and overhead fluorescent lights blinked on, revealing a ten-by-ten-foot concrete room with a gleaming tile floor. A ceiling-mounted camera over a metal door pointed at her. She took her cover off, exposing short blonde hair and green eyes. She stood tall at five feet, two and a quarter inches. They wouldn't let her put the quarter inch on her ID. She waved at the camera. Electric gears hummed and rolled as a locking mechanism released, and the four-inch-thick steel door swung open. She entered a space with an elevator door.

She noted levels "L" to "5" across the top with "3" glowing in bright red. She pressed the down arrow—kind of redundant since down was the only direction. After entering the car, she took a key from around her neck and inserted it into the emergency key slot. She turned it right, then left. The doors closed, and the elevator descended, passing floors one through five, stocked with Mark 50 torpedoes, and then another two hundred feet below the bottom level. The doors opened into another ten-by-ten-foot anteroom with a security camera on the bulkhead and a biometric palm reader by the door.

She put her right hand on the purple fluorescent outline of a hand. The reader emitted a bright flash of a photocopier, and a green light illuminated on the console. There was a loud, metallic *thunk*, and a blast-proof door pivoted open. She entered the most sophisticated intelligence collection operations center in the world, which did not belong to any government agency.

"Hi, Becka." Max Lindy turned around in the supervisor's chair. "How was your day?" Max was also a USN officer with LCDR oak leaves on his collar. He was about five foot ten, brown hair, 180 pounds, with a small gap in his front teeth when he smiled.

"Nothing exciting. I went for a run on the beach." She tossed her cover on the desk, which also had a gold oak leaf on the front. "Anything going on?"

"Naw, all quiet. The director called and said you were going to research pending drug shipments into Port Tampa Bay, the Church of Illuminology, and something called the Holy Ship. The regional centers are handling everything else. I moved the air asset from the fraternity at UCF to the Church of Illuminology complex. No communication intercepts. They're running a jamming system. Israeli, I think."

"Roger. The director briefed me earlier. I got it. Enjoy your day."

"I stand relieved."

"On the floor, this is LCDR Kendall; I have the watch."

"Aye, LCDR Kendall has the watch," the team responded in unison.

The team comprised six intelligence analysts, divided by geography, to cover the entire United States. They supported the regional centers set up in every major American city.

Max got up from the supervisor's chair and went to grab his Navy windbreaker. Becka sat down. She put her CAC card into the computer monitor, and the comprehensive, integrated intelligence feed of the US government came up on her screen:

Buxton D-Wave on Line

HUMINT	*TECHINT*	*NSA*	*SCOTUS*
GEOINT	*MEDINT*	*DOD*	*White House*
MASINT	*Intelligence Portal*	*CIA*	*DIA*
OSINT	*Cryptanalysis*	*FBI*	*DOS*
SIGINT	*Meteorological*	*DEA*	*Cabinet*
Optrint	*DHS*	*State*	
Spy satellite	*FININT*	*DNI*	*Local*
TEMPEST	*CYBINT*	*Congress*	*Universities*
Traffic analysis		*Omni*	*Labs*
NASA	*Industry*	*FAA*	*ATF*

CHAPTER 59

Gabi picked up the gun case holding Lilly to slip it into the cargo area of her rented white Chevy Tahoe next to a backpack, stealth sheet, and ghillie suit. A third party cutout who often rented vehicles for the church had put the Tahoe in his name. He'd parked it in the long-term lot at Orlando International Airport, while Rafi scrambled the security cameras. Following the usual procedure, the cutout would return it at the mission's end unless problems led them to report the vehicle as stolen.

Gabi shut the liftgate, walked to the driver's side, climbed in, and pressed the ignition button. The Chevy rumbled to life. She pulled out of the parking complex and followed the Highway to Heaven to the Church of Light Boulevard at forty-five miles per hour, then took a left. She stopped at the twin lighthouses, which were illuminated to call in the true believers, and took a right on 192 East. After 186 confirmed kills, she didn't believe in any religion.

She followed Route 192 for twenty-three miles and exited right onto Sweetwater Drive. After about a mile, the pavement gave way to a dirt road. She followed the path until she saw a sign for the Three Forks Conservation Area North Trailhead, and she pulled into the dirt parking lot. She drove through it, switched to four-wheel drive, and headed down fire trail 5A while continually scanning the right side of the road. About five miles in, she spotted the flat rock leaning on a tree. She pulled the Tahoe off the fire trail into the woods, put the truck in park, and killed the engine. The world suddenly got very dark and quiet.

She reached up and turned off the dome lights so they wouldn't shine when she opened the door. She sat in silence for about ten minutes until her eyes adjusted to the dark. She reached into the center console and pulled out her Kenai chest holster, which contained her stainless Ruger GP100 357 Magnum. She had six cartridges of Buffalo Bore Outdoorsman 180-grain flat-nosed bullets in a nickel-plated brass casing with boxer primers. The round would generate 783 feet per pound at fourteen hundred feet per second muzzle velocity. It would end the four-foot predator that swims and the two-foot asshole who walks. She slipped her arms into the chest holster and pulled the straps tight. She pulled the latch on the door and kicked it open—time to go hunting.

Bri tried counting sheep, blinking her eyes a hundred times and willing each body part to fall asleep, but nothing worked. She stared up at the ceiling, and tears welled in her eyes. She thought of her mom, her sister, and her dad. *How did this happen? I'm supposed to be a college student worried about finals, boys, and next Saturday night, not this.* She rolled over and looked at the clock: 1:59. *Fuck this. I'm not lying here like a victim.* She sprang out of bed, turned the light on, and headed to the bathroom for a shower—*game on, bitch woman.*

The phone rang in Captain Moreno's cabin. He rolled over and pulled the handset off the bulkhead. "Captain."

"Good morning from the bridge, Captain. This is your zero two hundred wake up call."

"Thank you. Start making turns for eight knots and follow the track line to the pilot station. I'm going to take a shower, and then I'll be up."

"Aye, Captain."

Captain Moreno put the handset back in the cradle and turned on the rack light over his head. He swung his feet over the edge of the rack and sat up. The ship vibrated as the engines came up to speed. Butterflies churned in the pit of his stomach. *Is this our final run? Everything has an endpoint: a life, a marriage, and a smuggling run. Will blue lights be waiting for us on the pier?*

He stood up and headed for the shower to wash away the doubt—time for another dance with the devil.

Gabi pulled up the liftgate on the Tahoe and slid out the case for Lilly. She opened the latches, eased up the top, and pulled Lilly from her foam padding. Lilly was an IWI Dan .338 Lapua Magnum sniper rifle topped with a Leupold Mark 6 scope. The IWI Dan is a bolt-action rifle with a ten-round detachable box magazine and sub-MOA accuracy at a range of twelve hundred meters. The Mark 6 delivers three to eighteen times magnification in a compact and extremely durable scope. Lilly had a collapsible stock and an adjustable bipod mounted on the front of the barrel. Gabi could drop ten-inch targets at one thousand yards with every shot. Her nickname in the Mossad was the machine. She never missed.

Gabi leaned the 15.2-pound rifle against the edge of the liftgate and pulled her Israeli Defense Force night vision goggles from the rear storage area, slipped them on, and pressed the energize button. The blackness of night became an eerie green. Her folded custom "Marshy" ghillie suit was attached to the back of her backpack with bungee cords. Her stealth blanket was rolled up and secured to the top of her pack, where a sleeping bag would typically fit. She lifted the pack out of the SUV and put it on. She hefted Lilly with her left hand and shut the liftgate with her right.

She walked around the front of the Tahoe to a game trail matted into the grass, stood on the trail, and looked north. A line of infrared dots snaked through the marsh. They were attached to trees, stumps, and rocks to mark the path to the blind site. She followed the shadowy trail, guided by the dots and her night-vision goggles. Invisible, she kept her eyes on the ground, looking for gator nests and snakes. She moved through the swamp for about three miles until she came to the edge of the Saint Johns River Marsh, which connected Lake Washington and Sawgrass Lake. She found the blind, lifted the top, and peered in to check for any unwanted visitors. It was clear. She stepped into the blind and pulled the cover down. Intertwined synthetic and real marsh grass concealed the roof of the blind, so it blended perfectly into the foliage. The marsh reclaimed all the disturbed soil years ago, so it was invisible to the casual observer.

The blind, constructed out of fiberglass, was built off-site two years before and buried there. It contained two molded benches on either side with a padded shooting bench in the center. The blind was ten by ten feet and seven feet deep, complete with a sanitary disposal system designed for boats. The holding tank drained into the marsh. Not EPA legal, but then the EPA never came around.

She placed Lilly on two sandbags that were lying on the shooting bench. She unsnapped her chest strap and slipped off her pack, which she leaned on the right-side seat. She lay down on the left bench to take a nap. Twilight wasn't until 0615, with the sun coming up at 0630. She would probably be shooting around 0645 or 0700, so she could catch a quick nap. She set her watch for an 0530 alarm.

CHAPTER
60

Josh's alarm licked his face. He cracked his eyes and looked at the clock on the table next to the sofa bed: 0455. "Really, you can't hold it for another hour?" Syrin licked his face again, jumped on the floor, and headed to the door. "Fine." Josh rolled out of bed, found his running clothes, laced up his sneakers, and headed to the door. "No running ahead. Florida drivers are crazy."

Josh pushed through the door and headed to the elevator. The lobby was quiet except for the sound of vacuum cleaners and cascading waterfalls. They rode the elevator down to the first floor and exited the hall into the warm Florida morning. Josh looked at his watch. He wanted to get going at 0600, so it would be a short thirty-minute run. Syrin headed for the closest grassy area for her morning constitutional. Josh checked his pocket for a waste bag in case his princess decided to take a dump. Nope, just a tinkle.

Josh ran circles around the hotel to keep Syrin out of the traffic, staying on the grass. Syrin went into kennel point at minute twenty-six. Josh pulled out the bag, scooped up the poop, and dropped it into a garbage can at the front entrance. "Ready for some breakfast?" Syrin barked yes and headed for the door.

Captain Moreno leaned over the railing of the starboard bridge wing to watch the pilot boat approach. The ship rigged a ladder over the side, and two sailors stood by the cutout in the ship's railing to drag the pilot aboard. The *Garcia Asombrosa* was maintaining bare steerageway with flat seas and only a hint of a breeze. It would be a smooth recovery.

The pilot was standing outboard of the safety railing on the pilot boat, ready to leap on the ladder. The boat made an approach and pinned its port bow to the container ship's side, matching the ship's speed. The pilot stepped onto the ladder and scrambled on board.

Everybody wants to be a pilot on a beautiful day with calm seas. Nobody wants to be a pilot in driving rain, with eight-foot seas, and thirty-five knots of wind. Captain Moreno turned back to the pilothouse. "Come right to course zero eight zero."

"Aye, Captain."

Gabi's watch vibrated on her wrist. She sat up and took three deep breaths, opened a side pocket in her backpack, and took out a power bar for breakfast. When she finished the power bar, she used the "boat" facilities and started prepping her shot. At the end of the blind closest to the water, she unlatched a partition and pushed it outward. The separation pushed the marsh grass down. She picked Lilly up off the shooting table and laid her on the molded bench on the left, and pushed the end of the shooting bench through the opening in the blind.

From her backpack, she removed the bungee cords holding her ghillie suit, which was custom made to her measurements. She had completed the exterior camouflage herself. The suit would break up her shape and blend her into the grass and marshy environment around the blind. Nothing in nature had perfectly straight lines, so equipment like rifles and antennas often betrayed concealed positions. She also pulled out a ghillie suit for Lilly and put both suits on the bench.

Next, she unstrapped her stealth blanket. With the advanced technology of UAVs and infrared technology, detection from the air was a concern. Her ultrathin stealth sheet would reflect infrared light rendering her invisible from overhead exposure. Her cover incorporated black silicon, commonly found in solar cells. Black silicon absorbs light because it consists of millions of microscopic needles called nanowires, all pointing upward like a densely packed forest. Infrared light becomes entrapped in the blanket. She had six sheets in her inventory with various camouflage patterns. This cover was marshland green.

She picked up her ghillie suit, put in her legs and arms, and zipped up the front, which was an open pad to provide comfort in the prone position. She reached into her pack, pulled out a single .338 Magnum round, opened the bolt on the rifle, inserted the cartridge into the breach, and closed the bolt. She also grabbed a box magazine with ten rounds, inserted it into the gun, and banged it home with the palm of her hand. Her final piece of equipment was a pair of Canon 18x50 IS Image Stabilizer binoculars, which she strung around her neck. She zipped Lilly into her ghillie suit, climbed up on the shooting bench, and crawled out the front of the blind, dragging her stealth blanket. At the end of the bench, she reached back and slid the bean bags to the front to support the rifle while she waited. She snapped the front bipod down, set the gun on the bean bags, and pulled the stealth blanket over her head. It was still pitch black, but the sun would be up soon. She rested her head on her right arm and listened to the lonely screech of an owl hunting for a morning meal.

CHAPTER 61

They came for her at 0550, probably expecting to catch her running around in a mad dash to be ready by 0600. There was a knock on the door. Bri sat on the edge of the bed, dressed in a pair of *Garcia Asombrosa* dark-blue coveralls with her white sneakers. The pin was firmly in her hair over her right ear, and a sharpened toothbrush was rolled into the waistline of her underwear and white T-shirt in the front. "I'm on the bed."

The door swung open, and her heart sank as "The Rock" filled the door frame. He walked in and stood in front of Bri. "My name is Julius, and you are not going to give me any problems today. Do you understand?"

Bri nodded her head yes, unable to get the word out over the disappointment of seeing a giant. She didn't stand a chance.

"Put out your wrists." The Rock had a pair of handcuffs swinging on his right index finger.

Bri stuck out her wrists, and the Rock snapped on the cuffs. The steel felt icy and hard on her skin.

"Stand up. Walk out of the door, and get in line." The Rock stood back.

Bri stood up and walked out of her prison. A line of six girls was along the wall to the right dressed in identical coveralls with their wrists handcuffed in front. They all had their heads down in submission, so they would be no help. She walked to the end of the line.

The Rock and the black dude from yesterday stood near Bri. Two more dudes were in the front. One of them called out, "All right, ladies, let's move. Stay in line, and no fucking talking."

The line moved forward. Bri followed along. They walked to the end of a dormitory hallway and up to two flights of stairs. One of the men in front held a door open. The line snaked outside into the morning twilight. The sun wasn't up yet, but it was getting lighter. Bri exited the building and looked left. A blue and gold motor coach with black windows loomed in front of a black Cadillac Escalade with dark tinted windows. Both vehicles were running. The smell of diesel exhaust and the rumble of an engine filled the air. The rear door of the Escalade on the passenger side was open. A towering black and white lighthouse stood menacingly off to the left with a cross on the side. It's rotating light bounced over a basketball arena; they weren't near water.

At the sight of the cross, Bri looked up at the sky. *Please, God, help me.* As the front of the line passed the Escalade on the way to the bus, Bri felt a large, powerful hand grab her shoulder. It was not the hand of God. It pushed her into the Escalade.

"You're not riding on the bus." Julius shut the Cadillac door and climbed into the front. The black dude got in the driver's side. Bri watched the other six girls get onto the bus. Like sheep to the slaughter, every girl followed orders, afraid even to acknowledge the loss of anyone in the flock.

Becka reached for her China Art mug of coffee perched on her desk next to a half-eaten bran muffin. She'd made them fresh the morning before. She took a sip of coffee and nearly dropped the mug at the sound of the target alarm and a flashing red light. A picture of Bri Castillo's face looking up at the sky flashed on the alert screen with her name across the bottom, and a running video started playing on the display mounted to the right.

"What's the source and location of the video?" Becka grabbed the phone on her desk.

"It's real-time from the bird over the Church of Illuminology," the analyst shouted from his station.

"Roger. Track the Escalade." Becka punched in the number for Josh.

"Roger," came the reply.

Josh picked up on the first ring. "Becka, what can I do for you on this fine morning?"

"Code red. We are currently tracking a target vehicle with Bri Castillo inside." Becka put her hand over the phone. "Direction?"

"Just turned on Route one ninety-two, headed east." The operator took control of the JSTAR drone and started following the Cadillac.

"Vehicle is a black Cadillac Escalade headed east on Route one ninety-two."

"Roger. Rolling now."

Josh stood up from the breakfast table at the hotel's free, cooked-to-order breakfast area.

"They just got a confirmed sighting of Bri Castillo. She's in a black Escalade headed east on Route one ninety-two."

"Holy shit!" Elena pushed away from the table.

"You get the truck, and I'll get Syrin." Josh ran for the elevator. He slapped the elevator's up button. "Come on, come on." The elevator made a slow descent, stopping at floors twelve and six before finally opening in slow motion at the lobby. Two older couples exited the elevator at the speed of February molasses in New Hampshire. *Jesus Christ. Can you move any slower?*

He rushed into the elevator, pulled out his badge to stop anyone from getting on, and hit the button for the twenty-fifth floor. *Of course, we're on the top floor.* He rode the elevator to the top with no stops along the way. When the elevator opened, Josh hit the stop button. The alarm blared. He sprinted to his room, swiped his card at the door, and pushed it open. Syrin danced at his feet. "Let's go." Syrin shot out of the room to follow a sprinting Josh to the elevator. Another couple was making a run at the stopped elevator. "FBI. Do not get on that elevator." Josh held up his badge to the startled couple.

"Sorry for the inconvenience, sir." Josh and Syrin ran into the elevator, and he hit the stop and lobby buttons. The alarm cut off, and the doors closed. The elevator descended sluggishly. He had to badge two groups of guests to keep them off the elevator before reaching the lobby. The doors opened, and Josh and Syrin sprinted for the exit. The Shelby was parked in front of the entrance. Elena sat in the passenger seat, and the rear passenger door was open. Syrin jumped in. Josh shut the door, ran to the driver's side, climbed in, and stepped on the gas.

The truck rocketed through the parking lot and fishtailed into a hard-right turn on Palm Bay. Josh slammed on the brakes one hundred yards from the on-ramp to I-95 North behind a solid wall of commuters on their morning slogs to work. Josh smacked his hands on the steering wheel. "Fuck me! So, close."

Becka looked at the screen and asked, "Where's the Escalade now?"

The analyst said, "Ten miles east of the church entrance, still heading east at fifty-five miles per hour. Let me see if we can get a tag number."

When she zoomed in, the screen changed to a picture of Bishop Avery giving a sermon. "And on this day, God brought forth a new kingdom on earth."

"What the fuck is that?" Becka walked from her desk to the analyst station.

"We're getting jammed." The analyst changed channels, but the jammer switched with every change.

"Jesus. Did the Russians decide to show up? Get my picture back." Becka pulled her phone out of her pocket and dialed Josh.

"Becka, we're caught in traffic at the I-ninety-five on-ramp. Where's the target?"

"We lost visual."

"What do you mean, you lost visual?"

"The church is jamming us."

"Son of a bitch. Call me if you get the video back. I've got to get around this traffic." Josh clicked off.

CHAPTER 62

The blackness faded with a faint glow in the east as the sun began its transit across the sky. A sandhill crane meandered on the shoreline to Gabi's left, oblivious to the patch of marsh grass looking at her. A northern harrier sounded off with two notes lasting about two seconds each, and a bald eagle swooped low, looking for breakfast.

Gabi trained her binoculars on a compound five hundred yards across the river marsh. Two moored airboats with ten seats each floated at the dock. A cement walkway from the boat docks led to a circular snack bar with a covered roof. Two sidewalks split off from the snack bar. One path led to an office and ticket booth. The other way led to the gift shop and gator pen. A paved parking lot extended out from the office and snack bar to the entrance off Route 192.

Farther left of the gator pen were three identical small cinder block homes with faded yellow paint and rust stains on exterior walls. The front door to the first house banged open, and a male figure walked out and headed to the gator pen. Gabi focused the binoculars. *Michael Dibble, dressed in khakis and a green polo shirt. I should put a bullet in this son of a bitch and do the world a favor.* She did a quick scan of the other houses. The one on the far left was Howard Dibble, the elder of the bunch. Dave Dibble, his son, was in the middle house, while Dave's sons Michael and Kevin shared the end house.

The Dibble women had died young to ovarian cancer and a heart attack. Gabi had to admit, they did serve a purpose, but it didn't make it right.

The Escalade slowed about three miles before it would have reached the exit to I-95 and turned just past a sign for the Dibble Brothers Gatorland Airboat Adventures. A mile down the road, they pulled into the parking lot. A steel swing gate mounted between two poles blocked the path. An older gentleman in tan khakis and a green Gatorland Adventure polo shirt was waiting for them. He pushed the gate open and waved them in. The Escalade drove through the parking lot to the house on the end and stopped. Julius got out of the Cadillac and nodded at Dave and Kevin Dibble. Dave was pushing fifty. He wore the same green polo shirt and tan khakis as his father, Howard. His thinning gray hair drooped in strings over a beaten-down face. His twenty-something son Kevin sported a black mullet and a gold earring in his right ear. He wore the same Gatorland outfit and a matching baseball hat. His pants bulged with a raging hard-on because he knew what was coming.

"The bishop wants this done tonight. No extended play period. Are we clear?" Julius eyed the two rednecks.

"Yeah, we're clear. Open up the back, and let's see what we got." Dave craned his neck to see around Julius.

Julius walked to the back of the Escalade and opened the rear door. "Out."

Bri slid out of the Cadillac and squinted in the growing sunlight.

"Oh, Pa, she's a redhead, and she's pretty. I never been with a redhead." Kevin practically creamed his jeans.

"Easy, boy. Dave walked over and grabbed Bri by the arm. "We got it, Julius. Did the bishop send the payment?"

"It should be in your account. Remember, tonight, or you will feel the wrath of God." *I should've said Gabi, not God, but it's the same thing.* Julius shut the rear door and climbed into the front of the Caddy. They turned around and headed back to the church, leaving Bri standing with the descendants of the hillbillies from *Deliverance*.

Josh inched forward in the traffic. It was slow going since there was a light at the on-ramp, and any car trying to turn right on red had to wait for a steady stream of traffic turning left from the other side of the intersection. "Call nine-one-one. We're going to need an escort through this shit. I need to get some lights and a siren on the truck."

Elena pulled out her phone and dialed 911. "This is U.S. Marshal Elena Diaz, badge number six, one, eight, three, two, five; I am one hundred yards south of the I-ninety-five on-ramp on Malabar Road in a red Ford F one-fifty. We are on a code three response for kidnapping, and we need a police escort. Roger, thank you." Elena clicked off the call and put the phone in her jacket. A siren started blaring behind them. "Cavalry is rolling."

Josh looked in his rearview mirror. He could see a Brevard County Sheriff's Office green and white cruising up the shoulder with lights and siren. Cars were inching left to get out of his way. Elena put her window down and held her badge and credentials out of the window. The cruiser got abreast of them and gave the thumbs-up.

Josh pulled in behind the cruiser with his flashers on. The deputy followed the shoulder the entire way and turned up the on-ramp with the F-150 on his ass. At the top of the ramp, the cruiser got in front of a white Mercedes and stopped traffic. Josh stepped on it and waved to the deputy as he flew by and entered I-95 North.

"Call Becka." She picked up right away.

"Where are you?"

"Just got on I-ninety-five North at the Malabar Exit. What do you have for me?"

"Nothing. We're still watching the sermon."

"Damn. Fuck them. Are there any buildings or structures between the church and I-ninety-five?"

"Wait, one."

"What are you thinking?" Elena looked at Josh.

"If they make I-ninety-five, there's nothing we can do. They're gone. Our only shot is they stopped somewhere for disposal." Josh changed lanes to the right, flew around a green Mazda, and cut back in.

"The main thing between their last know position and I-ninety-five is something called 'Dibble Brothers Gatorland Airboat Adventures.'"

"Bingo. What better way to get rid of a body than feed it to a gator?" Josh pushed the truck to one hundred miles per hour, at seven hundred horsepower, barely cruising. "Thanks, Becka."

"God, I hope you're wrong." Elena leaned back in the seat and grabbed the armrest and the console.

"Me too." The exit for Palm Bay Boulevard flew by. Josh started to move right. The next exit was Route one ninety-two.

CHAPTER 63

Bri took in her surroundings. She was at some airboat tourist attraction, and she didn't think they were going to take her for a ride and a cheeseburger. Those two rednecks were not the sharpest crayons in the box, but from the look on the younger one's face, she was the entertainment.

Dave dragged Bri over to Kevin. "Take her to your house, and chain her up. I'll go get your brother." He started walking to the gator pen.

"Come on, sweetheart. Let me get you out of the heat." Kevin grabbed her handcuffs and led her to the first house. He opened the door and dragged her inside.

The house smelled like a locker room, stale beer, and some nasty flowery scent. Through the door was a kitchen with dirty dishes, empty beer bottles, and pizza boxes everywhere. A lone Renuzit air freshener sat on the corner of the counter, fighting a losing battle.

"I knew you were coming, so I put out an air freshener. It's violets." Kevin pointed at the counter. He dragged her to a steel pole support, which marked the separation of the kitchen from the living room. A chain was attached to the pole at the base. Kevin picked up the chain and threaded it between Bri's cuffs and her body. He then locked the chain back to the pole. "You can sit on the bed." Kevin pointed to a tan dog bed with a dark gray stain. “I’ll show you my bedroom later.” Kevin dropped the chain and headed out the front door.

Josh exited to Route 192 West as fast as he could with all four wheels on the pavement. Three miles down the road, he saw the sign for the Dibble Brothers Gatorland Airboat Adventures. He took the crossover to Route 192 East, pulled into the entry road, and stopped.

“So, how do you want to play this? By the looks of this place, there are probably ten rednecks with shotguns sitting around waiting for a nubile black princess like yourself to show up for breakfast. We also don’t know if the girl is here. I’d hate to get in a shootout for no reason.”

“I got an idea.” Elena looked at Josh. “Do you still have Bri’s scent marker?”

“Yeah, it’s under the seat in the back. What are you thinking?”

Bri stood in the center of the room and listened for any sound from a backroom or outside. No sounds except a window unit rattling in the back. She reached up into her hair and pulled out the bobby pin without the rubber tip, and jammed it into the ratchet side of the handcuffs. She then smacked the bobby pin on the steel pole, driving the pin into the latch, and the cuffs snapped open, and the chain fell to the floor. She repeated the procedure on the other side. *Now, how do I get out of this shit show?*

She checked the house. There were two bedrooms in the back and one thoroughly disgusting bathroom. No rear door and all the windows had a direct view from the compound. She could run out the front and race the rednecks to the highway; she could not beat a bullet. There had to be another way. Another look around, and she saw what she needed in the corner of the living room.

Kevin walked over to his approaching dad and brother Michael. "Michael went first last time. It's my turn. Plus, he always leaves them bleeding and crying."

Dave looked at his boys. "You know the rules, Kevin. You shake for her, but the loser gets to kill her."

"Motherfucker, not fair." Kevin stuck out his fist, followed by his brother. "One, two, three, shoot." Kevin stuck out a rock, and Michael stuck out paper. "No fucking way." Kevin stormed off to the gator pen.

"Don't worry, little brother. I'll warm her up for you." Michael did a hop and a skip to his house, feeling the rise in his jeans. He pushed open the front door. "Honey, I'm home." He slammed the door behind him and caught a baseball bat flush in the side of his head with a hollow *thunk* like a dropped watermelon on the pavement. He fell to the floor, convulsing with blood oozing out of both ears. After what seemed like an eternity, he stopped thrashing around like a fish on a pier and became very still. His eyes locked open.

Bri stepped over the body and looked out the window. *One down. One to go. Come on, chuckles—time to show me your bedroom.* Bri leaned the bat on the wall and dragged Kevin's body into the living room, out of sight from the doorway. She kicked the dog bed over the pool of blood and picked up the bat.

Josh drove around the swing gate, through a small swale, and into the parking lot.

He pulled to the center of the lot and stopped in front of a male, probably about fifty. Josh hopped out of the truck, followed by Elena and Syrin. They left the truck doors open.

The male waved them off. "We're closed for maintenance. Come back tomorrow."

Josh saw a shadow pass the open gift shop door, another suspect in the shop. "My wife needs to use a bathroom, and we were hoping to get something in your gift shop." Elena nodded her head at the mention of the gift shop. Syrin started running around the truck, getting her wind. She stopped near Josh. "Seek." Syrin barked and ran straight for the first house on the end and barked at the front door.

The male in front drew a black automatic from behind his back and started to level it at Josh. Both Elena and Josh drew their sidearms and fired simultaneously. Two rounds struck big Dave's center mass, driving him to the pavement before he could fire. The automatic skidded across the asphalt. Both Josh and Elena moved to the cover of the truck as a burst of automatic weapons fire sprayed out of the gift shop door. Rounds whistled through the air, striking the F-150 and the pavement. Another male rushed from the building to the left with a shotgun. Josh dove through the rear door as a blast of buckshot peppered the side of the truck. One round creased his leg. He pulled the rear door shut as another barrage of buckshot slammed the side of the truck. Josh hit the release on his rear seat armory. He handed the Benelli shotgun to Elena and pulled out his MP4.

Josh rolled out of the truck near Elena. He sighted the MP4 through the gift shop door and squeezed off three shots; the reports echoed off the buildings. Elena sprinted to the first house to cover Syrin and whoever was inside. She banged through the front and ducked as a baseball bat whistled over her head.

"Whoa, whoa, friendlies." Bri dropped the bat and collapsed into her arms. "It's okay, baby. You're safe now. Is there anyone else in the house?" Bri shook her head no. "Is there a back door?" Another no. "Ok, sweetie. You stay here with Syrin. She'll protect you. I need to take care of two more assholes. Syrin, stay." Bri wrapped her arms around Syrin, who gave her a big lick.

Elena came out and gave Josh a thumbs-up as she turned left and went around the back of the house. She kept her eye on the gift shop and followed the shoreline to a back porch. She hopped over the railing and peered inside. A male bent over a counter was pointing an AR-15 at Josh through the open door. Elena sighted through the window and pulled the trigger. Three pellets of Grex buffered 00 plated buckshot followed by a Winchester PDX1 segmenting slug exited the barrel at fourteen hundred feet per second, blasted through the window glass, and slammed into Chuckle's side, bouncing him off the cash register and driving him to the floor.

Elena raced to the end of the gift shop and peered around the side. She gave Josh a thumbs-up and sprinted for the snack bar. The old-timer tracked her with a shotgun from the office door until Josh fired three rounds through his chest, blasting him so hard his head slammed down on a desk while his arm threw the gun to the ceiling.

Elena made her way back to Josh. "Thanks for the cover. Bri's in the house with Syrin."

"No shit?" Josh turned to look at the house. Bri and Syrin burst from the front door, running to Josh. Tears streamed down Bri's face. She ran to Josh and gave him a big hug.

"Thank you so much. How did you find me?" Bri stepped back and looked at Josh.

"Long story. We need to call your mom." Josh reached for his phone.

"Did you find the other girls?" Bri looked from Josh to Elena.

"What other girls?" Josh stopped mid-dial.

Gabi watched the entire scenario play out through her binoculars. *Not good. Two feds and a dog, and these aren't ordinary feds. No, "Come out with your hands up." Just* bang. *Fuck you. I can appreciate the professionalism.*

Gabi eased Lilly's scope reticle from Josh, to Elena, to Bri. The range registered at 625 yards. She focused on the target, held her breath, let it halfway out, and squeezed the trigger. The recoil slammed her shoulder, and the three-hundred-grain Sierra HPBT MatchKing round screamed to its target at 2,790 feet per second.

CHAPTER 64

Captain Moreno stood on the port-bridge wing and watched Captain Ben, the Tampa pilot, pass commands to his tugboats via VHF FM radio. Captain Ben had black hair with a matching mustache, a green "Port Tampa Bay Pilot" polo shirt, tan Dockers pants, and lace-up blue deck shoes. The *Garcia Asombrosa* approached Hooker's Point berth 211 in Port Tampa Bay at bare steerageway. Two tugs, the Tom and the Brady, pushed the ship sideways into the berth beneath two large orange-and-white-striped gantry cranes. Line handlers on the pier waited for the *Garcia Asombrosa* deckhands to throw monkey fists on the dock with three-inch blue poly mooring lines attached. When the ship nudged the dock, "Put over all lines" blared from the ship's speakers. Six monkey fists arched over from the ship to the cement berth. The handlers on the pier grabbed the lines and hauled them in—four spring lines, a bowline, and a stern line.

Captain Moreno looked down the pier to the stern of the *Empress Express* moored at Berth 212. Her crew of twenty-three was seated on the berth in a straight line with their hands behind them in handcuffs. Six Customs and Border Protection vehicles occupied the pier near the gangway with their lights on. A handler wove a drug dog among the crew to pick up any drug residue.

"What's going on?" Captain Moreno pointed to the *Empress Express*.

"Drug bust. I think they found ten keys of cocaine." Captain Ben replied.

"Wow, that sounds like a lot. It won't interfere with our offload, will it?" Captain Moreno leaned over the bridge wing to make sure all his lines were clear of any obstructions on the pier.

"No, Customs will be tied up with that for hours. They need to do a stem-to-stern search. Your containers should move quickly. Well, Captain, I think that completes our trip. Can I get you to sign my ticket?" Captain Ben handed over his trip ticket.

Captain Moreno took the ticket to the bridge wing handrail and signed on the master's line. "Thank you for an exceptional transit. My first mate will escort you off. Lope?"

Captain Ben shook hands with Captain Moreno and retrieved his ticket. "Fair winds on your next trip, Captain." Captain Ben headed for the pilothouse.

Captain Moreno went back to the bridge wing railing and looked across the container stacks at the Port Tampa Bay container terminal. Neat stacks of boxes lined up six rows deep. He knew the odds were with him. Customs only inspected 3.7 percent of the nearly eleven million containers that arrive in the United States each year. So far, the Church of Illuminology had not come close to getting caught smuggling drugs. Customs always pulled a couple of random boxes to inspect but took them from the first fifty off the boat. The church only used the diversion of busting a nearby drug-run every third time to keep Customs happy, and they never used the same ship twice.

Captain Moreno looked back at the *Empress Express* crew lined up on the pier. *I wonder what kept Customs happy when Hooker's Point was the largest cattle shipment port in Florida, sending beef to Key West and the West Indies? Captain William Brinton Hooker reigned as cattle king of Florida with over ten thousand head of open range cattle. I don't think they name ports after cocaine smugglers. Oh, well. I bet cocaine pays better than beef—also, a lot less smell.*

CHAPTER 65

Josh looked at Bri, waiting for an answer. Syrin bumped the back of her leg, Bri started to bend to hug her, and the world slowed down. Bri's head snapped sharply to the right, and a red mist sprayed Josh in the face. Josh wiped his hand across his face and reached out to catch Bri, who was falling to the ground. *What the fuck is going on?* A rifle shot thundered across the water. *Sniper!* "Get behind the truck!" Josh caught Bri with his left arm, clamped his right hand on the left side of her head, and sprinted to the tailgate of the F-150 with Bri limp under his arm. Elena was already moving to the truck at the sound of the shot, and Syrin beat them both.

"Any idea on the direction?" Josh held his hand firm on Bri's head.

"No. Can't tell with just one shot, especially between buildings. It's definitely from across the water, so it's all angle now." Elena looked at Bri. "Is she still alive?"

"Yes, I can feel her heartbeat, but she'll bleed out if we don't do something. The truck is supposed to be bulletproof, and I have a trauma kit in the back. So, which side do we choose?" Josh looked at Bri, then at Elena. "Fuck it. You stay here with Syrin. If I pick the wrong side, use the other."

"Fuck that." Elena sprinted to the right rear door, expecting to catch a bullet in the head. She pulled the door open and dove into the back.

“Syrin, move.” Syrin jumped after Elena into the truck and hopped into the front passenger seat. Josh sprinted to the door and set Bri in the back.

Elena already had the trauma kit out. She grabbed a package of Celox hemostatic gauze pads and ripped it open. Josh took his hand off Bri’s head, and blood streamed from a jagged laceration running the length of her scalp. Elena pressed five-inch pads across the whole length of the bloody scalp, pressed down with her hands, and looked at her watch. Josh pulled out a Celox bandage.

“Sixty seconds.” Elena took her hands off Bri.

Josh tightly wrapped Bri’s head with the bandage, covering all of the gauzes. Blood started to seep through the dressing. “Damn, we need to get her to a hospital.”

“You get in the driver’s seat, and you can kiss your ass goodbye.” Elena closed her eyes in prayer.

Gabi watched everything unfold. She had gone for a headshot, which was a mistake. *Should have gone center mass. Headshots are always risky. Targets love to move their heads even when a fucking dog doesn’t give them a push. But it could’ve worked beautifully--watermelon the head and pop the other two in the confusion. Maybe even get the mutt. But no ambiguity in these two; they reached cover before I finished jacking a round. They also picked the safe side of the pickup. Go for the driver’s side, and I would drop you before you could reach the door—time for a new plan.*

Gabi moved her crosshairs to the driver’s side and sighted just over the steering wheel. “Okay, cowboy, I know your little girl is bleeding pretty good. Why don’t you climb up in the driver’s seat and play the hero? Come to Momma.”

"Well, we can't sit here." Josh looked at the limp form of Bri on the floor of the truck. "I hope the low bidder didn't win the contract to modify this truck." Josh peeked above the center console, hoping to see something, but that was just a wish. He started to crawl over the console to the front of the truck. Syrin licked his face. "Thank you, baby girl. Back seat." Syrin hopped over Josh into the rear compartment. Josh crawled into the passenger seat with his head on the door. He rolled his legs into the driver's seat and shifted his torso, so he didn't nail his nuts with the gear shift. He moved his feet to the floor, curled into the driver's seat while keeping his head down, depressed the brake, and pushed the ignition switch. The Shelby rumbled to life. He shifted the truck into drive, stomped on the gas, and sat up.

Movement and a head flashed into Gabi's sight picture, so she squeezed the trigger. Lilly slammed into her shoulder. She worked the bolt, seated another round, sighted at the front of the truck, and squeezed off another shot. Lilly thumped her shoulder again. Worked the bolt, sighted at the red F-150, and squeezed off another round. Lilly pounded her shoulder. Worked the bolt and searched for a target. Three 300-grain Sierra HPBT MatchKing rounds screamed toward their destinations at 2,790 feet per second, in rapid succession.

Josh watched the bullet impact the windshield directly in front of his eyes. The hit clouded the entire windshield like a dense fog, obscuring the view, as millions of nanites dissipated the energy across the whole glass. The flattened copper bullet slid down the glass, and the windshield cleared. "Holy shit. It worked. Thank you, President Byrne." Another round slammed into the front of the truck and ricocheted with a whine, and another round hammered the front right fender as Josh accelerated into a hard-left turn and stepped on the gas. Seven hundred horses galloped toward the swale. He slowed a bit. "Hold on." He sloshed all four wheels through the swamp grass, righted the Shelby, and stepped on the gas. "We need to find a trauma center."

"Holmes Regional Medical Center, thirteen fifty Hickory Street, Melbourne. I got it on my phone. Head east on Route one ninety-two, and step on it." Elena cradled Bri's head in her lap.

"We're going to need an escort." Josh pressed the phone button. "Call nine-one-one."

"Where is the location of your emergency?" came over the truck's sound system.

"This is FBI Special Agent Josh Martin. We are currently headed East on Route one ninety-two in a red F-150. We have a medical emergency and need an escort to Holmes Regional Medical Center."

Gabi lifted her head in disbelief as the red pickup accelerated out of the parking lot. *No way did I miss three times. I can drop ten-inch targets at twelve hundred yards. I know I can hit a truck at six hundred yards.* "What the fuck? Son of a bitch."

She pulled out her phone and called Sari.

"So, girlfriend, what good news do you have for me?"

"None," Gabi replied.

"What do you mean, none?"

"The feds and the dog showed up." Gabi moved back into the blind.

"You're shitting me."

"Nope. They dropped all the Dibble brothers like a bad habit and got the girl."

"And?" Sari asked.

"And I dropped the girl, but it was not a clean kill. I'm not sure if she's dead or alive."

"Fuck, what about the feds?"

"They scooped her up, loaded her into their truck, and split."

"Why didn't you take them out?"

"I can't believe I'm saying this, but I missed. Three times." Gabi shook her head.

"Wait. You missed three times? That's not possible."

"I know, but they're driving away, and I'm sweating my ass off in a blind."

"All right. Head back to the church. Michael's going to have to bat clean up."

"Agent Martin, an ambulance, and a BCSO escort are waiting for you at the Dunkin' Donuts a quarter mile on the right, once you pass under I-ninety-five."

"Roger. I know it. We went there for breakfast." Josh kept the hammer down, holding the truck steady at one hundred miles per hour with his emergency flashers blinking. "How's she doing?"

"The bleeding stopped, and she's breathing but not responsive." Syrin leaned on Elena and whined, looking at Bri. "It's okay, girl. She's going to be okay." *Please, God, don't let this girl die. Send your heavenly angels to protect her.*

Josh eased off the gas, tapped the brakes, and moved to the right lane as he approached the intersection at the I-95 interchange. "Please turn green. Please turn green." The light held at a steady red with eight cars waiting to go through. "Fuck it." Josh pulled the truck onto the shoulder, passed the cars, waited for a green Honda to pass in front, and cut in front of a purple Dodge truck. Horns blared, and the driver of the Dodge flipped him off. Josh waved. "Shouldn't drive a piece-of-shit Dodge." He stepped on the gas and blew through the intersection. Dunkin' Donuts appeared on the right. "How's she doing?"

"She's doing…no, no…Josh, she's not breathing. She's not breathing. Come on, Bri. Come on, Bri." Elena tilted Bri's head back and started to give her CPR and mouth-to-mouth resuscitation.

Josh turned right into the lot and parked behind a red Brevard County Fire Rescue ambulance. Two paramedics dressed in blue T-shirts and blue pants stood near a gurney behind the ambulance. Josh kicked the door open. "She stopped breathing!"

One of the paramedics pushed the gurney up to the Shelby. The other grabbed an orange kit, stenciled *Airway*, out of the back of the ambulance and ran to follow his partner. The paramedic pulled the rear driver's side door open. Syrin hopped out.

"She's not breathing." Elena slid out of the truck.

A paramedic got in the back, and the other passed in an Ambu bag and got on the radio.

"Brevard County Dispatch, this is unit four. We have a Caucasian female with a gunshot wound to the head, who is not breathing and unresponsive."

CHAPTER 66

Zeus rumbled up to the warehouse double door riding a Harley-Davidson Road Glide Special with a custom paint job in dark blue with yellow lightning strikes. At night, the luminous strikes would glow. When the door opened, Zeus pulled into a large open warehouse with containers stacked throughout the six-million-cubic-foot facility.

Angels Logistics Center had two large warehouses separated by a center road parallel to the lanes that went end to end through the middle of each building. Bloated asphalt ovals surrounded the structures and overlapped at the road. They made for easy access to eight transfer areas with four loading docks. Trucks brought in full containers for unloading and empty ones for loading. Container forklifts scurried about with pallets wrapped in plastic. Twenty-five percent of one building supported cold storage.

Zeus parked the bike next to a blue and gold motor coach with black windows. Five other bikes were lined up where a hallway led to a conference area, a suite of offices, and a break room. He kicked the stand down, leaned the bike over, and stepped off. He pulled off his helmet, hooked the strap on a handlebar, and headed toward the hallway.

JB walked out of an office that exited by the bikes. He looked like a skinhead with jeans, Doc Martin boots, and a T-shirt with *Ride Me* on the front. He stopped when he saw Zeus. JB was the club accountant with a bachelor's from Princeton and a master's from the Sloan School of Management at MIT. "Hey, Boss, how was the ride?"

"Not bad. The scenery is starting to improve. It should be a good time on the beach tomorrow. Speaking of which, how's our cargo doing?" Zeus tilted his head at the motorcoach.

"All set up in the conference room with cots and HBO. Can't say they're watching much TV. We'll bring in four-point-six million for all twenty-eight—one million each for the two virgins, and a hundred thousand each for the other twenty-six. After splitting with the bishop, we'll net two-point-three million. Money transfers tomorrow when we complete delivery to the ship." JB walked over to a container positioned near the office door. "We'll ship the girls in this container." He patted the side of the box with his hand.

"How are we doing the drugs this time?" Zeus walked over and stood next to JB.

"Oranges." JB walked around the motorcoach, followed by Zeus. On the far side, ten tables lined the edge of their quadrant with a barrel full of oranges at each end. Each table held a stack of green vinyl hard-sided coolers, cans of coffee, and an ice chest full of frozen gel packs.

JB walked up to a table, grabbed a cooler, and unzipped the top. He reached in and pulled a tab on the bottom, which opened to reveal a false compartment. "We'll put a kilo of product in here. Fill in the rest of the space with coffee to mask the scent, close the lid, top with oranges, and an ice pack to keep the oranges fresh. Zip the top, the cooler is ready to roll, and it fits perfectly in a bike storage compartment."

"Dude, you're a genius. Does coffee really mask the scent?" Zeus picked up a cooler and inspected it.

"Not if the dog is skilled and trained on masking scents, but every little bit helps. We have seven hundred and thirty-two members at this rodeo, so we'll still have to store one thousand, two hundred, and sixty-eight keys. We'll keep them in their original packing and containers until we move them. I set up a three-person security rotation. Someone will always be sitting with the dope."

"When does the shipment arrive?" Zeus put the cooler back on the table.

"Our contact just called. The ship moored, and they're waiting for Customs. The boxes should be here around fifteen hundred. We can start packing when it gets dark. I figure we can process a hundred and twenty kilos an hour, six to seven hours to complete the job."

"Excellent." Zeus put his arm around JB. "Why don't you take me inside and show me what a million-dollar pussy looks like."

CHAPTER 67

Josh leaned on the truck as the BCSO cruiser and ambulance accelerated out of the parking lot with lights flashing and sirens wailing. Traffic stopped as the little convoy turned right on Route 192 and screamed down the road to the Holmes Regional Medical Center. Elena leaned next to him, and Syrin sprawled on the ground at his feet.

"Doesn't feel like mission accomplished." Josh put his arm around Elena and hugged her. "You did great."

"Yeah, I hope we did enough. It's in God's hands. What do you want to do now?" Elena looked at Josh.

"Make the call I'm avoiding." Josh pulled out his phone.

"The director?"

"Exactly." He pressed the contact for El Jefe, and the phone started to ring.

"Tell me you have good news, Josh. Becka just gave me a quick update. Did you find Bri?"

Josh pushed the speaker button. "I'm standing here with Elena. We just watched an ambulance speed out of here with Bri, but I'll be honest with you, it doesn't look good."

"Oh shit, what the hell happened?"

"They sent her to a disposal crew. Someplace called Dibble Brothers Gatorland Airboat Adventures off Route one-ninety-two in Melbourne, I think. We rolled up and put Syrin out for a whiff. She picked up Bri's scent, and the shooting started. Elena and I put down three, and Bri took out one with a baseball bat."

"Oh, Jesus, how am I going to tell the senator that?"

"We were standing in the parking lot, and a sniper shot at us from across the water. Bri took a round along the side of her head. Pretty deep crease and it bled like a stuck pig. Elena bandaged her up with Celox, and we just rendezvoused with an ambulance crew for transport. They're taking her to Holmes Regional Medical Center. It's supposed to be the best trauma center in the area."

"All right, do you guys need anything? Dave Tuly's crew just landed in Tampa, and some of your old compadres are headed your way from North Carolina."

"Sounds good. We need a cleanup crew at the Gatorland shit hole, and you should station security outside of Bri's room. Someone may try to finish the job. I would use our folks. I also need some air support to move around between Tampa and Melbourne."

"Roger on all. What are you going to do?"

"Bri said there were more girls in play before she got clipped. We also got the possible drug shipment into Tampa, and we need to deal with the Church of Bullshit. I think our shooter's part of the Israeli team."

"Okay, good luck. I'll have your North Carolina support add an extra bird to their package for you. I need to call a senator. Be safe." Vince clicked off the call.

Josh pushed off the truck. "What do you say, partner? Time to send a message?"

"What message is that?" Elena rubbed her hands on her pants to try and get the blood off.

"They took the wrong girl, and payback is a bitch!"

Director Santiago leaned back in his chair and stared at his phone. *I hate making these calls. I pray to God I'm never on the receiving end.* He turned around and pulled a Diet Coke out of his office refrigerator, pulled the tab with a pop of carbonation, and took a long swig. He put the can on a stone coaster with an Army "A" in the center and pressed the call button for Senator Alonzo. The phone barely rang.

"Vince? Any word on my daughter?"

"Donna, I wish I could do this in person, but time may be of the essence."

"Oh, Vince, no. Not my baby. Oh, God. Please, no."

"Our team rescued Bri, but an unknown assailant shot at them during the operation. She's at the Holmes Regional Medical Center emergency room in Melbourne. I have a G five-fifty holding for you at Andrews to take you there. A car and driver are currently parked in front of the Hart Building, waiting for you."

"What's her condition?" Vince could hear the change in her voice from a mom to a pissed-off senator.

"Unknown. Josh just called me with the report." There was a long pause on the line. "Donna? Do you need anything else?"

"What's the status of our agents? Are you bringing them back?"

"No. They are going to find and deal with whoever is responsible for the abduction and shooting of your daughter and the gassing and killing of the UCF college students."

"Thank you, Vince—for finding my daughter…and for the justice to come. I would like to thank Josh and Elena in person when the operation is over. I'm headed to Florida. Take care." The line went dead.

CHAPTER 68

Customs Inspector Calvin Jackson opened the black binder in front of him to scan the manifest for the *Garcia Asombrosa*. Unlike some of his contemporaries, he still looked good in the dark-blue CBP uniform, with short black hair and a black-and-gray goatee. "So, you have three hundred and fifty containers of automobile engines?" He flipped the page. "And you're going to depart with three hundred and fifty containers of engine parts? Is that correct?" He picked up a mug of coffee from the captain's cabin table, took a sip, and looked at Captain Moreno.

"Yes, Inspector, that is correct. No change; regular run for us. How's your daughter doing?" Captain Moreno pushed a thick, sealed envelope across the table.

"She's doing great. Harvard agrees with her but is very expensive." Calvin picked up the envelope and slipped it inside the cover of his binder. Nothing but the very best for our daughters, eh, Aimon? How's Isabel doing?"

"Almost seven and growing like a weed. I get off shift in about a month. I can't wait to get home. Gets kinda old cutting water between Veracruz and Tampa, but the pay is good."

"Well, let me get out of your way so you can start earning some of that pay." Calvin stood up and took another sip of coffee. "Delicious coffee, by the way. You're cleared."

Captain Moreno stood up, and they shook hands. "Thank you, Inspector Jackson. We'll make another run in about two weeks. I can make another contribution to your college fund. Be safe, my friend."

"I look forward to it, Aimon. Thank you for the coffee." Inspector Jackson picked up the black folder and headed to the door.

When his cabin door closed, Captain Moreno picked his cell off the cabin table, scrolled through his contacts, found the one he was looking for, and pressed send. The caller picked up.

"Yes?"

"Shipment is cleared for offload. We should depart in two days with the new cargo."

"Excellent. Let me know when you're underway."

On the way back to the hotel, Josh and Elena stopped at Staples to get supplies: two easels, four large pads of easel paper, tape, a three-in-one printer, ink, a marker, pens, and two packages of eight-and-a-half-by-eleven writing pads. The world was digital, but no way to hack paper. They also stopped at Sam's Club and loaded up on beer, soda, water, snacks, deli meat, condiments, and bread. They tipped Jason an extra forty bucks to bring everything to their room. On their way through the lobby, they stopped at the reception desk and rented the rooms adjacent to their suite on both sides. Elena headed to the shower, Syrin assumed her observation position on the couch with her eyes closed, and Josh checked out the other rooms. They were all identical. When he exited the suite on the right, he saw Jason pushing a luggage cart, followed by two other valets.

"Yo, Jason, over here." Josh gave him a wave.

"Where do you want all this stuff, Mr. Martin?" Jason stopped the cart near the room on the right.

"Put all the food and drink stuff in this room." Josh tapped on the door to the right. "Put all the office supplies in the room on the other side of ours." Josh pulled a wad of hundreds out of his pocket, peeled off six hundred-dollar bills, and handed each valet two. "I also need eight ballroom chairs put in each adjacent room. Can you boys handle that?"

"For two hundred bucks, we'd fill each room with chairs." Jason laughed.

"One more thing." Josh peeled off another hundred each. "You three are our eyes and ears. Anyone starts asking questions about us, you see anyone new, or something doesn't look right, you call me." He handed each valet his business card. 'If anything you tell me pans out, I got a thousand for the tip. Any questions?" Their eyes got wide, and they shook their heads no. "Also, you don't tell anyone about us or what we set up. You break that rule; I send you to prison. Are we clear?"

"Yes, sir. We're clear." All the valets nodded yes.

"All right, boys, let's get busy." Josh swiped his card, walked back into his room, and pulled the door closed.

"Are you done terrorizing the help?" Elena stood in the doorway between the sitting area and the bedroom, drying off her hair with a towel. She wore a US Marshal olive-green tactical uniform.

"Don't you look all kinda official?" Josh walked over and grabbed Syrin by the snout. She growled and shook her head. "Are you done using all the hot water?"

"Yeah, I'm done. Not my fault; we're on the top floor. Besides, I hear squids like cold water." Elena turned and threw the towel at Josh, who caught it with his left hand.

"Did you leave me any of these?" Josh held up the towel and threw it back at Elena, who ducked at the return fire.

"One. If you're taking Syrin with you, you'll have to share." Elena laughed.

"I'll pass on that. Plus, I don't think she's leaving the couch for a while." Josh headed for the shower.

Zeus punched the off button on his cell phone, took a swig of Bud Light, and set the bottle on the office desk. "Hot damn." He walked out of the office spaces into the warehouse. Twelve bikers crowded around JB, who demonstrated how to load a cooler using a kilo-size bag of sugar wrapped in packing tape.

"Compadres, I am the bearer of good news." Zeus walked up to the crowd of bikers and put his arms around the group. "I just got off the phone with Pablo Escobar. Our shipment cleared Customs, and it will be here in a couple of hours." A cheer went up from the group. "Learn well, my friends. Ten-thousand-dollar bonus to whoever packs the most coolers." Another roar of approval from the group.

"How about a trip around the world with one of the sorority sisters?" came a call from a red-headed biker with a beard.

"Sorry, Stinky Pete, the babes are off-limits. Use the ten grand to buy a hooker. I bet even you can get laid for ten grand." Another roar from the bikers and some back-slapping for Stinky Pete.

Zeus walked around the motorcoach to the far wall and dialed another number.

"How's my favorite old biker?" Sari asked with a smile in her voice.

"Rock hard and ready to roll all night long, baby."

"A little blue magic doesn't count, stud. Whatcha got for me?

“Everything is a go. The girls are ready. Shipment is cleared, and we should be all packed up by the time the cock crows in the morning.”

“That’s good news. Remember. Anyone crows in one of those girls, and Gabi will take the head off the rooster.”

“I know. I passed the word.”

Josh ran a towel through his hair and walked into the sitting area dressed in green tactical pants and a green T-shirt tight across his chest. Elena sat on the couch, checking her phone with Syrin’s head in her lap.

“Hey, do you remember what the patch said on Bri’s coveralls?” Josh asked.

Elena looked up and searched her memory. “The first word was ‘Garcia.’ I don’t remember the second. I think it started with an ‘A.’ Why?”

“I don’t know. Something’s bothering me. She looked ready to stand deck watch on a ship.” Josh walked over and picked up his phone off the counter near the sitting-area sink and dialed a number. Becka picked up on the first ring.

“Hey, Josh. Glad to hear you guys are okay. We have a crew at the gator location doing the cleanup. I think the real gators are going to eat well tonight. The counter-sniper team found the hide across the marsh. It’s been there a while. It was made out of fiberglass like a pool, and they didn’t find any physical evidence. What can I do for you?”

“That sounds great. I hope the gators don’t get sick on Dibble meat. Do you have any stills of Bri getting into the vehicle?”

“We do. That’s how we got the alert.”

“Can you tell me what she was wearing?”

"Let me take a look." Becka typed on her computer. "Okay, she's in dark-blue coveralls."

"Is there a patch on it?" Josh looked at Elena and motioned for her to get a pencil and some paper.

"There's something. Let me see. 'Garcia.' I'll spell the next word: 'Alpha,' 'Sierra,' 'Oscar,' 'Mike,' 'Bravo,' 'Romeo,' 'Oscar,' 'Sierra,' 'Alpha.'"

"So, I copy 'Garcia,' next word 'Alpha,' 'Sierra,' 'Oscar,' 'Mike,' 'Bravo,' 'Romeo,' 'Oscar,' 'Alpha.'" Elena gave Josh a thumbs-up. "Good copy. Did you find anything on Holy Ship?"

"The only thing we could find was an annual electronic dance music festival held aboard the NCL cruise ship *EPIC*, with two back-to-back sailings leaving out of Port Canaveral, Florida, with stops in the Bahamas."

"Yeah, I don't think the cruise ship is moving significant weight between the US and the Bahamas. What about…? Wait a minute." Josh looked at a waving Elena. "Amazing? Amazing what?"

Elena held up her note pad with: "'Garcia Asombrosa' means 'amazing grace' in Spanish…Holy Ship!"

The light went off in Josh's head. "Son of a bitch."

"What's the problem?" Becka asked.

"No problem. Do a check for a vessel named *Garcia Asombrosa*."

"Checking…Got it. It's a small container ship. Makes regular runs between Veracruz, Mexico, and Tampa carrying engine parts and engines. It's currently moored in Tampa."

"Bingo." Josh did a Tiger Woods fist pump. "Call the Coast Guard Captain of the Port and have them put a hold on the ship. Also, call the CBP port director and stop all cargo operations and restrict the crew to the ship. Did Dave Tuley's team make it to Tampa?"

“Yes, they got there about an hour ago,” Becka said.

“Okay, send them to the ship. Have them set up a perimeter. No one on or off the ship.”

“Roger on all. Do you need transport?”

Josh looked at Elena. “Transport?” She nodded her head, yes.

“Yes. See if you can get a Pave Hawk out of Patrick. We’re going to gear up.”

“Good Luck.” Becka clicked off the call.

CHAPTER

69

"Hi, sweetie, how are you? Daddy misses you very much." Captain Moreno stood on the port bridge wing. He had his phone to his left ear, and he was counting off boxes on a pad of paper—number thirty-five just hit the pier. Lope and the escorts were on the deck to keep an eye on the significant boxes. They were going off as numbers 200 and 201. The gantry crane cycled back to the ship. It got over the deck and shut down. Captain Moreno walked forward on the bridge wing so he could see on the deck. He looked at Lope, who shrugged his shoulders on why the crane stopped. *Something must have broken on the crane.* He looked up at the crane operator, who opened his cab door, exited his operating station, and started down the crane steps toward the pier.

"Hey, sweetie, Daddy has to go. Tell Mommy I love her, and I'll see you guys soon. Love and kisses." He clicked off the call. Captain Moreno scrolled through his contacts and found Calvin. He pressed the number. The phone went straight to voice mail. "Calvin, this is Aimon. The offload just stopped. Call me back. I don't know if the crane broke or if we have a problem." Captain Moreno looked over the railing again. Lope started to make his way across the deck to the gangway to find out what was going on. He looked farther up the pier at the *Empress Express*. Four Customs officers in uniform started walking toward the *Garcia Asombrosa*. Out of the corner of his eye, he spotted a Coast Guard cutter headed toward his boat at a high rate of speed with blue emergency lights flashing. The cutter slowed off his stern and took station about a hundred yards off his starboard beam.

Captain Moreno reached out to grab the bridge wing railing to keep from falling. His world started to spin, a pit formed in his stomach, and his balls retreated to his spine. *How did they find out? Oh, fuck, no, no, no.* He stumbled onto the bridge, the tears started to stream down his face, and he exited the bridge. He made the long, slow march to his cabin. Fortunately, he didn't meet anyone on the way. He entered, slumped into his desk chair, and opened the top right-hand drawer of his desk. An HK VP40 sat on a pile of pads like a sentry guarding the drawer. He pulled the pistol out and set it on his desk in front of the keyboard. *It will only hurt for a second.*

Sari found Bishop Avery, dressed in her white preaching robes, on the church stage, working through her Sunday sermon. She stopped on the edge of the stage. No one interrupted the bishop when she was in the zone. She glided stage left, stopped, eyed the empty arena, paused, headed to stage right, paused, and came back to the center of the alter. She moved like a choreographed ballerina. She learned the steps first then filled in the words, music, and drama. Music, words, theatre—preaching performance ideals instilled by the great Reverend Avery, when the bishop was only thirteen.

"So, what brings you to disturb my walk with God, Sari?" Bishop Avery looked over at the troubled angel.

Sari strode over to meet the bishop. "Good news and bad news. What do you want first?"

"Give me the good news since I'm feeling good in the presence of God almighty." Bishop Avery turned to face Sari.

"The shipment cleared Customs, Zeus is ready to take delivery, and we'll transfer the girls to the ship tonight." Sari paused.

"Let me guess; the bad news is the lioness." Bishop Avery stamped her foot, and evil crossed her face.

"Our two feds and the dog tracked her to the Dibble brothers. Gabi said they did not act like feds, more like professionals. *Pop*, *pop*, *pop*—no more Dibbles. The feds found Bri in one of the houses. They were standing in the parking lot. Gabi lined up a shot on the girl and missed."

"Missed? Missed? How does Gabi miss? Gabi never misses. She's the machine." The bishop's face turned red, and saliva formed at the corner of her mouth.

Sari stepped away from the face of the devil. "It wasn't a total miss. The round creased the side of the girl's head. She's at Holmes Regional Medical Center. Our source inside said she's in a coma and not expected to make it."

"So, not all bad news." Serenity returned to the bishop's face. "Any chance we can help her along on her path to heaven?"

"Not at her present location. Some type of private security showed up. It's not the police or hospital rent a cop. There's someone with her twenty-four-seven."

Bishop Avery pursed her lips. "That's too bad. The Valkyrie may have to fly again, and a lot of other people will die, but that girl cannot wake up."

Josh accelerated up the ramp onto I-95 and pulled into the light flow of traffic. Twelve miles in, he edged down Exit 188 and took a right at the bottom of the ramp to the Pineda Causeway East. The truck passed over the Indian and Banana riverways and exited to Patrick AFB. At the bottom of the ramp, Josh turned north and stopped four cars back from the entrance gate. He followed the four cars up to the guard shack. A young female Security Forces Airman with an M4 strapped to her back stuck out her hand.

"Bring back any memories?" Josh lowered his window.

"A few, but I was usually freezing my ass off and not working on my tan."

Josh passed his credentials to the airman. "FBI Special Agent Josh Martin and U.S. Marshal Elena Diaz. We're catching a Pave Hawk to Tampa."

"Yes, sir." The airman twirled her finger in the air. "Please follow the police vehicle."

An Air Force vehicle emerged from a pull-off with its lights flashing. The airman walked behind the truck to stop traffic. Josh pulled ahead and got in behind the police vehicle at a blistering twenty-five miles per hour.

"They do know we're in a hurry." Elena looked back at the military police officer. "I used to be that young."

"Now, you're just a crusty old marshal." Josh smiled.

"If I'm old, you're ancient. Why don't you tell your escort to pick it up? I could walk to Tampa at this pace. Isn't that right, Syrin? Ready to go for a ride with some sexy pilots?" Syrin stuck her head between the seats, and Elena hugged her.

"Good thing you're up to date on your shots, girl. You never know where those flyboys have been. Plus, they're helo pilots. Real men fly jets," Josh said.

"You don't listen to mister driving slow. He's not used to speed." Elena laughed.

They crawled through the base past medical, the commissary, the exchange, and a bunch of brick office buildings and barracks. The escort finally pulled in front of a gray hangar and parked. The driver got out and pointed Josh to a slot at the end of a row of parking spots marked by an *Official Visitor* sign. Josh pulled the Shelby in, put the truck in park, and killed the ignition. He, Elena, and Syrin piled out of the cab. They were both dressed in identical green BDUs with tactical vests. Josh's had *Police FBI* across the back. Elena's said *Police US Marshal.* They dragged their gun cases out of the rear and walked over to the escort.

"I just called in. They're coming right out," the escort said.

As if on cue, two men and a woman walked out of the hangar door dressed in flight suits and carrying helmets. A blonde with pilot wings and oak leaves on her collar stuck out her hand. "Amanda Barr. This is Captain Isaac Smithfield and Chief Denny Strutton. We got orders to fly you to Port Tampa Bay."

They shook hands all around.

"Thanks for the lift, Amanda. My name's Josh, this is Elena, and our four-footed partner is Syrin. Syrin, say hi." Syrin sat and lifted her right paw.

Amanda shook her paw. "You're a real sweetheart. Are you ready to go for a ride?"

Syrin barked.

"I'll take that as a yes. Your chariot awaits." Amanda started walking to her bird.

CHAPTER

70

Dave Tuley wove his dark-blue Ford Explorer through the rows of stacked containers and pulled in near the gantry crane positioned over the *Garcia Asombrosa*. His two trail vehicles pulled in behind him. He slid out of the SUV and headed over to a gaggle of uniformed Customs officers huddled near the ship's gangway. Dave wore a DHS Homeland Security Investigations dark-blue tactical uniform. On some other day, it could be the FBI; he never knew until the mission was set. His Oakley Radar EV shades were tight to his short-cropped blond hair, and his heavily muscled six-foot frame pushed against the seams of his uniform. The gaggle looked up at his approach. He didn't feel any zaps on his wrist, so no insiders in the group.

"Gentlemen, good morning. I hear we have an issue with the *Garcia Asombrosa*. Possible drug smuggling?"

"We may, but who are you? No one called HSI. I think we have a handle on it." A heavy-set Hispanic man with dark black hair, silver oak leaves on his uniform epaulets, and *Sanchez* on his name tag stepped away from the group.

"Port Director Sanchez, nice to meet you. My name's Dave Tuley." Dave extended his hand.

Sanchez shook his hand. "Sorry you had to ride all the way out here, Dave, but I think we can handle it."

"Okay, Director, I understand. We'll wait in our vehicles in case you need help," Dave said.

Sanchez looked over at the Explorers at the mention of the word "we."

"Suit yourself, Dave, but I think we'll be fine. Nice to meet you." The port director walked back to his staff meeting.

Dave headed back to his Explorer, pulled out his phone, and dialed Director Santiago's number. "Vince, good morning. We may have a problem with Customs."

"Are you at the port?" Vince said.

"Yes, sir. I just talked to the port director, Ignacio Sanchez. He's conducting a cluster fuck on the pier and protecting his turf. We have no Black and White on the scene. How far out is Josh?"

"He was wheels up about an hour ago and should be in your AOR in about twenty minutes. You guys sit tight. I'll make a few calls."

"Roger. Out." Dave clicked off the call and put the phone back in his pocket.

Lope banged on the cabin door. No response. "Captain Moreno?" Still no response. He entered the cabin. Captain Moreno was seated at his desk, bent over his keyboard. "Captain? Customs shut everything down. They've got about ten officers on the pier, and there's a Coast Guard boat off the starboard side. What's going on?" No response. He walked farther into the cabin and saw the handgun on the desk in front of the Captain. *Oh, shit!* Lope backed out and ran for the gangway.

He moved quickly across the deck and headed off the ship. A Customs officer stopped him at the bottom.

"Gangway is closed. An inspection team is getting ready to board your ship. No one is allowed off or on until the inspection is complete."

"It's my captain," Lope said, out of breath.

"What about your captain?"

"He's up in the cabin, sitting at his desk with a loaded handgun. I have nothing to do with whatever's going on."

"Oh, shit! You stay right here." The Customs officer headed to the cluster fuck.

Major Barr banked the Pave Hawk to the left and cruised by the port side of the *Garcia Asombrosa* at eighty knots. "Is that your target?"

Josh keyed the mike on his headset. "Yes. Can you set us down close?"

"Let me look." Major Barr did a pedal turn left, and put the helo in a hover.

It was about 150 miles from Patrick AFB to Port Tampa Bay. The Pave Hawk's cruising range was a little over five hundred miles, especially with a light load of two pilots, a flight engineer, two agents, and a dog. She usually carried a crew of four, two gunners, and twelve troops in the back. They had made the trip in a little over an hour.

Major Barr did a quick scan of the container lot. The right side all the way back to the rail line was empty since the *Empress Express*'s load was under hold. She keyed her mike.

"All clear on the north side of the terminal. Are you guys okay with a little walk?"

Josh questioned Elena with a thumbs-up, and she returned the gesture. He said, "Yes, Major, no problem. Are you going to recover at MacDill?"

"We can do whatever you want. Our orders are to support you in any capacity until you release us," Major Barr said.

"Roger. No need to wait in the hot sun for us. Recover to MacDill, refuel, use the facilities, and get a cold drink. I'll call you when I need you." Josh pulled a business card out of his pocket, tapped the flight engineer on the shoulder, and handed him the card. Chief Strutton gave him a thumbs-up.

Major Barr did a slow transition to the north, entered a hover, and set the helo down, sweeping the cement clean for about fifty yards in all directions with the downdraft. When the chopper landed, she killed the engines; their fast, high-pitched whine slowed and deepened. When the rotors stopped spinning, Chief Strutton gave them the all-clear to exit the Pave Hawk.

Josh unbelted his seat harness, pulled off his headset, and put it on a hook behind his seat. He reached over to undo Syrin's harness and take off her ear protection. He got a lick for his efforts. Elena exited the helo and pulled her gun case and backpack with her. Josh and Syrin followed her out. Josh walked to the front of the chopper, tapped twice on the side, and signaled Major Barr with a thumb in the air. They both started walking toward the *Garcia Asombrosa*. A dark-blue Ford Explorer weaved around a gantry crane and headed in their direction.

The SUV pulled to a stop near them, and the driver's side window slid down. "Hey, baby, you know you can do better than this candy-ass if you are looking for something to do tonight." Dave Tuley laughed out of the window.

Josh did a double-take at the comment and then started laughing.

Elena looked at them both and said, "I take it; you two know each other."

"Yes, Elena, this is Dave Tuley. He helped me out of a jam up North. Dave, this is my new and better partner, Marshal Elena Diaz."

"Pleased to meet you." Elena shook Dave's hand through the window.

"Why don't you two and the real professional in your threesome pile in, and I'll take you to the circus," Dave said.

"That bad?" Josh asked.

"Yup, that bad." Dave closed his window.

CHAPTER

71

Amado Arias pulled out the drawer beneath his *Garcia Asombrosa* rack, lifted out his Galil SAR compact assault rifle, and laid it on the mattress. He also removed a green tactical vest with six, thirty-five-round magazines double stacked in three pouches, slipped his arms in, and tightened it to his chest. He released the magazine from the rifle, checked the 5.56mm rounds, slammed the mag home, and pulled the charging bolt to put a bullet in the chamber. He retrieved his wallet, passport, and a ten-thousand-dollar stack of hundreds, then stuffed the items in various pockets and checked his rack for anything important. He ripped the picture of his wife, Gabriella, and son, Jose, from the head of his bed, kissed it, and slipped it into a pocket. A knock on the door startled him.

"Yes? Who is it?" Amado pointed the Galil at the door.

"It's me, Berto. Open up."

Amado pulled the door open, and Berto rushed in and slammed the door shut. He wore the same tactical outfit as Amado with an identical Galil.

"What are we going to do?" Berto asked.

"I don't know." Amado leaned back on the door. "Did you get everything? Money? Passport?"

"Yes, I got everything. What are we going to do? The Coast Guard is on the water with a cutter and a small boat, and Customs is on the pier. They closed the gangway. I also heard the captain is in the cabin with a pistol." Berto paced in the tiny stateroom. "Maybe they won't know we're the ones protecting the containers."

"No, we're the only crewmembers who joined the ship in Veracruz, plus one of the *pendajos* will rat us out for a deal." Amado straightened up with the resolution of a decision. He grabbed Berto by the vest. "We're done, my friend. If we do nothing, El Padron will kill our families and then kill us in prison. We need to make it look good and take as many of these motherfuckers with us as we can. If we kill enough, maybe we can get a car and get out of here."

Berto nodded his head in resignation. "Let's do this."

Dave Tuley pulled up to the other Explorers, parked, left the engine running, and hopped out. Elena and Josh joined him. Syrin jumped into the front seat to enjoy the AC. They approached the Customs officers.

"Port Director Sanchez, this is FBI Special Agent Josh Martin and U.S. Marshal Elena Diaz," Dave said.

Sanchez shook hands with Josh and Elena. "Finally. CBP HQ told us to wait for your arrival before boarding the ship. What's going on?"

"Sorry for the wait; we had to catch a flight from Patrick Air Force Base." Josh pointed to the Pave Hawk across the container yard. "DEA has intel this ship is smuggling a significant amount of drugs into the country."

Port Director Sanchez whistled. "Whew, baby, double-dip. We just pulled ten kilos of cocaine off the *Empress Express*. How do you want to play this?"

"The drugs are all yours; I'm only interested in a conversation with the captain," Josh said.

“That may be a problem. The captain is sitting at his desk with a loaded pistol in his lap.” Sanchez took off his uniform cap, wiped his sleeve across his forehead, and put it back on.

Josh paused for a moment. “You guys secure the ship. When you’re happy, give us a call, and we’ll come to take care of the captain. I even brought a narcotics dog to find the drugs for you.”

“Sounds good to me. Easy day. Let’s go, boys.” The port director started to walk toward the gangway with the Customs contingent of ten officers in tow.

Josh turned to Dave and Elena. “The only easy day was yesterday!”

Amado and Berto opened the watertight door between the house and the main deck and searched both sides of the containers. They were empty. Most of the crew was on the mess deck waiting for Customs. They knew the drill. They also knew there was no way to connect them to the drug shipment. They were all paid in cash, and they had no idea about the location, smuggling method, or type of drugs. It was just another day in the lives of merchant seamen.

Amado stepped out onto the deck and turned to the starboard side, keeping low below the railing, so he was not visible from the Coast Guard cutter. He crept alongside the containers and stopped amidships, then crouched behind an end container. He had a clear shot at the first ten feet of the gangway entrance as it opened onto the ship.

Berto followed him out and headed to the port side. He kept low to be obscured from the pier and duckwalked to the port railing, then tucked in behind a fueling manifold with a clear shot along the entire port side forward, including the gangway entrance amidships. He pulled the Saint

Nicholas medal from inside his shirt and kissed it. *Please, Saint Nicholas, get us the fuck out of this.*

Port Director Sanchez started up the gangway with a bounce in his step. Two drug busts would get him the promotion. *"Area Director" has a nice ring to it.* At the top of the gangway, he reached for the ship railing and saw Amado pointing a gun at him. "Gun!" He dove for the protection of a container on the right, just as Amado pulled the trigger. The two officers behind him heard the shout and dropped to the floor of the gangway. The third officer didn't get the memo, and the 5.56 round hit him square in the forehead. His head snapped back, and he dropped over the gangway railing onto the pier fenders, then slid into the water.

Berto watched Sanchez dive to the protection of the container. He sighted just behind the man's right ear in case he was wearing body armor and squeezed the trigger. The Galil bumped Berto's shoulder, the port director's blood painted the container's side in red, and he slumped to the deck. Berto got to his feet and raced to the gangway to shoot the fish in the barrel. Amado reached the gangway at the same time. They both turned their guns on the fleeing Customs officers and had the same thought: *Mow these fuckers down, and we're home free!*

Josh stood near one of the gantry crane supports and watched the Customs officers march up the gangway. He turned to Elena. "How do you want to handle…?"

Instinct and training kicked in at the sounds of "gun" and two rifle shots, so his hand raised his Glock 22 and pointed it at the gangway. Port Director Sanchez dove onto the ship, two officers behind him, hit the deck, and the third officer took a bullet in the head, then fell over the rail with a thud and a splash. The other officers started falling over each other to get off the gangway, and the two officers who hit the deck were getting to their feet and running down the ramp to freedom. Two figures in tactical dress appeared at the top of the gangway and pointed rifles at the fleeing officers.

Josh gauged the distance at fifty yards, focused on his front sight, and squeezed off fifteen rounds as fast as he could pull the trigger. The pistol hammered his hand, but he kept firm on his sight picture. His goal was to force the shooters off the gangway to seek shelter and not shoot the fleeing Customs officers. Dave and Elena drew their sidearms and advanced under Josh's cover fire to get between the Customs officers and the shooters. When they reached the bottom of the gangway, the shooters disappeared behind the railing of the ship.

During the firefight, Dave's TAC team bailed out of the Explorers with their M4s and took position behind the vehicles. Ready to play "whack an asshole" if anyone stuck his head over the ship's railing, one of the team leaders called out, "In position to cover." Josh, Elena, and Dave retreated to the safety of the vehicles at the command. They ducked behind their Explorer.

"Well, that didn't go well." Josh ejected a magazine from his Glock, pulled out a new one, and rammed it home. He tossed the spent mag into the SUV. He looked over at the gaggle of Customs officers racing behind a stack of containers to get out of the shooters' lines of sight.

"Now, what?" Dave asked. "If we try to assault the gangway, they can pick us off the minute we step on the ship."

Josh surveyed the ship through the Explorer's rear window from bow to stern. "Bow line."

"What does that mean?" Elena asked.

"Get your shotgun and follow me." Josh pulled his M4 out of the back.

Amado raised his rifle to fire, and bullets started whizzing by his ear, banging into the rail of the ship, the container behind him, and one grazed his shoulder. He quickly dropped down behind the ship rail. "Fuck me." Berto fell in next to him.

"Holy shit, that fucker was fast." Berto rolled to the edge of the rail. "What are we going to do now?"

"The same drill," Amado said. "You crawl back to your position, and I'll go back to mine. Pick them off when they storm the ship. Then we take one of the Explorers."

"Okay, see you on the other side." Berto crawled back toward his manifold.

Josh did a quick peek around the rear of the Explorer. All clear. "Dave, did you bring a shooter with you?"

Dave nodded yes.

Josh said, "Put him up in the crane to limit any movement on the ship. We want them fixed in one spot."

"Roger."

Dave looked back at his team and pointed up. "Jason. Topside in the crane."

Jason nodded yes and scurried to the crane stairs, carrying his M24 sniper rifle—the military and police version of the Remington Model 700. He quickly climbed the stairs and found a perch with a clear view of the deck from the operator's platform.

Josh leaned over to Dave. "We're going to need one more for this adventure, preferably one with a nautical background."

Dave squinted toward his crew, called "Washington," and made a *come here* sign with his hand. A large and heavily muscled black operator pushed away from the fender of the next Explorer and slipped in next to Dave.

"Josh and Elena, this is Ray. Ray, this is Josh and Elena. Ray's a former member of your old fraternity," Dave said.

"Glad to meet you, Ray. What class?" Josh asked.

"Two-eighty-four," Ray said. "What about you?"

"Two-seventy-seven, the first coastie class," Josh said.

"Outstanding. What are you thinking? Sit and scoot on line one?" Ray asked.

"Exactly, then we sweep the main deck fore and aft and call up the troops when we reach amidships." Josh and Ray bumped fists.

"Can you please translate that into plain language, so us lowly Army grunts can understand it?" Elena asked.

"Sorry, we're going to climb the line from the pier to the bow and then clear the main deck of assholes until we reach the gangway, then call up Dave's team," Josh said.

"Now, was that so hard? Let's kick some ass." Elena lifted her Benelli shotgun and started toward the bow of the ship.

CHAPTER 72

Captain Moreno looked up at the sound of gunfire. *The escorts are probably defending their turf. It's a no-win situation. Do nothing, and the cartel will kill you in prison along with your family. Fight back, the police will kill you, but the cartel might spare your family, unless they want to send a message.* Captain Moreno picked up the pistol and looked at the custom grips and the Vickers Elite Battlesight. It was an excellent firearm.

Captain Moreno pulled back the slide and jacked a round into the chamber. *At least this way, the two million dollars in the offshore account will set Isabel and Ana up for life. The cartel won't come looking for a dead man.* He placed the HK to his right temple and prepared to squeeze the trigger.

A series of gunshots rang out. He stopped his finger squeeze. *Maybe it's better if I take a couple of police officers with me.*

Josh grabbed the three-inch poly bow line with his hands, wrapped his legs around the rope, and rapidly pulled himself up the line to the rail of the ship. He peered over the lip—all clear—then hopped over the railing and unslung his Colt M4 from his back. He signaled back to the crew below and took up a cover position with a clear line of sight to the edge of the containers at the curve of the bow.

Dave swung over the railing, tapped Josh on the back, and took up a similar position on the starboard side. Elena came over the rail next and crouched next to Josh, followed by Ray, who tapped Elena on the shoulder and said, "Last man." Ray got behind Dave.

Josh looked at Dave and hand-signaled him to move out. Dave nodded affirmatively and started to creep forward. Josh moved to the edge of the first set of containers, did a quick peek around the corner, and snapped his head back.

Josh keyed his mike. "Shooter is on the deck behind a fuel manifold port side, fifty feet from the gangway entrance. Sierra One, do you have a shot?"

"Negative. Sierra One has no shot."

"Roger. I'm going to start shooting at him. When he flushes, pop him."

"Sierra One. Roger. Good copy."

Josh took three deep calming breaths, slipped around the corner of the container, found the prone green figure in his sights, and fired three shots. The rifle barely moved in his hands as the weapon cycled through the three 5.56mm rounds, and the brass casings ejected and bounced on the deck. No need for the sniper follow-up; all three rounds found their mark, and the target slumped over on his back.

"Target is down. Advancing now." Josh and Elena started edging down the port side.

A loud rifle shot cracked from overhead. "Target is down. Amidships," came the report from Sierra One."

"Roger. Any other movement?" Josh looked up at the Sniper.

"Negative movement. Sierra One is clear."

"Roger, advancing now." Josh and Elena cleared the entire port side of the ship to the gangway. They stopped to check the body of Port Director

Sanchez. He was gone. Elena checked the body of Berto to confirm he was dead. Josh looked left, and he saw Dave and Ray checking Amado. Dave made a cut sign under his chin to indicate Amado was gone. Josh stood on the gangway and waved up the remainder of the tactical team. They rapidly stormed up the gangway.

Dave Tuley walked over to Josh. "What do you want to do now?"

"Have your team sweep and secure the ship. Most of the crew is probably sitting on the mess deck, waiting for the smoke to clear. The first mate and chief engineer may be a problem. No way they didn't know what's going on. Elena and I will head to the cabin."

"Roger. Got it. Stay up on comms in case you need help," Dave said. He motioned to his team, who headed off in pairs. Josh and Elena went to the pilothouse.

Captain Moreno turned his chair to face the cabin door. He held the pistol in both hands and rested it on his lap. The shooting had stopped, which meant they were coming for him. Captain Moreno raised the gun and sighted. *The first face I see is catching a bullet.*

Elena and Josh moved through the pilothouse and up two ladders to the deck below the bridge. A mounted *Cabin* sign with a red arrow pointing to the right was just outside the ladder well. Josh followed the passageway to a door with *Captain Aimon Moreno* stenciled in black letters. Josh paused just outside and pulled out his cell phone and hit the send button. Becka picked up.

"What can I do for you, Josh?"

"Hey, Becka. I need everything you can send me on Aimon Moreno, captain of the containership *Garcia Asombrosa*, and I need it in about five minutes. Focus on wife, kids, and immigration status. Also, contact Customs. Two of their officers are down, and we need someone to take control of the seizure when we find the dope."

"Roger. I'll send you what I can find." Becka clicked off the call.

Elena slipped past Josh and got on the other side of the door. "How do you want to play this?"

Josh looked at the door. "Homeslice is in there with a gun in his lap, so he's either dead, or he's waiting for us to kill him, which means it's currently pointed at the door." Josh pulled an M84 out of his vest. "I think we give him a little Black and White Club wake-up call."

Elena nodded in agreement. Josh passed her the flashbang and counted with his fingers. *One*, *two*—Elena pulled the pin—*three*. Josh cracked the door three inches, five gunshots boomed in the cabin, and five rounds slammed into the door. Elena tossed in the flashbang, and Josh pulled the door closed. They each covered their ears with both hands.

The M84 bounced onto the cabin deck and lit off within two seconds. The magnesium-based pyrotechnic charge ignited, sending a 180-decibel sound wave and eight million candelas flashing through the cabin.

After the detonation, Josh pushed through the cabin door. Captain Moreno thrashed on the deck, holding his head. Josh grabbed the HK VP40 off the carpet, ejected the magazine, and racked the slide to the rear, sending a round bouncing on the deck. Elena went to Captain Moreno, turned him on his stomach, and cuffed his hands behind his back. Josh tossed the gun onto the cabin table and reached down to help Elena haul Captain Moreno to his feet. They threw him into a chair, still shaking his head.

"Hey, are you guys okay?" Dave Tuley asked over the radio.

Josh keyed back. "Yeah, we're fine. We used an M84 on the captain."

"Ouch. I'm sure he enjoyed that. We found most of the crew on the mess deck. We're still looking for the chief engineer. The first mate was with the crew."

"Roger. We're going to talk to the captain; then we gotta find the dope. Customs should be coming back to get their folks and take control of the ship."

"I'll let you know when we find the engineer," Dave said.

Josh keyed his mike twice and sat down opposite Captain Moreno. Elena stood directly behind him.

"So Aimon, I'm going to talk, and you're going to listen. I'm going to call you Aimon since captain is a sign of respect, and you've lost all respect as a dope-smuggling, sex-trafficking asshole." Josh pulled out his phone and scanned through Becka's text.

Aimon stared at him with vacant eyes and a ringing in his ears. His head was down, and his posture broadcast defeat. "I would like a lawyer."

"So, here's the thing, Aimon; the marshal and I are not exactly law enforcement at this time, so I don't give a fuck what you want, but I'm not totally unreasonable. I'll give you two options. You can talk to us, or my partner will shoot you in the forehead, uncuff you, and dump you on the deck. I know you'd prefer the second option since you wanted us to shoot you when we came through your cabin door. But here's the rub, If my partner does shoot you in the head, your wife Ana and your daughter Isabel are not going to live a comfortable life after you're gone." Josh saw a flicker of anger in Aimon's eyes. *Gotcha.*

"Hey, Josh?" Josh keyed his mike. "Yeah, Dave, what's up?"

"We found the engineer. He was under one of the deck plates in the engine room. We cuffed him and dragged his ass to the mess deck. We segregated the first mate and the engineer from the crew. What do you want us to do now?"

"Sit tight. We're negotiating with Aimon now. If you hear a gunshot, the negotiations are over."

"Roger. Out."

"So, Aimon, back to Ana and Isabel. One of my associates tells me Ana is on a green card from Venezuela, which is not exactly a vacation spot right now. Still, if you take option two, some agents of mine are going to make a house call at one-oh-one Cunningham Avenue in Saint Johns, Florida, giving your wife Ana a lift to the airport to catch a charter flight to Caracas tonight. Which brings me to your daughter, Isabel—since you're dead and your wife's digging through the trash in Caracas, your seven-year-old daughter becomes a ward of the state and not just any state. I'm thinking about New York. Maybe the Bronx in New York City. What do you think?"

"Yellow envelope, the top right drawer of my desk. My family is not part of this." Aimon had the look of a scared husband and father.

Elena walked over to the desk, opened the drawer, pulled out a yellow eight-and-a-half-by-eleven-inch envelope, and gave it to Josh. Josh opened the flap, pulled out a picture and a white piece of paper, and spread them on the table.

"I'm guessing the photograph of this pretty girl on the swing is your daughter." Josh tapped the picture with his right index finger.

Aimon nodded his head, yes.

"What are the numbers zero, six, one, zero, two, five and one, zero, two, one, two, seven?" Josh asked.

"They are the container numbers for the shipments," Aimon said.

"Okay, Captain, you get a little respect back since I think the cartel is squeezing you to move the drugs. How does it work?" Josh watched Aimon for any tells of a lie.

"We make regular runs between Veracruz and Tampa. From Tampa to Veracruz, we carry engine parts; on the return trip, we transport engines. About once or twice a month, I receive a yellow envelope at the quarterdeck in Veracruz. It always contains a recent picture of my daughter and a container number. We also add a crewmember who escorts the container to make sure nothing goes wrong. We had two on this trip, one for each box.

"Yeah, I think we met them earlier. They're catching a few rays up on the main deck. Tell me about the girls," Josh said.

Captain Moreno lowered his head and closed his eyes as the tears started to flow. "You must believe me. I had no choice. They would kill my wife and daughter." Aimon shook his head and sniffed a couple of times to regain his composure. "On some return trips, we carry a special container. The escort will tell us when we have a return shipment. Sometimes it's girls; sometimes it's cargo. I think the cargo is money."

"Do you have a return shipment on this trip?" Josh asked.

"Yes, it is supposed to arrive tomorrow morning when we start loading containers around zero nine hundred," Aimon said.

"So, walk me through what happens after you tie up." Josh reached for his phone, selected the camera mode, and pressed record.

"Before we arrive, there's always a decoy ship with a small amount of drugs to occupy Customs. This time, it was the *Empress Express* tied up in front of us. Once we arrive, Inspector Calvin Jackson boards the ship. I meet with him in the cabin, we exchange pleasantries about our daughters, I pass him an envelope with ten thousand dollars cash, he clears our manifest, and we start unloading. I call the designated number and tell the person on the other end of the line that Customs cleared the shipment. I call the number again when we pass the sea buoy headed back to Vera Cruz. When…"

"Ah, shit." Josh stood up.

"It's the truth. I swear, it's the truth," Aimon pleaded.

Josh waved him off. "Is Inspector Jackson, a Customs officer?"

"Yes, of course." Aimon nodded his head.

Josh looked at Elena. "We need to find Inspector Jackson or the other girls are dead."

CHAPTER 73

Inspector Jackson sipped his coffee, comfortably seated in his office checking email. It was mostly bullshit. He turned at the sound of officers running by his door. Rich Roncone stuck his head in.

"Let's go. Gear up. Shooting at Hooker's Point onboard the *Garcia Asombrosa*. We got two officers down, including the port director." Rich banged his hand twice on the door, and he was gone.

Inspector Jackson paused for a moment to think. *What the fuck? What would cause a shootout on a container ship? No way they found the dope. That would require a full inspection. No way that's happening. Must be a stowaway or disgruntled mariner.* He grabbed his vest off the hook on the wall, picked up his keys off the desk, and headed to his car. *One way to find out.*

Josh and Elena escorted Captain Moreno down to the mess deck to join his crew. They stuck him with Lope and the chief engineer. Dave Tuley walked over.

"Find anything?" Dave took a sip of bug juice over ice.

"Yeah." Josh handed Dave the piece of paper with the container numbers on it. "The dope is in these containers."

"No, shit? Just like that? This is good bug juice, by the way."

"Yup, just like that, and I'll pass on the bug juice," Josh said.

"What's bug juice?" Elena asked.

Josh pointed to the drink dispensers on the mess deck. "Sailor talk for any Kool-Aid-type drinks onboard ships. It's usually nasty."

Dave took another sip of his bug juice. "Obviously not a connoisseur of the finer things in life. What do you want to do now?"

"We need to find a Customs inspector named Calvin Jackson before he starts running. Did you call Customs?" Josh asked.

"Yes, I told them we secured the ship and crew, and they had two officers down. Speak of the devil." Dave pointed at two Customs officers walking toward them.

"I'm looking for FBI Special Agent Josh Martin; a couple of your boys topside said he was in charge of this shit show."

"I'm Special Agent Martin, and I'm sorry for your loss." Josh stuck out his hand.

"Assistant Port Director Dan Kim and this is Port Operations Officer Adele Willis." They all shook hands. Kim was Korean with dark black hair, a little shorter than Josh, but thick through the shoulders like a gymnast. Adele's uniform was loose like she'd lost a lot of weight, and her face was shrunken like she was battling an illness. Her gray hair was pulled back into a ponytail.

"I wish we could have met under better circumstances, but unfortunately, I have to be direct. Lives are at stake," Josh said.

"Okay, what've you got?" Dan asked.

"We need to speak to one of your inspectors, Calvin Jackson," Josh said.

"Why do you need to speak to him?" Adele asked. Her hands immediately went to her hips.

Defensive—not the first time Inspector Jackson was on the carpet. Josh pulled his phone out of his pocket, found his camera, and said, "This is a recording of Captain Moreno, who is the gentlemen over there in handcuffs." Josh hit play and pointed at a dejected Captain Moreno seated with his head down. Moreno's voice said, "Once we arrive, Inspector Calvin Jackson boards the ship. I meet with him in the cabin, we exchange pleasantries about our daughters, I pass him an envelope with ten thousand dollars cash, he clears our manifest, and we start unloading."

"Ah, shit." Assistant Port Director Kim ran his hand through his hair. "This day keeps getting better and better. Can I get a copy of that tape?"

"Absolutely," Josh said. "And I'll give you the seizure." Josh held up his paper with the container numbers. "These containers are packed with engines, and each engine has a large quantity of narcotics hidden inside."

"And what do I have to do for such largesse?" Kim asked.

"I get ten minutes with Jackson; you take care of all of this." Josh waved his hand. "And you owe me a favor."

"Done," Kim said.

The two shook hands. Josh gave him the paper with the container numbers and sent him a copy of the tape.

Kim handed the paper to Adele. "You take care of this, and Agent Martin, let's go find the son of a bitch."

Calvin Jackson crossed the railroad tracks into Port Tampa Bay's container yard in his Customs white with blue trim Ford Explorer and stopped just past the first line of containers. He had a clear view of the *Garcia Asombrosa* and a gridlock of government vehicles, private vehicles, work vehicles, and a lot of people standing around, running around, and walking in all types of uniforms and work outfits, representing all kinds of agencies—so, the definition of a cluster fuck.

He parked the SUV and got out, leaving it clear of the congestion, so he had an easy exit if needed. He walked to the end of the pier near the bow, which gave him an unobscured view of the ship. He leaned over the edge of the dock. Four Coast Guardsmen struggled to get a body dressed in a Customs uniform out of the water and into a stokes litter.

Oh man, who's that poor bastard? He walked closer to the gangway to get a better angle. He looked up and saw Assistant Director Kim at the top of the gangway and someone he did not want to meet in a dark alley behind him dressed in tactical gear.

Kim waved. "Inspector Jackson, we need your help with something."

"Yes, sir, what do you need?" Jackson moved to the end of the gangway. *Something's not right. You've got an army of people, and you need my help.*

Kim got to the bottom of the gangway along with the tactical dude who had *FBI* stenciled on his uniform. The FBI guy did not look happy.

Fuck. They know. Jackson turned and ran.

Josh watched him run with Assistant Port Director Kim in pursuit, so he rushed to the Explorer and opened the rear door for Syrin to hop out. "Syrin, come." Josh ran clear of the crowd with Syrin in the heel position. He pointed at the two running figures. "Syrin, bite."

Syrin accelerated. *I hope they trained her to bite the guy running away and not the guy pursuing. That would put a quick end to Dan Kim's favor.* Josh ran after Syrin. Syrin reached her top pursuit speed of thirty miles per hour and was quickly closing the gap on Jackson. An average human running at fifteen miles per hour equates to a six-minute mile. Usain Bolt can run at twenty-eight miles per hour for one hundred yards. Jackson wasn't Usain Bolt, but neither was he running a six-minute mile.

Syrin blew by Kim and slammed into Jackson, latching on to his right arm and driving him onto the cement.

"Ah, motherfucker. Get off me." Jackson tried for his service weapon with his left hand. Syrin kept shaking him and biting down on his arm with 195 pounds of pressure per square inch, dragging him on the concrete.

Kim arrived first and drew his weapon. "Jackson, if your hand reaches for your weapon again, I'm going to shoot you."

"Okay, okay, I give up. Get the dog off me! He's tearing my arm off!" Jackson went still.

Josh ran up behind Assistant Port Director Kim. "She's actually a girl, and she doesn't like dirty cops. Syrin, hold." Syrin stopped shaking Jackson. Josh moved in to remove Jackson's Glock from his holster and stepped back. "Syrin, *lass es*." Syrin let go of Jackson's arm, barked at him a couple of times, and walked over to Josh. Josh grabbed her by the ears and gave her an easy shake. "Good girl. Nothing like a little asshole rundown to get the blood flowing."

"Fuck you," Jackson said from the ground. "I want a lawyer."

The assistant port director moved in, snapped handcuffs on Jackson, and hauled him to his feet. "You're going to need a good lawyer and maybe some protection once the crew finds out you're responsible for Sanchez and Rosa getting shot."

Josh ejected the magazine from Jackson's Glock and put it in one of his vest pockets. He racked the slide to the rear and picked up the ejected round off the ground. "I'm ready for ten minutes with him in my car. It's over by the containers by the end stack."

"Sure thing," Kim said. "Take as long as you want. Shithead isn't going anywhere."

"I want a lawyer and a doctor. I think the fucking dog broke my arm."

CHAPTER 74

Zeus paced the office and kept looking at his phone, willing it to ring. He checked his watch—almost noon. *Damn, Jackson is never this late. Something is fucked up.* He picked up the phone and pressed send. The call went straight to voice mail. *Fuck me.* Zeus walked out of the office area into the warehouse. JB and six other bikers were playing poker around a card table.

"JB?" Zeus walked to the end of the motor coach away from the card players.

"Yeah, Boss." JB kicked back his chair. "Deal me out." He joined Zeus.

"No call yet from the fed, and his phone goes straight to voice mail," Zeus said.

"Oh, man, that's not good. What are we going to do with twenty-nine chicks if this goes south?" JB pulled out a pack of smokes, lit one up, and blew the smoke in the air away from Zeus.

"Take Stinky Pete and head down to the port to see if anything's going on. I'll call the God Squad and see what they want us to do with the busload of liability."

"Got it." JB nodded his head. "Yo, Stinky Pete, we're going to take a ride. Let's go."

JB headed to the exit.

Stinky Pete stood up. "Any of you assholes take any of my chips; I'm going to cut you."

The two bikers next to him slapped him in the head and split his chips. "Cut this bitch, now get the fuck outta here." One of them booted him in the ass on the way to the door. "Bring us back some beer." Stinky Pete gave them the finger as he walked out the door.

Zeus punched in the number for Sari. She picked up on the second ring.

"Tell me it's snowing in Tampa."

"No, still hot and sunny," Zeus replied.

"You're kidding me. What the fuck?" Zeus could hear the anger in her voice.

"No call from the fed, and his phone goes straight to voice mail. He's never been this late before. I sent two guys to take a ride down to the port to see what's going on. What do you want us to do with the girls?" He waited for a response, but none came. "Sari, are you still there?"

"Yes, I'm still here. Not my problem. Possession is nine-tenths of the law. Do not call me again unless the shipment shows up." The call ended.

Zeus looked at the phone. "Fuck me." He walked over to the card game. "Time to earn your pay, boys. He pulled out a wad of hundreds, peeled off three, and tossed them on the table. "I need six five-gallon cans of gas, full, two propane tanks, some road flares, and three sets of king-size bed sheets."

The bikers scooped up the money and headed toward the door.

Zeus turned to look at the motor coach. *I wonder if it will burn.*

Josh opened the passenger door and stuffed Jackson into the seat.

"Hey, easy on the arm. As I said before, I think the dog broke my arm, and I want a lawyer. I'm not saying…"

Josh slammed the door, and Jackson's mouth kept moving.

Josh walked around the front of the Explorer and slipped into the driver's seat. He pulled out a tablet from the edge of the seat and the center console. Dave Tuley got in behind Jackson, and Elena got in behind Josh. Syrin moved over to the shade of a container and lay down.

Josh powered up the tablet, pressed the icon for Becka, and she appeared on the screen. "Hi, Becka. I'm with Elena, Dave, and Mr. Jackson. Did you get the information I needed, and are the guests ready?" Josh asked.

"Yes, on both counts. Mr. Jackson's wife's name is Liza. They've been married twenty-four years. He has two daughters: Jade, who is a junior at Harvard, and Divinity, a freshman at the University of Central Florida. They own their home in Tampa, and they have a summer place on Deer Point Lake. I'm switching to our guests now."

Becka pressed the video button. Two faces filled a split-screen: Mark A. Davenport, commissioner of US Customs and Border Protection on the right, and Vincent Santiago, special assistant to the president, on the left.

"Mr. Jackson, do you know who I am?" Commissioner Davenport asked.

"Yes, Commissioner," Jackson stammered.

"Good. Effective immediately, you are no longer an employee of US Customs and Border Protection. For the sake of you and your family, tell them what they want to know." Commissioner Davenport's screen went dark.

"Mr. Jackson, my name is Vincent Santiago, special assistant to the president. By order of the president, you are a domestic terrorist and sentenced to death. My employees currently in the vehicle with you are authorized to carry out that sentence on you and your family. They are accessories to terrorism." Director Santiago's screen went black.

"Whoa, wait a minute, you can't do that. I want a lawyer. This isn't right." Mr. Jackson thrashed in his seat. "Hey, hey!" He banged his head on the window and yelled to the assistant port director, who looked back at him with a poker face. "Dan, Dan, these fucks are going to kill me."

Dave Tuley racked the slide on his silenced Glock 22. "Shut the fuck up, or I'm going to put a bullet in your back."

"This isn't right." Jackson started to break down. "Please. This is America. I have rights."

Josh waved to Assistant Port Director Kim, who was on the phone, through the window. Kim was nodding his head up and down. He got off his call and gave Josh the thumbs-up. Josh rolled down the window. "Syrin, come." Elena opened the back door, and Syrin hopped over her and landed between Elena and Dave. She gave Dave a lick.

"Who's a good girl? I hear you ran down the terrorist in the front seat. We're going to go pay his wife a visit."

Josh started the Explorer, put it in drive, and pulled past the gantry crane.

JB and Stinky Pete accelerated down Business Route 41 into Port Tampa Bay. They both had Port Tampa Bay identification badges as temporary stevedores. They would drive new cars off the car carriers into the port for shipment to dealerships throughout the Southeast. It was easy money, and they got to drive new vehicles. Plus, sometimes the cars would disappear from the lot when a club member needed a new ride.

At the point where Business Route 41 became South Twenty-Second Street, they took a left turn into the Crescent Causeway parking lot. New cars filled the north half of the lot; the south end was empty. They drove out to the Ro-Ro berth and parked the bikes.

JB kicked his stand down, eased the bike onto the support, and stepped off. He stripped off his helmet and gloves to set them onto the seat. He opened a rear luggage bin and pulled out a pair of Celestron 71454 Echelon 20x70 black binoculars. Stinky Pete parked his bike and followed JB down to the south end of the pier. They had a clear view of Hooker's Point and the *Garcia Asombrosa*.

JB took the endcaps off the binoculars and focused on the ship. A Coast Guard cutter with a flashing blue light filled his field of vision. Another smaller Coast Guard boat was off to the left, near the stern of the *Garcia Asombrosa* and the berth.

"Fuck me. Not good." JB handed the binoculars to Stinky Pete, who took in the scene.

"The gantry crane's not operating. They're not unloading," Stinky Pete said.

"I gotta call Zeus." JB pulled out his phone and pressed the contact button for Zeus.

"Yo, my brothers, what's the good word with our cargo?" Zeus asked.

"Not good, Prez. Coast Guard is on scene, and the cranes aren't moving. No containers are getting unloaded."

"Maybe there was an accident. Any way you guys can get closer?"

"Not without attracting attention. Our port badges are only good for access to the Ro-Ro berth and parking lot. What do you want us to do?"

"Head back here. We got some cleanup to do, and it's not going to be pretty."

"Roger. We're headed back now."

"What did he say?" Stinky Pete asked.

"He wants us back at the warehouse for cleanup. Let's go." JB headed back toward the bikes.

"Do you think he'll let us party with the girls?" Stinky Pete started breathing hard just thinking about it. "I really like the blonde chick with the pretty mouth."

"Don't get too attached." JB made a finger gun. He pointed it at his head and pulled the trigger.

"Once Josh made it past the containers, he pressed the navigation button on the steering wheel. "Navigation, address, nine-one-eight West Peninsular Street, Tampa, Florida." He pressed the start button on the screen.

"Come on, man, that's my home address. You can't do this. My family's not involved in this. This isn't right." Jackson squirmed in his seat. "What do I need to do to make this right?"

Josh stopped the car. "Where do they take the containers?"

"I don't know. I just clear the shipment, and I make a phone call when the containers depart the port," Jackson pleaded. "You gotta believe me."

"I don't have to do shit," Josh said. "Who's your contact?"

"I don't know. I've never met him. Street name is Zeus."

"What number do you call?" Josh looked back at Elena.

Jackson gave him the number, then slumped back in his seat.

"If you were doing this operation, what would you do?" Josh asked.

Jackson thought for a moment. "I'd use one of the transshipment facilities close to the port to minimize exposure. They could break down the shipment in a warehouse without anyone watching them and move the product in a new method of transport."

"How many are there?" Elena asked.

"Around six, with the facilities to unload and repackage car engines." Jackson looked back at Elena.

Elena pulled out her phone and opened the notes app. "What are their names?"

Jackson lowered his head to think. "JJ Taylor Distributing, Eagle Transport, Port Consolidated, Angels Transport Logistics, Dillion Transport…"

"Wait, back it up," Josh said. "Angels Transport Logistics?"

"Yes," Jackson said. "They're run by some church organization—plenty of money."

"That's gotta be it," Elena said.

"Dave, call your boys." Josh pulled out his phone and pressed a number for Assistant Port Director Kim. "Dan, yeah, it's Josh. You can come pick up your inspector. He confessed like a sailor to his wife after a port call in Thailand." Josh clicked off the call.

"Wait, this was all a setup?" Jackson asked with a surprised look on his face.

"No. If you didn't tell us what we wanted to know, I would have shot you in the head," Dave said from the back seat.

CHAPTER 75

Zeus unscrewed the caps on the twin fuel tanks for the motor coach. They each held 125 gallons of diesel fuel. Diesel fuel doesn't burn as quickly as gas, but in its vapor form, it will catch fire and explode, especially when you add oxygen and a road flare, which burns at 2,650 degrees Fahrenheit.

Zeus looked up at the sound of Harleys rolling in. The garage door started to go up, and his gas can brigade rode in.

"Where's all the stuff?" Zeus asked.

The boys parked their bikes and stepped off. "Paulie's got it in the van." They headed to help Paulie offload.

"Put everything in the corner. I want it out of sight before we load the girls," Zeus said.

A biker named Curly hung back. He was bald with a gut pushing over his turquoise belt buckle. "Are you sure you want to do this? We could just ride out of here. No way those girls are going to make us."

Zeus leaned down to Curly's face. "Do you want to live constantly looking over your shoulder, waiting for the knock on the door from the cops? Kidnapping is twenty years federal time. Add on sex trafficking, and you will never see the outside of a jail cell. Make it a trifecta of drug smuggling, and they will throw away the key. Not to mention, the God Squad may just show up to take care of loose ends. Now, quit bitching, or you can take a seat on the bus," Zeus said with a flex of his chest, arms, and shoulders.

"No, Boss, I'm good." Curly quick-stepped over to the group stacking the gas cans in the corner. They ripped open a package of bedsheets, pulled out a top sheet, and draped it over the gas cans, propane tanks, and flares.

Zeus turned at the sound of more Harleys. JB and Stinky Pete rolled in, kicked down their stands, set the bikes, stepped away, and pulled off their helmets and gloves.

"I think they got the load," JB said. Stinky Pete nodded his head in agreement. "What are we going to do about the girls?"

Zeus walked to the stack of gas cans and pulled off the top sheet. "Bonfire."

"Becka, please send building schematics on Angels Transport Logistics to me, Elena, and Dave. Their address is six-oh-three-one Madison Avenue, Tampa, Florida." Through the windshield, Josh saw three Explorers headed in his direction, one with blue and white US Customs markings. "Hey, Becka, I gotta go. Thanks for the help."

Josh clicked off the call and slid out of the SUV, followed by Elena and Dave. Dave opened the front passenger door and pulled out Jackson.

The Customs vehicle pulled to a stop, and two large Customs officers in uniform piled out. They grabbed Jackson and shoved him toward the rear passenger seat without opening the door. "Oh, my bad," exclaimed Officer Janzen as Jackson banged off the door and fell to the ground. "I thought Officer Hernandez opened the door."

Officer Hernandez opened the door, and Officer Janzen picked Jackson off the ground to throw him into the back seat. Jackson's head bounced off a headrest, and he landed on the floor. Officer Janzen followed Jackson into the back and kicked him on the ass. "Move the fuck over." Hernandez shut the door and walked over to Josh.

"Thanks for your help in rooting out this *pendejo*." Officer Hernadez jerked his thumb at Jackson.

"No problem. Glad we could help," Josh said. Josh shook his hand, and Hernandez climbed into the Explorer, then the SUV headed back toward the *Garcia Asombrosa*.

"Think he's going to make it to federal lockup?" Dave asked.

"Maybe fifty-fifty," Elena said. "If it was one of ours, no chance." She fist-bumped Dave.

The other two Explorers pulled into the spot vacated by the Customs vehicle, and Dave's eight tactical operators piled out.

"Gentlemen, welcome to the party, and thanks for coming out." Josh reached into the Explorer and pulled out his tablet. Scrolling through his texts, he found the one from Becka with the schematics, opened the file, and put the tablet on the hood of the Explorer. Dave and Elena did the same thing. "This is our target: a logistics warehouse—actually two warehouses—called Angels Transport Logistics. We're looking for members of the Lightning Strikes Motorcycle Club. This is the head scumbag." A picture of Zeus appeared on the screen.

"They're responsible for the death of two DEA agents, and we suspect they are holding girls for sex trafficking, so the gloves are off," Elena said.

"How do you want to play this?" Dave asked.

"We put a shooter at each corner of the two buildings, so we have three-hundred-sixty-degree coverage of anyone coming or going." Josh pointed to the corner of each building. "Put Jason here on the end between the buildings." Josh looked at Jason. "Try to get on the roof of either building to increase your shooting arc."

"Roger, Boss," Jason said.

Josh turned to Dave. "You, Me, Elena, and Syrin will do recon in one of the Explorers. If we see any possibilities, Syrin will find the warm bodies. Any questions, problems?"

"What are the rules of engagement?" Ray Washington asked.

"Weapons-free. Just remember, we may have an unknown number of civilian females in play." Josh scanned the faces of the tac team. "Any more questions?" They all shook their heads no. "All right, boys. Be safe. Let's go." Josh smacked the hood of the SUV twice.

"All right, ladies, let's go." Zeus held the office door open for the line of girls, who filed past with their heads down. "The journey is just about over. Get on the bus." The bikers lined the route to make sure everyone got on the bus. JB and Stinky Pete escorted each girl to their place on the bus and zip-tied them to their seats.

Stinky Pete blinked his eyes twice when the blonde girl with the pretty mouth stepped on the bus. Her head was down with her arms wrapped tightly around her chest. Stinky Pete touched her elbow and guided her to a seat in the middle of the coach on the aisle so she wouldn't see what was coming. *What a waste.*

"Put your hands on the armrest," Stinky Pete said. "I won't pull it too tight."

The blonde girl put her hands on the armrest, and Stinky Pete zipped them in place. He kept his head down; he couldn't look at her face. It would haunt his dreams forever. *This is not right.*

When all the girls were in place, JB and Stinky Pete stepped off the bus, and Zeus locked the doors. The tinted windows would prevent the girls from seeing anything outside of the bus. Zeus walked over to the pile of gas cans and ripped off the sheet. He slipped a folded Buck knife out of his pocket and snapped open the four-inch blade. He cut the sheet into strips, unscrewed the spouts off five gas cans, and stuffed each can opening with a piece of cloth. He picked up the sixth can and poured gas on each piece of sheet, which created five big Molotov cocktails.

"Put two cans behind the rear axle, two in the middle, and one behind the front axle. Spread the remaining sheets under the bus." The bikers opened the remaining packages and spread the sheets under the bus, and placed the cans. Zeus picked up two road flares, unscrewed the tops, wrapped each flare in a cloth strip, and walked over to the coach diesel tanks. He stuffed a flare into each tank opening and poured gas over them. He sloshed the rest of the gas on the sheets under the bus and tossed the empty can on top.

He then put a propane tank under each diesel tank, ripped off the plastic cover, and turned the valve fully open. Propane gas started to vent under the bus.

"All right, Strikers, let's get ready to ride." Zeus unscrewed the top of a flare.

CHAPTER 76

"Six, this is Sierra One. I'm on the roof of the southern building. All units are in place. I have three-sixty coverage. The only vehicle is a white van parked in front of the second loading dock on the north building. How copy? Over."

"Good copy, Sierra One. Can you get a plate number off the van?" Josh looked at Elena. "No way it's the same van; they can't be that stupid. Look up the tag."

"Wait a sec," came Sierra One's reply.

Elena checked Becka's last report on the Angels, Zeus, and the van. "Florida tag: Foxtrot, Zero, Seven, Six, Tango, X-ray."

"Six, this is Sierra One. Florida plate: Foxtrot, Zero, Seven, Six, Tango, X-ray."

"Roger, Sierra One, good copy. Break. All units, the van is registered to the motorcycle club. Tangos are on site. Stand by; we're rolling." Josh put the Explorer in drive and turned between the two buildings. The van was nosed in near the loading dock overhead door on the right. Josh pulled the Explorer behind the van, blocking its exit, and shifted into park. He left the engine running.

"One, this is six. Move up to our position," Josh said.

"Roger. Moving now." Ray Washington moved south from his position on the corner.

Josh slipped out of the SUV, pulled his M4 out of the back, and met Ray behind the white van. Elena and Dave joined them. Dave cradled his M4 under his left armpit, and Elena carried the Benelli. Josh looked over at the overhead door and a white entry door to the left of the truck entrance.

"What do you think?" Josh asked.

"Two options," Dave said. "We can ram the overhead door with the Explorer or breach the entry door and toss in some flashbangs."

"I think we breach the door. For all we know, the girls are sitting in front of the overhead door." Josh looked at Elena. "Do you have any breaching rounds?"

"Yeah, let me configure the shotgun." Elena walked back to the Explorer and laid the Benelli M1014 automatic shotgun on the rear seat, then ejected eight rounds. She looked back at the entry door—three hinges. Elena pulled three M1030 breaching rounds out of her vest. The rounds were twelve-gauge, two and three-quarter-inch shells with a forty-gram projectile made of powdered steel, bound with wax. She followed the breaching rounds with five rounds of Winchester PDX1 rifled slug and three buck pellet ammunition. She lifted the shotgun off the back seat and walked back to the end of the van.

"Ready to rock," Elena said.

Nine of the eleven bikers walked over to their bikes, grabbed their helmets off the handlebars, straddled their bikes, turned their switches to ignition, and pressed the run button near the throttle. Donovan headed to the door to drive the white van.

Stinky Pete paused, turned, and walked toward Zeus. "Zeus, man, this is bullshit. There has to be a better way. Let's just ride away. The girls won't remember shit, or we can threaten them."

In one smooth motion, Zeus pulled a Glock 17 from a side holster, pointed it at Stinky Pete, and pulled the trigger. The 9mm round caught Stinky Pete flush in the forehead, snapped his head back, and exited out the back of his skull, sending bone, brain, and blood spraying. Stinky Pete dropped to the floor.

"Does anyone else have an objection?" Zeus asked. "Curly?" Curly shook his head no. "All right, start your engines. We'll rendezvous back at the clubhouse." The Harleys roared to life, and exhaust filled the warehouse. Zeus walked over, pressed the green up button. The overhead door started to rise, and Donovan opened the entry door.

Elena focused on the top hinge, started to squeeze the trigger, and froze at the sound of gunfire on the other side of the door. She looked back at Josh.

"Hold." Josh turned to Ray and Dave. "What do you think?" Their reply was drowned out by the sound of nine Harleys rumbling to life. The overhead door started to rise, and the entry door opened in their face.

Elena slammed the butt of the shotgun into the face of the surprised biker, driving him back into the building and flat on his ass. She turned her head and covered her nose at the overpowering smell of gasoline pouring out of the open door, driving them back along the sidewall. She kicked the door, and it snapped shut. Nine Harleys flooded out of the overhead door; the roar of their engines echoed off the buildings. Several bikers pulled pistols and started firing in their direction.

Josh ducked at the sound of bullets whining past his head. He switched to full auto and squeezed the trigger. The M4 bucked in his hands, trying to climb his shoulder with the recoil. He kept the barrel centered on the mass of motorcycles and unleashed an entire clip into the side of the exodus, sending four bikes and riders flaying on the ground. The other five bikers roared off, firing back in their direction. The perimeter shooters quickly cut them down with five rapid shots. The bikes dropped and careened down the road, with dead bikers flopping on the ground.

Josh caught movement on the left. He turned his head and saw Zeus pointing a gun at them from the far corner of the overhead door. "Gun!" Josh reached out and grabbed Elena's TAC vest and dropped to the ground, pulling Elena with him at the precise moment Zeus pulled the trigger. The round burned a crease across Josh's left shoulder, and he winced at the pain.

Zeus squeezed off six more shots booming them from the doorway. Two rounds missed high, where Josh was just standing. Dave Tuley screamed, "I'm hit!" as two rounds smacked his vest with the sound of a hammer hitting steel, driving him to the ground. Ray Washington cartwheeled backward toward the SUV, struck by an unseen force.

Zeus broke right, running into the building. Josh gained his feet, pulled his Glock 22, and sprinted for the door. Josh rounded the corner to see Zeus throw a flaming stick under a bus. The undercarriage of the motor coach erupted into a sheet of flame. Josh stopped as recognition flooded his brain. *Bomb.* He turned and ran toward Elena.

"Bomb. Run, and don't stop." Josh ran to a thrashing Dave Tuley, grabbed his vest, flipped him on his shoulder in a fireman's carry, and ran for the far building. Elena darted ahead of them as the thunderous blast of heat and flame shot out of the open overhead door and shattered every window in both buildings. The concussion wave plowed through them, knocking them to the ground—most of the overpressure dissipated up and out.

Zeus did a double-take when the garage door went up, and the two Feds from the club were standing there with two other operators in tactical uniforms and long guns. He pulled his Glock 17 and tried to get a clear shot between the roaring parade of motorcycles and choking exhaust fumes. The boys pulled their weapons and fired poorly aimed shots at the feds, trying to drive and shoot at the same time. One of the feds fired a full-auto burst into the mass of riders sending four sprawling on the ground.

"Fuck," Zeus squinted his eyes in the fumes and tried to focus on the fed who'd just fired into the motorcycles. He squeezed the trigger, just as the cop yelled something, grabbed one of the operators, and fell to the ground. The pistol bucked in his hand. He squeezed off six more shots in the general vicinity of the feds and ran toward the front of the motor coach. He paused, lit the flare, and tossed it under the bus, which instantly ignited the fumes and gas in a whoosh of flame, then ran for the exit across the warehouse, expecting a bullet in the back or the flaming hand of God to strike him down.

The vapors in the five gas cans exploded at nearly the same time. The force of the blast lifted the coach off the ground and ignited both diesel and propane tanks, which exploded in a giant fireball, vaporizing the front half of the bus and sending out a massive overpressure wave. The wave instantly killed the girls as the tiny air sacs in their lungs burst from the pressure just before the flames incinerated them. The onslaught expanded, overtaking the fleeing Zeus and bursting his eardrums, lungs, and bowels. His last thought on earth: *I just shit my pants.*

Josh stood up and shook his head to clear the ringing in his ears. Dave Tuley was rolling on the ground with two rounds impacted in his vest.

"Get…get the vest off me…can't breathe," Dave said.

Josh bent down, pulled the Velcro straps on the sides of his vest, removed it over his head, then tossed it on the ground.

"Thank you. Much better, but my ribs are killing me. What about Ray?" Dave asked.

Josh shook his head no. "He wasn't moving after the initial folly of rounds, and no way he survived the overpressure." The smell of smoke filled the air. Josh looked at the warehouse, which was now a fully involved structure fire. "We need to get out of here. Can you move?"

"I think so," Dave said.

Josh and Elena got under each arm and pulled Dave to his feet. Elena steadied him, and Josh opened the rear door of the Explorer. Dave slid into the back seat, and Josh pushed the door closed. Elena hustled around to the passenger seat. Josh climbed in the front, started the engine, and pulled the SUV clear of the burning building to a spot abreast the top of the southern building just as Jason hit the bottom rung of the roof access ladder. Jason trotted over. Josh rolled down his window, and Jason leaned in.

"No one exited the building, so if anyone was inside, they didn't make it," Jason said.

"Roger. I'm going to take Dave to the ER at Tampa General Hospital. Did you call for fire and police?"

"Yes, sir. I also called for a clean up and containment crew. They're on the way. What about Ray?"

"Didn't make it, brother, sorry," Josh said.

"Damn." Jason smacked the window track with his fist and lowered his head. He rubbed his eyes and looked up. "Okay, we've got this. Take Dave to the hospital. I'll back brief you on what they find inside."

"Roger." Josh powered up the window and headed for the exit.

CHAPTER 77

Sari opened the refrigerator in the break room to pull out a can of Diet Pepsi, popped the top, and took a long swig. She glanced at the TV with a picture of a warehouse on fire with the caption: *Explosion and shoot out at Tampa logistics center, an unknown number of casualties.*

"Fuck me." Sari ran back to her office, picked up her cell phone, scrolled through her contacts, found the one she wanted, and pressed the green phone button. Chris Del Torro picked up.

"It's not good," Chris said.

"How bad?" Sari slumped into her chair.

"Customs and Coast Guard got the load. There was a shootout on the ship. Two Customs officers, including the port director, are down along with the two Colombian escorts. Some DHS tactical team showed. No one knows where they came from."

"Let me guess; they also had an FBI agent, a U.S. Marshal, and a dog along for the ride."

"Yes, how'd you know?"

"Lucky guess. What about the girls and the warehouse?" Sari rocked in her chair, thinking about the next move.

"The same TAC team hit the warehouse. Your boys blew up the warehouse and the girls. The TAC team took care of the bikers, no survivors. I'm taking off. The feds got Calvin Jackson; they can't be too far behind me."

"Roger. Good luck." Sari clicked off the call and leaned back in her chair. She started to playback the loose ends in her mind. *Zeus and the bikers are gone. Drug shipment is gone, along with the load of girls. Fraternity guys are gone. Dibble brothers are gone. Calvin Jackson and Chris Del Toro are still in play, but there's no way to tie them to the Church.*

That only left two: a girl in the ICU at Holmes Regional, and two mother fucking feds and a fucking dog. She slammed the Pepsi can in the trash.

Josh pulled up to the emergency entrance patient drop-off for Tampa General Hospital and put the SUV in park. A nurse, two orderlies, and an ER doctor quickly raced over to help Dave get out of the Explorer and onto a gurney, then they whisked him away inside. Two men in dark-blue suits walked over when the medical entourage departed. Josh felt two zaps on his wrist.

"Skip Eastman, and this is my partner, John Perreault." Everyone shook hands. "Director Santiago sends his greetings. He would like you to give him a call when you get a chance. Everything's under control at the port and the warehouse, and we'll look after Dave Tuley. Time to focus on some payback for Ray."

"Roger that. Thanks for your help, guys. See you around." Josh waved and hopped back in the SUV.

"Who was that?" Elena asked.

"Club members." Josh put the truck in drive and pulled away.

"Well, that explains the reception. What are we going to do now?"

Josh looked over at Elena. "We're going to church."

Sari spotted Bishop Avery barricaded behind stacks of books at her conference table in the office reception area. She pulled one copy of God's Choice at a time from a box with open flaps, signed it, laid it like a brick in a wall on the table, and quickly reached for another. Julius carried them to Eleanor, who packaged and shipped them to the faithful worldwide for $99.99. Bill Gates wouldn't bend over to pick up a hundred-dollar bill; Stephanie Avery wouldn't relinquish her autograph for two pennies less than that. Richard Wagner's *Die Walküre* played in the background, and a glass of red wine sat on the edge of the table: support to get through the tedium of signing.

"How many do you have left?" Sari took a seat next to the bishop. They wore matching polo shirts and tennis shorts. The bishop's gold cross shimmered on her chest against the white polo fabric above her baby blue shorts. A matching blue ribbon tied her hair back in a ponytail.

"Too many." Bishop Avery leaned back in her chair. "I try to do one hundred a day." She took a sip of wine. "Would you like a glass?"

"Definitely," Sari said.

"What kind do you want?" Bishop Avery put the glass back on the table and added another book to the finished stack. "This is a Rothschild twenty-fifteen." She tapped the glass.

"That's fine, thank you."

"Jean-Paul? A glass of wine for Sari. The same one I'm drinking," Bishop Avery said.

"Yes, Bishop," came the reply from the overhead speaker.

Bishop Avery put her book-signing pen down and turned to Sari. "So, not a good day for the home team. What's your assessment?"

Sari tapped her hands on the table and looked at Bishop Avery. "Depends on what you want to do in the future."

Bishop Avery thought for a moment. "I want to go legit. We need to separate ourselves from anything overtly illegal for probably the next ten years—no drugs, girls, or guns. We get my sister elected president of the United States for two terms, and then we shift to a more acceptable line of work like kickbacks, pay for access, government contracts, and political favors."

Sari turned her head at the sign of movement. Jean-Paul shuffled across the marble floor and placed a glass of wine in front of Sari.

"Anything else, madam?" Jean-Paul asked.

"No, thanks, Jean-Paul. This is great," Sari said.

"Can I get you anything, Bishop?" Jean-Paul asked.

"No, thank you, Jean-Paul. What's for dinner?" Bishop Avery and Sari each took another sip of wine.

"Salmon with a honey glaze, wild rice, fresh green beans, and homemade apple pie for dessert. I'll leave you two to your wine." Jean-Paul shuffled back to the kitchen.

Sari took another sip of wine and set the glass down. "I ran through the variables. We only have two outstanding issues we need to clean up, and they aren't easy.

"They never are," Bishop Avery said. "One has to be Senator Alonzo's daughter, Bri. What's the other one?"

"Two feds and a dog," Sari said. "They show up everywhere, and this time with a tactical team of eight. I don't think they're going away, especially after the warehouse with the girls."

"So, what's your plan?" Bishop Avery picked up her pen and tapped it on a book.

"I think the Valkyrie flies again—the only way to eliminate the girl, and Michael's going to clean our favorite feds' room." Sari stood up.

"Sounds like a plan; go forth and do God's bidding." Bishop Avery signed a book with a flourish. "I need to make another ten-k."

Sari started across the floor. *God's bidding. That's a good one. I don't think God would approve of killing a couple of hundred hospital patients.*

CHAPTER 78

Josh pulled the SUV into an empty slot in the emergency room patient parking lot and pressed the phone button. "Call El Jefe."

"Calling El Jefe" came over the Explorer's speakers, and the phone rang.

Director Santiago picked up immediately. "Where are you?"

"We're in the parking lot of Tampa General Hospital. We just dropped off Dave Tuley. I'm here with Syrin and Elena. You're on speaker," Josh said.

"Hi, Elena," Vince said. "How's Dave?"

"Hi, Director. Dave took two to the vest, but he'll be okay. I think he may have a couple of broken ribs and a world-class bruise," Elena said.

"That's good news," Vince said. "On the bad news side, they found a lot of remains in the ashes of the bus."

"Fuck no. The girls." Josh lowered his head. "Zeus lit it off before we could gain entry."

"Roger, we also found three dead bikers inside. Two burned to a crisp by the entry doors, and one intact about halfway across the warehouse floor with blood coming out of his ears, but no other sign of trauma. Probably died from overpressure. Facial recognition and fingerprints identify him as Adrian Stanhope, aka Zeus."

"Good riddance, but it does eliminate a tie to the church. How's Bri doing?" Josh asked.

"No change. Still in a coma and unresponsive. It doesn't look good, which brings me to the reason for my call. You've completed your assigned mission, located Bri, and eliminated the motorcycle group responsible for her abduction," Vince said.

"Vince, I can't speak for Elena, but we haven't completed our mission. The church of bullshit is behind everything. We just need some time to tie them to everything and then take out the trash. We also need to find out who gassed the fraternity house and eliminated the ones in the UCF jail cells. The campus police computer geek didn't punch holes in those kids' eyes. The shooter's still out there, and it wasn't one of the bikers. I saw their crappy shooting up close."

"Roger. Elena, what's your assessment?" Vince asked.

"I agree with Josh; we're only getting started. Those girls on the bus deserve some justice."

"Okay, just what I needed to hear. I agree with both of you, but we'll have to convince the executive committee. Bear in mind, the Church of Illuminology is the biggest contributor to the president's reelection campaign. I'm headed to a meeting when I get off this call. Josh, the president would like to meet with you. I have a G five-fifty waiting for you at MacDill. Elena, the Patrick Pave Hawk is also on deck at MacDill. It will take you and Syrin back to Melbourne. Your tactical team just checked into your hotel. You can bring them up to speed. Any questions?"

"No, sir," Josh and Elena replied.

"Roger. Godspeed." Vince clicked off the call.

Sari pushed into the Angels' break room. "What's up, bitches?" Gabi, Rafi, and Michael were seated around a conference room with a set of building plans spread out on the table. An ice bucket from the Tropical Suites Hotel anchored one side, and a tan box with tiny stainless steel fans secured the other end. They were drinking Heinekens and wearing T-shirts with workout shorts. They felt the plush white carpet with the toes of their bare feet.

"Waiting on your slow ass," Michael said. "You missed a good workout. Where've you been, dressed like you're playing a set with Serena Williams? There's cold beer in the fridge, courtesy of Gabi."

"You're welcome." Gabi clinked bottles with Michael.

"I was up talking to the bishop about the future." Sari walked over to the fridge, opened the door, pulled out a Heineken, and snapped the top off with a Church of Illuminology bottle opener hanging by a blue lanyard on the door. The breakroom consisted of a full kitchen, a pool table, a foosball table, four brown leather chairs facing a ninety-eight-inch 8K TV mounted on the wall, and the oak conference table.

"So, what's the verdict?" Rafi asked.

"We're going legit—not totally legit, but moving to white-collar stuff. No more girls, guns, or drugs." Sari walked over to the table and took a seat.

"Why the change?" Gabi asked.

Sari took a drink of beer. "Plan is to get big sister elected president of the United States. Drug smuggling, sex trafficking, and arms dealing would not look good in a campaign ad. So, how are we coming with plan B?"

Rafi spread her hand across the blueprint of the Holmes Regional Medical Center. At six feet and two hundred pounds, the collegiate powerlifter dwarfed her fellow angels. She was also the brains of the group, with advanced degrees in electrical engineering and cybersecurity. "Our intake vents are right here." Rafi pointed to four large AC fan intakes on the roof of the medical center. “Our target is this fan, closest to the building near the Helo pad. It feeds the ICU.” Rafi reached for the tan box with the fans on the end of the table and placed it in front of her.

“That thing is empty, I hope,” Sari said.

“Yes, I cleaned and flushed it after we deployed it on the fraternity. They required a five-minute burn for the cyanide gas; we’re going to need a ten-minute burn for the hospital because of the size of the area. Valkyrie only has a run time of fifteen minutes with a full load, so we need to be close for launch and recovery.”

Rafi pulled a Google Earth photo from under the hospital blueprint. “I circled the three possible launch locations: Fee Avenue Park, the Melbourne Military Park next to Our Lady of Lourdes school, and the Melbourne City Cemetery. I recommend we use the cemetery.” She tapped her finger on a triangular patch of green grass dotted with white stones. “Industrial buildings surround the site, so we should have no one in the area at zero two hundred. We can use the back of a pickup truck for launch and recovery, drive in and out in under twenty minutes. The chance of detection is almost zero.”

“How are you going to configure the drone?” Sari asked.

Rafi turned around and picked up a Valkyrie Wing S1000+ drone, which could carry up to a nine-point-five-kilogram payload for fifteen minutes. The drone’s modified Zenmuse gimbal carried the cyanide gas generator. She also picked up a plastic drone housing and set them both on the table.

“I’m going to paint Holmes Regional Medical Center markings on the drone housing along with Advent Health North. On the cyanide gas generator, I’ll put drug container delivery markings. Anything goes wrong; we land the drone on the helo pad and split. By the time anyone figures out something’s off, we’re gone.”

“Sounds like a good plan.” Sari took a sip of beer. “How long to get everything ready?”

"I should be ready for a test run by tomorrow night." Rafi sat back in her chair.

"Great, what about Michael's hotel warming gift for our favorite law enforcement officers?" Sari asked.

CHAPTER 79

The light flashed on Vince Santiago's secure phone, and the voice of Lisa, his executive assistant, came through the speaker. "Executive committee meeting in ten minutes."

"Thanks, Lisa." Vince stood up, grabbed his dark-gray suit coat off the hook, smoothed his red power tie, and buttoned the jacket. He walked out of his office and over to the elevator doors with "Gates of Hell" written in bold red letters over a scene of hell, complete with the devil, fires, and lost souls. The initials JLF were in the lower right corner of the mural for James L. Flattery, Major, USAF. Major Flattery worked for Presidential Contingency Programs, and he was a talented painter. Vince always laughed at the door. Military folks in all branches of service had unique senses of humor.

Vince put his palm on a pad with the outline of a hand. A blue light scanned his prints like a copier scanning a document. The elevator doors opened, and he stepped in. Then the doors closed. A computer voice from a speaker in the ceiling said, "*Please state your name.*"

"Vincent Santiago," Vince said.

"*Identity confirmed,*" said the computer voice, and the elevator started to descend. It was a little disconcerting since he couldn't watch the floors tick off. There was just a sense of falling. The elevator stopped, the doors opened, and Vince walked into the Black and White Club secure conference room. Katherine Rich, Speaker of the House, and Carlo Virgilio, Chief Justice of the Supreme Court, were already seated at the conference table.

"Good afternoon, Vince," Speaker Rich said. Justice Virgilio raised his Diet Pepsi can in a salute. He wore black pants and a black T-shirt with *The Judge* in white block letters. Rich was in a white open-collar shirt with gray pants. Her matching jacket hung off the back of her chair. They were both drinking Diet Pepsi.

"Madam Speaker, Chief Justice, good afternoon." Vince walked in and took a seat next to the chief justice.

The judge put his right hand on Vince's arm. "Vince, do you think we can skip the song and dance? I have no desire to see the burnt remains of twenty-nine girls. Your last presentation was bad enough. I had nightmares for a week. Let Josh keep doing what Josh is doing until all the bastards responsible for these atrocities are no longer walking the earth. I'm not interested in any jail time, negotiations, or plea bargains. What do you think, Katherine?"

"I agree one hundred percent," Katherine said. "I bet Donna feels the same way. What happened to her daughter is beyond tragic and should not happen in America."

"She does feel the same way," Vince said. "She's not making the meeting to remain in Florida with her daughter. Per the club by-laws, I'm acting as her proxy. I vote no change."

"Splendid, I'll break the news to the president when he arrives," Carlo said.

As if on cue, the elevator dinged, and President Brian C. Byrne strode through the doors with Vice President Amelia Evelina. The president set the leather case with the nuclear launch codes near the elevator so as not to forget it. The military aides would torment him endlessly if he left the football behind. Both the president and vice president wore dark-blue suits with matching blue ties.

"So, I see the party has already started," President Byrne said. He walked over to the table and pulled out the chair next to Vince for the vice president.

"Thank you, Mr. President," Vice President Evelina said as she sat down. "Good to see you, Vince. We need to get together on better occasions than these meetings."

The president took the seat next to his vice president. "So, by the look on your faces, it's been decided."

"Yes, Mr. President," Carlo Virgilio said. "No change. I asked Vince to spare us the pictures of dead girls."

"Amen to that," Vice President Evelina said.

"Okay, I'm good with that. We let Josh keep running this to ground," the president said. "In the spirit of full transparency, I asked Josh to fly to DC to meet with me to discuss the case. I've known Bishop Avery for over twenty years; I can't believe her church is involved in any of this. I would like to meet with Josh to get his first-hand evaluation of these tragic events. Anyone is welcome to attend the meeting." The President scanned the faces around the table. "Vince, when are you on the schedule?"

"Ten hundred in the Oval Office, Mr. President," Vince said.

"Perfect, thank you. So, are we in agreement? Josh keeps operating under the original assignment?" the president asked. Everyone nodded, yes. "Vince, are you speaking for Senator Alonzo?"

"Yes, Mr. President," Vince said.

"Okay, motion carries. The meeting is at ten hundred in the Oval Office tomorrow if you want to attend. Meeting adjourned." The president smacked his hand on the table and stood up.

Josh climbed the stairs of the Air Force Gulfstream G550 aircraft, waved goodbye to Syrin and Elena from the top step, smacked the side of the plane twice for good luck, and stepped inside the executive comfort of the cabin. The G550 seated nineteen and could sleep eight, so plenty of room for one frogman. With a cruising speed of 488 knots and a range of 6360 miles, the aircraft could get you anywhere in the world in comfort.

Josh ran his hand across a tan leather seat in front, which felt like an expensive leather coat, then strolled back to two opposing seats next to oval windows. He slid into the forward-facing chair and buckled his seat belt.

The cockpit door opened, and a fit woman in dark-blue pants and a white shirt with short blonde hair stepped out and headed in Josh's direction. Josh looked at the leather couch next to her, which probably folded out into a bed. *Hmmm, mile high club!* His fantasy faded in an instant after two zaps on his wrist. *Damn, club member, not Air Force.*

The blonde smiled, buckled into the seat in front of Josh, and extended her hand. "Welcome, Agent Martin. My name is Trisha. I'll be your companion for the next two and a half hours. We should land at Andrews just after eighteen thirty."

Josh shook her hand, "Hi, Trisha. Please call me Josh. Sorry for my appearance." He gestured at his tactical uniform. "They didn't give me time to change. I hate to dirty up your beautiful plane."

"Please, this plane usually transports Undersecretary Shithead from Washington to some meeting in Paris. It's about time it carried someone useful. Are you hungry?"

"I'm starved. I haven't eaten anything since breakfast." The plane started to vibrate under Josh's seat, and the engines whined. The runway whizzed by the window, and Josh felt the lift as the plane took off, shuddering when the landing gear retracted. A silence and quiet comfort filled the cabin.

Trisha unbuckled her seatbelt and leaned forward. "Steak, chicken, or fish?"

"Steak, please, and a glass of red wine." Josh unbuckled his seat belt. "You're not going to yell at me because the seat belt sign is on, are you?"

Trisha laughed. "Nope, brain damage won't change a coastie much if he hits his head on the overhead."

"Ouch, I didn't think you were military," Josh said.

"I'm not." Trisha stood up, squeezed by Josh, and headed to the aft galley.

Josh eased back into his seat and fell asleep in twenty seconds.

Elena watched the G550 taxi to the runway from the MacDill passenger terminal. The plane turned to line up on the white center line, accelerated, and took off. Syrin whined at the sight of the plane leaving. Elena stroked her head.

"Don't worry, girl; he'll be back." Elena kneeled and hugged her. "You and I are going to have a ladies' night in. What do you say to a movie and some ice cream?" Syrin barked and wagged her tail.

"Marshal Diaz, are you ready?" Chief Strutton asked.

Elena looked over toward the departure door at the sound of her name. Crew Chief Denny Strutton held it open with one foot. "Yeah, Chief, we're ready. Come on, Syrin."

Elena and Syrin exited the terminal and headed about one hundred yards to the Pave Hawk prepped on the tarmac. Syrin hopped into the helo and lay down in the back. Elena followed her and strapped into the seat closest to her. Chief Strutton stepped in and pulled the door closed, then latched it shut. The engines whined as the RPMs increased, and the rotors started to spin. The helo began to shake as the rotors got up to speed. The chopper lifted off, and Elena and Syrin fell asleep before it crossed the perimeter of the airfield.

Rafi stood up, grabbed the mount under the Valkyrie drone, and moved it to the floor along with plastic housing and the gas generator. She reached over and picked up the Tropical Suites ice bucket from the edge of the table, put it in front of her, removed the lid and the plastic liner, then set them next to the bucket.

"So, here's how we take out the feds in their hotel room. I've got a steel liner insert for the bucket. Once it's in place, I'll put a block of C4 with a remote cell phone detonator at the bottom. I'll cover the explosive charge with stainless steel ball bearings and reinsert a cutdown version of the plastic liner to cover the bomb and the steel liner. Fill the bucket with ice, put it in the room, call the number, and duck."

Sari shook her head. "Rafi, you are a genius. Remind me not to piss you off. Michael, any word on our feds?"

"Still not back in the room. Probably filling out paperwork from Tampa. Do you think they'll be back? They got the kid and the dope." Michael launched her beer bottle, which banged into the trash can near the edge of the kitchen counter. "Yes! And the crowd went wild."

"They'll be back. Someone's going to want justice for those twenty-nine girls," Sari said. "Rest up, angels. Things should get interesting in the next couple of days."

CHAPTER

80

"Wake up, sailor boy; chow is ready," Trisha said.

Josh cracked an eye and looked across the aisle. Trisha smiled and held a glass of red wine toward him. The aroma of steak permeated the cabin, and Josh's stomach growled.

"That smells great." Josh rolled out of his seat and slid into the one opposite Trisha. He looked down at his plate: New York strip, baked potato, garden salad, and green beans. "Now, *this* is how the other half lives." He picked up his glass of Cabernet Sauvignon and offered a toast: "We drink to those who love us; we drink to those who don't. We drink to those who fuck us, and fuck those who don't."

Trisha laughed. "A true poet." They clinked glasses and dined on the feast.

Josh finished the steak, potato, beans, and salad. He would have licked the plate, but that wouldn't earn him any bonus points toward the mile-high club.

"I can't believe the meat and wine are this good on a plane," Josh said. "And I also don't believe you are a flight attendant. So who are you?" Josh took another sip of wine.

"Pretty perceptive for a sailor." Trisha took another bite of her New York strip.

"And still dodging the question," Josh said.

"A girl doesn't spill all her secrets on a first date. Your momma should have taught you that," Trisha said. "Maybe there will be a second date, and things will get interesting. Not jump-in-the-fold-out bed interesting, but interesting." Trisha sipped some more wine and smiled.

"And I see you can read minds." Josh leaned back to enjoy the moment.

"Not all minds, but male thoughts are pretty straightforward. Food, sex, and sleep—maybe not in that order." A brief shudder and drop went through the plane to signal a speed and altitude change. Trisha looked at the overhead and her watch: 1800. "I'm afraid we're going to have to cut our date short. We should be on the ground in thirty minutes." Trisha stood and carried her tray with its half-full plate and glass to the rear galley and crew compartment.

Josh drained his goblet and slid out with his tray to follow her to the rear of the plane. The view was extraordinary.

Elena waved to the Pave Hawk flight crew, turned, and ambled over to the Shelby F-150 with Syrin in tow. She clicked the fob, the lights blinked, the doors unlocked, and she pulled the front passenger seat door open. Syrin hopped in, and she pushed it closed. Elena went around the front, pulled the driver door open, and slid into the leather seat, feeling the comfort surround her. *A girl could get used to this. How does a door kicker afford this? I need to ask for a raise.* She depressed the brake and pressed the start button. Seven hundred horsepower rumbled to life. "Now *that's* what I'm talking about, Syrin."

It was a quick trip back across the Pineda Highway and I-95 to the Tropical Suites Hotel. Elena pulled the truck into the valet lane, put it into park, and hopped out.

"No Agent Martin today?" Jason asked as he wheeled a luggage cart over.

"Hi, Jason. Not today. Just us girls. Syrin, come." Syrin bounced across the seats and jumped to the ground. Elena handed Jason the truck fob. "Same rules apply, but if anything happens to this truck while I'm driving it, they will not find your body."

"No worries, Marshal. We'll take good care of it. Also, some large friends of yours took up residence in the two suites on either side of your room."

"Great, my brothers have arrived. They are also very fond of this truck. Please send up my luggage when you get a chance." Elena clapped Jason on the shoulder. "You can hit Agent Martin up for the tip when he gets back. He's got all the money." Elena and Syrin started walking to the lobby.

"Yes, ma'am. No problem. You're paid up for the rest of your visit."

Elena pushed through the lobby doors, walked over to the bank of elevators, pushed the up arrow, and stepped in with Syrin when the doors opened. The doors closed, and they started their ascent to the twenty-fifth floor.

Michael stopped midway across the lobby with her housekeeping cart and watched Syrin and Elena get onto the elevator. She continued across the reception area to get a better view of the entrance. The valets were parking the red truck—no cowboy in sight. Michael continued across the lobby and up a ramp to a section of first floor rooms. She swiped a key for suite 101, stepped into the room, pulled the door closed behind her, and took out her phone.

Sari picked up on the first ring. "Can you bring some fresh towels to suite sixty-nine?"

"Fuck you. Gabi gets the next shit detail—and I mean shit. People are disgusting. Two out of three just returned to their room." Michael put her head near the door in case anyone was coming in.

"Who?" Sari asked.

"The marshal and the mutt. No sign of the cowboy. Do you want to go forward with the ice bucket challenge or wait?"

"Set it up for tomorrow. Rafi completed the retrofit, so it's good to go. If the cowboy makes it back for the party, it will be a bonus."

"Roger." Michael clicked off the call.

Josh walked down the G550 steps to the tarmac. He stopped at the bottom, turned, waved to an empty door, then shook his head. *I guess no send-off for the military hero. That was one weird plane ride.* When he scoped the surrounding area, a dark SUV blinked its lights twice, so he headed in that direction. The driver's side window lowered on a black Chevy Tahoe as he approached.

"Agent Martin?" the driver asked.

"Guilty as charged," Josh said.

"Sergeant Duffy, from the White House. I'm your ride to quarters." The driver's side window went back up.

Josh walked over to the passenger side, pulled open the door, and slid into the seat. "Josh Martin." He extended his hand.

"Glad to meet you," he said as they shook hands. "I'm taking you to the Presidential Inn. It sounds better than it is, but the sheets are clean." Sergeant Duffy started the Tahoe and turned off the tarmac.

"Well, that sounds better than a foxhole and a poncho liner," Josh said.

"Hooah! It sounds like you did some time in the field with the Army green machine." Sergeant Duffy took a left on First Street.

"I just finished up a training stint at Fort Bragg," Josh said.

“What outfit?” Sergeant Duffy maneuvered through Arnold Street and took a right on Menoher Drive.

“The one that shall not be named,” Josh said with a laugh.

“No shit, Delta. Not bad for a fed. Delta usually doesn’t play well with others, especially government bureaucrats, no offense. But then, I’ve never seen a fed fill out the BDUs like you. Your palace is up on the right.” Sergeant Duffy turned on California Avenue and pulled under the wide, covered VIP reception area at the Presidential Inn to park.

“Thanks for the lift.” Josh pulled the door handle, kicked it open, stepped out, and shut the door. Sergeant Duffy met him at the back of the SUV.

“Here’s your room key. Suite one fifteen. No need to check in at the front desk. I’ll meet you tomorrow at zero eight-thirty in the lobby. You have a meeting at ten hundred with the boss.”

Josh took the key. “Thanks, Joe. See ya tomorrow.” They shook hands, then Josh headed for the lobby, pushed through the double doors, and felt the rush of cold air on his face. The inside looked like a typical civilian hotel, except the tile floors gleamed from constant waxing and cleaning. *If it moves, oil it. If it doesn’t, paint it. If it’s tile, wax it.* Josh smiled at the thought. The reception desk on the left was empty. A gold sign with black numbers on the far wall indicated rooms 100 to 120 were to the left. Josh followed the sign and waved his card at the silver lock for suite 115. The light turned green, and Josh stepped into the room. The smell of military disinfectant washed over him. *The fragrance you never forget.*

Elena and Syrin stepped out of the elevator and headed right to their suite—2501. They stopped at suite 2502, and Elena knocked on the door. After some rustling noises on the other side, the door popped open to reveal Sergeant Mike Jamison in flip-flops, red Nike workout shorts, and a gray Army T-shirt. She felt two zaps on her watch. Sergeant Mike no longer needed peas on his nuts.

"Mike Jamison, they let you out in public?" Elena asked.

"Only for our most important clients. Speaking of which, where's Granite?" Sergeant Mike stepped aside to allow Elena and Syrin into the room.

"He's in DC, meeting with the president and Director Santiago. He'll be back tomorrow." Elena and Syrin stepped into the room, and Sergeant Mike shut the door.

"Thanks for all of the snacks, beer, drinks, and supplies; we usually don't live this large. Who's your four-footed friend?" Sergeant Mike took a seat in the armchair, and Elena sat on the couch.

"You're welcome; it was the least we could do. Thanks for coming down. This is Syrin. She's Josh's dog. Say hi to Sergeant Mike, Syrin." Syrin walked over, sat down, and lifted her right paw for the sergeant.

Mike shook her paw and rubbed her head. "Nice to meet you, Syrin. Is she trained?"

"Like you wouldn't believe. Drugs, explosives, takedowns, and guard duty. She will kick your ass and make you call for your mommy. Where's everyone?" Elena asked.

"Koichi is in the other room finishing up the link analysis and the target list; the rest of the boys are out for a run. Do you want to take a look at the intel picture?" Sergeant Mike stood up.

"Absolutely, it's about time we took some of the players off the board." Elena headed to the door.

Josh walked into the room, which looked like 1980 called and wanted its furniture back. There was a full kitchen on the left, a living room with a brown fabric couch, and an armchair with a small dinette table straight ahead. A full ice bucket sat on the end of the kitchen counter with three Dos Equis Amber beers sticking out. Josh pulled one out, snapped the top with an opener on the counter, and walked into the living area. He continued through to stick his head into a bedroom. Navy PT gear, sneakers, socks, underwear, T-shirts, towels, khaki shorts, a polo shirt, and docksiders adorned the bed. He saw a notecard on top of the towels next to a small white box.

Josh walked in and picked up the card. *Check the closet. I hope everything fits. Welcome to the Brotherhood of Warriors. Vince.*

Josh picked up the small white box and lifted the lid. A pair of gold cufflinks with an Army "A" monogrammed on the front gleamed from a bed of cotton. Josh blinked his eyes a couple of times to push back the tears. The memory of a similar gift of cufflinks flooded his mind and emotions. He sat on the edge of the bed, looked at the present, and remembered his graduation from the Coast Guard Academy; his mom gave him a pair of eighteen-karat-gold square cuff links with a monogrammed *M.* Kat was with him when he opened the box. *God, I wish she were here now. I miss her so much.* Josh wiped the tears from his eyes with his left sleeve, put the lid back on the box, and set it back next to the towels. He stood up and made his way to the closet.

The closet had a full-length-mirror sliding door. Josh opened it. Hanging in the closet was a Zegna Milano Pin Dot Trofeo wool notch lapel suit in dark gray, next to a white 100FILI cotton shirt with French cuffs and a blue silk tie with white microdots. On the floor was a pair of Siena Flex calfskin derby shoes in black with a matching leather belt rolled up next to dark-gray socks.

Josh ran his hand over the fabric of the suit. *Now,* these *are some beautiful Sunday go-to-meeting type of clothes. Vince has excellent taste, or his wife does—definitely his wife. No way an Army grunt picked out these clothes. I wonder if he put them on the corporate card.*

CHAPTER 81

Sergeant Mike swiped his key for suite 2500 and came in with Elena Diaz. "Big brain, we got company."

Koichi Fukumato turned around from writing on easel paper. "Marshal D., good to see you." Koichi went over and gave her a big hug. They both felt zaps on their watches.

Koichi was a Japanese American from Hawaii and an intelligence analyst on loan from the CIA. He stood barely five feet tall in shoes and kept his black hair closely cropped. He wore khaki shorts, flip flops, and a Pittsburgh Steelers T-shirt. His seven languages included Arabic and Farsi, and his wizardry with numbers centered on probability analysis. The team protected him like one of their own.

Elena scanned the room. Large sheets of paper lined the walls with pictures, diagrams, link analysis, and target assessments. Boxes of documents and folders lay stacked on the lone table and the floor. "Looks like you've been busy, my friend. How do you get any work done hanging out with the Neanderthals?"

Koichi laughed. "They bring me some of the finest whiskey from all over the world. I get the attention of beautiful women, and no one fucks with me at a bar."

Sergeant Mike bumped fists with Koichi. "You got that right. Give me some."

Elena asked, "So, other than whiskey, women, and bullshit, what do you have for me?"

"I finally have the target package. Becka sent over a lot of information, and I did a link analysis on the data. With 87 percent certainty, which is high for us spooks—most solid intel comes out at around 80 percent—I have identified these individuals as involved with the conspiracy around the Church of Illuminology, the fraternity deaths, the abduction of the girls, drug smuggling, and the shooting of Senator Alonzo's daughter."

"Well, let me see who's who in the zoo," Elena said.

Koichi led her to a series of three sheets taped to the wall over the back of the couch: one marked *Church*, one labeled *Affiliated*, and one identified as *Uncorroborated*.

On the church sheet were captioned pictures of Bishop Stephanie Avery, Aria Rafael (Rafi), Maya Sarno (Sari), Mila Gabel (Gabi), Romi Michelson (Michael), Julius Montgomery (the mowing Samoan), Eleanor Davis (the personal assistant), and Jean-Paul Dalisma (the cook).

"Why are the bodyguard, the secretary, and the cook included?" Elena asked.

"They've all had access to the bishop's personal and private life; statistically, there's no way they're in the dark about illicit activities. Also, we have a picture of Julius with Bri before they took her to the Dibble brothers for termination."

"Who do you think shot Bri Castillo?" Elena studied the pictures.

Koichi tapped the picture of Gabi. "Mila Gabel was a world-class sniper for the Mossad before she went missing on an op in Syria. She placed second and third in a couple of the annual international sniper competitions. She's the shooter, and I would make sure to stay out of her crosshairs."

"I'll remember that. Who shot the kids in the cell?" Elena asked.

Josh walked out of the bedroom in a T-shirt and gym shorts, plopped on the couch, and spied the two remaining beers sticking up out of the ice bucket. *No sense in letting beer go to waste.* He climbed off the sofa, retrieved a bottle, an opener, and his cell phone from the counter then returned to his spot. The couch looked ugly, but it felt comfortable. He popped the cap off the beer, took a long swig, laid it on the table, and pressed the second soft button on his phone. The dial pad lit up. He scrolled through the contacts, found his mom, and pressed the call button.

Sarah Beatrice Martin picked up. "Josh, is that you? Are you okay?"

"Hi, Mom. I'm fine. I just completed my training exercise, and I should be home in a couple of weeks."

"Oh, that's excellent news. Pops and JJ are down at the calving barn. One of the cows is having a tough delivery, and your sister's at work. They're going to be bummed they missed your call."

"Do you have a wedding date yet?" Josh asked.

"Not yet. We are waiting for you. You and your sister are the ones with the tightest schedules."

"Just pick a date after the first, and I'll be there. How are JJ and Pops doing?"

"They're both doing great. Pops drives his new truck everywhere and lets everyone know his sons bought it for him. Our new business venture on the twenty-three-thousand-acre Phillips Brook watershed is moving along. We found ten more maple groves on the site, along with the original nine confirmed tracts. Ten of the planned one hundred hunting, fishing, and snowmobiling cabins are complete, and we're booked solid on those ten units. The biomass conversion power generation facility passed the 50 percent-completion mark, and we just signed contracts with Northern Woods Lumber for logging rights on five thousand acres."

Josh could hear the excitement in his mom's voice. "Sounds great. Who's Northern Woods Lumber? I've never heard of them."

"Some outfit out of Canada. JJ's going to head up and check on their operation in the next couple of days, depending on calving operations."

"Tell Pops to hurry up and make an honest woman out of you. I'll pay for the honeymoon. I gotta run, Mom. You take care. I love you."

"I love you too, Josh. Be safe."

"I will. Bye." Josh clicked off the call. *Northern Woods Lumber. I need to check on them.*

Koichi pointed to the picture of Romi (Michael) Michelson. It was either Michael or Sergeant Joe Friday of the UCF Police Department. Koichi tapped Sergeant Friday's image on the *Affiliated* sheet. The statistical analysis was split even at 50 percent.

"You gotta be shitting me. We're working the case with him." Elena stepped back in disbelief. "How'd you tie him in?"

Koichi walked over and picked the targeting matrix for Sergeant Friday, and glanced at his notes. "Let's see, started working with the UCF Police Department about ten years ago, about the same time the Golden Knight drug ring appeared on campus. Top five NRA small-bore shooter in the country. Link analysis connection to the Delta Faros Fraternity, Chad Brown, Margaret Thorne, and a card-carrying member of the Church of Illuminology. He knew the detention cell location for the two fraternity brothers, and he had ready access."

"Son of a bitch." Elena shook her head. "A lot of bad connections, but not a smoking gun."

"Based on forensic accounting, Sergeant Friday owns or controls accounts with over seven million dollars in assets, which is two and a half times the probability based on saving and investing his salary for thirty years. No indication of inheritance or lottery winnings." Koichi looked up from his notes.

"Bang. I think the gun just went off," Sergeant Mike said. "Always follow the money."

"Damn. Ain't that the truth? That little fucking weasel worked with us. Who popped Thorne?" Elena asked.

"Again, I'm not sure. It was a statistical split, either Michael or Sergeant Friday." Koichi walked back to the couch.

"No more 'sergeant' reference. He's no longer a police officer, just a scumbag. So, the scumbag is a drug dealer at best and a double murderer at worst," Elena said. "But either way, he earned a Black and White Club bullet."

"I would say that is correct," Koichi said.

"Who else is on the affiliated list?" Elena looked at the chart. "Who's Chris Del Toro?"

Koichi pulled another piece of paper out of his targeting stack and checked his comments. "Chris Del Toro was an intelligence analyst with Customs and Border Protection, who failed to show up for work yesterday and is now in the wind. He called in the alerts on the decoy ships for the past six years. Inspectors found two thousand kilos of cocaine on the *Garcia Asombrosa*, so he's responsible for a shitload of drugs getting into the country. He was six months short of retirement. He paid cash for a forty-acre spread with a cabin on Smokey Mountain Lake in Tennessee and put almost one-point-five mil in an offshore account in the Caymans."

"Are we going to track him down?" Elena asked.

"Right now, the direction is to let Customs do it. He's on our list in case Customs comes up dry," Koichi said.

"Anyone else on the affiliated list?" Elena asked

"No one alive and free," Koichi said. "Adrian Stanhope, Lightning Strikes Motorcycle Club, Delta Faros Fraternity UCF Chapter, the Dibble Brothers, and Margaret Thorne are all deceased. Calvin Jackson and the crew of the *Garcia Asombrosa* are in custody."

"How'd they gas the fraternity?" Elena asked.

CHAPTER

82

Rafi lifted the Valkyrie drone and set it on a catering cart, then she picked up the cyanide gas generator and put it on the bottom shelf below the drone. Even though it was a trial run, they would have to attach the generator to get the weight right. She wheeled the cart out of the breakroom and headed for the garage. Gabi met her at the elevators. Both women wore black pants, black T-shirts, and black tactical boots. They both had lightweight black jackets and balaclavas in the truck.

They rode the elevator down to the garage and pushed the cart to a rented F-150 Crew Cab parked next to the BMW M8. They lifted the drone into the bed of the Ford, covered it with a tarp, and secured the tarp to the sides of the truck with bungee cords. They put the gas generator on the floor behind the front seats and covered it with a sheet.

"We still have a couple of hours before go time. Do you want to play some pool?" Rafi asked.

"Sounds good to me." Gabi shut the doors on the truck. "At least we're not cleaning toilets like Michael. She's going to be a bitch for the next couple of weeks. We also need to swing by the armory to get some long guns in case things go sideways."

"JSTARS recorded a drone launch at zero two twenty on the night the fraternity got gassed. The drone flew to the mansion, hovered for five minutes, and returned to its launch location. The drone ID was a Valkyrie Wing S-one thousand-plus, which can carry up to a nine-point-five-kilogram payload for fifteen minutes. The drone launched from the top of a UCF student parking lot. The camera system for the parking lot went dark from zero two hundred to zero three hundred." Koichi walked over to the fridge and pulled out a Sprite. "Do you want anything?"

"No, I'm good. Syrin and I are going to have a ladies' night in with plenty of ice cream. Did we put up a geofence at the hospital?" Elena asked.

Koichi walked back to the couch. "Yes, we also put one up over the hotel. I didn't feel like smelling almonds in my sleep."

"Roger that. Tell me about the uncorroborated list." Elena tapped the paper sheet.

"Uriel, Raguel, and Remiel are archangels of the Church of Illuminology, but unlike Michael, Raphael, Gabriel, and Saraqael, they hold ceremonial titles. They're the largest individual donors. The titles can change hands if someone wants to donate more money to sit on the stage with the bishop for the church service. No flags on any of them, other than they have too much money." Koichi took a sip of Sprite.

Sergeant Mike walked over when he saw the name of President Brian C. Byrne on the sheet. "Holy shit! You ran an analysis on the President of the United States?"

"Yes, at the request of Director Santiago. In fact, we ran an analysis of all the executive committee members. They all came back clear. The president got flagged because he personally knows Bishop Avery and her sister, Lieutenant Governor Rachel Avery Collier. Plus, the Church of Illuminology is the largest donor to his reelection campaign."

"Wait a minute. The bishop and the lieutenant governor are sisters? She tried to push us off the fraternity shooting and the massacre at the mansion. She has to be involved," Elena said.

Koichi checked his notes. "The only connection is sibling, campaign donations to the president, conduct during fraternity investigation, and the phone number eight, five, zero, seven, one, seven, nine, two, one, zero."

"The phone number sounds familiar. What is it?" Elena asked.

"It's the number Captain Aimon from the *Garcia Asombrosa* called every time he arrived in port and departed. The phone number connects to the central administration for the state of Florida in Tallahassee." Koichi tossed his notes on the table. So, that's the target list."

"Pretty thorough work, Koichi. Thank you, but I still think the lieutenant governor is involved." Elena turned to look at Sergeant Mike. "So, now we gotta figure out how to send a bishop, four angels, a scum bag, and the hired help to hell!"

Josh swiped to the next page of *Blue Moon* on his kindle. He wiggled his feet at the bottom of the bed. Joe was right; the sheets were clean. His phone buzzed on the nightstand. He reached over, picked it up, and checked the caller ID to make sure his extended warranty wasn't expired. The screen showed *Marshal*. He pressed the green accept button.

"Syrin snoring?" Josh asked.

"I'm looking at her right now. She is indeed snoring, and she's a bed hog."

"I should have warned you about that. You may wake up with a paw in your face. How was your day?"

"I went over the target set with Koichi and Sergeant Mike. I think the lieutenant governor is involved. After dinner, Syrin and I had ice cream cones, and now I'm lying in bed listening to her snore."

"Well, that sounds like a full day. Ask Sergeant Mike how his nuts are doing." Josh laughed. "I agree with you on the lieutenant governor, but that's a big whack; we would need a direct tie for that."

"I know, but a lot of kids didn't get a chance to grow up, and everything points to a bunch of Karens running a criminal enterprise dressed up as a church. Have you seen the list?"

"No. I flew back to Andrews, and now I'm racked out at the Presidential Inn, enjoying the quiet and reading a book."

"There's one surprise on the list," Elena said.

"Joe Friday?"

"How'd you know?"

"You called it. How did someone know we were holding Kyle and Dillion in the UCF detention cell? There were probably six different options. The killer gained access in less than twenty hours. That screamed inside job. Plus, how can you trust someone named Joe Friday?"

"He's got over seven million dollars in cash and assets."

"Whew, I need to get a job as a UCF police officer. The pay's pretty good. So, he's the Golden Knight. Are you guys putting together some target packages?" Josh asked.

"Yes, your boys are going over the options tonight and tomorrow, before you get back. What time do you meet with the president?"

"The meeting is set for ten hundred hours. I'll catch a flight after the meeting, probably back at Patrick around fifteen hundred. I'll call you when I'm airborne with an ETA. Please send someone out to get me."

“Will do. Tell Vince I said hi.”

“Roger. Kiss Syrin for me. I’ll see ya tomorrow.” Josh clicked off the call, picked up his kindle, and got back to Jack Reacher.

CHAPTER 83

Gabi opened the rear door to the truck and pushed in her cased Savage MSR 10 long-range AR chambered in .308 and topped with a Bushnell 3.5-21x50 Elite Tactical DMR II-i scope. She also tossed in a range bag with five twenty-round magazines, shut the door, and climbed into the passenger seat.

Rafi stepped out of the elevator carrying her fanny pack with a Glock Model 17 9mm and three spare seventeen-round magazines, then headed to the truck, popped the door, and slipped into the driver seat. She put the fanny pack on the floor behind her feet, started the F-150, and plugged her iPod into the sound system.

"Do you have a preference?" Rafi asked.

"Play some Luke Combs. Maybe *One, Too Many*?" Gabi leaned back in her seat and closed her eyes. She didn't have to worry about Rafi's driving.

Rafi backed the truck out of the slot and pressed the audio button. "Play *One, Two, Many*."

Luke Combs sang while Rafi pulled out of the parking garage. She wound her way through the complex at thirty-five miles per hour and took a right on Route 192 heading due east to the ocean. Traffic was light at 2300, so she made good time. Before long, she nudged Gabi. "Just passed the Melbourne Mall."

Gabi sat up, rubbed her neck, and shook her head. "Any cops?"

"Only one BCSO cruiser. It turned onto I-ninety-five." Rafi pointed. "There's Crane Creek Preserve. The next mark is the one-ninety-two East New Haven split."

At the split, Rafi stayed left on 192, then turned right on South Harbor City Boulevard. She pulled into the Dunkin' Donuts parking lot at the intersection of East Hibiscus Boulevard.

"Do you want anything?" Rafi asked.

"Get me a large French vanilla, hot with crème and swirl." Gabi checked her holstered Glock. *Still in place. I'd rather take the Savage, but crossing a main road with a gun case would earn a call to the cops.* Gabi keyed her mike, "Test, one, two, three."

"Loud and clear," Rafi replied.

Gabi opened the door and stepped out. The warm air hit her face. *Still hot at midnight. But I'll take heat over cold every day.* Gabi shut the door and walked over to the sidewalk along East Hibiscus Boulevard and turned left.

Rafi pulled into the drive-through lane.

Jason, Sierra One, rearranged his position on the shooting mat next to the southeast corner AC vent on the roof of the Atlantic Orthopedic Group. His location gave him a 270-degree shooting arc and complete coverage of the Melbourne City Cemeteries. Similar overwatch positions were also set up at Wells Park, Melbourne High School, the Melbourne Military Memorial Park, and the Fee Avenue Park. A four-person quick reaction force in two SUVs was stationed on either side of the hospital. BCSO and the Melbourne PD were on standby to shut down intersections in a 360-degree perimeter around the Holmes Medical Center.

Jason watched a figure cross East Hibiscus and head north on the train tracks along the far edge of the cemetery. The subject wore black and moved like a soldier. Jason shifted his M24A3 sniper rifle to track the movement and peered through his heavy AN/PAS-13B(V) 2-night vision scope. The subject appeared in his field of vision. *Female. Bingo.* “Six, this is Sierra One. I have movement on the edge of the cemetery. One female subject, dressed in black, no visible weapons.”

“Roger. We’re going to head your way. We’ll hold on the outer perimeter.”

Jason keyed his mike twice.

Gabi proceeded to the edge of the train tracks and surveyed the cemetery. No movement and no sound except the highway traffic behind her. She continued north, keeping to the tree line on the left of the tracks. The gravel crunched under her feet, but everything else was still. The silence and the cemetery nighttime vibe sent a chill down her spine. She stopped every ten steps to check things out. She finally reached her destination, the caretaker’s office at the cemetery midpoint, which consisted of two garage bays and an attached building with an office, a conference room, and two restrooms with exterior doors. She checked all the entries. Everything was locked. A single carport on the south side of the building was empty.

“Everything is quiet. The carport is empty, and the doors are all locked. You are good to go,” Gabi said.

“Roger, I’m rolling now.” Rafi pulled out of the Dunkin’ Donuts parking lot and turned left on South Harbor City Boulevard, and then another immediate left on East Hibiscus Boulevard. She crossed over the train tracks, turned right at the second dirt road entrance into the cemetery, switched to parking lights, and followed the dirt path to the caretaker’s building. She pulled into the carport and killed the engine.

"Six, this is Sierra One. A white Ford F-150 crew cab just joined the party. The truck pulled under the carport at the caretaker's office. The driver just exited the vehicle. Female, dressed in black. Both subjects are now in the bed of the truck removing a tarp. Tailgate is down; they are taking a drone out of the truck bed and setting it on the ground. Subjects are now in the back of the truck. They are removing a large metal box and carrying it to the drone. Six, I don't think we can let this thing fly even with the geofence."

"Roger, Sierra One. We are closing on your position now. Put one in the drone and the truck. Engage tangos if you see a gun."

"Roger, Six. Engaging now." Jason put his crosshairs on the drone center, held his breath, left it halfway out, and squeezed the trigger. The M24A3 thumped his shoulder, and a .338 Lapua Magnum Hornady 225gr SST/IB round boomed to its target at 3,150 feet per second. Jason worked the rifle bolt, shifted his aim to the right front fender of the truck at the engine's midpoint, and squeezed the trigger. *Boom*, another round to its target. Jason moved his crosshairs back to locate the two subjects.

Rafi bent down to attach the generator to the drone, and the drone exploded in her hands. Plastic shards stung her hands and face. She jumped back at the impact, and a rifle shot boomed across the cemetery. A loud metallic crack slammed the front of the truck, and steam rose from the hood, then another rifle shot echoed across the buildings. She stared at her hands in disbelief. She tried to comprehend what was happening. Two vehicles with bouncing headlights rapidly closed on their position from East Hibiscus Boulevard.

Gabi sprinted to the rear of the truck at the sound of the first shot and ripped the door open. She jumped as another round slammed into the F-150 engine. "Rafi! Come on; we gotta move." She pulled the gun case out of the back, unzipped it, and grabbed the Savage MSR .308. She leveled the gun at the bouncing headlights in the lead vehicle, aimed for the front driver's side windshield, held her breath, let it halfway…Her head exploded in a red mist, and her headless body collapsed into the dirt. She never heard the rifle report boom across the cemetery.

The impact of the bullet into Gabi's head snapped Rafi back into reality. "Oh shit! Oh shit! Oh shit! They knew we were coming." She ran to the front of the truck, opened the driver's door, and yanked her fanny pack off the floor. She unzipped the pouch, removed the Glock 17, pointed it at the advancing vehicles, and squeezed off two rounds, which flew aimlessly into the night. The hand of god then bounced her off the truck, sending her to the ground with a large red splotch in the center of her chest and another boom resounding among the gravestones.

"Six, this is Sierra One; both targets are down. Jason leaned back against the AC unit and pointed at the sky. "That's for you, Ray, and the twenty-nine girls who didn't make it home." Jason picked up his shooting mat, rifle, and range bag, then headed for the ladder off the roof.

Josh's phone started playing the Tommy Lee Jones outhouse speech and vibrating on the nightstand. He rolled over, picked it up, and hit the green accept button. "If you are drunk dialing me, I'm gonna have Syrin bite you."

"Guess what I'm doing?" Elena asked.

"I don't know, knocking boots with Sergeant Mike. What time is it?" Josh searched for the alarm clock time.

"Tempting, but no. He's more like a brother, and it is zero two hundred. I'm standing in a cemetery looking at a shattered drone, an F-one fifty with a round in the engine block, and the bodies of Mila Gabel—Gabi—and Aria

Rafael—Rafi—both graveyard dead. Rafi is missing her head. We had to ID her with fingerprints."

Josh sat up, fully awake at the news. "Give me the abridged edition."

"Gabi and Rafi attempted to launch a drone from the Melbourne City Cemeteries' caretaker's house. It's about a mile east of the medical center. Dave Tuley's shooter, Jason, was on overwatch and put them both down when they broke out the guns."

"This is good news." Josh ran the options in his head. "We can get a warrant to search the church for any sniper rifles, drones, gas generators, and evidence of Bri. So we got the two responsible for the gas attack on the fraternity and for shooting Bri Castillo. Tell Jason I owe him a steak dinner."

"I will. I already called Becka, so she's working on the warrant with DOJ. We should have it by the time you get back to Florida. Now, go to bed. It's not every day you get a meeting in the Oval Office."

"Yeah, roger that. Thanks for the call. See you this afternoon. I'll call you when I'm wheels up." Josh clicked off the call and laid back down in bed. *Two down and four to go. Maybe five, if we can find anything on the lieutenant governor.*

Sari and Michael stared at the TV in disbelief. They were watching *Whose Line is it Anyway* when the breaking news about a police-involved shooting at the Melbourne City Cemeteries interrupted the show. A reporter stood in front of a cluster of police and emergency vehicles and gave the update. Two individuals were shot and killed by police. No further information on the identity of the police officers involved in the shooting or the identity of the victims.

Sari redialed Rafi's number. The phone went straight to voice mail. "Shit." Sari tossed her phone on the break room table and put her head in her hands. Michael stared at the TV with a blank expression, trying not to cry.

"Are you going to wake up the bishop?" Michael asked.

Sari lifted up her head and wiped the tears from her eyes. "No, I'll let her sleep. No reason to ruin everyone's night. She was very fond of them. This sucks. We got too confident. We should have known the feds would figure out the drone option. I mean, how else do you gas a house without going inside?" Sari looked at the Tropical Suites ice bucket on the table. "Are you still good with this? They might be waiting for you."

"I'm good. Time to send a little payback, plus it will complicate their investigation if we can remove the primary investigators from the equation, and I get to watch them go *boom*. Do you want a beer?" Michael stood up and walked to the fridge.

"Yeah, I'll take a beer; we've got work to do. We need to get everyone up and sanitize this place to remove any trace of Rafi, Gabi, and the fucking virgin. All the guns got to go, and we need to wipe all of their digital footprints." Sari stood up and retrieved her phone off the table.

Michael pulled two Heineken's out of the fridge, popped the tops off, and handed one to Sari. She held up her bottle. "Let us not forget Rafi and Gabi, but remember them always, for they have earned our respect and admiration with their lives. We knew them, we remember them, and they will not be forgotten. To our fallen comrades!" Michael and Sari clinked bottles and took a big pull on their beers.

"Why don't you take your present down to your car. We don't want the feds to find that. It would ruin the surprise." Sari gestured at the ice bucket. "Shoot some video on your phone of the aftermath. I want to see all the whining and crying. Rafi and Gabi would appreciate the send-off."

CHAPTER

84

From the driver's seat of a dark-blue Chevy Tahoe, Sergeant George Duffy watched Josh walk out of the Presidential Inn. He pushed open the door, slid out of the seat, and walked around the front of the SUV. The DC heat was just starting to kick in. He opened the passenger door for Josh. "You look like a billion bucks in that suit."

Josh walked over to the car. "I know. It's tough being this good looking, but somebody has to show the Army how to dress."

"Funny. I'll set up a photoshoot with GQ. Since you'll be modeling, be careful not to sit on the wet coffee stain upfront. Would you rather squeeze into the cargo area?"

Josh slid into the passenger side, and George shut the door. The car was suit-wearing cold, which was a nice touch. Josh snapped on his seatbelt and pushed his seat all the way back.

George got in, started up, and pulled out of the reception area. "How did you sleep last night?"

"Like a baby," Josh said. "You were right about the sheets and the room. Did you get breakfast? I could use some Dunkin' Donuts coffee. I'm buying."

"I'm good on breakfast, but I'll never turn down free coffee. There's a shop just outside the front gate on Allentown Road." Joe navigated off the base, pulled through the Dunkin' drive-through for two extra-large black hazelnut coffees, and picked up the Suitland Parkway into the city. There were no accidents, so despite the traffic, he made decent time into the city.

"I don't know how you put up with all of these crazy drivers," Josh said. "I probably would have shot someone by now. How long is your tour?"

"You get used to it after a while. Some folks don't make it and wash out. The standard tour is three years. If they like you, they'll ask you to stay for a fourth. It takes a lot of training to become a master driver. On the plus side, you get your pick of assignments after the job."

"Where do you want to go?" Josh asked.

"I promised the wife Hawaii; I have thirteen months left on the tour. I signed for the fourth year of driving with a thirty-k bonus. There's your stop up ahead on Seventeenth Street. Director Santiago's going to meet you out front. I'll pick you up at the west entrance to the White House after your meeting." George pulled to the curb.

"Thanks for the lift. Wish me luck." Josh checked the traffic, climbed out of the car, and shut the door. He gave George a wave and stepped up on the curb in front of the New Executive Office Building, part of the eighteen acres which comprised the White House complex. Josh looked up at the front of the red brick building with its glass entrance. A white 725 sat above the presidential seal over the front door next to *New Executive Office Building* in large, raised brass-colored letters. *My life has definitely changed since the last time I stood here.*

He surveyed the stream of bureaucrats and contractors exiting from the building and quickly spotted Director Vance in a dark-blue suit, white shirt, and red tie. He felt three zaps on his watch for the leader of the Black and White Club.

Director Vance sidestepped around a security bollard and walked over. "Damn, you look good. How much weight did you put on? Twenty pounds?" They shook hands.

"About twenty-five pounds," Josh said. "Thank you for the suit and the cuff links." He pulled back the sleeve on his suit to show the gold A.

"Hooah." Vince smacked him on the arm. "You earned them. How was your trip up?"

"Outstanding. The aircraft and the company were five stars. Who's Trisha? Is she one of us?"

"That's the real reason for your trip." Vince put his arm around Josh's shoulder. "Let's go meet with the boss, and you can find out."

Elena sipped her coffee and looked at Syrin sitting next to her and watching everyone move around the breakfast area. *What a beautiful dog. I need to get one. Makes a better companion than a man.* Elena reached out to scratch her head, and Syrin rubbed her fur into Elena's hand.

Sergeant Mike walked up, carrying a tray with an omelet, bacon, toast, juice, and coffee. Koichi trailed him. Mike said, "Do you mind if we join you, ladies?"

"Not at all. Please, pull up a seat. Syrin and I were just contemplating the problems of the world and how great it felt to sleep in after a busy night."

The sergeant sat down across from Elena, and Koichi slid into the chair to her left. He said hello and laid down his trayful of pancakes, sausage links, hash browns, and coffee.

"And what was your solution to the world's problems?" Sergeant Mike asked.

"A lot of them can be solved by a Lapua Magnum to the side of the head," Elena said.

"Can't argue with that." Sergeant Mike took a bite of the omelet. "They make a great breakfast here."

Koichi took a sip of coffee. "The coffee is also good. It usually sucks in a hotel. Anyway, as for business, I hear I can scratch two off the list."

"Yes, both Mila Gabel—Gabi—and Aria Rafael—Rafi—caught the express train to hell last night," Elena said.

"Who punched their tickets?" Kochi asked between bites of pancakes.

"Jason Cook from Dave Tuley's team," Elena said.

"How's Dave doing?" Sergeant Mike poured hot sauce on his omelet.

"Bitching at the staff and looking for his clothes." Elena laughed. "They had to hide them so he wouldn't check out on his own."

"That sounds like Dave," Sergeant Mike said. "Did one of the shooters from last night fire the round at the senator's daughter?"

"Yeah, we think Gabi was the shooter. She had the skill." Elena's phone buzzed on the table. She looked at the caller ID: *Holmes Regional Medical Center.* "Shit." She picked up the phone and pressed the green accept button. "This is Marshal Diaz."

"Senator Alonzo would like to see both you and Agent Martin in the ICU as soon as possible."

"Roger. Can you tell me what it's about?"

"I'm sorry, no. That's the only information I have."

"Thank you; I'm on my way." Elena clicked off the call.

"Who was that?" Sergeant Mike asked.

"The hospital. They want to see Josh and me now." Elena stood up from the table.

"Oh, that can't be good," Koichi said.

CHAPTER

85

Sari set the rubber container in the rear of the church box truck and stepped back to look at the load. She wore dark-blue construction coveralls. Boxes and bins with all of the executive team's electronic hardware, paper files, and office contents filled the twenty-six-foot vehicle's cargo space. IT had erased all digital data, including the backup storage cloud in Texas. Sari turned at the sound of footsteps behind her.

Michael, dressed in the same coveralls, pushed a box into the rear of the truck. "That's the last one. Julius already departed with the armory's contents, and the cleaning crew is doing another deep clean on all the holding rooms used for the girls. All the congregation members involved in the care and feeding of our guests are on a charter flight to a church compound in Seattle. I think we're done." She wiped the sweat off her forehead with a coverall sleeve.

"Okay, that sounds good." Sari pulled the door down until it slammed into the lock. She rotated the door handle to secure the door, took a padlock out of her pocket, slipped the shackle through the handle, and snapped it shut. "Time for you to take a shower and get ready for work." She hugged Michael. "Be careful. Anything looks wrong; just walk away. I'll give the bishop an update."

"Roger." Michael let go of Sari and started walking to her car.

Sari watched her go. *I hope this isn't the last time I see you.* She turned to head over to the elevator and pressed the up button. The elevator dinged and opened. Sari stepped in and pushed the button for floor five. The door closed, and a Bishop Avery sermon started playing from the overhead speaker. The elevator stopped rising and dinged open on the fifth floor. She turned left and walked over to Eleanor, who was busy feeding papers into a shredder.

"Is she in her office?" Sari asked.

"Yes, she's at her desk, I think. You can go on back. Sorry to hear about Gabi and Rafi." Eleanor returned to her shredding.

"Thanks, Eleanor. Make sure all of the shredder clippings go into the burn bags." Sari walked into the reception area across the marble floor and stopped at the archway entrance into the bishop's office. She glanced at the Château Mouton Rothschild 2015 nestled on a wooded tray in the wine fridge. *I could use a bottle of that.* She knocked on the wooden arch.

"Yes." Wearing a burgundy dress to mark the somber occasion, Bishop Avery looked up from her desk. The small gold cross almost gleamed in contrast to the deep red of the fabric behind it.

Sari walked in and took a seat on the art deco white mocha metal swivel chair in front of her desk. *The chair still sucks. Glad to see some things don't change.* "We've sanitized everything. The armory is empty, and the support staff is on the way to our compound in Seattle. Are you sure you don't want to join them?"

"I thought about it, but that would look like I have something to hide. Plus, I would miss the expressions on the faces of the federal officials when they get our payback. Everything is still on track, I trust?"

"Yes, Michael just left with our package in her car. She's going home to take a shower before she heads to work. Everything's a go. We still don't know the location of the cowboy, but we'll catch the marshal, the mutt, and a bunch of operators who are working out of the hotel rooms."

"Excellent. How does that song go? 'Two out of Three Ain't Bad?' Why don't you take a bottle of wine when you go? You look like you could use it. I'm sorry about Gabi and Rafi. I really loved those girls. Taken too early."

Sari stood up. "Your chairs still suck but thank you for the wine. You read my mind. It's been a long day. It was tough cleaning out Rafi and Gabi's stuff, so many memories. Hopefully, we'll get some different breaking news on the TV tonight."

Josh and Vince turned left on Pennsylvania Avenue and headed to the northwest security checkpoint. Pennsylvania Avenue was one big open mall with crowds of pedestrians, contractors, government employees, and tourists mixing for a view and a snapshot of the White House as a backdrop. President Clinton closed the avenue to traffic in May of 1995 after the bombing of the Alfred P. Murrah Federal Office Building in Oklahoma City, Oklahoma. They kept to the right of the black wrought iron security barriers, which lined the front of the White House perimeter fence line and stopped at a white granite security building.

Vince turned to Josh and handed him a White House Blue Badge. "Put this around your neck. You're now 'official' with unescorted access to the White House; just stay off the second floor and no swimming in the back pool."

Vince stepped up to the entrance, and the door buzzed. He pushed it open and stepped inside, followed by Josh. The air conditioning hit them in the face. Large, clear, bulletproof glass atop marble counters dominated the space on either side of a single security line through a magnetometer. An X-ray security belt ran down the right side, and a counter-assault team member dressed in black with an MP5 stood in the left rear corner. Two uniform Secret Service security personnel in blue operated the security line.

Vince put his badge on an access reader on the right, the light turned green, and he pushed through a turnstile. Josh did the same thing. They emptied the contents of their pockets and removed their Rolex watches, and put them in trays, which went through the X-rays. They both walked through the magnetometer without a buzz and retrieved their belongings.

The counter-assault team member opened the exit door for them. “Good morning, Director.”

“Good morning, Kevin. This is Special Agent Josh Martin with the FBI.” Vince nodded at Josh.

Josh felt two zaps on his watch. “Pleased to meet you.” Josh put out his hand.

“Welcome to the White House,” Kevin said. He shook Josh’s hand. “Stay off the second residence floor, and no swimming in the pool.”

“Roger. I got that.” Josh followed Vince outside onto the White House grounds. “I gotta admit, as a kid growing up in New Hampshire, I never thought in a million years I’d be walking around the White House. What’s up with the residence and pool comment?”

“All members of the CAT team are members of the club. The residence and pool comment tells me everything is secure. If they ask you to take a swim in the pool or visit the second floor, there’s a problem. It’s how we keep tabs on the president.”

Vince strode up the driveway toward the West Wing with Josh at his side. “All the major news outlets have press briefing locations on the right. When anyone is reporting live from the White House, this is their location.” Vince pointed to fifteen mini studios along the driveway.

Halfway up, Josh spotted a Marine on station in front of the West Wing entrance. “What’s up with the Marine? Is that a permanent guard post?”

"That's how you tell POTUS is in the Oval Office. Any time the president is in the Oval Office, there's a Marine on the front door."

Vince stopped just short of the West Wing reception overhang and pointed at the North Portico. "If you walk under the North Portico and look up, you can see scorch marks on the marble from when the British burned the White House on August twenty-fourth, eighteen fourteen."

"Wow, I love authentic history. That's why I appreciate the Smithsonian. Everything's real." Josh held his breath involuntarily at the sight of the White House looming over its impeccably manicured lawn. He felt struck by the contrast between this oasis of tranquility and the bustling international crowd of tourists snapping photo after photo from Pennsylvania Avenue. "This is amazing."

"Are you ready for your first Oval Office meeting?" Vince asked.

"Lead the way." Josh stood up a little taller in his new suit.

CHAPTER 86

Elena fought through traffic to navigate to the Holmes Regional Medical Center. Between white-haired local drivers, white-haired drivers with out-of-state plates, and long red lights, the traffic sucked. *I hope this isn't a trip to tell me Bri died.*

"Do you see any parking spots, Syrin?" Elena did a lap around the medical center, hoping to find an easy spot to put the truck, but no luck. *So, put it in the garage or walk from an outlying parking lot.*

"Looks like we're walking, Syrin. I'm not listening to Josh bitch about a scratch on his truck."

Elena pulled into patient lot D4 across from the Heart Center entrance and found a spot five rows in. Dressed in her green tactical uniform, she hopped out of the truck, followed by Syrin with her FBI vest. It was already starting to get hot. *Please don't be dead. Please don't be dead.*

They crossed Hickory Street following a concrete path around the edge of the building and pushed through the Heart Center doors. An unarmed security guard in a light-blue shirt and dark-blue pants stood near a single X-ray portal. He was going to say something about Syrin until he saw the vest. Elena walked up and pulled out her credentials.

"Elena Diaz with the U.S. Marshals Service. I'm armed, and I have a meeting with Senator Alonzo in your ICU."

"Please wait here, Marshal." The rent-a-cop raised his hand, and two DHS tactical officers in full gear carrying M4 carbines appeared from the back of the lobby.

Elena felt two zaps, so they were on the home team. "Good morning, fellas—Marshal Elena Diaz. I have a meeting with the Senator."

"Please follow us, Marshal."

Elena and Syrin walked around the X-ray portal and trailed the operators to the elevators. They all stopped at the doors, and one of the operators keyed a mike.

"Lead, this is Post Four. I have Marshal Diaz. She's coming up with one FBI canine."

"Roger. Send her up." The operator keyed his mike.

"Fourth floor, Marshal. Someone will meet you there." The operator pushed the button, and the elevator opened.

"Thanks, guys. Come on, Syrin." They stepped in, and the door closed. She pushed button four. They rose—with the butterflies in her stomach leading the way. *Please, God, don't let this girl die.* Memories of all the grief around the death of her baby sister flooded back as they reached the fourth floor, and the doors dinged open. She stepped into the hallway.

Michael combed her hair in the mirror. A hot shower had eased her tense muscles and provided a retreat from the world for a few minutes. She wiped the fog from the mirror and looked at her reflection. *Is this it? It's been a hell of a ride, but I'm not ready to go out in a blaze of glory. Maybe I should just say fuck it and ride off. I could use a change of scenery.* She brushed her teeth, swiped on some deodorant, and put on a gray T-shirt and blue workout shorts.

She walked into the living room, found her iPod, located "Last Time for Everything," and hit play. Brad Paisley crooned about memories. She dropped into her favorite leather chair and thought about the long line. *Every minute someone leaves the world behind. Gabi and Rafi went last night. Everyone's in line without knowing it. We never know how many people are ahead of us. We cannot move to the back of the line. We cannot step out of the line. We cannot avoid the line. Is this the end of my journey? Is this my last time for everything?*

When the song stopped playing, she stared at the ceiling and went over the plan in her head. *Drive to work. Start shift. Place package between two stacks of towels for concealment. Wear belly band holster with Sig Sauer P365 and two extra magazines. Put Beretta Model 70 with a six-inch silencer inside a pile of towels in case someone needs to move up their departure time in the line. Start cleaning rooms on the twenty-fifth floor. Roll by suite 2501 to check on availability. If clear, place the package. Keep cleaning rooms until the target returns to the room. Ditch the cart in an empty suite. Place the Beretta in a folded towel and head to the southwest stairwell. Call the cell phone and record the destruction and response on the phone. Pull the fire alarm and calmly walk out of the hotel—mission complete. If something fucks up, go to egress plan B.*

Michael rolled out of the chair and padded to the kitchen. *If this is my last hurrah, I'm not going out hungry.* She pulled out two hamburger patties and a bottle of Heineken, grabbed a spatula off the top of the fridge, and headed to the grill on the patio. *I gotta stop all this thinking bullshit. Sari finds out; she'll shoot me!*

Vince and Josh walked up to the West Wing north entrance; the Marine sentry pulled open the door, came to attention, and saluted smartly as Vince walked by. "Good morning, Director."

Josh walked over to the Marine. "Thank you for your service. You look great." Then he followed Vince into the lobby.

"Josh, I want you to meet Rita. She's the West Wing receptionist." Vince gestured to a young twenty-something with long black hair and an understated blue dress. She sat behind a wooden desk on the right side of the lobby.`

Josh walked over and extended his hand. "Josh Martin."

Rita shook his hand. "Rita Davis. The president is expecting you. You can head back."

"Thank you, Rita," Vince said, and he headed down a hallway to the left.

"Doesn't this place feel like a museum?" Josh asked.

"Yeah, it does," Vince answered. "But you get used to it. On the right is the Roosevelt room named after Teddy, who built it, and FDR, who renovated it. Theodore Roosevelt's Nobel Peace Prize for settling the Russo-Japanese War is on display on a shelf in the back. Bathroom is right next to it in case you need to use it."

"No, I'm good," Josh said.

Vince stopped at the end of the corridor and pointed to a door across the hall on the left. "Cabinet room is in there."

Josh stuck his head in the door. Seventeen brown leather chairs ringed an oval mahogany conference table filling most of the room. One chair was slightly higher than the rest. Josh turned to Vince. "Let me guess; the taller chair is for the president?"

"You would be correct," Vince said. "The table was a gift from President Nixon in nineteen seventy. Each cabinet member is assigned a position at the table according to the date the department was established. The president occupies the taller chair at the center of the east side of the table. The vice president sits opposite. The secretary of state, ranking first among the department heads, sits on the president's right. The secretary of the treasury, ranking second, is to the vice president's right. The secretary of defense, who is third, sits to the president's left, and the attorney general, who's fourth, sits to the vice president's left. When cabinet members conclude their terms of service, they are permitted to purchase their cabinet chairs, which bear brass plates indicating their cabinet position or positions and dates of service."

"You sound like a tour guide," Josh said.

"You would not believe how many West Wing tours I have given for family, friends, business associates, and club members. Come on; the president's in here." Vince turned right and headed down the corridor. Two Secret Service agents in dark-blue suits stood on either side of a doorway. Vince walked between the agents. Josh followed, expecting to get thrown out at any minute.

President Brian C. Byrne looked up from the Resolute desk when Vince and Josh came into the Oval Office. "Vince, Josh, come on in and have a seat. Charlie, can you please shut the doors." One of the Secret Service agents pulled the office doors closed.

Josh felt two zaps on his watch. *I forgot the president was tagged.* He looked around, trying to figure out where to sit. Two armchairs against the wall on the opposite side of the room faced the Resolute desk. Their legs dug into a plush beige carpet with the presidential seal monogrammed into it. Between the chairs and the desk were two large white couches that faced each other with a coffee table in the middle.

The president, dressed in a dark-blue suit with a white shirt, red tie, and shined black shoes, walked over to one of the couches and sat down. Vince sat down on the sofa opposite him. Josh moved in next to Vince. He tried not to be obvious about looking around the office, but the sense of history overwhelmed him.

"Pretty impressive, isn't it?" the president asked.

"Yes, Mr. President. I'm a student of history, and the history of this office is extraordinary."

"Well, Josh, I hope we have a long and close relationship, so eventually, you'll see this as just another office. Can I get you guys anything to eat or drink? One of the perks of the office is outstanding coffee." The president briefly raised his hand, and five seconds later, the office door opened, and a female steward in a white uniform and blonde hair walked in.

"Yes, Mr. President?" the steward asked.

"Coffee service for three, Hannah."

"Yes, Mr. President." The steward did an about-face and exited.

"Military?" Josh asked.

"Navy," Vince said. "Which means they won't spit in your coffee, but I'm not so sure about mine."

"I don't know, Vince. Since he became a warrior of the brotherhood, they may make an exception. You look great, Josh, by the way. Army life agrees with you," the president said.

"Thank you, sir, but I think I'll stay with my day job." Josh sat back on the couch and tried to relax.

"Speaking of your day job, thank you for your efforts in Florida. What a nasty mess. I hear you have a target package." Byrne looked at Josh.

"Yes, Mr. President, we execute a search warrant tomorrow."

"Excellent. Well, let me tell you the reason I dragged you to Washington."

CHAPTER 87

Elaine Bishop, Senator Alonzo's chief of staff, smiled when Elena and Syrin stepped off the elevator. Elaine wore a green polo shirt over white shorts with sneakers. Her blonde hair barely touched her collar. She was forty-something with a brilliant smile. "Thank you so much for making the trip down. I know traffic is terrible."

"Is everything all right?" Elena asked in a halting voice.

"Yes, everything is fine. I'm sorry I couldn't tell you over the phone, but security was adamant about not releasing any information. This must be Syrin." Elaine bent down to stroke the top of Syrin's head. Syrin wagged her tail.

"Careful, you get any closer, and she'll give you a lick. So, what's going on?" Elena looked around at the bustling pace of the ICU floor.

"Why don't you follow me, and you can find out for yourself." Elaine turned to the right and headed down the corridor. Elena and Syrin followed her down the hall, past the nurses' station, and over to a private suite in the corner. One uniformed tactical officer stood near the station, and another stood outside the corner suite. Elaine opened the door and walked into the room, followed by Elena and Syrin.

"Look who I found," Elaine said.

Elena looked around the room and saw Bri in a blue hospital bathrobe sitting in a tan recliner playing cards with her mother. An ace bandage wrapped her head.

“Oh my God, you’re okay. I was so worried driving over here.” Elena rushed over and grabbed her hand. “How are you?”

“I’m fine,” Bri said. “The doctor said I could go home in a couple of days, and I owe it all to you guys.” Tears welled up in her eyes. “I didn’t think I was going to see my family again.” She wiped her eyes on her bathrobe sleeve and spotted Syrin. “Hi, Syrin. Come here, girl.” Syrin walked over to put her head in Bri’s lap, and Bri hugged her. “Where’s the big guy?” Bri asked.

“The big guy’s in DC. He’ll fly back this afternoon. He’ll be thrilled that you’re okay. I just can’t believe it. We thought you were gone.” Elena squinted to try and hold back tears.

Senator Alonzo eased out of her chair and wrapped her arms around Elena. “Thank you so much for bringing my baby home and saving her life. The doctors said Bri would not have made it without you stopping the bleeding and getting her to the hospital. I can’t thank you enough.”

Elena regained her composure and stepped back. “You’re welcome, Senator. I’m so happy it worked out.”

“You can call me Donna. You and Josh are now family, and I will never forget.” Senator Alonzo squeezed Elena’s hands.

Elena leaned in and glanced at Donna. “Can I talk to you in private?”

“Yes. Bri, I’m going to talk to Elena in the hallway. Keep Syrin company.”

“Okay, Mom. We need to get a Syrin.”

“Just what I need: another dog for her to leave at home. Let’s go out in the hall. Elaine, please make sure no one gets too loud.” Donna tilted her head at Bri. “We’ll be right back.”

Donna headed out, followed by Elena. Once outside the room, she glanced up and down the hall. No one was within earshot except the security officer, who was a member of the club. She turned back to Elena. "What's up?"

"We have a target matrix of everyone involved in the abduction of your daughter. We're going to execute a warrant tomorrow," Elena said.

"That's amazing, but why execute a warrant? You have the authorization to eliminate them all and do humanity a favor."

"For two reasons: one, we want to make sure we have the right people, and two, we want to make sure we have everyone. Do you know anything about the Church of Illuminology?"

"Sure, it's headed by Stephanie Avery. Her sister, Rachel Collier, is the lieutenant governor. They're huge supporters of the president's reelection campaign and big donors in my last campaign. Why do you ask?"

Elena hesitated.

"Oh shit, they're involved? That doesn't make any sense. The Church makes about a hundred million a year, and Bishop Avery's probably worth ten times that." Donna involuntarily shook her head no.

"The two people killed last night attempting a gas attack on this hospital, and your daughter were employees of the church. We believe the two individuals were also responsible for the gas attack on the UCF fraternity. One of them shot your daughter."

Donna stepped back. "How sure are you?"

"One hundred percent on Bishop Avery, and only fifty percent on the lieutenant governor, which is why I wanted to talk to you in the hallway. I'd like to show Bri some pictures to confirm we have the right folks. Does Bri know about the girls burned on the bus?"

"No, not yet. I want to give her some time before we head down that road," Donna said.

"Okay, I can understand that. You also have to ask Elaine to wait out here since some of the people in the pictures are going to disappear," Elena said.

"Wow, that's a lot to process." Donna paced in the corridor and ran her hand through her hair, sifting through the information and possible courses of action like a politician, which quickly shifted to mom mode. "Why am I even thinking about this? Let's go. I'll give a stirring eulogy at their funerals."

The Navy steward wheeled a cart into the Oval Office with three mugs of coffee, boxes of White House M&Ms, and a plate of chocolate-covered strawberries. She placed cups of coffee on White House coasters in front of everyone, along with four boxes of M&Ms in front of Josh and Vince, and a plate of six colossal chocolate-covered strawberries on the coffee table. "Anything else, Mr. President?"

"I think we're good, Hannah. Thank you." The president picked up his mug of coffee and tasted it. "Hot, but always good."

Hannah wheeled the cart out of the Oval Office and shut the door.

Josh and Vince took sips of coffee.

Vince tossed his boxes of M&Ms to Josh. "I have cases of these in my office if you want more. Send them back to your family; they'll get a kick out of them."

"Thank you. Anyway, can I get a box for one of those strawberries? I think Elena would like that."

"Absolutely," the President said. "After what you two accomplished, I'd throw you a state dinner, which leads to the reason for this meeting. Vince, why don't you lead off."

"Yes, Mr. President. So, Josh, in this line of work, you have a limited shelf life before you start to question what you're doing and why you're doing it. You and I are warriors. We protect those who cannot defend themselves, and if someone shoots at us, we shoot back. The gray area comes when we ask you to remove someone who is not a physical threat to you, especially if that someone is young or a woman. Your target package in this assignment is made up of mostly women." Vince paused and took a sip of coffee.

"This is probably not the best example of a gray area. Twenty-nine dead women burned in a bus, and twenty-two students gassed; I have no problem putting an end to the Church of Bullshit," Josh said. He took another sip of coffee. "This is good coffee, especially for the Navy. Usually, it's burnt sludge in the bottom of the pot."

"You're right on this case, Josh, but it does highlight an issue," the president said. "Your mom raised you after your dad died, so you have a protective instinct for women, and we don't want you to get lost in the ethics of eliminating someone you know nothing about other than an order to carry out the mission."

"Something tells me you have a solution," Josh said.

"We do," Vince said. "You met her."

"Elena?" Josh sat back on the couch.

"No, Trisha," Vince said.

"I didn't think she was a flight attendant." Josh opened an M&M box and popped two in his mouth. "What's her story?"

"What do you know about psychopaths?" Vince asked.

Josh took another sip of coffee. "It's been a while since I took psychology, but from what I remember, they lack empathy, guilt, conscience, and remorse. I think most serial killers are psychopaths."

"You are correct," Vince said. "And if you go by the book definition, you can also add shallow experiences of feelings or emotions, impulsivity, superficial charm, failure to accept responsibility, and a grandiose sense of their worth."

"So, fifteen years ago, we started a program out at Langley," the president said. "We identified people with diagnosed psychopathic tendencies, who were young and wards of the state with no living relatives. Not a very big candidate pool, as you can imagine."

"And Trisha fit the profile?" Josh asked.

"Yes. Her dad died when she was three from colon cancer. Her mom was gunned down by two teenage girls at an ATM in front of her when she was ten, so she has no love lost for women or teenagers. She was an only child, both sets of grandparents were dead, and there were no aunts or uncles. At a series of foster homes, she exhibited violent and anti-social tendencies, so she was diagnosed as a psychopath, then transferred to a state mental hospital." The president paused and took a drink of coffee.

"The state notified us, and we brought her to the farm at Langley," Vince said. "We gave her coping skills for her violent outbursts. Taught her self-control, and gave her the finest education in the world, including a particular skill set."

"Let me guess—she kills people," Josh said.

"We prefer the term 'finisher,'" the president said. "Elena finds them. You kick down the door, and Trisha puts a bullet in their heads."

"Trisha is the leader of a group we call Echo Team. Instead of solving crimes and then taking action like you, Echo Team eliminates people or organizations deemed a threat to our nation by the executive committee. On certain occasions, we would like you to be a part of that team. Do you have any problem with that?" Vince asked.

"No, sir, I go where I'm needed, and there are a lot of people who need finishing in this world. Do I need to pass an initiation or test?" Josh asked.

"You already did. The minute you told Trisha you were worried about getting her plane dirty, she approved you. She also likes your company," Vince said. Both Vince and the president laughed.

"Now, let me get you two boxes for your strawberries," the president said. "You can bring one for Trisha. She'll be going back with you to Florida to finish your target matrix."

CHAPTER

88

Senator Alonzo stepped back into the suite, followed by Elena. "Elaine, could you give us a moment, please?"

"Yes, Senator." Elaine walked out of the suite and pulled the door closed. She was used to some secrecy around meetings and events on the senator's schedule.

Bri looked up from patting Syrin, whose head was still in her lap. "Mom, what's up?"

"Elena wants to show you some pictures of people who may be involved in your abduction and confinement. Are you up for that?" Senator Alonzo walked over and stood behind Bri.

"Of course, anything to prevent this from happening to someone else provided I get to meet the big guy. What's his name?" Bri asked.

Elena laughed. "His name is Josh, Josh Martin. I'll make sure he comes over to see you when he gets back." Elena walked over next to Bri and placed her phone on Bri's lap next to Syrin, who barely moved.

Bri picked up the phone and tapped the screen, and a picture of Bishop Avery appeared. She then started swiping through photos. She stopped on Maya Sarno—Sari. "This woman stuck me with a shank I made out of a toothbrush. I think she was in charge. She's very strong and quick. I found out the hard way."

Bri touched the side of her face. She continued with the photos and stopped at Julius Montgomery. "This black dude put me in the back seat of the Escalade and dropped me off with the chuckle twins."

She continued through the rest of the photos without IDs. "That's it. I don't recognize anyone else." She handed the phone back to Elena.

"Do you remember anything else? Where you were held? How you got there?" Elena asked.

"I know exactly where they kept me: The Church of Illuminology main campus. I saw the life-size replica of the Cape Canaveral Lighthouse next to the stadium building right before they put me in the Cadillac. I left proof of life, proof I was staying in my room—basement floor, fourth room on the left from the entrance stairs."

"Outstanding," Elena said. "What was it?"

Josh and Vince walked out of the west side entrance from the West Wing and stopped under the awning. George stood by the Tahoe with the door open. Josh and Vince shook hands.

"Good luck in Florida. Give my best to Elena. You can start your thirty-day vacation clock whenever you touch down in New Hampshire. I assume that's where you're going," Vince said.

"Yes, my mom's getting married. I'm going to be there for the wedding; otherwise, if you need me, I'll be fishing." Josh walked over to the SUV and slid into the seat. George shut the door. Josh gave Vince a wave as George pulled out of the White House complex.

"How was your meeting?" George asked. "I see you have parting gifts. M&Ms and strawberries?"

"Yes, I guess they're popular items." Josh felt himself sink into the seat as the White House adrenaline wore off.

"First-timers always get both. Once you've been here a while, it's just a strawberry and one box of M&Ms. The Secret Service has a pretty cool souvenir shop in the Eisenhower Building. You can get lighters, stationery, leather folders, and holiday-themed stuff. You also get an autographed large Christmas card from the president during Christmas, and you can buy the annual White House ornament from the White House Historical Society." George looked over at Josh, who was asleep. *It's going to be a quiet ride to Andrews. You can always tell the professionals. Sleep whenever you can. Never miss a meal. Never walk by a bathroom without using it.*

Michael walked out of her house and climbed into the red Toyota Corolla. She looked over at the cherry-red Porsche Carrera Cabriolet convertible parked next to her in the driveway. *I can just imagine the comments of the housekeepers if I pull up to work in that. Who's she fucking?* Michael backed out of the driveway and eased out of the Bayside Lakes development at twenty-five miles per hour. *Funny how a bomb makes you drive like a law-abiding citizen. Except Sari. Sari never drives like a law-abiding citizen.* She smiled.

It was an uneventful trip to work, and Michael pulled into a slot in the back for employees. She walked around the rear of the car and popped the trunk. She pulled out a large green canvas bag, which contained a change of clothes, the present from Gabi and Rafi, and the Beretta. The SIG 365 9mm was snug in her belly holster on her right side, with an additional magazine in a pouch on the left. *If I need more than twenty rounds, I'm not making it.* If anyone asked about the bag, it was a change of clothes for a date after work.

Michael slammed the trunk and headed for the rear entrance. She swiped her card at the door access reader, and the light turned green. She opened the door and strode in. *No turning back now. I hope I'm not moving to the front of the departure line.*

Bri sat up in the recliner, the feeling of payback swelling in her chest. *I would pay to see the look on bitch woman's face when they find my proof of life.* "There is a folded wad of toilet paper on top of the water feed line in the back of the toilet with my pee on it. I also put a strand of my hair in every corner of the room and the bathroom along the edge of baseboards."

Elena smiled. "Smart girl. I know this sounds gross, but can I get a pair of your used panties in a Ziplock bag?" Both the Senator's and Bri's foreheads crinkled into *what the fuck?* looks. Elena pointed at Syrin. "It's best in a case like this if the evidence is found by a K9 trained to locate people by scent. Your roommates gave us one of your dirty UCF T-shirts. That's how Syrin found you in the house. We used it as a scent marker."

Both the senator and Bri laughed. "Okay, that makes sense," Senator Alonzo said. "I'll get the bag, and Bri can dig through the dirty laundry." Senator Alonzo headed to the door, and Bri walked over to the bathroom, dragging her IV stand.

Bri walked out of the bathroom with a pair of white cotton panties between two fingers just as her mother came back with a gallon Ziplock and another bag with *Holmes Regional Medical Center* stenciled on a blue background.

"I didn't think you wanted to walk around with dirty panties in clear plastic," Senator Alonzo said, holding up the blue bag.

"Spoken like a true mom," Elena said.

Senator Alonzo held open the Ziplock bag, and Bri dropped the panties in. She then went back into the bathroom to wash her hands. Senator Alonzo zipped it shut, put it in the medical center bag, and handed it to Elena. "You don't need to bring these back."

"Roger that." Elena took the bag and felt her phone vibrate in her pocket. She pulled it out and looked at the text message. *Wheels up. ETA two hours to Patrick –Josh.*

"That's Josh. He's two hours out from Patrick. I gotta run. We'll drop by tomorrow and let you know how our church visit goes. One more thing—do you think you can get the lieutenant governor to come by for a visit tomorrow?"

"Sure. But why?" The Senator gave Elena another look.

"I have a hunch." Elena pointed at the bathroom door.

CHAPTER 89

Josh put his phone back in his jacket pocket, waved to George, and climbed the steps into the G550. "Honey, I'm home."

Trisha walked up from the aft cabin. She wore tan pants and a white polo shirt—ready for a day of shopping on South Beach. "My, don't you look fancy in your Oval Office suit," she said. "You could pass for a politician, except you look like you're an athlete and not a doughboy. Put your jacket in the closet by the door. The boys dropped off your stuff from the hotel room, so you're good to go. Not sure about the packing job. Flight time to Patrick is two hours. Do you want some lunch?"

Josh opened the closet door and hung up his suit coat next to a light blue windbreaker, which must have belonged to Trisha. "That would be wonderful." He closed the closet door. "I came bearing gifts." Josh handed her the box with the chocolate-covered strawberry.

She cracked the top and peered in. "Oooh, a chocolate-covered strawberry. I know where you got this. Did you get one for Elena?"

Josh held up the other box. "Of course. She's been babysitting Syrin. I had to bring something back."

"Who's Syrin?" Trisha slipped into a forward-facing seat and buckled her seatbelt.

"She's my dog, a trained working dog. She's incredible, but don't tell her that, or she'll get a big head." Josh plopped down opposite Trisha and strapped in. He could hear the door closing behind him. The engines whined as they came online.

"Well, I can't wait to meet her. Vince called and said you accepted the invitation to join Echo Team. You don't have a problem with my back story?" Trisha watched him for his reaction to the question. The plane started to shake as it taxied to the runway for take-off.

"I judge people on how they treat me, other people around me, and animals. I don't care if you are Black, White, Asian, Latino, gay, straight, rich, or poor. If you treat me fairly, I will return the favor. So far, you're great company and a nice person. We'll deal with the other stuff as it comes up."

Josh grabbed the armrests as the plane accelerated down the runway, forcing him toward Trisha. "You must have talked to Elena." The aircraft lifted into the air, and the wheels retracted into the plane with a *thunk*.

"I did. She said you were the best partner she's ever had. Great personality, calm under fire, easy on the eyes, and you can drop three dirtbags with MP5s by firing three headshots in ten seconds. That's how I judge people." Trisha unbuckled her seat belt. "What do you say we get some lunch? I'm buying."

"Sounds good to me." Josh released his seatbelt and followed Trisha to the aft cabin. The view was still spectacular. *Maybe this will turn into a problem.*

The elevator opened, and Michael pushed her cart on to the twenty-fifth floor. The floor was a square around the central atrium with twenty-five rooms on a side, a stairwell in each corner, and four elevators located at the center point of each side. She pulled the cleaning chart out of her pocket:

fifteen check-ins and seventy-five occupied, so it would be a busy night, not that she was going to do much cleaning. *Make the bed with the old sheets, replace the towels, and watch some TV until it's payback time.* She glanced at suite 2501. The green maid service sign hung on the doorknob like a beacon of sunshine. The red do-not-disturb signs still hung on 2500 and 2502. They were up all the time. *I'll have to keep an eye out for the Japanese guy in 2500. He doesn't look like an operator, which means he's an intel guy and probably knows me on sight. I guess I'll start at that end of the floor.*

Michael pushed the cart around the corner and started down the hall. The Japanese guy walked out of 2500, pulled the door shut, and started walking in her direction. *Shit.* She looked right at suite 2018, slipped her hand under the first stack of towels, removed the Beretta model 70, and placed it down her right side. She glanced up to see the Japanese guy closing on her position, and she swiftly scoped out the hallway in her peripheral vision. *Empty. I could just pop this little bastard and stuff him under a bed.*

Elena maneuvered the truck through the medical center traffic and turned left on Route 1 North. Syrin bounced in the front seat like she knew they were going to pick up Josh. It was a slow slog down to the Pineda Causeway. *Glad I left early. I would never hear the end of it if they were waiting on me. I wonder if Trisha's going to be with him. Josh would make an exceptional addition to Echo Team. I hope he said yes.*

She turned East on the Pineda Causeway over the Indian and Banana River bridges and took the exit to Patrick Air Force Base. At the bottom of the ramp, she turned left at the light and rolled up to the security gate. When she got abreast of the booth, she lowered the window and passed her credentials to an Asian Security Forces Airman with Lee on the name tag.

"Marshal Elena Diaz, I'm picking up two at the VIP Hangar."

Airman Lee checked her credentials, looked at her face, raised his right arm over his head, and twirled his finger. “You’re good to go, Marshal. Please follow the escort vehicle.” Airman Lee stepped into the next lane and stuck out his hand to stop traffic; then a Patrick Security vehicle pulled out from the right with its lights flashing.

Elena raised her window, waved to the Airman, and fell in behind the security vehicle at a brisk twenty-five miles per hour. *Killing me. Good thing he’s got his lights on; I’d hate to run over a retiree. It must be a slow day.* She looked at her watch. *Shit, it’s going to be close.*

The escort vehicle wound its way through the base, stopping at every light, stop sign, and crosswalk full of pedestrians. It finally passed into the flight operations area and turned left toward three gray hangars. A sleek Gulfstream G550 sat off to the right with a fuel truck alongside. A fit dude in a suit with a striking blonde next to him stood in the shade from the hangar.

“Ah, shit.” Elena pulled the truck up next to the couple while the security vehicle turned off, killed the lights, and headed back to the road. Syrin spun and jumped in the front seat at the sight of Josh. Elena put the truck in park, opened the driver’s side, and stood clear as the hair missile launched from the F-150, hit the ground, and did a high-speed run around the front of the truck directly at Josh.

Josh squatted down and caught her full in the chest with head shakes, growls, and barks. “Who’s my good girl? Did Aunt Elena stop at the beauty parlor? I could have melted, waiting in the heat for her slow ass.”

“Funny. Florida traffic sucks, and the Air Force Security personnel are pussies.” Elena walked over and hugged Trisha. “Welcome to Patrick. How was the trip?”

“Really smooth, and the company was fantastic,” Trisha said.

“Yeah, he does clean up pretty good. Nice suit. No way you picked that out, Josh,” Elena said.

Josh stood up. "Hey, I have some taste in clothes, but the suit was a gift from Vince. Check out the cufflinks." Josh pulled his sleeve up to reveal the golden Army As.

"Wow. I bet you don't wear those in mixed company," Elena said.

"Yeah, probably not wearing them to the next frogman reunion." Josh reached down to pat Syrin's head while she danced around his feet. "I see Syrin survived. Trisha, this is Syrin."

Trisha bent over and reached her hand to Syrin, who walked over and gave her a sniff. After a momentary pause, Syrin danced around Trisha's legs. "What a good girl." Trisha scratched her ears.

"Wow, you got the welcome dance. Elena only got a lick the first time she met Syrin. Now that we're all acquainted, what do you say we hop into the truck and go plan our church wedding?" Josh headed toward the truck with Syrin in tow. "Do I need to do a walk around to make sure there are no scratches on the baby?"

CHAPTER

90

Michael turned, swiped her card on suite 2018, the light turned green, and she pushed through the door, which closed behind her. She stepped up to the peephole and watched Koichi walk by. *You almost made the head of the line, dickhead.* The peephole provided a 180-degree view of the hallway, so she saw Koichi get on the elevator. When the elevator door closed, she opened the suite door and stepped back into the walkway, grabbed her cart, and turned right. She slipped the Beretta back under the stack of towels.

She was just about to suite 2502 when the radio on her belt squawked. "Sam, twenty-five fifty-four needs two towels and two face cloths." She unclipped the radio and pressed the talk button. "Roger. I'm headed there now." She put the radio back on her belt and leaned her head on the door to room 2502. Silence. *Meatheads must be out lifting weights.* She pushed the cart in front of 2501. She swiped her card and pushed open the door.

"Housekeeping." No reply. She did a quick walk through the suite. Empty. She returned to her cart and removed the package from the bottom. She went over to the counter near the sink, removed the ice bucket, and replaced it with the special package. She looked around the suite and found what she wanted on the table next to the couch. She picked up a pad and pen, and scribbled something on the paper, and put it next to the ice bucket. Satisfied, she walked into the bathroom and placed the ice bucket in the shower. She headed back to her cart, shut the door, and pulled the green maid service card off the handle. She leaned into the cart and started toward suite 2554.

Nothing to do now but wait…wait and decide where I'm going. Without Rafi to erase the hotel video, I'll be a hunted felon.

Josh exited the base and went up the ramp to the Pineda Causeway. Elena sat up front with Josh, and Trisha was in the back seat, making friends with Syrin.

Elena looked at Josh. "I just remembered what I forgot to tell you."

"What's that?" Josh looked left and accelerated into traffic on the causeway headed west.

"Bri's doing fine," Elena said.

"Wow, that's great news. How did you find out?" Josh glanced at Elena.

"I was at the hospital when you sent me the text. Senator Alonzo asked me to stop by. I thought she was going to tell me Bri was dead. When the swelling in Bri's brain from the round's impact went down, she woke up. She was playing cards with her mom when I walked into the room. They also want you to stop by, so they can say thank you."

"We can add that to the list after we finish with the church," Josh said.

"But it gets better," Elena said. "I showed Bri pictures of our target matrix. She positively identified Maya Sarno and Julius Montgomery."

"That's good news," Trisha said from the back seat. "We can definitely scratch those two. What about the lieutenant governor?"

Elena turned to look at Trisha. "Unfortunately, no. She's still at fifty percent. But I asked the senator to invite the lieutenant governor to the hospital tomorrow."

"What are you thinking?" Josh asked.

"I think Bri may be able to identify her in person," Elena said.

"Plus, it will bring the lieutenant governor closer to us. It saves us a trip to Tallahassee," Trisha said.

Josh made good time sticking to the Pineda Causeway and I-95, with no timid drivers or lights to slow them down. He rolled into the valet lot at the Tropical Suites Hotel and put the transmission in park. Everyone piled out of the Shelby, and Jason headed over from the valet stand.

"Welcome back, Agent Martin. I made sure we took care of your truck while you were away."

"Thanks, Jason. Elena wasn't doing doughnuts in the parking lot?" Josh passed him the truck fob wrapped in a twenty.

"No, sir, she said she drove like she stole it." Jason suppressed a smile, and Trisha snickered at the comment.

Elena said, "I told you that in confidence, Jason. It does shimmy a little at one-eighty! Come on, Trisha, let me show you to our suite." The girls walked arm and arm to the lobby entrance. Elena stopped and turned back. "Come on, Syrin, you can come, too. This is a girls' party." Syrin ran up to join Elena, and they disappeared into the lobby.

"Oh, so that's how it is, Syrin. I'll remember that tonight. You're sleeping on the floor." Josh turned to Jason. "Bring up the luggage. Dump the bags in twenty-five zero two and put the truck in the usual spot."

"Yes, sir." Jason climbed into the truck.

Josh marched to the lobby. The cold air hit him in the face when he went through the automatic doors. The girls waved to him as the elevator closed.

Josh looked around the lobby and spotted Sergeant Mike and some of the guys at the bar. Sergeant Mike waved him over.

Michael walked out of suite 2075 when the elevator at the far end of the hallway opened for two women and a dog to step out. She spotted the Belgian Malinois and quickly ducked behind the cart to rearrange towels. The pair of women went around the corner and down the hallway to suite 2501 with the dog trailing behind. As the couple got closer, Michael recognized Marshal Diaz. *No idea on the blonde. Oh well, sucks to be her—showtime.*

Marshal Diaz swiped her card at the door and pushed it open. The blonde and the dog followed her in. Michael quickly pushed her cart to the southwest stairwell and stuck it in a corner. She grabbed the Beretta from the stack of towels and backed out of the hallway.

From the stairwell, she had a direct view of suite 2501 through a small window in the door. She pulled out her phone, found the number for the package, and brought it up on her screen. Her finger hovered around the green send button.

Elena closed the suite door. "It's not much, but it's not a hole in the desert."

"Amen to that," Trisha said. "Only one bedroom. You and Josh doing the horizontal refreshment?"

"I wish. He just lost his wife and spent six months with Delta, but he's been nothing but a perfect gentleman. He sleeps on the pullout couch with Syrin. He's easy on the eyes, and I bet dynamite in bed. Some girl is going to wake up lucky with that catch."

Syrin barked, stared at the ice bucket, and sat down.

Elena looked at Syrin. "What's up, girl?" Syrin barked again. She crept closer to the ice bucket and sat down. Elena walked over and saw a note on a pad of paper next to the bucket.

From Rafi with love, if you leave this room, I'll detonate the bomb. Enjoy your night.

"Fuck me; we got a bomb." Elena stared in disbelief.

CHAPTER

91

Josh took a sip from a mug of Coors Light beer. The boys were drinking pitchers of Coors, playing pool, and throwing darts. Josh was at a table with Sergeant Mike, Koichi, and David Drouin. Dave was a delta operator from San Francisco. He was about five foot nothing with broad shoulders and a black mustache. His team nickname was Hercules.

"So, Koichi, what does a satisfied woman say when she gets out of bed?" Dave asked.

"Oh, Koichi san, you do me so good," Koichi said. Everyone laughed.

"Old joke, Dave," Sergeant Mike said.

Josh felt his phone vibrate in his pocket. He pulled it out and looked at the caller ID: *Marshal.* He pressed the green accept button. "Miss me already?"

"Josh, there's a bomb in our room," Elena said.

"Wait, what, a bomb? Are you sure?' Josh asked. Everyone stared at Josh.

"Yes, Syrin alerted, and the bomber left a note: 'From Rafi with love, if you leave this room, I'll detonate the bomb. Enjoy your night.'"

"OK, shit, let me think. Koichi, do you have plans for the twenty-fifth floor?" Josh asked.

"Yes, let me pull them up on my phone." Koichi started scrolling.

"What are you thinking?" Elena asked.

"If the bomber can see you leave the room, they must be on the twenty-fifth floor, but the question is where? Where is the bomb?"

"It's in the ice bucket on the counter next to the sink in the sitting room," Elena said.

"All right, barricade yourself in the bedroom. Stack up the mattresses and the box springs, and get in a corner. Also, open the door to the patio to help release some of the overpressures if the device goes off. It can't be too big if it is in an ice bucket."

"How about we switch places if it's not too big," Elena said.

"Yeah, sorry, poor choice of words. We'll get things rolling. Hang in there. Let me know when you're in the corner. Put a vest on Syrin."

"I already did. Find the asshole and take her out. It's got to be one of the angels. I'll call you when we're ready." Elena clicked off the call.

"Here's the schematic." Koichi passed Josh his phone.

Josh scrolled around on the schematic checking rooms with a sightline to suite 2501. "OK, the bomber is either in the southwest stairwell or room twenty-five seventy to twenty-five seventy-five. They would all have a clear shot of twenty-five zero one."

"Or the bomber is just playing for time while they get out of Dodge," Sergeant Mike said.

"Yeah, that's a possibility, but it doesn't change the fact we need to clear the rooms and the stairwell. Dave, grab Clovis and head to the twenty-fourth floor in the southwest stairwell. Hold that position. No one up or down."

"Roger, Boss." Dave headed to the pool game to grab Clovis.

"Koichi, head to the front desk. Have them start calling rooms to get everyone out. Also, call BCSO for their bomb squad. Sergeant Mike, you and I are headed to the twenty-fifth floor. Let's find our bomber.

"Sounds like a plan. Let's go," Sergeant Mike said.

Michael peered through the small window in the stairwell door. The floor was empty.

The marshal and blondie had to have found the bomb and called someone. Hopefully, the cowboy's on his way up to save the day. Michael checked her watch: 1520. *I'll give them ten more minutes; then I'll blow the room and get the fuck out of the country.*

Michael dialed a number on her phone. The person answered on the first ring. "Be in the position for evac in ten minutes," Michael said.

"Roger, ten minutes to evac." The caller clicked off.

Josh and Sergeant Mike exited the elevator on the twenty-fifth floor and turned right to room 2570. Josh spotted the housekeeping cart tucked into the corner by the southwest stairwell.

"Gotta be the stairwell," Josh said. Sergeant Mike nodded his head in agreement.

Josh pulled his phone out of his pocket and dialed Elena's number. She picked up right away.

"Yeah, we're in the corner," Elena said.

"Change of plans. Get to the room entrance. When the shooting starts, run like hell to the left. Give Syrin the 'guard' command. She'll stay with you."

"Are you sure?" Elena asked.

"Yes, you should get clear of the blast range before she can detonate the bomb, especially if she's dodging bullets. You got three minutes to get in position."

"Roger. Moving now." Elena ended the call.

Josh looked at his watch, then at the sergeant. "Three minutes, I'm going to start shooting at the window in the stairwell door. I'll fire five rounds, then you rush the stairwell door, and I'll go through and engage the target. Clear?"

"Crystal," Sergeant Mike said.

Michael re-checked the hall. It looked like there was some movement on the right. The shadows and light kept changing. She looked again, and the safety glass exploded, sending shards into her face, and something clipped her left ear. Five gunshots boomed in the hallway, and bullets whizzed through the empty hole in the door. Rounds impacted the cinder block walls behind her, sending bits of concrete flying. Shouts of men and footsteps rang out from below.

"Fuck me." Michael turned and raced up the stairs to the roof. She heard the door below bang open and footsteps starting up the stairs. At the landing before the roof entrance, she pressed the green send button on her phone. A thunderous roar vibrated through the building, and the hotel's fire alarm system kicked on. She pointed her Sig down the stairwell and fired five rounds in rapid succession. The gunshots echoed in the staircase, amplified by the concrete and confined space. *That should freeze the fuckers for a few minutes. That's all the time I need.*

Michael slammed the emergency bar on the door and exited onto the roof. She sprinted toward the far end of the building, where a black Bell 505 Jet Ranger X helicopter rapidly approached, trailing a Jacob's ladder.

Josh froze as the five rounds ricocheted through the stairwell. Sergeant Mike ran up to his side. "Distraction rounds. Are you ready?" Josh asked.

"Like a fat kid on a devil dog. Let's roll, brother," Sergeant Mike said.

Josh told him, "I'll go first through the door to draw any fire. You follow and take out any shooters."

"Roger, Boss. Run fast." Sergeant Mike tapped Josh on the shoulder.

Josh took the stairs two at a time and stopped at the roof door. When Sergeant Mike caught up, Josh slammed through the door and sprinted toward an AC unit for cover. Automatic weapons fire from a helo door gunner tracked him, sending gravel and bits of tar flying. He slid in behind the unit as rounds slammed into the metal box.

Sergeant Mike ran out and started toward the helo. He stopped at the sound of automatic weapons fire and emptied the entire magazine from his Glock 17. Fifteen 9mm rounds peppered the opening, striking the shooter in the body and bouncing him like a puppet on a string. The corpse fell forward out of the helicopter.

At the sound of Sergeant Mike's gunfire, Josh sprinted from behind the AC unit and closed the distance to the helicopter. A female figure clung to a Jacob's ladder beneath it. As the gunner pitched out of the aircraft, Josh fired five rounds into the cockpit windshield, shattering the glass and striking the pilot who slumped forward in his harness. The helo pitched, yawed, and slammed its rotor blades into the side of the Tropical Suites Hotel. The blades disintegrated, and the aircraft body fell twenty-five stories straight down with all the aerodynamics of a rock, dragging Michael down to punch her departure ticket from the line and incinerate her flesh on impact.

Josh headed toward Sergeant Mike when his phone rang. "Yeah?"

"It's Elena. We're in the lobby. You need to come. It's bad. It's really bad."

CHAPTER 92

Lieutenant Governor Rachel Avery Collier stared at the breaking news story on the TV. *Explosion, fire, and helicopter crash at the Tropical Suites Hotel in Palm Bay, Florida. An unknown number of casualties. Tune in for an update at eleven p.m. on News Nine.* She picked up the remote and turned the TV off.

It is going to be tough to win the White House with shit like this. Reporters will be asking questions about the church, employees, dead girls, drug trafficking. How did it get so bad? How can I solve this problem? She paused for a moment and drummed her manicured fingers on the desk, and then the solution came to her. She picked up her phone, scanned through the contacts list, found the one she wanted, and pressed send. The caller picked up.

"Yes, madam?"

"It's time you came back to Tallahassee."

"Yes, madam. When?"

"Tonight."

"Yes, madam. I will be there tomorrow. Anything else?"

"Yes, bring the gold cross."

"Oui."

Lieutenant Governor Collier ended the call and tossed the phone on her desk. *I better check on transportation. Can't say no to the almighty Senator Alonzo. We should have snuffed that little bitch out when we had the chance.*

Josh raced down the stairs from the roof and sprinted along the hall of the twenty-fifth floor to the elevator. *Please don't let it be Syrin. Please don't take her.* He hammered on the elevator button. "Come on, come on, come on. You slow piece of shit." After an eternity, the elevator dinged open. Josh stepped on and pressed the number for the lobby. The elevator started its slow descent. *Please, please, please, please, God, don't let anything bad happen to my dog. She's all I got.* Tears welled at the corner of his eyes. He wiped them with the back of his hand.

The elevator bounced on the bottom, and the doors opened. Josh flew out of the elevator. He saw Syrin across the lobby with Elena and Trisha. *Thank you, Jesus!* "Syrin!"

Syrin turned at the sound of her name, saw Josh, and bolted for him with her nails scratching on the lobby tile, trying to gain traction. Syrin jumped on Josh and licked his face. Josh wrestled her down to happy growls. "Who's my good girl?" Syrin did her happy dance and barked.

Josh looked over at Elena and Trisha, who headed in his direction. "So, I count Elena, Trisha, and Syrin. What's really bad?"

Elena waved him over. "It's outside."

Josh followed Elena and Trisha through the lobby doors and over to the valet stand. Syrin stayed on Josh's right hip. The parking lot was full of fire trucks, police cars, hoses, and spraying water. The firefighters were dousing the remnants of the helicopter, which had fallen on a line of vehicles. Josh looked at the flames, and he spotted the front end of a red Shelby F-150 sticking out from the bottom of a blazing inferno. "My truck! Not my fucking truck. You got to be kidding me!"

Jean-Paul walked into Eleanor's office, carrying a tray with four plates of chocolate chip cookies and four glasses of milk. Eleanor sat hunched over her desk, and Julius leaned back in one of the reception chairs, checking the sports on his phone.

"With all the bad news, I thought everyone could use a little cheering up, so I made a batch of chocolate chip cookies. They're hot." Jean-Paul put a plate on Eleanor's desk along with two glasses of milk.

"Bless your heart, Jean-Paul. Thank you," Eleanor said. She picked up a cookie and took a bite. "Mmm, so delicious, as usual. Come get one, Julius."

Julius put his phone down and walked over. "I'm going to take a couple, Miss Eleanor. I'm a growing boy." Julius picked up three cookies and walked back to his chair. "Thank you, Jean-Paul. The bishop and Miss Sari are at the conference room table. I know they could use some hot cookies to cheer them up."

Jean-Paul nodded his head. "You're welcome." He walked into the reception office and spotted the two seated at the end of the table, lost in thought. They both looked up when he walked into the room.

"Now, here comes the answer to my prayers and a blessing on this tragic day," Bishop Avery said.

"I thought you might like some fresh chocolate chip cookies and a nice glass of milk." Jean-Paul walked over and put a plate of cookies and two glasses of milk on the table. Bishop Avery and Sari each picked up a cookie, took a bite, and washed it down with milk.

"Thank you, Jean-Paul. Very thoughtful of you," Bishop Avery said.

"If there's nothing else, Bishop, I'm going to turn in for the night."

"No, Jean-Paul, nothing else. Have a good night. Thank you for the cookies." Bishop Avery took another bite.

Jean-Paul carried the tray down to the break room and left two more plates of cookies for the night crew, and then he walked back to his small apartment just off the kitchen. He pulled out a small overnight bag and packed a change of clothes, some small personal items, his passport, and about fifteen thousand dollars in cash. He sat on his bed and looked at the clock.

Thirty minutes later, he stood up and draped the bag over his shoulder. He pussyfooted through the reception area on the way to the elevator. He rode to the ground floor, shuffled out into the parking garage, and turned toward a car under a gray cover. He pulled off the fabric to expose a 1985 Cadillac Fleetwood Brougham d'Elegance. He popped the trunk, dropped his shoulder bag into it, and stuffed the car cover beside it. He opened the driver's door, sank into the seat, and pulled a small gold cross and chain from his pocket. He put the chain around his neck and shut himself in the sedan. He would make Tallahassee in about five hours.

CHAPTER

93

Josh looked across the breakfast table at a smiling Elena. "It's not funny. I loved that truck. That truck saved our lives."

"No, it's pretty funny," Trisha said. Both she and Elena laughed robustly.

"Well, if you guys are done hooting, I think it's time we went to church." Josh pushed away from the table and headed to the lobby dressed in a full dark-blue FBI tactical outfit. Syrin followed. Trisha and Elena joined him dressed in U.S. Marshals tactical uniforms. Josh walked through the hotel lobby and out into the bright Florida sunshine. The air still smelled like burnt plastic. Three dark-blue Chevy Tahoes filled the valet lane.

Sergeant Mike gave a thumbs-up from the driver's side of the second Tahoe. Josh opened the door on the first Tahoe and held it for Syrin, who jumped from the driver's seat into the shotgun position. He nestled behind the wheel and prepared to hit the road. Trisha and Elena piled into the back. Josh led the procession out of the hotel parking lot.

"Anyone taking bets on what we're going to find?" Trisha asked.

"I think the place is empty, and they're in the wind," Josh said. "Elena gets a chance to earn her pay and find the assholes. It's not going to be easy with the amount of money and resources under church control. The Israeli is probably already in Tel Aviv, making nice with the Mossad. She'll be tough to get."

The procession got up on I-95 and exited at Route 192. Josh turned by the twin lighthouses. "Someone should C4 those monstrosities," Elena said. "In fact, I think I remember someone talking about burning the whole thing down."

Josh looked at Elena in the rearview mirror. "It's still early." He turned onto Road to Heaven Boulevard. Two miles ahead, the Cape Canaveral Light House loomed over the orange groves and the church stadium. Empty parking lots extended forever on the right, and immaculate lawns and flower beds flowed from the parking lot to the church.

"This place looks like Disney World," Trisha said. "Or maybe the Garden of Eden."

Josh turned into the parking garage and pulled into the slot marked for Angel Parking. "I bet we find the serpent on the fifth floor," Josh said. He kicked open the door and marched back to a waiting Sergeant Mike, who had his window down.

"You guys do a sweep of the building and the grounds. When we're all clear, I'll bring in Koichi and the lab gremlins."

"Roger, Boss." Sergeant Mike raised his window and pulled into a slot next to a Barcelona Blue BMW M8 competition convertible. The other SUV pulled into the next spot, and twelve operators piled out of both trucks. They jumped right into their weapon and comms checks.

"Six, this is Three. Radio check," Sergeant Mike said.

Josh keyed his mike. "Loud and clear. We're going to the fifth floor to see if we can find Lucifer. By the look of things, I think the Devil went down to Georgia; she's probably looking for Charlie Daniels." Josh keyed his mike twice and looked at Elena and Trisha. "Are you ladies ready?"

Both women nodded their heads yes. "I've been dying to go to church," Elena said.

"Syrin, guard," Josh said. Syrin took position on Josh's right hip. He walked over and pressed the elevator button. The door dinged opened, and they stepped inside. He pushed the button for the fifth floor. When the cab reached its destination, Josh stepped out of the elevator. "Oh, shit."

Lieutenant Governor Collier looked out the window of the state-owned Cessna Citation Latitude aircraft as they approached the Melbourne Airport's south runway. The Citation made a smooth landing, and she gripped the armrests as the pilot applied the brakes. The plane turned and taxied to the VIP terminal, stopped, and the pilots cut the engines, which whined to a stop.

Linda Faircloth, the lieutenant governor's chief of staff, wearing a dark-blue skirt with a white blouse, leaned across the aisle. "We have a ninety-minute meet and greet with the airport commission, and then I have a car waiting to take us to the meeting with Senator Alonzo."

"Sounds good, Linda. The sooner we get this over with, the better. We need to get back on the campaign trail if we're going to make a run at the White House." The lieutenant governor undid her seat belt.

Josh drew his Glock and gingerly moved toward Eleanor's office with Trisha and Elena flanked on either side. An older female sat with vacant eyes face down on a large brown desk. A drizzle of vomit lined the edge of her mouth and puddled on the blotter. A plate with three chocolate chip cookies sat next to her. Her right hand clutched a partially eaten cookie over a note pad.

Josh did a quick peek around the corner and spotted a large black male sprawled on the floor with vomit around the edge of his mouth, too. Two cookies had tumbled to the floor next to a cell phone, and a partially eaten cookie was in his right hand.

"Okay, I don't think anyone should eat a chocolate chip cookie," Josh said.

"Roger that," Elena replied. She walked over to get a better look at the dead lady at the desk. "This is Eleanor Davis, and the black gentleman on the floor is Julius Montgomery. We can scratch two off the list."

Josh moved to the edge of the reception room and spotted two figures slumped on a large conference table at the far end of the room. He walked farther in with Syrin at his side while Trisha and Elena were moving to his left. Josh pointed to an archway through the wall ahead of him. "Syrin, seek." Syrin bolted through the arch. After a few minutes, she returned to Josh. "All clear." Josh holstered his gun.

Elena walked over to the slumped figures. A plate of chocolate chip cookies sat between the bodies with two partially filled glasses of milk. Both bodies had vomit on the edges of their mouths and partially eaten cookies in their right hands. She peered at them. "The one at the head of the table is Bishop Avery, and the one on the right is Maya Sarno. We can scratch two more."

"I think they were killed in the reception room, with a chocolate chip cookie, by the baker," Josh said.

"Let me guess, you played *Clue* as a kid," Trisha said. She holstered her gun and looked around the room.

"Every rainy day in the summer," Josh said. "So, who is the baker?"

"We're only missing one. Gotta be the chef, Jean-Paul," Elena said.

Josh keyed his mike. "Three, this is Six. We got four dead bodies on the fifth floor—any sign of our chef?"

"Negative, Six. We have four dead uniformed security guards. No old black guys. Don't eat the chocolate chip cookies."

"Yeah, we figured that out. Call Koichi and get the lab guys rolling. We're going to the hospital."

"Roger. Out," Sergeant Mike said.

Josh pulled out his phone and looked at Elena and Trisha. "I'm going to call Vince and find out what he wants us to do about the lieutenant governor."

CHAPTER

94

Josh brought the SUV up to the hospital entrance and pulled into a spot marked *Official Police Vehicle*. He stepped out of the Tahoe, and Syrin jumped across the seat to follow him out. Trisha and Elena joined him. They entered in lockstep, and Security Guard Paul waved them through. Josh's phone buzzed in his pocket. He looked at the caller ID: El Jefe. "I'll meet you guys upstairs."

Elena and Trisha stepped onto the elevator without him.

Josh made his way to a corner by a vending machine with Syrin watching everyone go past.

"Good morning, Vince."

"Good morning, Josh. I talked to the president about the lieutenant governor. It's going to be an arrest. We don't want to make her a martyr if she disappears. Politically, the president wants her supporters and financial backers, especially with a high-profile trial."

"He's not worried about the church and the lieutenant governor being a huge supporter of his reelection campaign?"

"Nope. His administration brought the church to justice despite their financial backing."

"Roger. She should be here shortly to meet with the senator. I'll take her into custody. Are you going to send a transport team?"

"They're already en route. One more thing: you can scratch Joe Friday and Chris Del Toro off your to-arrest list. The DEA picked Friday up, and Customs Special Operations Unit picked up Del Toro at his Tennessee lake house. Both agencies owe us huge favors."

"Sounds good to me. So, after I stuff and cuff the lieutenant governor, I can go on leave?"

"Yes. What are you going to do about transportation? Sorry to hear about the truck. The president just ordered a new one, but it will take six months to build."

"I'll figure it out. Tell the president thank you. At this rate, he should probably order a spare."

"I'll tell him, Josh. Excellent job on this mission. Call me in thirty days—good luck with the fishing." Director Santiago ended the call.

"Come on, Syrin. Let's go say goodbye to your girlfriend." Josh and Syrin rode the elevator to the fourth floor. They stepped off and walked over to the nurses' station, where a woman pointed them to the corner suite.

Josh and Syrin walked over to the room. "I hear some beautiful girl is going home today."

"Josh!" Bri jumped out of the corner chair and gave him a big hug. She wore gray sweatpants, a black and gold UCF T-shirt, and white sneakers.

Josh stepped back and looked at her head, which was still wrapped in an ace bandage. "How's the head?"

"No problem. The stitches come out next week." Bri spotted Syrin. "Syrin!" She bent down to hug her.

Senator Alonzo came over and embraced Josh. Tears streamed down her face. "I don't know what to say but thank you. Thank you for bringing my baby back to me."

"You're welcome, Senator, but it was a team thing," Josh gestured at Elena and Trisha.

"Yes, of course, thank you all. We're holding a big bash next month for Bri's birthday. I hope you all can come."

A tactical security officer stuck his head in the door. "The lieutenant governor is on her way up."

"Thank you, Derek," the Senator said. "One more thank you, then we're out of here."

Josh moved over to Elena and Trisha. "It's going to be an arrest."

"Roger," Elena said. "Can we let the meeting play out before we arrest her? I got a hunch."

"Okay with me," Josh said.

As if on cue, Lieutenant Governor Rachel Collier breezed into the suite trailing the scent of Tom Ford Lavender Extreme behind her. She walked over and hugged Donna. "Donna, so good to see you."

The scent of lavender filled Bri's nose, and recognition filled her brain. The sound of the lieutenant governor's voice made her bristle. The feel of the firm hand pressing on the small of her back, pinning her to the X and that voice: *"Hmmm. A nice slice of lettuce!"*

Bri stood up from patting Syrin. Rage filled her body. She walked over to the lieutenant governor, tightened her fist, and nailed her with a sharp right cross to her jaw, knocking her to the ground.

Senator Alonzo stood back in shock. "Bri, what the hell?"

"She was there, Mom. She was there the night I was taken. How's that for a nice slice of lettuce, you fucking bitch?" Bri screamed.

"Good hunch, Elena," Josh said. "I would have paid good money to see that. Do you want to do the honors?"

"Thank you; it would be my pleasure." Elena pulled her handcuffs from behind her back and walked over to the prone lieutenant governor. *No, not lieutenant governor now, just scum bag.* She snapped the cuffs on the groggy Rachel Collier and hauled her up.

"Rachel Collier, you have the right to remain silent. Anything you say can and will be used against you in a court of law. You have the right to an attorney. If you cannot afford an attorney, one will be provided for you. Do you understand the rights I have just read to you?"

"You can't do this to me. I'm the lieutenant governor. I'm going to be president of the United States," Rachel said in a groggy voice.

Elena spotted the transport team outside the door. "All yours, boys. Read her rights to her again; I don't think she heard them the first time."

"Will do, Marshal." Two escort U.S. Marshals dragged Rachel out of the suite and down the hall with her chief of staff in tow.

Josh walked over to Senator Alonzo. "Sorry, Senator, we had to be sure."

"You knew?" Donna looked confused.

"We were fifty percent sure. Now, we're a hundred percent sure. The president ordered an arrest warrant this morning." Josh put his arm around Bri. "We got them all, Bri. Everyone involved in your kidnapping and confinement is either dead or in jail."

"Thank you so much," Bri said. "Mom, do you think we can leave?"

"Yes, sweetheart. Come on, let's go home." Donna put her arm around Bri, and they left the suite.

“Now, that’s what I call a satisfying arrest,” Trisha said. “Nice right cross. Well, if you will excuse me, I have a baker to find. Elena, are you going to help?”

“Yeah, I’ll be right there in a minute,” Elena said.

“Okay, I’ll meet you in the lobby.” Trisha headed to the elevators.

Elena strode over to Syrin and kneeled to hug her. “I’m going to miss you, girl. You take care of Josh.”

Syrin gave her a goodbye lick. “Oh, thank you for that.”

Elena stood up and went over to Josh. She patted him on the chest and kissed him on the cheek. “Take care, cowboy. I’m sure we’ll get a chance to ride the range again.”

Josh gave her a big hug. “You’ve got my number. If you ever need anything, give me a call.”

“I will. I’ll let you know when we find Jean-Paul.” Elena stepped into the hallway, paused at the nurses’ station to say thank you, and headed for the lobby.

Josh looked at Syrin. “Are you ready to go home and see Bob and Brady?” Syrin barked and danced at the names of her partners in crime. Bob and Brady were his mom’s dogs and Syrin’s favorite playmates. *Speaking of Mom, I better call her to tell her I’m coming. I can just taste the fresh corn chowder and biscuits.*

Josh pulled out his phone, highlighted the contact for his mom, and pressed send. She picked up on the first ring.

“Josh, your brother is missing!”